TANGIER

TANGIER

WILLIAM BAYER

Thomas Congdon Books · E.P. Dutton · New York

All the characters in this novel are fictitious. Any similarity to actual persons is coincidental.
Grateful appreciation to Penguin Books, Ltd. for permission to quote from the R. S. Pine Coffin translation of St. Augustine's Confessions, *copyright © R. S. Pine Coffin, 1961.*

Copyright © 1978 by William Bayer
All rights reserved. Printed in the U.S.A.

No part of this publication may be reproduced or transmitted in any form or by any means, electronic or mechanical, including photocopy, recording or any information storage and retrieval system now known or to be invented, without permission in writing from the publisher, except by a reviewer who wishes to quote brief passages in connection with a review written for inclusion in a magazine, newspaper or broadcast.

Library of Congress Cataloging in Publication Data
Bayer, William.
Tangier.
"Thomas Congdon books."
I. Title.
PZ4.B356Tan [PS3552.A8588] 813'.5'4 77-11150
ISBN: 0-525-21410-0

Published simultaneously in Canada by Clarke, Irwin & Company Limited, Toronto and Vancouver

10 9 8 7 6 5 4 3 2 1

First Edition

To Paula Wolfert

Prologue

Tangier in the rain: it's as if our whole gleaming city is bathed in tears. As the rains lash the streets, the Moroccans pull up the hoods of their djellabas and hurry for shelter beneath the arcades. Men push vegetable carts through deep puddles on Rue de Fez, and in the cafes of the Socco Chico one sees abandoned lovers hunched over their coffees and the haunted, glazed eyes of the smokers of hashish. Suddenly Tangier seems filled with stricken people. Arrayed at the tables in the Cafe de France are the faces of our dispossessed.

Passing Madame Porte's pastry shop last February, one might have seen the agony of the old architect Leo Fischer through the broad window that looks out on the intersection of Rue Goya and Rue Musa Ben Nusair. He was sitting at the corner table sipping from a cup of tea. Were those tears streaming down his cheeks or an illusion, caused by the raindrops that washed the windows of the shop?

Madame Porte's, in the center of the busy European quarter, was built in the 1940s with a refinement that has well withstood the many vicissitudes that have buffeted our town. Its marble floors and Art Deco moldings make a pleasant contrast with the seediness of the central area. But its elegant architectural details did not interest Fischer that miserable, rainy February day. This man, whose fine leonine presence had come to grace our streets a year or so before, was feeble with illness on the verge of his discharge. One prefers to remember him at his best. Those of us who lived on the Mountain saw him often on our trips back and forth to town. He'd be strolling among the awful shanties of Dradeb, deep in conversation with his assistant, Driss Bennani, talking always of their plan to rehabilitate the Moroccan slum.

Fischer had a magnificent dream. Under contract to the Moroccan government as an advisor on urban renewal, he had lobbied bravely for his vision in the ministries and had even given a series of public lectures in Tangier. "A Visionary Architecture for the Third World" he called them, moving us with his passion to design decent housing for the poor.

"We must give these people sanctuaries," he'd say, shaking his great white mane, rapping on the lectern with his fist, "sanctuaries for living built of the forms they understand. They need the dome and the minaret. Their bricks cry out to make the arch and the fine, sharp edge that reveals the splendor of their sun. . . ."

Arches and domes, plazas and minarets—this was the stuff of Fischer's dream. But his plan to transform Dradeb into a "new Moroccan village" was lost in the papers that clogged the desks in city hall. The Moroccans wanted a sky-

line; they wanted to replace the slum with a high-rise development, and nothing Fischer could say would change their minds. Finally he was devastated. As the Moroccans plotted ways to send him home, he walked the muddy alleyways, turned this way and that among the awful shanties, speaking to the still bedazzled Bennani of the plan they both knew was doomed. A routine examination by his friend and doctor, Mohammed Achar, revealed that his heart had suddenly grown weak. He left Tangier in the rain to join his son in California. A few months later we heard that he was dead.

Poor Fischer. His dream for Tangier is forgotten now. He's remembered for his San Francisco synagogue, the masterpiece of his "brutal period," a monumental hunk of twisted steel and slashing triangles of glass.

Perhaps he could have saved us, but we did not listen to him well enough. That failure—our failure—would lead in time to the convulsion that shook apart the sweet limbo in which we lived, shattering our illusion that to live as a European in Tangier was a cheat against all the miseries of the world and a revenge against the inevitability of our deaths.

Hamid

In the basement of the Tangier Sûreté there were a number of large holding cells and several small ones reserved for madmen or politically contaminated detainees. On the second day of May Hamid Ouazzani had one Spaniard down there, denounced by a thirteen-year-old boy for rape on the Malabata beach, and a long-haired American youth who'd been caught that morning at the airport trying to board a plane for Paris with a suitcase full of hashish. Neither prisoner interested him very much, and toward the end of the afternoon he was poised at the third-floor window of his office staring down at a mob of veiled women waiting patiently for a glimpse of their incarcerated sons.

He'd been brooding the whole day. A vague malaise, accentuated by the harsh insistence of the wind, which had been blowing for a week and which had turned the May Day parade into a feast of dust, gnawed at his even temper, made him nervous and aloof. His assistant, Aziz Jaouhari, sensing this unease, worked quietly at the smaller desk, adding notations to dossiers. But occasionally he glanced up at the Inspector's back, framed in frozen tension against the unwashed glass.

After a while Hamid turned back to the office. Its only decoration was a cheaply framed photograph of the King. "I'm going out, Aziz," he announced, starting toward the door. "If you need me, you'll find me at La Colombe."

Turning down Boulevard Pasteur, he plugged a cassette of Egyptian love songs into his dashboard recorder, then slowed his car. At Bazaar Marhaba he saw his brother standing aimlessly in the doorway of his shop. Tourists were prowling the Boulevard, blond Scandinavian girls with huge, awkward packs on their backs, accompanied by unburdened youths on the lookout for sellers of kif. The usual hustlers were eying them, while a pack of children, offering badly made caftans and fake Berber jewelry, surrounded a tour group trudging wearily toward the Chellah Hotel. At Claridge he caught sight of the American Consul General, Daniel Lake, deep in conversation with his assistant, Foster Knowles.

At the Cafe de Paris the four Anglo-American novelists—Kranker, Klein, Townes, and Doyle—gesticulated wildly like an out-of-tune string quartet. On Rue Belgique men were already dismantling the plywood arches erected for the May Day parade. He passed a mad Spanish lady he'd been observing for several years: she promenaded each evening at six o'clock, marching like a robot, her face white as chalk.

He stopped at Bourbana to buy flowers from a Riffian woman who'd set up shop beneath a eucalyptus beside the road. Tessa and David Hawkins rode by on their magnificent matching Arabian geldings, cantering lightly up the Mountain, their blond hair gleaming in the failing sun.

He turned and followed the Jew's River to the base of the Mountain Road. Then he parked, a few doors above La Colombe, snapped off the Egyptian music, and scanned the front of the shop. It was past six then, but still he could make out the silhouette of Peter Zvegintzov bustling inside. From time to time Zvegintzov's head was obscured by a poster afixed to the glass. It announced the Tangier Players' latest production, due to open in two weeks at the auditorium of the Spanish Polytechnical School.

It was impossible to see who else was in the shop, but Hamid could recognize most of the cars parked in front: the white Buick of the Manchesters; the black Fiat of Françoise de Lauzon; and the silver Mercedes that belonged to the retired French general Gilbert Bresson.

Patiently he waited for them to leave. It had been five months since he'd been inside the store. He was not at all sure why he'd chosen this day for a confrontation that he knew would be difficult, and that he'd been dreading the entire afternoon. It had simply seemed to him that his relationship with Zvegintzov should be resumed, that five months was long enough to dull the sharpness of their break.

And, too, he was curious to see how the Russian would react. Zvegintzov was unpredictable, a man of many moods. The scapegoat of foreigners to whom he offered his elaborate service—handling their mail, taking care of their villas, providing them with luxuries few Moroccans could afford—he knew more about what happened on the Mountain than any man except Hamid. He talked to everyone, steamed open letters, offered himself as a confidant. Though most of his customers abused him terribly, they told him things they would not dream of telling anybody else.

Hamid had discovered him years before, then carefully developed him as a source. In the old days he had stopped by the shop every day, but then there came a time when he could enter it no more. Aziz took over, while Hamid waited in the car outside. For five months it had been like that.

When he finally walked in, triggering the little bell that clasped the door, Zvegintzov was at the counter with Countess de Lauzon demonstrating some expensive preparations for cleaning rugs.

"This one's quite good," he said, looking up. For a moment he stared, searched Hamid's face. "Makes a good foamy lather, then dries out in the sun. Afterward you vacuum the foam away."

"But that's so *complicated*. Why not soap and water?"

"Of course," said Zvegintzov, "I can sell you soap if you wish. But even the dullest servants, I assure you—"

"Some good mild soap will do very nicely. And I'll take this *Connaissance des Arts*."

Zvegintzov shrugged, rang the charges up. General Bresson was next—he had come with a bitter complaint.

"Three days ago I told you my telephone didn't work, but still you haven't set it right."

Zvegintzov screwed up his canny Russian face and stared across at the old warrior's chest. He was used to humiliations, even seemed to welcome them, as if by his patience he could shame his tormentors into acknowledging his infinite good will.

"Excuse me, General. My man's been sick. I'll have it fixed tomorrow night."

"I don't like to think about *little* things—that's why I subscribe to your service. But I insist on promptness and that you keep your word. Otherwise there isn't any point."

The General stalked out of the shop, grasping a *Le Figaro* on his way. For a moment there was silence, then Hamid shook his head.

"What a difficult man. And so abrasive."

"The General needs his phone. I understand."

"But he's very rude."

"No, no, Inspector. My clients are wonderful people. A little hard at times, but underneath they have good hearts. They're human, after all. We all have our moods. Really I think they appreciate what I do. I make their lives here easy, give them peace of mind. I'm a cushion for their difficulties, and always they're grateful in the end. They know that if I weren't here their lives would be too complex. I have no doubt that some of them would leave."

As he spoke Zvegintzov danced behind the counter, straightening his display of cigars, arranging and rearranging his jars of English jams and marmalades. Hamid watched him, pitying his tension, but Zvegintzov's platitudes made him want to wince.

"Tell me," he said. "How do you manage to fix their phones?"

Zvegintzov smiled. "I know a man who works at the PTT. I slip him a little something and he works for me at night."

"Yes." Hamid nodded. "Clever—I admire that."

"It's the only way to get them repaired. Morale is bad at the company. It takes them weeks to process a complaint. There are, at this moment, over six hundred lines out of order in Tangier. Did you know that? Extraordinary! So you see, if we were to go through channels, the proper way, half the lines on the Mountain would be out right now. And that would be a tragedy for my clients, of course, *but not only for them.* If you think about it a moment you'll see what I mean. I'm speaking, of course, from your point of view." He winked. "If there were no phones, after all, then there wouldn't be anything to tap—"

He stopped then and let out a little gasp. He realized he'd been babbling and had dangerously overstepped.

"*Kalinka,*" he said suddenly, in a whisper. "How is *she?*"

Hamid stared at him.

"Yes, yes, I know," said Zvegintzov. "Your life together is good. I know that. I've heard. I hear everything, you see. They tell me she was sick last month. I wanted—but still I care for her. It's foolish. I know it's foolish."

Hamid wanted to say something, to put this conversation to an end. But Zvegintzov continued, at a new, more frantic pitch. "I wish she'd come by the shop sometime, early in the morning, before my customers come in. I so long for that—to see her face, feel her hand, her cheek—"

The telephone rang. Zvegintzov turned abruptly and fled to the rear of his shop. Hamid looked after him for a moment, then backed out into the street. It was dark then, still windy. The air was cool, but his face was flushed. He'd seen tears behind the thick lenses that shielded Peter Zvegintzov's eyes, and this glimpse of pain, so sudden and acute, filled him with alarm.

As he slid into his car, he noticed a Volkswagen with diplomatic license plates parked farther up the street. The American Vice-Consul, Foster Knowles, sat behind the wheel. As Hamid passed, he had the impression that Knowles was watching the shop.

He began to drive about the Mountain aimlessly, wandering up and down the little lanes. The Manchesters' Buick was parked in the gateway of their pink stucco monstrosity, and at General Bresson's sumptuous villa he could see light behind the grills. He wandered past the homes of numerous foreigners, Camilla Weltonwhist's gray fortress, the Cotswold cottage of the Australian inventor Percy Bainbridge, and the home of Peter Barclay hidden behind a privet hedge.

The thought, the very thought of Zvegintzov's wrinkled hand on Kalinka's cheek.

He drove then to the region of walled estates, the homes of Tangier's rich. He passed the great old manor of Rachid El Fassi, built a century before by his ancestors from Fez; the beige extravaganza of the Paraguayan painter Inigo; the black-floored palace of Patrick Wax. He passed Jimmy Sohario's "Excalibur," built on a fortune's worth of Chinese laundries; and at the end, at the Mountain's highest point, he paused before the great gates of "Castlemaine," where the American millionaire Henderson Perry was in residence a few weeks a year.

From here it seemed to Hamid that he had a commanding view of his terrain. He knew them all, these rich Americans and Europeans, knew their houses, their cars, their habits, and roughly how much each of them was worth. He knew who they saw and what they did, their cliques, their vices, their complicated whims. And there were many others he knew as well—hundreds more, diplomats and commercial people who lived in apartments in the town, hippies and dope peddlers who lived in the medina, the eccentrics of the Casbah, the doctors, barons, retired naval officers, and desperate divorcees who lived on the Marshan or on the Charf. From here he could see everything, from the Mountain to the foothills of the Rif, the whole raging town and, between Peter Zvegintzov's shop on the Jew's River and the Italian cathedral on the edge of modern Tangier, the place where he was born, the great sprawling slum, Dradeb.

Zvegintzov, Zvegintzov! Who could understand a man like that?

Since he'd been a boy, Hamid had been enamored of the European colony of Tangier—its impoverished duchesses, vicious homosexuals, doctors without medical degrees, artists, hustlers, fools. He was fascinated by these expatriates, their endless *danse macabre*. He observed with wonder all their attempts to acquire stunning lovers, their intrigues, their bizarre affairs. For years they'd been his obsession, and now, facing the wind before the huge gates of Henderson Perry's estate, he saw them laid before him like a banquet, ready for him to taste, digest. He looked to his left across the water, toward the beckoning lights of the coastal towns of Spain. Europe was close—it seemed as if he could touch it if he wished. But the Straits of Gibraltar loomed in the night like an uncrossable abyss between. *And that,* he thought unhappily, *is the way it is for me.*

He knew these strange people, and yet he did not. Though he had spent years learning their languages, studying the women and boys they fought over and loved, hearing their confessions, observing the results of all manner of their crimes, still there was a wall that separated him from them, a wall he longed to breach.

It made him furious when he thought of it, but an instant later he was resigned. There was no point in considering the possibility that sometime when he was small and had gaped at everything foreign and longed to comprehend it, he'd taken upon himself a terrible burden, wandered by error into an inescapable maze. He had lavished too much of himself already to even consider the possibility of that. Rather, he knew, he must continue to strive until, in some night of insight, their mystery would be revealed. But if at times he was amazed by emotions he could not understand—Peter Zvegintzov's tears over Kalinka, as fresh as if five months had never passed—still he was driven to look deeper, uncover more, examine all the combinations until he discovered the secret of their unfathomable European game.

He drove back down the Mountain, then slowed as he passed La Colombe. Foster Knowles was still waiting in his car. *Why? What was he doing?* Now, too, he would have to think about that.

As he drove through Dradeb, a hundred yards or so before the mosque, his headlights caught the figure of a man standing in the middle of the road. He was waving his arms, motioning traffic to the side. A crowd of men and youths surrounded a large tourist bus ahead. Hamid rolled down his window, caught the sound of angry cries. But the wind was too loud and he could not make out the words. He pulled over, parked, then walked into the mob. Looking up, he could see the tourists, their frightened faces peering out. Angry men were pushing at the driver, who was babbling furiously to two uniformed police.

He strode quickly up Rue de Chypre, the lane that led to Achar's clinic. The moment he entered he could smell the disinfectant. It came upon him like a blow across his face. It was eight o'clock and still there were people waiting to be helped. They sat in rows of hard benches, some in casts, others holding their stomachs, a tall, thin girl with a soiled bandage wrapped about her head. He avoided a wet patch on the floor, something thick and yellow sprinkled with a layer of sawdust that had not yet soaked it up. From the cubicles where the doctors worked he could hear moans and a few kind words.

He ran into Achar at the operating room door. The doctor's white gown was spotted with dark red stains. His large hands, firm and covered with black curls of hair, grasped at Hamid's arm.

"What happened?"

"A little girl. Impossible to save her." Achar shook his head. "Come," he said, leading Hamid into his little office in the back. They sat down amidst the clutter. Achar smoothed his mustache, then yelled for someone to bring them tea.

"Did you see the accident?"

"No. I was driving through. It must have happened a few seconds before."

"Pointless, of course. The bus was going much too fast. They have no business taking tourists through these streets."

"It's the best way back from Cap Spartel—"

"Yes. Of course. Do you know what they say—the guides on the buses? They have to keep talking, you see. If there's nothing 'touristic' to point out then they have to make something up. When they come through here they say 'This is a typical Moroccan village, settled by people from the Rif who have left their farms to seek their fortunes in Tangier.' How absurd! I have no doubt the cameras click away."

Hamid nodded. He was used to Achar's rage. "What happened tonight?"

The doctor shrugged. "A typical incident. There's no water in Dradeb during the day, so when the public taps are turned on at night the children are all waiting with their jugs. Probably this little girl was late, and ran across the street to get a place in line."

Hamid began to think of his boyhood in Dradeb, fetching water for his mother, carrying bread to the ovens on a board on top of his head.

"Suicide Village."

"What's that?"

"That's what they call Dradeb."

"Who calls it that?"

"The foreigners, Mohammed. My friends on the Mountain."

The tea arrived and they both began to sip.

"My beautiful friends. They zoom through here in their cars, and always there are donkeys and sheep and little children running about. There are old women who are deaf, and old men who ignore their horns. So it seems to them that this is a place filled with animals and people who want to throw themselves beneath their wheels. Suicide Village—do you see?"

"Oh, I see," said Achar. "An amusing little name for a place which unfortunately they can't avoid. Well—I'm a surgeon. One of these days all your friends will have to leave. Or else we'll have to cut them out."

Hamid looked at him, neither nodding nor shaking his head. There were men at the Sûreté who would use such a statement as a pretext to start a black dossier.

"Aside from all that," Hamid said finally, "have you had a good day?"

"Terrible! This afternoon a woman was brought in. Literally she was bleeding to death. She'd tried to abort herself with an uncurled coat hanger. She punctured herself, of course, infected her entire womb. I gave her massive doses of sulfa drugs and tetanus, everything I had. Tomorrow I'll operate—if she's still alive, and if I can get sufficient blood."

His anger over all this misery showed brightly in his eyes.

"I envy you," said Hamid.

Achar began to laugh.

"No. I envy you. You're a scientist. You can be certain about the truth. The diagnosis may be right or wrong, but moral questions don't arise."

Achar gave him a curious look. "Really, Hamid, that's one of the silliest things you've ever said. Here in Dradeb all the questions are moral ones. This woman with the coat hanger—don't you see? She was pregnant and wanted to abort. That's a social issue. She committed a political act. No, don't envy me. Here we have far messier days than you in the police."

They finished off the tea, then Hamid rose to leave. He was at the door when Achar suddenly looked up.

"My love to Kalinka," he said.

The tourist bus had left, and now people were running back and forth across the street as if the accident had never occurred. Big cars blew their horns, but nobody turned. Foreigners were driving to dinner parties on the Mountain or in the town.

Hamid parked outside his apartment house on Ramon y Cahal, gathered up his flowers, and carefully locked his car. The wind, blowing even more furiously, seemed to have upset the neighborhood. Pausing at the front door of his building, he could hear the cries of children and insanely barking dogs.

The elevator, a black cage, moved slowly with irregular jerks. When he entered the apartment he found it dark, except for a thin bar of light beneath the bedroom door.

"Hamid? Is that you, Hamid?" She was lying on their bed, her pipe in her hand. The thick, sweet smoke of hashish hung about her like a veil. "Soon I'll get you dinner, Hamid. But first sit down, tell me why you're late."

"There was an accident in Dradeb. Then I stopped to see Achar."

He sat beside her, and she began at once to caress his hands. Her dark Oriental eyes and ivory-colored skin, diffused by the smoke of her hashish, held the promise of mysterious ways of making love.

"I bought a nice fish for you today. And strawberries for dessert."

He picked up her pipe, put it on the little table beside their bed, then bent down to kiss her lips. She was Eurasian, half Russian, half Tonkinoise—his fragile, strange *métisse*.

"I'm hungry."

"Soon you will be fed."

"What did you do today?"

"I smoked all afternoon."

When she finally pulled herself up, he followed her to the kitchen, stood and watched while she heated oil in a pan.

"I saw Peter today," he said. Between themselves they always spoke French.

"Oh? Does he still look the same?"

"Exactly the same, of course."

"He was surprised to see you. I have the feeling he was surprised."

"Yes, he was surprised. But he pretended he wasn't and talked too much. He became impertinent toward the end."

"The same shabby suit?"

"What?"

"Was he wearing the same suit—the brown one, frayed at the cuffs?"

"He wants to see you."

She flung the fish into the pan. "I don't want to see him. Sometimes I feel him following me, but I never turn around."

"He follows you?"

"I don't know. I think he does. But since I never look back I can't be sure."

It was typical of her, this sort of dreamy remark that offended his sense of order, his restless need to observe everything and seek out its cause. But she was different, full of things half sensed, visions she could not be sure she'd seen, or only imagined while she smoked.

He left the kitchen, took the flowers, arranged them in a vase. When she brought out the food he waited for her to notice them, and when she didn't he pulled one out by its stem.

"A good bouquet, don't you think? These are the first agapanthus of the year."

"Yes," she said, staring closely. "I saw some at the market. I knew you liked them, so I brought them home."

"No, no, Kalinka. I bought these for you. I bought them from an old woman late this afternoon."

She looked across at him and smiled. "Oh! Then I forgot. I paid the flower lady, I remember that—but then I must have left them in a taxi, or maybe at the butcher's stall."

It was possible, he thought, and then again she might have been thinking of a purchase she'd made a year before. He would never know—her vagueness was endemic, a sort of poetry that maddened him yet gave him the sensation that in her presence he could always rest, enveloped in her soft cocoon of dreams.

For a long while he lay awake in bed, listening to the wind. It rattled the windows, loose in their old frames. Dogs barked like madmen in the night. He turned to Kalinka, who was breathing evenly by his side, her eyelids fluttering like the petals of a yellow rose. Who was she? He had never understood her, and supposed he never would. She was a cipher, and he a mad cryptographer fumbling for the key to her strange utterances, the pattern of her actions, so random, so obscure.

For years he'd seen her in Zvegintzov's shop, huddling in the back on the stool which Peter used to reach the upper shelves, or else on the yellow hassock he kept between the ice cream freezer and the counter of children's toys. For years Hamid had seen her, but not really well—she was like a fixture in the shop, a part of the decor, an Oriental girl who'd come with the Russian, a relic of his past life, his life before Tangier.

Then, for some reason, their paths began to cross. She'd be walking the streets aimlessly, wandering in her long Oriental dress, white silk trousers flashing through the slit, moving like a sparrow or a butterfly, sometimes with flowers in her arms. When he'd see her he'd pull over in his car, sit and watch her as she passed. Her face was oblivious and gay, as if she had no notion she was being watched.

One night the previous autumn he came upon her in the Casbah standing in the shadows of the wall, looking out across the Straits. He couldn't remember why he'd come, except that he was feeling lonely and wanted to gaze down upon the city lights. The Place de Casbah was deserted, except for the one-legged man who watched the cars. Hamid's footsteps rang on the old stones, but she did not turn when he came near. Then, when he greeted her, she nodded at him and smiled.

"It's a good evening," he said.

"Yes," she said, "thanks be to God."

They stood side by side in silence for a while, then she floated away across the vast, dark square, disappearing through a massive arch without a sound.

Suddenly, it seemed, they saw each other every day—in the market early in the morning, before a gas station, or in unexpected places, on narrow side streets, in odd corners of the town. It became a game with him: Where could he go, what obscure quarter of the city could he visit, without seeing her pass? Even in Beni Makada one day, where he'd gone after a man who'd stabbed a tourist with a knife, even there, amidst rotting garbage and dust, in the maddening, punishing heat, he caught a glimpse of her talking with a potter in his shed, their heads close together, her hand squeezing clay. He could not stop then, but afterward, when his quarry was safely handcuffed, he questioned the old man, who showed him a sketch she'd made, a design for a vase for flowers. He was amazed—it was so perfect. It must have taken her hours to draw. All the shadings were fine, and she'd even drawn in the shadows and made the high points glow as though they reflected light. The signature was tiny, fragile—KALINKA, the letters compressed to form a seal.

So, he thought, there is some purpose to her walks; she moves about on errands, fills her days with little things. But there was something odd too—a feeling he had that she was lost.

He became interested and wondered if she noticed how frequently they met. Why? Why did he, busy with police work, and she, on her little errands—why did their paths so often intersect? What was there in common about their lives? What drew them together in this teeming town?

He tried to study her when he visited La Colombe, tried to watch her as he and Peter talked. Sometimes he'd catch her eye and then she'd smile as if to say: "We have a secret—we see each other, have knowledge of each other's life." Did he imagine this?

Around Zvegintzov she was docile, never said a word. No wonder he'd never noticed her there—she came alive for him only when he saw her walking by herself.

One day, on a tip from an informant, he and Aziz Jaouhari raided a strange cafe in the medina. They raced up three flights of dark, stale-smelling stairs, then suddenly burst out onto a roof. The sunlight was blinding, the air sweet with the fumes of hashish. A dozen Chinese puffing on long cane pipes lay on reed mats beneath a panoply of freshly laundered sheets. No one turned as they stood watching from the door, panting from their climb.

"Who are these people?"

"Isn't that Zvegintzov's wife?"

Aziz pointed, and Hamid recognized her at once. Her head was covered by the hood of a black djellaba drawn about her dress. It was all so strange—he'd never noticed that there were Chinese in the city before, never imagined that there was a Chinese group. He stared and then withdrew, muttering to Aziz as they descended that they should start a Chinese file.

What was she doing there? Impossible to know. When their eyes met in the shop he felt confused.

He saw her sipping tea with an Italian smuggler in a small cafe near the bus terminal at the end of Avenue d'Espagne. He knew the man, knew for a fact that he was ruthless and corrupt. *What was she doing? Why?*

Another time, when he was driving down Pasteur, he saw her talking with his brother, Farid, in the doorway of his shop. He raced around the block and parked, then ran to the corner just in time to see her leave.

"So," he said to Farid, "you know Madame Zvegintzov?"

"Yes, Hamid, she's come by several times. Thank you for sending her, but I don't think I can help. The sort of horn she wants—copper and very long—I haven't seen one like that in years."

"She said I sent her?"

Farid narrowed his eyes. "You did, didn't you? I'm sure she said you did."

He turned away, his hands trembling. She'd sought out his brother, used his name. What did she want with a long old-warrior's horn? Perhaps she wanted to convert it into a lamp.

After that she was fixed firmly in his brain. Her implacable gaze, her masklike face—he saw it everywhere, even when he closed his eyes. What was happening? He was in love with her. Yes, he loved her—he realized it then. But what to do? Was she playing a game? He must find out, must corner her somewhere, force her to speak. Where? She was always moving, slipping away. In the shop? Impossible! With Peter watching? No!

He began to lose interest in his work, to wander about by himself at night, hoping to run into her, to find a situation where they could talk. He went to the dark place by the Casbah wall, but she did not appear. He stood gazing down at Tangier and its bay, watching the night pour over the Mountain like thick, black ink, watching until he could no longer see the towers of the mosques.

He became obsessed, and during the day at unexpected times he would think of her, imagine her coming toward him down a street, smiling, stooping every so often to pick a wild herb or rip a flower from a hedge. Yes, she was tracking him, tracking him inside his mind. At the shop their eyes would lock and she would smile. As he stood talking to Peter he felt tense, certain she was watching his back. Afterward he would go to his car, or move to the shadow of some doorway, and rub away the moisture from his palms.

He thought only of her and whispered her name over and over to himself: *Kalinka, Kalinka.* Her name sounded like the ring of a bell.

One day he went to Farid's bazaar, prowled for an hour among the antiques. Finally he couldn't contain himself—the words pulsed with passion as they escaped his chest. "Find me the sort of horn she wants," he panted. "Find it and sell it to me."

"Oh, Hamid, she has cast a spell on you. I can see it in your eyes—she has made you mad."

"Find me this horn, Farid," he begged. "I will pay anything, but find it. Find it soon."

He found a chicken's foot in his mailbox. Who put it there? A thief, perhaps, someone he'd caught and sent to Malabata prison? *Why?*

The next night it was cold. The wind was blowing hard, and he could barely sleep. Suddenly a knock on his door. He was living on Rue Dante then, in a small apartment on the top floor of a building full of Spaniards. He stumbled out of bed, tried to turn on the light. Nothing. The electricity had failed.

He opened the door. Peter Zvegintzov stood in the dark hallway, a thick, black overcoat hanging from his arm. Hamid could feel tension. The taste of brass filled his mouth.

"Why do you come here, Peter?" he asked.

"My wife wants to leave me. She tells me she's in love with you."

They stood facing each other in the darkness. He could feel menace in the Russian, and also great despair.

"I know nothing of that," he said. But at the same time he felt joy.

"What has happened, Hamid? What has passed between you?"

"I don't know anything about it. I doubt we've exchanged a dozen words."

"But she says—"

"Yes! Yes! Tell me what she says."

Zvegintzov was silent. *Had he betrayed himself?* Hamid stepped back.

"She says you meet all the time, everywhere in the city. She says she's been lying to me, that when she goes out it is never to the places she has said. She says she follows you, and that when you come into my shop you pretend to listen to me but use your eyes to speak with her."

Zvegintzov stepped into the doorway. A bit of light from the street cut a triangle across his head. There was anger in his face. Down the hall someone yelled "Quiet!" in Spanish. Hamid took another step back.

"I don't understand why you've come here in the middle of the night."

"How can you say a thing like that? My wife tells me she's leaving. Of course I've come to you. What difference the time of night? I have come for an explanation. I'm the husband. I have certain rights."

Hamid stared.

"For a long time I have helped you, Hamid—invited you into my place of business, told you things that have helped you with your work. You could not force me to do this. There is no pressure you could bring against me. I talked to you of my own free will. Now I learn that you will take away my wife. I confront you and you deny it. Is Kalinka a liar then? Tell me, tell me to my face."

He stood blocking the door, defiant, enraged. Finally Hamid answered him, but not without exerting an enormous effort to meet his eyes.

"Yes, I love her. But I never knew she loved me until you told me so tonight."

"Ah—then it's true." His voice was filled with resignation, all the anger drained away. He brushed past Hamid, walked to the center of the room. "I'm a fool," he said. "A fool. You're an inspector of police and I'm a fool."

From a sleeve of his coat he drew a short, stiff riding crop. Then he dropped it on the floor. "I brought this so I could slash your face. She does this to me, you see. Drives me mad, makes me miserable, makes me act the fool."

He stood for a time, his head bowed. Hamid watched him, unable to tear away his eyes. Zvegintzov began to gasp and then to weep—strange sounds, whimpers of agony stifled finally by his heavy Russian cough.

"Forgive me for coming. I can't control myself. I am helpless. You see that."

He wept some more, then left. Hamid watched him from the window, watched him move slowly down the street. The wind was blowing hard, the street lights flickered. Then a hailstorm began. Pellets the size of marbles were falling upon Tangier.

He and Peter did not speak again. The next day he sent Farid to fetch Kalinka and bring her to Farid's bazaar. In the back room she told him she was in love with him, and that if he wouldn't take her to live with him she would leave the town.

"For years I saw you," she said. "Sometimes I waited the whole day thinking of nothing but that soon, perhaps within the hour, you would come to see Peter in our shop. I wanted to see your eyes, hear your voice. I trembled when I saw you watching me on the street."

He asked her about Peter, and she swore to him then that she was not his wife, had never been, either in law or in deed. He was amazed, and his policeman's temperament, his skepticism, all his control ebbed away. He felt helpless in the face of her passion, her strange inflections, her enigmatic eyes. He took her hand. They kissed and moaned. She lay her fingers upon the high bones of his cheeks.

Later he went to see his mother in Dradeb. She was ironing when he came into the house.

"Ah, Hamid, you have always been in love with foreigners. Ever since you were a boy. Now the foreigners will dislike you. It's bad for a Moroccan to steal a Nasrani's wife."

"No, mother," he said. "I'm an inspector of police. Now it doesn't matter what the foreigners think. It only matters what I think of them."

She nodded, but she didn't understand. To her Tangier would always be a city which the infidels controlled. Later, when he brought Kalinka, his mother looked into her eyes.

"This woman smokes hashish."

"I know. I know."

It had bothered him at first, but he came to realize that the smoke was a part of her, part of the aura of dreaminess and mystery that he loved.

"Perhaps," his mother said, "she will cause you pain."

She hadn't yet. She served him, cooked for him. She polished his moccasins and arranged them on the floor in pairs. Farid finally found the horn and gave it to them as a gift. They kept it standing straight on the floor beside their bed. It was as tall as Kalinka, and its end, shaped like a bell, reminded him of her name.

At the Sûreté they said she was the best thing ever to happen to him. Once he overheard Aziz speaking to a colleague in the police canteen. "Of course Hamid understands the foreigners," he said. "He lives with a Chinese woman now, has learned all their secrets from her."

A Chinese woman—she was not that, but he understood why they thought she was. Just as all foreigners were infidels, and all infidels were Christians, so all Orientals were Chinese to them.

The wind. The wind. It blew so often in Tangier. When he thought back over that time he remembered the wind and the tears that flowed from Peter Zvegintzov's eyes. It pleased him that he lived with a woman who could inspire great love and break men's hearts. To love a woman—yes, that he understood. A woman could charm a man, cast a spell upon him, drive him mad. He was himself, he knew, bound to Kalinka by invisible bonds of passion that only she could break.

Who was she? Why had Peter lied and said she was his wife?

The wind, blowing hard outside, steady, raw, drove him finally into sleep. His last thought before falling off was of Peter's misery and the way Kalinka haunted him, lived on in his heart even after her betrayal.

Lake

It was three o'clock in the morning, and still Lake couldn't sleep. The wind was bothering him, ripping at the palms in the Consulate garden. He stared up at the ceiling and thought of faucets that leaked, appliances in the basement that didn't work. He couldn't bear a smudge on a window or a puddle of grease beneath a car.

He stole out of bed, went to the bathroom, snapped on the light, splashed water on his face. Then, as he stared into the mirror, he practiced a stiff salute. His curly hair was dull, not glossy as he liked, and there was a bald spot toward the back. There was a terrible ticking too—something like a bomb that threatened to blow up inside his brain.

He turned on the shower, adjusted the faucets until the water ran hot. Then he stood under it, trembling in the heat. It had been the same in Guatemala during the visit of the Secretary of State. He had almost had a nervous breakdown then, terrible chills in the tropic nights, insomnia, strange urges to fix things, clean things up. He'd felt caged in, restless, smoked too many cigarettes, and had been frightened by his inability to sleep. Was it happening to him again, all those strange symptoms that had come together and then nearly brought him to the brink? This time would he succumb? Would Tangier drive him mad?

He dressed and wandered into the stainless steel kitchen, opened the refrigerator, found a package of bacon, threw some strips into a frying pan, and began to scramble eggs. When he was finished he turned on the blower to remove the fumes, then set to work washing the utensils. Everything had to be cleaned and arranged as it was before. When the servants came they mustn't find a trace.

He went back to the bathroom, brushed his teeth and shaved, then rinsed out the sink and applied an acrid spray to purify his breath. He checked himself in the mirror again, noticed crow's-feet around his eyes. His jawline was becoming flabby. His muttonchop sideburns were turning gray.

He looked in at Janet—she was curled toward the wall. He envied the calm rhythms of her breathing, so unlike his own harsh gasps. In a shelf by their bed was his collection of self-help books, paperbacks worn out by use. He checked his sons, paused for a moment in the doorways of their rooms. Steven slept peacefully amidst his games. Joe slept quietly too, and Lake was moved by the disarray: various sneakers, unmatched, spread in odd corners of the room; a limp tracksuit on the floor.

He let himself out the back door, braced before the wind. It swept him across the garden, between the yuccas and palms. Looking back toward the residence, he was struck by its enormous size. The moon was only half full, and that annoyed him—he couldn't abide uncompleted things, unanswered mail, unpolished shoes.

He turned a key in the back door of the Consulate, entered, then locked himself inside. Suddenly the wind was cut off by the thick sliding glass. For the first time that evening he felt relief. Here in the empty building he could be alone, sealed off from the wind, safe from his demons. Even the smell here made him feel good: the floors were cleaned in the early evening, and the odor of the cleansers still perfumed the air.

He took the elevator to the top floor, unlocked his office, sat back in his swivel chair, safe between his consular ensign and the American flag.

⟨ 33 ⟩

I am, he thought, *the Consul General of the United States.*

He loved the title. After tours in Guatemala, Beirut, Vientiane, he had come to Tangier excited by the prospect of two years of well-earned peace. For a decade he'd served in countries racked by street riots and guerrilla wars. Now at last he'd be able to rest, restore his balance, contemplate the dangerous world that lay beyond détente.

He'd been wrong. The post was a nightmare, and now the tedium stole his sleep. Too many lost passports to be replaced; too many hippies arrested on drug charges who had to be visited at the Tangier jail. He loathed his ceremonial duties, the endless, boring banquets with Moroccan functionaries and the irate tourists who wandered in, complaining because their reservations hadn't been honored at the hotels. His vice-consul disgusted him, and he felt no love for his Moroccan staff. The only friend he'd found was Willard Manchester, who'd once held the Coca-Cola franchise in southern Spain. But even Willard, full of advice on ways to cope, could not sustain him here. Thinking things over, pondering them for months, Lake had come to the conclusion that the Department had found him out. How had it happened? For years he'd gone to pains to conceal his disorders, used drugs to control his depressions, stayed clear of psychiatrists, bluffed his way through physical exams. Now they'd put him out to pasture, assigned him to Tangier. The town, so pleasant, so relaxed, had become for him a maelstrom where his demons gnawed without pity and his soul withered beneath the glittering sun.

It was so unfair. He loved the Department, loved to face foreign officials and say: "Speaking on behalf of the United States. . . ." What had happened? Were his symptoms really so bizarre? He didn't take off his clothes in public or sit in cafes speaking to the air. He was not one to teach a parrot dirty words or chase servant girls down scullery stairs. What was it then? Something not quite right, something that spooked people, an aura of failure that surrounded him like a cloud. Yes, that was it; he knew, could feel it in himself. There was madness at work inside, and that made him afraid.

By the light of half a moon he could see the wind tearing at

⟨ 34 ⟩

the trees. In the distance the Mountain was dark, except for the yellow lamps that lit the road.

Thank God for the files. They'd saved his life. Dating back to the time when the Consulate had been a full legation, they told tales of gun running, the recovery of stolen bullion, the sorts of intrigues that had given Tangier its fabled name. It was as if the city he read about was not the same as the place he lived, a dark night city of killers and spies, espionage, blackmail, double agents, dirty tricks. Now, at night, when he couldn't sleep, he'd leave his bed, shave and bathe, then steal across the garden to his office to immerse himself till dawn in tales of deceit.

There was much in these stories to entertain him—they were better than thrillers, though not so neat. And, slowly, they began to alter his perception of Tangier. Now this city of crumbling façades, so sleazy in its decline, became the backdrop for exotic dramas once played out on its shabby streets. He loved the tale of the defecting East German scientist, and the one about the Vichy agent whose body had been dumped in the Forêt Diplomatique. Then unexpectedly (by chance or fate?) he stumbled on the file on Z.

He'd almost missed it. He'd been prowling through a disordered drawer of gossip. He remembered a thin folder on Camilla Weltonwhist containing photos (clipped from an old issue of *Country Life*) of her recently sold Bermuda estate, and a fascinating report from Jakarta in which an informant ("usually reliable," it said) fingered Jimmy Sohario as a heroin racketeer, and his chain of laundries as a front. But Z's file was different, a special case. Over the next few weeks Lake would read and reread it, but he would never forget the exhilaration that seized him that first night.

ZVEGINTZOV, PETER PETROVITCH

This long-time resident of Tangier is believed to be a low-grade Soviet agent who has operated in northern Morocco for nearly twenty years. He emerged from deep cover in the early 1960s, at the time of the French Saharan nuclear tests. He was observed in contact with Col. Igor Prozov, coordinator of KGB activities in the Mahgreb. Subject is now believed inactive. Personal contact by consular officials not advised.

Z was born in Hanoi in early 1920s. Parents were White Russian. Education not known. Believed recruited by Soviets near end of World War II.

After service in the French army, Z returned to Hanoi, where he opened and operated a shop for five years. In the late 1940s he was put under surveillance by French colonial authorities who suspected that his shop was an intelligence drop, and that he was a Soviet agent working with the Viet Minh. Later, on the basis of captured enemy documents, he was accused of being a Soviet field officer responsible for the delivery of arms to caches along the coast. Subject denied accusations, but was expelled in 1952. Made his way from Hong Kong to Vladivostok, where he disappeared. In 1955 he resurfaced in Tangier on a Polish passport. Worked here in several banks and import-export houses. Founded La Colombe in 1959.

Z has regular habits and is considered highly reliable by his clientele. He is an accomplished linguist who reads and writes Russian, Polish, English, French, Spanish, and Vietnamese.

Thinking back to that night when he'd read the file for the first time, Lake tried to analyze its compelling effect. Why, he wondered, removing it from his desk, had he almost immediately begun to shake? What was it that had gripped him and started all those notions swirling through his brain?

He opened up the file, read it through again. There was much more than the covering summary, all sorts of things that belied the words "inactive" and "low-grade." He labored furiously with the documents provided by the Deuxième Bureau, trying hard to understand all the nuances in French. Red pencil in hand, he underlined his way through a maze of cold war intrigue. Z's life was filled with twists and turns. Why, Lake wondered, hadn't the case been closed?

Fantasies began to flood him as he let the papers slip back upon his desk. All his readings in the other files gave him material for a thousand dreams. His scenarios were rich pastiches of borrowed vignettes. He had a vision of himself following Z down narrow Tangier streets, observing meetings from dark archways in the Casbah, close calls in empty squares. There were suspicious transactions observed in rusting cafe mirrors, and mad chases up flights of wet stone stairs. He lost him in the Grand Socco, among a crowd of veiled women and hooded men, then picked him up again on a deserted beach at night, while the periscope of a Soviet submarine emerged slowly in the middle of the Straits. Prozov, the much-feared Prozov, was aboard, and Z was rowing out to him in a small black boat. Quick flashes of light from the sub, and a reply from Z. He would have to act now if he was going to intercept.

The water was ice cold against his body. There was danger in the currents, treachery in the tides. Something gelatinous and phosphorescent grazed his leg. His arms ached as he swam, then hoisted himself aboard. There was a mad fight then with the rough wooden oars. They dueled like savages while his hands bled, and when the boat capsized the salt water stung the damaged flesh. Finally he threw away his oar and went after Z with bare hands. A knee to the groin, and a fast chop against the neck. Z's eyes bugged out—he could smell the garlic on his breath. He grabbed his head and held it under water until he drowned. When it was done the Russian's spectacles bobbed away on a spumy wave.

Nine o'clock in the morning. Standing at the window of his office, Dan Lake could see the Mountain, bathed in sunlight, and the valley of Dradeb below. He was peering through binoculars at Willard Manchester's terrace, trying to hold Willard and Katie in focus against the pinkness of their house. There were pots of geraniums near the wrought iron table; a stainless steel coffee pot caught the light. Katie was writing—probably a shopping list; Willard was drawing on a pipe.

"Now tell me, Foster—slowly, please. And don't leave anything out."

Foster Knowles was sitting on a couch at the far end of the office, staring absently at the American flag behind the Consul General's desk. He looked at Lake's back, broad and straight against the window. Then he twitched a little and cleared his throat.

"Gee, Dan, there's not too much to tell. I watched the place all day. People go in and then they come out. There's sort of a buildup between ten and eleven in the morning—people coming back from the market, I guess. Then there's another rush between six and eight. At one he closes down and drives off for lunch. He opens again at four in the afternoon."

"Where does he go?"

"When, Dan?"

"For lunch, Foster. When do you think?"

"I don't know." Knowles shrugged. "I couldn't follow him. He might have recognized my car."

"You used your own car?"

"Well, what else could I use?"

"Christ!" Knowles was hopeless, his surveillance a flop.

"Look, Dan, I'm new at all this. If you'd just tell me—"

"Later, later—"

Lake let the binoculars droop around his neck, then looked at his vice-consul slouching on the couch.

"For Christ's sake, Foster," he said gently, "will you please sit up straight."

He moved around to his desk and shook his head. Knowles was an idiot. His blond hair curled down his neck and covered half his ears. He was exactly the same size as his wife, Jackie, who taught girls' gymnastics at the American School. They were vegetarians, smoked pot on the weekends, jogged around early in the morning in unisex sweatsuits like a matched pair of ponies parading on a course.

"All right," he said, settling into his chair. "What sort of people go in there, and what did you see them do?"

"Oh—people from the Mountain. The Manchesters, for instance."

"Willard Manchester goes in there?"

Knowles nodded. "Yesterday he went in twice."

"And?" Why hadn't Willard told him about the Russian and his past?

"The British. A lot of them. The Whittles. Vicar Wick. Retired people. People with big cars. They get their mail, pick up packages, buy newspapers—things like that." Knowles looked down at the rug. "I don't know—maybe I should have kept a log."

"That's all right, Foster. I just want a feel of what goes on. Any Moroccans?"

"Well, he gets deliveries. Ouazzani was in there last night."

"Inspector Ouazzani?"

"Yeah."

"Did he buy anything?"

"Not that I could see."

"OK, Foster." Lake yawned. "Thanks very much. You can go back to whatever you were doing now."

Knowles sat still. "You know, Dan, I've been thinking."

"Yeah? What about?"

"This whole business seems kind of crazy."

"Forget about it then."

"You mean forget the whole thing?"

"Uh huh. I thought you'd like it—snooping around. I sort of thought of you as a good snoop-around type. But I guess I was wrong. Forget about it. I'll handle it myself."

"Gee, Dan—"

"I've got a lot of paperwork this morning, so if you'd just—"

"Yeah. Right." Knowles nodded, unraveled himself, and started toward the door. Halfway there he paused and turned around. "There's one other thing, Dan, you ought to know. Might turn into a hassle later on. Couple of young Americans, hippies I guess, were camping out in the Rif. Seems they went hunting for psychedelic mushrooms and ate some poison ones by mistake. After a while they started feeling bad, so they hitched a ride to Tangier. They're at Al Kortobi Hospital now. According to the doctors they're really sick."

"OK. Keep me informed."

Knowles nodded and went out the door. When he was gone Lake made a fist and pounded it against the desk. Hassles! Psychedelic mushrooms! *God, what an asshole,* he thought.

He paced around the office for a while, feeling caged, bad-tempered, worn. He hadn't slept properly in a week, and now his mind was clouded by all sorts of things he didn't understand or know how to control. The wind was still blowing, though the sealed windows of the Consulate cut the noise. Outside he could see the palms thrashing and a small surf lapping at the sides of the Consulate pool.

He took hold of the binoculars again, trained them on the Mountain, found the Jew's River at its base and tried to move along it to La Colombe. *Damn those palms!* Just in the corner they blocked his view. He was about to call downstairs, order the gardener to cut them down, when he stopped himself and shook his head.

Madness, he whispered. *Mad! Mad!*

But a few seconds later he broke into a sweat. *Ouazzani!* There was some connection. He remembered it now. Through the winter Willard and Katie had talked of little else. Z's wife had left him for a policeman, Hamid Ouazzani, who headed the foreign section at the Sûreté. The Manchesters had been worried. Zvegintzov was despondent, and they were afraid he was going to close his shop. When he snapped out of it they'd been relieved. Now Foster said Ouazzani had visited Z. The whole setup began to stink.

Could it be, he asked himself, that Z planted the girl with the Inspector in order to infiltrate the police? With a police-man in his pocket he would have information on all the for-eigners in town. He could blackmail them, use them as couriers, employ them any way he liked. And he'd arranged his own protection too: with a link to the police his espionage operation could go on and on.

Lake toyed with the idea for several minutes, then slumped back into his chair. He knew he was being ridiculous, that all his fantasies were absurd. Z was inactive, a man much like himself, broken, put out to pasture, mired in failure and de-spair. He felt a surge of sympathy for him then. He and Z were a pair of relics, aging cold warriors stagnating in Tangier.

At lunch he was distracted, glum. He hardly listened as Janet rambled on about their social life, nodded absently when she asked him if he'd like her to get them tickets for the play. Joe said his French teacher was a queer. Steven said there was a kid at school with a mustache who threat-ened to take him into the bushes and "spread his ass." Janet was shocked and begged him to intervene. "You ought to call the headmaster, Dan. It's the very least that you should do."

He nodded, promised he would, but he was really concen-trating on Z. What could he do about him? Or might he do better to leave him alone?

When he crossed the garden again to his office, the wind had begun to slack off. There was a circular in his in-box, something from the Department asking how many square feet in the Consulate were devoted to offices, public areas, garage. "Foster—please take care of this" he jotted in the margin. Then he leaned back and groaned. It was asinine—a request like that, the sort of thing that could drive you mad. But he made certain that every memo received was answered by the following day. He insisted on "responsiveness" even if it meant that Foster would have to work at night.

He went to the vault, unlocked it, and walked inside. Here only Foster and himself were allowed. The cryptographic equipment lay immaculate on the table. The machine was quiet—no messages to be cracked. He walked along the bank of green steel filing cabinets, his fingers giving an extra twist to each of the gleaming locks.

Why had he been sent here? How could he convince the Department that he was cut out for grander things? Maybe he ought to come clean, admit to his instability, seek help, confess. But he knew the Department, knew there was no mercy there. Washington was littered with broken foreign-service officers, men like himself who'd cracked up overseas. He couldn't accept that. He had to educate his sons. On a disability pension he'd lose his self-respect—nothing to do, that's what was killing him. He needed action, crisis, work.

Feeling claustrophobic, he left the vault then carefully locked the door. Back in his office he was about to phone the school when he received a call from Knowles.

"Jesus, Dan—the shit's just hit the fan. One of those mushroom kids croaked, and it looks like the other may croak tonight."

"Christ, Foster! Do you have to use that word?"

"Sorry, Dan. What are we going to do?"

Lake thought a moment, back through his years of experience. When an American died overseas it was up to the Consul to take charge.

"Got a pencil, Foster? Get this down. First, find out the name of the next of kin and call him at our expense. Then get hold of the personal effects, put the consular seal on them, and store them away downstairs. Find out who handles corpses around here and get him to work. Be sure and get a death certificate from the hospital, and some documentation from the police. Have it all translated, make photostats of the originals, and prepare a covering letter for my signature, laying out the circumstances and expressing regrets. Then get in touch with the airlines about flying out the body. That'll wrap it up."

There was silence at the other end. Then he heard Foster gasp. "Gee, Dan," he said. "You really are a pro."

Lake smiled and hung up. *Yes,* he thought, *I've still got what it takes.* He'd done well in Laos, that never-never land of three-headed elephants. Even in Guatemala he'd been good—especially during the affair of the left-wing Maryknoll nuns. But here there was nothing—a lousy mushroom poisoning, for Christ's sake. How could he prove himself? What could he do? The question gnawed at him through the afternoon, as the wind subsided to a breeze. There seemed no way out of the dilemma. He was stuck in Tangier, boxed in.

Finally, at five o'clock, impatient with himself and his despair, he ordered his car brought around to the front of the building, then dismissed the driver and took the wheel himself. His intention was to drive out to Cap Spartel, park there, somewhere on the back of the Mountain, and stare down at the Atlantic toward the setting sun. But as he emerged from Dradeb, crossed the Jew's River bridge, he pulled up suddenly in front of La Colombe. It was time, he knew, to go inside and try to read the Russian's face.

Monday
at the Sûreté

Aziz Jaouhari had been working for an hour when Hamid walked in late. It was Monday morning and as usual there was much coming and going at the Sûreté. Civilians and police mingled on the bottom floor, and the basement was filled with people arrested over the weekend.

"Well, Aziz, what have we got this morning?" Hamid hung up his leather jacket and sat down at his desk.

Aziz was looking at his list. "Six tourists in the jug, Inspector—five of them members of a British ballet. They played Rabat, then came up here for fun. We caught them with little boys on Saturday night having an orgy at the Oriental Hotel."

"Robin, of course."

Aziz nodded. "He turned them in. They demanded to see the British Consul, but Mrs. Whittle told me he was out of town. Actually I think he was here but didn't want to be disturbed."

"Doesn't surprise me. He hates the queers." Hamid lit a cigarette.

"Then there's an American, brought in late last night. He

picked up a whore at Heidi's Bar. They were walking back to her place when she began to scream. That's his version, of course. She says he was going to break her arm. Anyway, a cop named Mustapha Barrada came along and found a kilo of hash in his jeans. There was a scuffle, and Mustapha beat him up. Doctor saw him early this morning, and I've been in touch with Knowles."

"Good, Aziz. Very good."

"There's more. The hustler they call 'Pumpkin Pie' wracked up Inigo's Mercedes on the Tetuan Road. In the process he hit an old man and crushed his legs. What concerns us is that Inigo reported the car stolen a couple of hours before, so we're holding the boy, whose name is Mohammed Seraj, until he comes in here and swears out a complaint."

"How's the old man?"

Aziz shrugged. "In pain. This Seraj is a wild one. Maybe he didn't even blow the horn."

"Right. Anything else?" Hamid felt weary already and wished he was back home in bed.

"The Prefect wants to see you this afternoon. And Vicar Wick, the one who runs St. Thomas Church, has an urgent matter that he will only discuss with you."

"Tell him to come in."

"You want the Vicar to come in here?"

"He's not a diplomat. I don't have to call on him."

Aziz beamed. "You interested in the ballet dancers?"

"Depends on who they are. If they're nobody special we'll expel them all tonight."

When Aziz finally left, Hamid turned to the window and groaned. It was like this on a Monday—people in jail, incidents from the weekend, trivial details that took up his time. Now he was concerned about Kalinka and found it difficult to concentrate on work. She'd always been strange—that was the secret of her attractiveness—but lately, it seemed to him, her strangeness had increased. She'd smoked the whole weekend, disappearing into a haze of incompleted sentences, utterances in Vietnamese he couldn't understand. It was as if she was trying to tell him something. So many times he had asked her, "Who are you, Kalinka?", and now, it seemed, she wanted to answer but couldn't find the words. She was such a puzzle. Often Hamid would pause to wrestle with her mystery. So far with no result, but still he hoped to find the key.

Aziz came back into the office. "Vicar Wick's on his way over now. The Prefect will see you at six. Inigo is here to make his complaint, and Knowles is with the American downstairs."

"Good. I'll start with Inigo. Then Knowles. Keep the Vicar waiting—half an hour at least."

Aziz gave him an admiring glance, then showed Inigo in. The Paraguayan painter was an extremely handsome young man, with the face of a Mexican saint.

"So, Inspector, you've got my little Pumpkin Pie. He's been a naughty boy. Good thing you locked him up."

Hamid smiled. He liked the artist, was a great admirer of his work. His paintings, all highly realistic, glowed with a translucent sheen. There'd been a time, when Hamid was a boy, when he'd thought a painter was someone who whitewashed a house.

"Yes, we have him, and since you're the owner of the car, the responsibility would normally fall on you. You reported it stolen so you seem to be absolved, but since Pumpkin Pie is your houseboy, it puts the affair in a curious light."

"Ha!" said Inigo, smoothing his long black hair. "I don't know where you get your information. Pumpkin Pie is my lover and does absolutely nothing around the house."

Hamid smiled again. "Yes. Of course. But to us, you see, houseboy and lover come to the same thing. What happened? Did you have a quarrel? How did he get hold of the keys?"

"Stole them, of course. As he's stolen nearly everything else. The boy's a kleptomaniac. There was a time when you would have cut off his hand."

"Yes. The old Koranic justice. Harsh, merciless, and irrevocable punishments. Sometimes we wish we could still mete them out. But we're trying to be civilized now."

"A big mistake, if you don't mind my saying so. When this country becomes civilized, it'll be time for me to leave. I came here for the barbarism. I like the feeling of being in a violent land. And the faces—gaunt, strong, primitive—they're the faces I dreamed of in Paraguay. Like yours, Inspector—a classic. Perhaps someday you'll be kind and model for me."

"I'm flattered, but I don't have the time—"

"A minute! Let me look closely!" Inigo stood up, leaned over the desk, and carefully inspected Hamid's face. "I swear I've seen this physiognomy before. Perhaps in one of the drawings by Delacroix." He sat down again. "It constantly amazes me—this sense I have that Morocco is still the same. Did you know that when Delacroix came here he spent days in the Socco sketching everyone who passed by? Hundreds of faces. Sometimes fifteen or twenty on a page. I'd swear yours was one of them. Has your family always lived in Tangier?"

"We're from Ouazzane. But enough about my face. The keys—did Mohammed have access to them? Was he normally allowed to drive your car?"

Inigo brought his fist up hard against his forehead, then squeezed shut his eyes. "Ah, Inspector, if you only *knew*—if you only knew the trouble I've had with that boy. He's a sadist, positively a sadist. Every day he tortures me to death. He steals my drawings, takes them to Madrid, and sells them on the street. Then he comes back penniless, makes sweet apologies, and I take him in again. He's not only a thief; he's a liar too. Constantly he lies about where he's been. With friends, he says, at some obscure cafe, and I nod, though I know perfectly well nothing he says is true. He's been in some shabby hotel with some disgusting British queer, acting the part of the rough street whore, probably beating the faggot up. I've bought him beautiful shirts, silk scarves, a motorcycle, the best perfume. My God, he was dressed in rags when I found him guarding cars in Asilah after a certain countess dismissed him from her staff. But the more I give him the more he takes. We've fought, actually come to blows. He once threw one of my paintings, still wet and unvarnished—threw it down a stairs! I bought a swan for my swimming pool. He captured it, strangled it with his bare hands! The boy's completely schizophrenic, but I need him, so what am I to do? Suffer, I suppose. Suffer! As people say an artist should. But why? Why should I suffer? My paintings have made me rich. I have the finest, absolutely the

⟨ 46 ⟩

finest house in Tangier. I live on the Mountain. Museums collect my work. Everything I paint gets snapped up. My prices climb. I get richer. And still my suffering goes on."

He removed his fist, settled back exhausted in his chair. "I must accept it, I suppose. My destiny. God's will, as you people say. It's written. *Mektoub.* But why? *Why?* Here I am, a great painter, perhaps the greatest technician since Velasquez, living with a nasty little street whore who uses me terribly and is way beneath my style."

Hamid listened, amused at Inigo's antics and the melodrama of his life. The artist, he knew, was fond of monologues, whose effects he always tried to gauge as he went along.

"I gather," he said finally, "that you're not particularly impressed."

"Oh," said Hamid. "I *am.* But forgive me if I keep my feelings to myself. In this office I've heard every sort of confession. I listen, I observe, but I refuse to judge."

"Ah. Then you're a student of human nature, a man much like myself. Still I'm glad I've told you this. Better for you to understand me than to think me mad for what I'm going to do. I want Pumpkin Pie released. I won't press charges, and I withdraw everything I've said. He didn't steal my car—I handed him the keys."

Hamid studied him a moment. "You realize, of course, that you'll have to pay damages, settle with the injured man? A Moroccan judge, knowing that you're rich, will want to teach you a lesson. It'll be extremely expensive—you can be sure of that."

"Yes, yes." Inigo waved his hands. "I understand. And I'm resigned. Money means nothing in the end. I simply want to return to my house, face my easel, and paint." He was quiet for a moment, then lowered his voice. "Tell me, Inspector. When will you let him go?"

"An hour or so. Aziz will show you where to post the bond."

"I brought my checkbook just in case."

"No guarantee, of course, that he'll return to your house."

"Oh, I know that. But he will. Sooner or later he will. He needs me, in his way, as much as I need him."

They both rose then, and Hamid shook his hand.

"I accept your decision, though I think you're making a mistake."

"Of course," said Inigo. "I'll pay for it later. I know that. But there's nothing I can do. It's my flaw—the flaw in my character, you see."

When Aziz came back Hamid asked him what he thought.

"The Nasranis are all mad," he said.

"Perhaps, Aziz. Perhaps. Now give me a few minutes to smoke a cigarette. Then bring in Vice-Consul Knowles."

The session with the Americans was quick. The prisoner was brought up, sat numb in his chair while Aziz read aloud from his dossier. When that was finished Hamid asked him if he agreed with the reported facts. The American shook his head and stared down at the floor.

"Listen here," Hamid said, "you'd do much better to confess. It's your word against a man of the police. Tell us who sold you the hash, sign a confession, and maybe the judge will go easy on you. But make us prove our case and the sentence will certainly be harsh." When he saw that this had no effect, he signaled Aziz to take him back to his cell. "Think about it," he shouted when the American was passing through the door.

He looked at Knowles, who seemed anxious and stiff. Hamid didn't particularly like him, though he wasn't certain exactly why. Sometimes in the mornings, driving to work, he saw the Vice-Consul and his wife jogging parallel to Vasco de Gama, appearing and disappearing among the trees and mists. He passed over the prisoner's passport, watched while Knowles copied the number down.

"Well, Mr. Knowles, what do you think?"

"You're asking me?"

"Why not?"

Knowles squinted, then shook his head. "A hippie. I think he's a hippie." He ran his fingers through his hair.

"But he denies everything—now why does he do that?"

"I don't know why you ask me, Inspector. I know nothing about the case."

"You know as much as I do. You're his fellow countryman. I was hoping you'd help me understand the processes of his mind."

Knowles shrugged. Hamid studied him for a moment, then decided to make a leap. "I have the feeling," he said, "that you don't much like this work."

"The work's all right. It's just, well—"

"Aren't you happy in our little town?"

"Yeah. Of course. Tangier's great."

"What is it then? Every time I see you you look disturbed. I know it's not pleasant to come into a police station, but I wonder if there's something more than that."

"I guess I'm a little nervous—"

"You know I've been observing you, Mr. Knowles."

"You have?"

"Oh, yes. Not you especially. But I watch everything, and I've seen you too."

Knowles turned away.

"A week ago, for instance, there were several occasions when you particularly caught my eye. You were sitting in your car outside Peter Zvegintzov's shop. Nothing wrong with that, of course. No crime. But I began to wonder. You seemed to be waiting for someone, though your wife wasn't in sight. Being a curious sort of fellow, I began to ask myself: Now why, why would a young man from the American Consulate be watching outside this particular store? And I never did figure it out."

Hamid fastened his eyes on Knowles, until the American finally looked back. He'd become extremely nervous—so much so that Hamid decided to change the subject.

"None of my business," he said. "You're your own man here. But forgive me if I give you some advice. Try to be helpful to the prisoners if you can. I know you're only required to give them a list of lawyers and a little counseling on our local laws, but your predecessor did a lot more. He was friendly to them, even used his own money to buy them soap and cigarettes. It's not very pleasant, you know, downstairs."

"I know." Knowles nodded his head. "But I don't want to get involved. Better to keep everything official—that's what our handbook says."

"Well, perhaps you're right. Still I admired the last vice-consul very much. He may not have liked the people he had to see, but he understood their pain."

When Knowles was gone Hamid waited a moment, then

went to the window to watch him enter his car. It was driven by a Moroccan chauffeur who for years had been one of his informants-without-pay.

He returned to his desk, lit another cigarette, and tried to clear his mind. Then he heard noises coming from the street and moved back to the window again. A middle-aged lady, a Riffian in a red-and-white-striped skirt, was struggling with two policemen and screaming for her son. A small crowd had gathered to watch the scene, and Hamid saw other inspectors watching from their windows too.

Why do we watch? he wondered. *Why are we all voyeurs?*

When he returned to his desk Aziz was waiting by the door.

"The Vicar's cooling his heels. You ready for him now?"

Hamid nodded, then began a shopping list in Arabic which he continued after the Vicar was shown in. When he was finished he turned the paper over and looked up at the Englishman with a smile. "Well, Vicar Wick," he said. "This is the first time you've been here, I think."

"Yes, Inspector Ouazzani. And I confess I'm not happy about it at all. A most unpleasant matter has forced me to come. As I explained to your assistant, I had to see you and no one else."

Hamid folded his hands and placed them on the desk. "Very well. You're here. Please tell us what we can do."

Vicar Wick, a short, stout, nervous man whose hair was slicked back with some sort of oil or cream, turned to look at Aziz. "It's most confidential, Inspector. I prefer to speak to you alone."

"Mr. Jaouhari is my *homme de confiance*. I promise you he's totally discreet."

"Still I'd prefer—"

Hamid shook his head. "Many people come into this room and say the most amazing things. It's necessary for me to always have a witness. Then if there's a misunderstanding later on—but I'm sure you understand."

"Hmmp! I see! Yes, yes." He turned back to Hamid. "Oh, very well." He was fidgeting. "This is a most delicate matter. Most delicate, indeed."

Hamid was becoming impatient. "Yes, Vicar, now please

tell us what it is. We have lots of work this morning. A number of your fellow countrymen have been arrested with Moroccan boys."

The Vicar's eyes began to flutter. Hamid studied him. The man chewed his fingernails. Another high-strung Englishman, he thought.

"You've heard of Mr. Peter Barclay, I presume?"

"I know him, of course."

"Good. Then you know the kind of man he is. And his importance to us British here. I needn't tell you that Mr. Barclay is from one of the greatest families in the British Isles—that his cousin is a duke and that he is related to Her Majesty in six different ways. He is, in short, a most distinguished person, and we count ourselves fortunate that he is a member of our little church."

"Yes, Vicar, we know all of that. Now please get to the point."

"I'm *getting* to it, Inspector, if you'll just let me tell this my own way. At our Sunday worship service there comes a time when we collect money from our parishioners. For the maintenance of St. Thomas, of course. Mr. Barclay, as one of our members, always takes charge of the plate. After the service he counts the money and enters the amount in our books."

Hamid nodded. Aziz, whom the Vicar couldn't see, looked at Hamid and rolled his eyes.

"Yesterday, Inspector, we had our service, and as usual there were a number of envelopes on the plate. I should explain that we provide them for people who wish to remain discreet. Discretion, you see, is most necessary, since the plate is passed hand to hand."

"Yes, I see that. Yes."

"Well, yesterday after the service Mr. Barclay began his usual accounting, and among the envelopes he found *this*."

The Vicar reached into his breast pocket and extracted a piece of paper wrapped in the cellophane from a package of cigarettes. "I took the precaution of putting it in plastic. Mr. Barclay and I both touched it, of course, but the culprit's fingerprints may be on it as well."

Hamid looked down at the item on his desk. "What is it?" he asked.

"It's a note, Inspector. A note. Without doubt the most malicious note that I have ever read. A note the likes of which has never before been handed to anyone in our church. A note which says things I cannot bring myself to repeat."

Hamid raised his eyebrows. "What does it say?"

"Please, sir, read it. Read it for yourself. In the strictest confidence, of course."

The Vicar glanced at Aziz, who was wincing with disappointment, while Hamid spread the paper out. The note was written in a violent shade of red ink; the handwriting was even, full of carefully modeled loops.

> YOU DEFILE THIS HOUSE OF THE LORD,
> PETER BARCLAY. A GOOD THRASHING IS
> WHAT YOU NEED. YOU'RE A PEDERAST, A
> TWO-FACED HYPOCRITE, BUT OUR LORD
> JESUS CHRIST CANNOT BE DECEIVED. LEAVE
> TANGIER, YOU SWINE, OR BE STRICKEN
> DOWN. THE LORD'S HOUSE WILL BE
> CLEANSED.

Hamid read through it quickly, then read it a second time with care. He wanted to be certain he understood all the nuances of the text. "It seems quite straightforward," he said finally, looking back at Wick. "Tell us what happened next."

"Nothing *happened*. This excrescence was simply read. The evidence before you speaks quite plainly for itself."

"Hmmm. Well, I'm afraid something is escaping me if this, in fact, is all."

"All! But don't you *see*? The most distinguished Englishman in Tangier, a man who but for the grace of God might have been a duke, is insulted in the British church by an anonymous note full of calumnies and threats."

"Yes, I see all that. What does Mr. Barclay have to say?"

"The poor man's been quite brave about it. He pretends to laugh it off, though of course he's deeply hurt. You see the gravity, Inspector? We simply must find out who wrote this and expel him before others are similarly attacked." He lowered his voice to a shaking whisper. "Oh, how I would love to know who among us has done this thing. With such a maniac in our midst we may all be driven from our church."

Hamid sat back. "All this is very interesting, Vicar, and I certainly understand your concern. But there's nothing we can do for you here. This isn't a matter for the police."

The Vicar sat up straight, angry and amazed. "Not a matter for the police! What else are the police for, may I ask, if not to solve cases such as this?"

"There's been no crime, Vicar. At least not under Moroccan law. No criminal act has been committed, so we're powerless to intervene."

Wick grasped the note, smudging any fingerprints that might have been left. "But the threats!" he said, shaking the paper in Hamid's face. "The threats! 'Stricken down!' 'A good thrashing!' These are violent threats."

"I myself see no threats. Only imputations, and entreaties to God."

"It's blasphemy!"

"Perhaps. I happen to be a Moslem and therefore not all that well acquainted with your faith. But the laws of my country are clearly spelled out. They say nothing about blasphemy in a foreign church."

"So that's it! The law doesn't apply to us."

"That's not true, but you may think what you like. I'm simply telling you I cannot help. You British must settle this among yourselves."

A long pause then, as the Vicar realized that Hamid could not be swayed. "I see," he said finally, standing up. "I see very well that I shall find no justice here. Good day, sir. I thank you for your time. And may I say that I think things have come to a sorry pass when the police refuse to deal with a foreigner's complaint."

He stalked out then, and when he was far down the hall Hamid and Aziz began to laugh.

"Another example of the Nasranis' madness, Aziz. Note it well!"

"I have, Hamid. I have. But please—what is a British duke?"

"A *grand signor*. A great lord. But the point is that Mr. Barclay is *not* a duke, though he would have everyone in Tangier think that he is. And what the note says is absolutely true—he *does* make love to boys. But enough of this nonsense. There's still work to do. Take care of the ballet dancers—call them up here, interrogate them, and make many thinly veiled threats. I'm going out for a while. I'll see you after lunch."

Hamid began to drive about the town aimlessly, in an attempt to clear his head. He passed the Emsalah Tennis Club, saw Omar Salah's car parked in the drive. He was tempted to go in then and play Omar a hard, fast set. But he knew he would feel guilty if he played during working hours, and, too, he knew what people would say. "Ah, Hamid Ouazzani is now an inspector of police and has become unbearably corrupt. He plays tennis in the daytime while the criminals roam Tangier. He has forgotten his humble origins, is now as rich and arrogant as Salah, whom he imitates."

He laughed at the thought, and at all his missed opportunities to become rich—all the bribes offered him, and sternly refused.

He turned down the road to Dradeb, then drove slowly so that he could look carefully at everything and see if there was something new. He often tested himself this way, believing that if he stared long and hard enough at familiar sights he might begin to understand them in a different way. He passed only one foreigner on the road, Laurence Luscombe, walking with an empty market basket from his home at the far end of the slum. Luscombe's face looked haggard, and there were pink blotches on his cheeks. His white hair was blowing in the breeze—gentle, thanks to Allah: the harsh winds of May had subsided for a time.

Hamid passed Dr. Radcliffe's car, parked as usual before the house of Deborah Gates. There was no trace of foreigners as he entered the heart of the slum. The shabby buildings, no more than a single brick thick, looked as though they might fall upon the street. Children in ragged clothing ran back and forth, and he thought of his friend Mohammed Achar busy in his clinic, struggling to keep up with the endless flow of the diseased. Often, now, when he drove through here he recalled his childhood and his struggle to get out, the old cherif who'd taken an interest in him, the year he'd spent preparing for the police exam. It had been difficult. He'd passed, and now he was free. Yet he knew that a part of him would always feel at home in this slum.

At La Colombe he slowed down, startled by the appearance of a black official car bearing the flag of the United States. It was the limousine of the American Consul General, Daniel Lake. Now he too was frequenting the shop. Hamid tried to look inside but the sun was in his eyes. He glanced at his watch, discovered it was nearly eleven, time for his weekly meeting with his favorite informer, Robin Scott. He turned his car and drove through Dradeb again, then up a narrow, winding road that took him by the Italian cathedral and onto the Marshan.

He saw one foreigner walking there, by the wall beside the municipal soccer field. It was the writer Darryl Kranker coming from the love nests near the Phoenician tombs. He was followed by three small boys who imitated his gait and made obscene gestures behind his back. Kranker was unshaven and in disarray. *Another pederast,* Hamid thought, *another one who likes small boys.*

He paused for a moment, watched as the boys passed his car. Kranker paid no attention to them, though they called to him in Arabic and wiggled their behinds. It was pathetic that so many people—painters, writers, British aristocrats—had found their way to Tangier in order to satisfy perverse needs. Hamid disliked nearly all of them, not for their sexual tastes, but for the way these tastes corrupted them and in turn corrupted the town. People had begun to say that it was the Europeans who had brought homosexuality to Tangier. Hamid knew this wasn't true—its existence had attracted the Europeans. Still their exploitation of the Arab vice offended him when it was coarsely and publicly displayed.

He'd had his own experiences with loving men when he was fourteen years old. He and his friends used to go fishing along the beach below the villas on the Mountain Road. Then they'd go into the bushes and play with each other for release. In those days all girls were kept at home, and women never walked the streets unveiled. There was no shame connected with having sex with one's friends—one grew out of it in time. But as he grew up he began to see it in a different way. It was something that made the Europeans leer as they tried to lure boys into their cars. He'd told his brother, Farid, who was beautiful and four years younger than himself, that if he had sex with a foreigner he would beat him up. Farid had done it anyway, and Hamid had forgotten the threat. Farid's affair had been with a notable, no less a personage than Patrick Wax. Out of that relationship, which had lasted three years, he'd earned enough to open up his shop. That was the way it was in Tangier, a good means for a handsome boy to advance. Perhaps Farid had been fortunate. He'd traveled to Europe, owned fine clothes, met princesses, been a guest aboard a yacht. A luxurious if degrading life for a time, but at least now he had his shop to show for all his pains. Would Pumpkin Pie be as lucky, or would he end up without a cent? Hamid could imagine him ten years older driving a taxi in Tangier.

He drove to Rue Haffa, parked his car, then walked down the narrow street. He loved the Haffa Cafe—the best of the traditional ones in Tangier. The mint tea there was flavored with orange blossoms in the spring, and with *shiba* all year around. Hamid liked to come here by himself at odd times, particularly in the autumn, when the hawks hung above the Straits and the air was so clear he felt he could touch Spain if he reached out. And, too, here he had his regular Monday meeting with Robin Scott, between eleven and noon, when no one else was around.

As he entered the cafe, mewing kittens ran between his legs. He found Robin in the garden in the back, seated at a small iron table scribbling in his notebook and sipping from a glass. He liked Robin. There was something endearing about his full, round face, dominated by the huge mop of heavily curled reddish hair. He sprang up when Hamid came into sight, making an elaborate flourish with his arm.

Robin looked healthy, and for the hundredth time Hamid wondered how he managed to survive. His needs were simple—he had a room in a fleabag medina hotel—but still Tangier was becoming expensive, and Robin's fortunes did not increase. The poems he wrote were infrequently published in obscure Canadian magazines, and he received only a stipend for his weekly column in the *Dépêche de Tanger*.

It was a gossip column, written in English and devoured by the Mountain crowd. They admired him for his well-aimed barbs but deplored him behind his back. He was too witty for them, dressed in shabby clothes, and was dangerous on account of his outspokenness and his unpredictable *beaux gestes*. Françoise de Lauzon had once told him that she didn't like his beard. He'd shaved it off the following day, then sent her the bristling hairs by express.

"Ah, Hamid, have you heard about the blowup at the English church?" Robin liked to begin their talks with bits of shocking news.

"The Vicar was in to see me this morning, in the *strictest confidence,* of course. He wanted a full investigation, which I refused. But I see the story's all over town."

Robin laughed, then pounded the little table with his fists. "Oh, the English, the English!" he said. "They're so antiseptic and they have such complicated lives." He laughed more, and then began to cough. He was fascinated by gossip, excited by it, collecting it the way other men collected stamps.

"We're holding a quintet of British ballet dancers on account of you."

Robin beamed. "Oh, Hamid. I loathed those nelly queens. They were rude to me—nasty little snobs." He did a quick imitation with a free-flowing limp wrist. "Wanted me to drink their sherry, share their Russian cigarettes, then thought I was a Philistine when I ordered beer and lit a cheap cigar. But I could tell at once they shared my vice. Mind you—with me it's all mental now, ever since my arrest."

"Yes," said Hamid. "Of course."

"Anyway, I heard around the Socco they were on the lookout for little boys. And I said to myself: 'My friend Hamid hates anything that smacks of the corruption of Moroccan youth.' Thought I'd do you a service and turn them in. A sweet revenge when I saw them taken away."

"Were they caught in the act? I didn't read the dossier."

"Caught with their pants down. A veritable orgy at the hotel. I could hear their squeals even in my room, though they were three floors above."

Their relationship had begun ten years before when Robin was twenty-five, and Hamid a mere detective in the foreign branch. When Hamid first saw Robin he was lying nude on a great, old, sagging bed with two boys working him over and another four looking on. Hamid had been furious, determined to see him expelled, but in their interviews something about the Canadian boy mitigated his disgust. Maybe it was his honesty, and his irony about himself. Whatever it was, Hamid had been touched, and when he'd discovered how much it meant to Robin to live in Tangier, how much he loved the town and wanted to stay, he'd offered him a bargain which in the decade that had passed he'd found no reason to regret. Robin would be allowed to stay on providing he kept clear of younger boys. In return he had to become an informer and turn in others indulging in his vice. To Hamid's great surprise, Robin had leaped at the chance. He loved to pry into people's lives and felt no scruples about being a traitor to his kind.

"What's going on with the Americans and Zvegintzov?" Hamid asked. "First it was Knowles, now it's Lake hanging around the shop."

"Yeah. Someone told me he and Lake have gotten thick, that Lake's in there a couple times a day."

"What's it all about?"

"Beats me. But the American's a curious bastard. Does his work all right, but his eyes are strange. He thinks he's some kind of mechanical genius. Always working on his car or down in the cellar fixing the water heater."

"I saw Luscombe on the way up. Looked awful. What's happening with him?"

"Poor Larry." Robin lit up one of his cigars. "Big brouha at the theater club. They're all ganging up on him, especially Kelly, who wants to take over the stupid group. There's a play Saturday. You ought to come. Even if it's lousy I'm going to give it a good review. Pathetic, isn't it, the way people take things so seriously here? These theater people, Larry excluded, are the worst trash in town. Mountain crowd's what interests me. Have you heard the latest on the Codds?"

Before Hamid could say he hadn't, Robin began his tale, twinkles embellishing his face as he came to the juiciest bits.

"Seems old Ashton and Musica were fighting a lot last year, and Ashton, bless him, told her off. Said he wanted an 'open marriage.' That's one of these arrangements where the husband and wife live together, Hamid, but get their sex in other people's beds. I got to hand it to Ashton—he's seventy-three. Musica, I think, is sixty-eight. They don't look like much now, but he's got a name, famous in Ireland, you know, though I think his poems all stink. And Musica isn't all that dried up—there's still a little juice in that bag of bones. Anyway, they spread the word among the younger set—bargaining fame for youth, or something like that. God forbid, of course, that anyone on the Mountain would hear. Someone told me they approached the Manchesters, though I find that hard to believe. No takers, finally, so the 'open marriage' idea faded away. But old Ashton, who's got a few quivers left in him, decided what they really needed was a good old-fashioned *partouze*. Seems they've actually approached some hustlers in the Socco, but nothing's happened yet because Ashton's too stingy to come to terms. But who knows what the future will bring? Ashton told me once that he's written five pornographic plays, all stashed away in some Swiss bank vault, to be released only after his death. Can't bear the shame now, poor man—afraid his friends in Dublin will turn their backs. Meanwhile Musica bides her time, planning to cut loose as soon as she gets her mitts on all his hoarded pounds."

Just the thought of those two old people making love with a hustler and a prostitute made Hamid shiver as he smiled.

"Makes you lose your appetite, doesn't it?" Robin said.

"Now that you've told me I don't think I can look them in the face."

"Never could myself."

They both began to laugh.

"By the way, is Barclay really upset about the note?"

"Doubt it. Man's a stone wall. Couldn't care less. But he's telling everyone what happened because he loves being in a scandal, and of course everyone listens and bows and scrapes. Wouldn't be surprised if he wrote the damn thing himself. Reminds me of an incident that'll show you how cold he is. Do you remember that weird case when David Klein was attacked by his houseboy in bed?"

"Yes. He was knifed by Achmed Ben Riffi. His penis was half cut off, and then Dr. Radcliffe sewed it back."

Hamid prepared himself for a good story, full of superbly imitated accents, expansive gestures, and pauses to build up the suspense.

"Yeah, the good doctor's greatest feat. Anyway, the instant

after Klein was stabbed, he reached onto his bedside table and picked up the phone. He was in shock, of course, so his mind wasn't functioning too well. Instead of calling the doctor or the police he rang up Barclay at his home. Typical. They all think Barclay can solve everything here. Anyway, David rings him up and Peter answers the phone. 'Oh, Peter,' David whines, 'the most awful, the most frightful thing has just happened to my cock. I think my Achmed has cut it off.' 'Sorry, David,' Peter says, 'but I can't talk now. I'm bidding for a slam.' Then he hangs up. Klein, you understand, was bleeding to death. Thank God he found Radcliffe at home. It must have been the only night he wasn't with pretty Miss Gates."

"Oh, Robin." Hamid was laughing away. "You know more stories than Zvegintzov, and certainly more than me."

"Actually I don't get around all that much. I'm not invited anymore into the great houses on the hill. But because of the column they still keep in touch. They come to me all the time and tell me terrible things. The malicious ones always bring the best. Like Kranker—he's full of dirt. I don't like him, so I try not to use his stuff. But every once in a while he gives me something good, and then I can't resist."

"Any new personalities you want to tell me about? I rely on your antenna, you know."

"Thanks, Hamid. I appreciate that. Aside from the church affair, Tangier's had a very dull week. But our high season begins in a month. Then everything'll pick up."

Hamid nodded. There was a pause. "I'm concerned about you, Robin," he said. "How long are you going to stay here and waste your life?"

"Now don't start that again—"

"*I will.* When we met you were a real hippie—not one of these imitations I see around today. You were wild and passionate about life, but now I see you're settling in your ways. You neglect your work and bury yourself in gossip. Watch out, Robin. The years will pass, and in the end you'll find you're just another Tangier writer, a shadowy presence who doesn't finish his books."

"Hmmm. Maybe so. But I'll have one distinction left."

"What's that?"

"I'll still be an informer for the police."

"Oh, yes. You'll always be that. Perhaps, as you've said, it's your real métier."

"You know, Hamid—" Robin began to laugh. "You're the only Tangerene who dares to speak to me like this. The others are too terrified because of the power of my column. They come around regularly to kiss my ass, and I adore them for it since I've kissed ass all my life and now, finally, I'm in a position where people must kiss mine."

"Still—"

"I know. You think I should leave, become serious, start a new life. Actually I'm thinking of starting a business here. My clients will be rich people who want to make it in Tangier. For an extravagant fee I'll set them up. Sooner or later they'll get to Barclay's for lunch—he'll try out anyone *once*. My final payment is delivered the day they get the invitation, but after that they must keep me on retainer if they don't want to be blasted in my column. I could make myself a fantastic living and enjoy the pleasure of being completely corrupt."

"But you wouldn't sell out your column, would you?"

"No. I suppose not. As much as I adore the idea of being your informer, and long to roll about in the gutter, the integrity of the column must be preserved. We're alike in that way, Hamid. I've often wondered why you haven't allowed others to make you rich."

"Oh—I don't know. I'm a simple man. I want to be respectable. An honest cop."

"Oh, Hamid, you're beautiful. And lucky too. I live alone, picking up scum here and there, whatever crosses my path. But you have Kalinka, and you're in love."

Back at the Sûreté at two o'clock, Aziz greeted him with a grin. "I've completely terrorized the ballet dancers. They want to see you and beg for mercy on their knees."

"Spare me, Aziz. You take charge of the case. If the prosecutor agrees, ship them out tonight. Take them in handcuffs to the airport. The humiliation will do them good."

"Marvelous idea. Why didn't I think of it?"

"Because you're only a detective. A long time yet before

you become the chief. I want you to contact our informants at the American Consulate, find out what you can about Zvegintzov and Lake. Has Zvegintzov been there for dinner? If he has, what did he say? See the butler and check with the maids. Also there's Kranker, the American. See the visa people downstairs and tell them to harass him a bit. When he comes in they should hold up his renewal. I think he's messing around with children, and I want him scared."

There were a few more matters to dispose of, then Aziz left and Hamid began to go through the motions of his job. He read dossiers and checked the status of his cases, but his mind kept returning to Kalinka. He thought of her sitting in their salon, or lying in their bed, smoking, filling her lungs with the harsh, acrid smoke of hashish. He must get her to stop, slowly, gradually, lead her out of her world of dreams. Then maybe he would marry her. But would she be different, a different person? Would he love her as much as he did now?

It was a difficult afternoon; the problem of Kalinka nagged until he grew impatient and telephoned her at home. She was in a daze, as usual, and there were long silences as they spoke. She asked him to buy her a television set. He said he'd think about it—it depended on the cost. He didn't think much of Moroccan TV—Saudi Arabian love dramas and propaganda from the Ministry of Public Works—but he knew she needed something to amuse her as she sat alone at home. She needed stimulation. In the summer, he promised himself, he'd take her regularly to the beach.

By the end of the afternoon he'd cleared up all his papers. A few minutes before six he set off for the Prefecture. He waited in the Prefect's anteroom for ten minutes, until a young man in a sharply tailored European suit approached him with a nod. "Inspector Ouazzani, I'm the Prefect's new assistant. He's ready to see you now." Hamid followed the assistant, a type he didn't like—glossy, smooth, educated at a French lycée, a young man destined to grow rich on bribes.

The Prefect was another sort, fat and charming, dressed in a traditional Moroccan robe. Hamid knew he was corrupt, but with a moderation his assistant would never understand. The Prefect stole just enough to keep his family in a decent style. It would never occur to him to milk a fortune from his job, or to look away from an injustice which might do a poor man harm.

"Sit down, Hamid," he said, waving toward a leather couch. "I already have one complaint today. The British Consul called, said you refused to investigate some nonsense at the British church. Well, don't worry. You did exactly right. I defended you, as I always have."

"Thank you, Prefect," said Hamid. "Now listen to a complaint of mine. Over the weekend we arrested some British ballet dancers. When they asked to see their consul, his wife lied and said he was out of town."

The Prefect laughed. "I'll remember that. Really, Hamid—you have the most difficult job."

"It's going to become even more difficult. Among the diplomats now we have two philanderers—Mr. Fufu, the UN man from Uganda, and Baldeschi, the Italian Consul. Both of them are accumulating mistresses at a greater than normal rate. Of course I'm grateful they're heterosexual—such a rarity among the foreigners here. But eventually someone's husband's going to find out, and then we're going to have one of those 'diplomatic affairs.' "

The Prefect laughed again. "I know you can handle it, Hamid. But I didn't call you here to gossip. A serious matter's come up. The Ministry of Interior has received information from Egyptian intelligence through our Cairo Embassy. The Egyptians claim an Israeli assassin is coming to Tangier."

Hamid was puzzled. It didn't make any sense. There were no important personalities in Tangier who could possibly interest an assassin, and as for the King, he espoused the Palestinian cause in a half-hearted way, but he was unpopular in the north and rarely used his palace in Tangier.

"Perhaps they've confused Tangier with Algiers. They've been that stupid before."

"Any ideas, Hamid?"

"The only thing I can think of is that there's an old Nazi here they want to get."

"Very good. Anyone in mind?"

"That's the trouble, Prefect. I don't think there're any left. But I'll look into it and let you know."

Driving home, he thought about the problem. A Nazi hunter made sense, but who could the target be? He thought and thought, sifting through hundreds of names. The implications were difficult to accept, for if he was right there was someone living in Tangier, someone quite poisonous, who lay dormant and had escaped his scrutiny for years.

That night when he made love with Kalinka all his tensions ebbed away. She was a mystery to him—she smoked hashish, her mind worked the opposite way from his. But none of that mattered when she touched him with her tiny hands, curled her long, thin legs around his thighs, tickled his genitals with her toes. Feeling himself grow hard within her, feeling her fragile, glistening body throb beneath him and hearing her gasps against his ear, he was inspired to a tenderness he had never felt with any other woman, a sense that she was exquisite and that it was his pleasure to make her body sing. In bed with other women he had cared only for himself, but Kalinka's moans and embraces made him as interested in giving as in taking, and so he let her guide him in his moves rather than thrusting to his own release. He treasured this new-found gentleness and loved her for provoking it. It was far better, he had learned, to make love to a woman than merely to use her to allay desire.

Yes, she had taught him about love, and now he could not imagine experiencing it any other way. She'd come into his life strangely, romantically, providing him with a refuge from the harshness of his work and from all the struggles that consumed Tangier.

A Night
at the Theater

Laurence Luscombe stood on the empty stage facing the place where the curtains met. He liked to do this on an opening night, stand silent, listen to the house fill up. He looked at his watch. Twenty to eight. In a few minutes *The Winslow Boy* would go on, and then all the agony of rehearsal, the tantrums and the temperament, would fade before the magic of the play. He would marvel then, as he had so many times, at the power of performance—the way it could seize an audience, hold it in thrall.

But suppose, he thought, *they all walk out?*

He'd had that anxiety for over fifty years, ever since he'd first gone on the stage. He couldn't overcome it—at the age of seventy-five he still couldn't rid himself of the nightmare of an empty house. He didn't act anymore himself, but the fear had followed him to Tangier. Here he'd founded the Tangier Players, his gift to the city that had embraced him in old age.

Peter Barclay had put it another way. "Thank God for Larry Luscombe and TP. They're something to talk about at our barren dinner parties, fill out our wasted afternoons." Peter was being amusing, of course. He didn't think *his* dinner parties were barren, or that he wasted *his* afternoons. Still Laurence believed his remark had been well meant, and now Peter, "pasha" of the Mountain, was a patron of TP and the club's most loyal fan.

It hadn't always been like that. The struggle had been lonely and hard. Laurence thought back as he stood on the empty set. At sixty-five he'd retired to Tangier with the dream of founding a theater club. He'd begun slowly, organizing readings in people's houses while he gathered the corps of loyal amateurs who shared his love for the stage. People had scoffed at first, Peter Barclay among them, but slowly the group had prospered and grown. Someone went to London and brought back lights. Someone else donated canvas and lumber. Gradually the productions grew more lavish and the ragged ends were smoothed. TP became a success, a permanent part of European life in the town.

But now, after all the struggles, the arduous climb to success, the club was facing its greatest crisis, a threat to its integrity and to Laurence's capacity to carry on. Kelly—that American swine, Joe Kelly—was trying to organize a putsch. He didn't yet have the backing, but if tonight's production failed there were people in the group who would take his side. The Drears, the Packwoods, the Calloways, Jack Whyte—that hard core of amateurs Luscombe had made into minor celebrities in the town—they'd turn on him sure as death, and TP would melt to mud.

Laurence knew what was going on, and what he hadn't overheard people made certain he found out. They were saying he was too old, losing his grip, that he couldn't control rehearsals, and that his tantrums were throwing everybody off. There was trouble in TP—no secret about that. People who'd accepted parts were doing the unpardonable and walking out. Others complained that Laurence got too much credit, while they were slighted in reviews. He wasn't disturbed—there was always temperament around a theater. What upset him was disloyalty—the disloyalty of the people he'd picked up along the way, plucked out of their mediocrity, straight out of the gutter in the case of the Drears, then taught and trained and made into stars.

For too long, he knew, he'd ignored the signs, and now he could smell resentment all around. How had it happened? He'd written the bylaws, made TP democratic. Everyone had an equal vote, though he'd always directed by consent. For years there'd never been a challenge or the slightest murmur of rebellion in the ranks. But now Joe Kelly had come to town, and it seemed all that might change.

Kelly! The man was a hack. He'd done years of radio soap opera in New York, played every kind of third-rate circuit in the States. Then he'd had an automobile accident and won himself a settlement in court, enough to come to Tangier, buy himself a little house, sniff around, and start giving little dinners at which he'd been clawing his way to popularity and trying to alienate Laurence's support. He even tried to ingratiate himself with the Mountain set. No chance of success, of course—he was far too grotty in his ways. But his mincing little efforts had caused confusion and, to Laurence, pain.

No sense brooding, he thought. *Too much work to be done.* He stroked the dusty curtains, then left the stage to check on things in back. Most of the cast was waiting in the wings. He went on to the dressing rooms to hurry the stragglers. In the men's section he found Jessamyn Drear watching Kelly apply powder to his ravaged face. They stopped whispering the moment he walked in. Jessamyn looked at him shyly. Kelly gave him a thumbs-up.

"Brings it all back, Luscombe," he said. "Smell of the greasepaint and all that. Never thought I'd troop the boards again, especially not in old Tangier. Not after the accident. Never thought I would." He raised his hands to his face. "Oh, the scars, Luscombe—the scars. I was a beautiful kid once. Can you believe it? But the years took their toll. Then the crackup in Connecticut, a year in traction, every damn thing broken and torn. They wrote me right out of *Suburban Wife.* I was in the hospital, listening to the radio one day, when one of the characters announced my demise. There were a few tears, and that was the end of that. No hope of work then. When you're sick they forget you soon enough. No pity. Not in show biz. Play's the thing. Course you know all that yourself."

Laurence was thinking of some way to respond when Jill Packwood stormed in, out of breath.

"Place is filling up, Larry. Looks like a full house. Derik says we can start on time."

He was about to answer her when Kelly interrupted. "Jill, sweetie, your dress is crooked. Better find a safety pin and hitch it up."

"Oh! Thanks, Joe. Wish me luck."

"Yeah," said Kelly, blowing her a kiss. "Break a leg, sweetheart. Break a leg."

When she was gone he put his arm around Jessamyn Drear, then leaned toward Laurence and stuck out his chin. "Jill's got nice little tits," he said. "Course I don't want 'em. Ha! Ha! Ha!"

Jessamyn giggled, but Laurence turned away, offended by Kelly's humor and the scent of liquor on his breath.

He'd been impossible at rehearsals, always interrupting, trying to give his own directions to the cast. The man was unprofessional, the way he kept cutting Laurence off. But he was clever too, knew how to handle amateurs, call them "sweetheart" and "darling" and blame everything on Laurence when he turned his back. Kelly told long anecdotes that wasted time, boring stories about his experiences on the road—that charade game, for instance, the one he'd played in Kansas City, where he'd acted out "He who steals my merkin steals trash."

No one, including Laurence, knew what a "merkin" was until Kelly smirked and then explained. "It's a female pubic hair wig," he said, then the vulgar, billowing laughter, the final "Ha! Ha! Ha!" Laurence couldn't stand it, wanted to fire him right out of the cast. But Kelly was good, a professional among amateurs. When he felt like it he had no difficulty standing out. Of course, he wasn't really top class, the way Laurence had been in his prime. Kelly could never have made it on the West End, where Laurence had worked for years. He'd been an actor's actor, not a star but a master craftsman admired in the ranks. His enemies called him "grand," but he'd never stooped to soap opera at least.

Between the wars, when he'd had a little fling with society, he'd been invited to Lady Astor's, where he'd met T. E.

Lawrence and Bernard Shaw. And he'd dined one summer at Villa Mauresque, with Noel Coward and Somerset Maugham. Willy Maugham had told a wonderful story that afternoon about the American writer Edna Millay. She'd come in uninvited, in the middle of a stag lunch, looked around at the house, the garden, and all the guests. "This is *fairyland,* Mr. Maugham," she'd said. He and Noel had chuckled through dessert.

Now *that* was funny. Real wit. Not like those vulgar nonsense things that Kelly came out with all the time. What had he said last night at dress rehearsal? Something obscene to Jessamyn Drear. Oh, yes, he remembered now—one of his vulgar "knock knock" routines.

"Knock knock."

"Who's there?"

"Fornication."

"Fornication who?"

"Fornication like this you ought to wear black tie. Ha! Ha! Ha!"

Jessamyn had doubled up with laughter. It was ghastly the way Kelly was winning them all. They were so weak in their characters, so flabby in their souls, that they couldn't see through his simpering guile. One day he'd have it out with Kelly, force a showdown, expose him raw. But for the moment he mustn't think of that. The important thing was that *The Winslow Boy* go on.

He left the dressing room, walked back around the stage to a door where he could watch the audience unseen. Many of the seats were taken, but the ones reserved for Peter Barclay and his group were still empty in the front. The Lakes, the Manchesters, and the Whittles were seated in the Consul General's row. Behind them sat Joop and Claude de Hoag, along with Claude's father, General Gilbert Bresson, and de Hoag's assistant, Jean Tassigny. Behind them he saw the Swedish dentist Sven Lundgren and Robin Scott, who would write the review.

The writer Darryl Kranker came down the aisle with a beautiful Arab boy, and behind him Vicar Wick followed by Countess de Lauzon, blue eye circles matching her hair, and Patrick Wax, in a gold-trimmed cape, holding a thin little pony whip in his hand. Fufu, the Ugandan, was with his wife and an assortment of distinguished-looking blacks. With them was Omar Salah, chief of customs in the port.

The Ashton Codds came next, along with Foster and Jackie Knowles. Laurence, noticing Inspector Ouazzani and his Oriental girlfriend, peered around to find Peter Zvegintzov slung low in a seat on the other side.

But where was the Barclay group? He needed Peter tonight, desperately needed the prestige of his praise. If Peter liked the play, then no one would dare speak against it, and Kelly's nasty little coup would be nipped right in its bud. But what if Peter didn't come? He'd promised he would, had reserved a whole row of seats, had even said something about a party afterward for friends. Laurence was counting on that—at the party Peter would put out the word. That night it would spread across the Mountain, would be all over town by the next afternoon. But what was Peter's promise really worth? Laurence knew not much. He was perfectly capable of forgetting the whole thing, or canceling out because it didn't suit his mood. That was the trouble with Peter Barclay, and everybody knew it too. He only did things that were in his interest, and cared only for himself.

Whew! It was desperate now, already three past eight. Still there were people coming in: Inigo, the painter, who'd refused to do the sets, and his Moroccan boyfriend, the one Countess de Lauzon called "Pumpkin Pie." He'd worked in her garden before Inigo had picked him up. His real name was Mohammed, but the Countess had so many of those around her place that she couldn't stand it when she yelled "Mohammed" and six Berber faces suddenly looked up. So she'd renamed them, squeezing their biceps while waiting to be inspired. There was "Celery Tops" and "Coffee Boy" and "Tender in the Night." But Pumpkin Pie was the prettiest of the lot—Inigo had something there.

Where was Barclay? The audience was restless. It was already eight past, and still no sign. They'd be having drinks somewhere when someone would say: "Oh, Peter, do we *have* to go to Larry's silly old play?" Peter would answer: "Of course not, darling." And none of them would give it another thought.

Laurence was worrying about that, still peering around, when Derik Law, his stage manager, came running up.

"Come on, Larry. We've got to start. It's twelve past. The hall's packed."

"There're still empties up front, Derik. We'll have to hold curtain a while more."

"But Larry," Derik moaned, "for heaven's sake. Everyone's nervous backstage. Joe says we've got to start or they'll all be too keyed up."

"To hell with Joe Kelly, and to hell with what he says! Where does he get the nerve to tell me what to do?" Laurence was furious, his face puffed out and red. "I've forgotten more about theater than that Yankee clod ever knew. Don't they see that, Derik? Don't you? That he's just a phony, trying to undermine me and bring TP down?"

Derik looked at the floor, then shook his head. "I don't think this is the time to get into that, Larry. At the next general meeting, maybe, but not tonight."

"All right. Never mind. We'll start in another minute, whether Barclay comes or not."

He was ashamed of his outburst, especially in front of Derik Law. Derik was his most loyal defender—when the crunch came with Kelly, Derik would stick by him to the end. Maybe, he thought, he *was* too hard on everybody. Maybe his temper *was* too short.

There was some commotion in the audience now. A couple of people had begun to clap. Well, all right, *damn them*. He'd start the thing. He was about to turn, make his way backstage, when he heard laughter coming from the hall. People were trooping in through the rear door. He turned back to look, and then he smiled. The Barclay group had arrived at last.

He might have known Peter wouldn't let him down. He was leading his crowd, that fat old moth Camilla Weltonwhist on his arm, followed by Percy Bainbridge, tall, elegant, and Colonel Brown in his formals, a row of medals festooning his chest. Vanessa Bolton, willowy and svelte, was with her current love, an Italian prince. Lord and Lady Pitt followed, Rachid El Fassi, his stunning wife, some good-looking people Laurence didn't know, with Skiddy de Bayonne bringing up the rear. Certainly they were the cream of the Mountain, the leaders of Tangier. Peter had outdone himself, and Laurence grew serene. Everything would be fine now. Peter Barclay had finally come.

He and Camilla Weltonwhist marched like royalty down the center aisle, and everyone in the theater, even the ones who hated and envied them, turned around to stare. Camilla's diamond collar gleamed, and Peter, handsome, his iron-gray hair combed back, craned his head, stuck out his leathery neck to render greetings to his waiting friends. "Hello, hello, hello," he said, shaking his cane. "Hello, darling. Hello. Hello." He said the word over and over, changing his inflection each time, so that each person received a smile, a special greeting reserved for him.

Even Patrick Wax, for all his airs, his gold-trimmed robes, and his palace of thrones and mirrors—even Patrick, the imposter, had turned around to gape. That was the source of Peter Barclay's power—that he alone among the British residents knew truly who he was. The others intrigued and entertained, moved about the Mountain as best they could, but in the end if they ever reached the top Peter was all they'd find. It was comical, the way they schemed and scraped, because Peter didn't care. Not for anyone, not even for his closest friends. (He called Camilla Weltonwhist "Mrs. Stout" behind her back.) But all that didn't matter, because he created an effect—which Laurence admired the same way he admired a fine performance by Gielgud or Olivier.

Thank God, he thought, *thank God he's come. Thank God that Peter Barclay is my friend.*

But the moment he thought that, he knew it wasn't true. Peter Barclay wasn't his friend, never would be, never could. They'd known each other all the years that Laurence had been in Tangier, and never, never once in all that time, had Peter had him in his house.

His mind turned back to the play. He let the door slip closed, moved into the wings, and gave the signal to Derik Law. The house lights dimmed, the theater went black, then the great curtains were slowly drawn. The audience applauded the set and settled down. *The Winslow Boy* began.

bear to stand in the wings on opening
ad to watch from the back. Here he
ions of the house, pace about, take
became too great he could slip out to

o a good start. He had a sixth sense
tell almost immediately when an
glued. He could feel it building now
it was on account of the play. He couldn't imag-
people not liking *The Winslow Boy,* with its commitment
to perseverance and family life.

He was thinking about that and about Peter Barclay's
praise (was counting on it now) when he felt a flash of pride.
TP might be an amateur group, but professional standards
were enforced. It wasn't like all those little clubs that Kelly
had been involved with in the States. And though every expatriate colony had its group, TP was among the very best in
the world. Word had gotten around about that. Some people
in Gibraltar had even come over for advice.

Laurence had done *Heartbreak House, Death of a Sales-
man,* and *King Lear,* then produced *The Cherry Orchard,
Hedda Gabler,* and *Ghosts.* Kelly, damn him, wanted to do
Boys in the Band. Said it would be "amusing to put a mirror
up to all those queers." Then he'd made a nasty crack about
the Shakespeare reading Laurence was planning for the fall.
"Bunch of queens playing kings," he'd said. "Let's can the
Shakespeare and write our own cabaret. We can beckon
them out of their closets, show them what they are. I've already got a title: *Queersville-sur-Mer.*"

It was a rotten, disgusting idea, and Laurence told him so
to his face. "Do what you want, Kelly, in your personal life.
But don't mess around with TP."

Laurence was wincing over the memory of that when he
heard footsteps in the lobby downstairs. A moment later the
rear door opened and a young man in police uniform appeared. Laurence brought his forefinger to his lip and
pointed toward the stage. The policeman nodded, then
moved closer to whisper in his ear.

"Have you seen Inspector Ouazzani?" he asked in French.

Laurence pointed him out. The policeman crept
aisle to Ouazzani's row, caught his attention, anc
him a note. Ouazzani read it, whispered something
woman, then stood up and walked back up the aisle.

"Sorry to leave in the middle, Mr. Luscombe," he sa
"But I've been called away to work."

Laurence nodded, and Ouazzani and the policeman left. It
was damn decent, he thought, of the Inspector to explain.

But what was happening? The hall was silent. No voices
were coming from the stage. Laurence turned to see Kelly
glaring out, hands on his hips, miming a slow burn. Silence,
then a "Hear, hear" from the front. Someone else whistled
from the side.

Laurence was aghast. The man had brought the play to a
halt. He was about to panic, run down the aisle and cry apologies, when Kelly gave a shrug, stepped back to where he'd
been, and resumed his part. Laurence was relieved, but only
for a moment. Then he realized that Kelly's acting was taking
a strange new turn. He was using a preposterous accent,
making fun of all his lines. The audience began to stir. The
whole tenor of the hall began to change. The spell that had
been building was broken now, and the other actors, terrified, were stumbling and missing their cues.

The audience began to laugh. There was scattered applause in the hall. Kelly, spurred on, bumped into Jill Packwood, then turned to the audience and winked. It was incredible. Kelly was behaving like a lunatic. It had all been so
beautiful, and now everything on stage was going mad. A
serious drama was being turned into a farce, and the audience, shaken by the change, was laughing like a herd of
fools.

Have they no pity for their friends? Laurence was appalled. It was all Kelly's fault. He would see to him, in the
dressing room between the acts. He ran out to the lobby,
collapsed in a fit of coughing, recovered, then ran around to
the stage door. He pounded on it. The damn thing was
locked. Thank God, he thought, they're near the end of the
act. He couldn't hear the lines anymore; they were sub-
merged in the cruel laughter of the house. He pounded on
the door again. Finally Derik opened up.

"What's happening, Larry? I don't understand."

"Horrible, horrible." Laurence could hardly speak. "It's Kelly. He's gone berserk. He's making a shambles of the play."

He pushed Derik aside and ran into the wings, catching the final moments of the act. All the lines were correct as far as that went, but the tone had gone cheap, turning them to rubbish in the actors' mouths. Finally the curtain was drawn, and a great surge of applause erupted from the house. Laurence covered his face and ran off to the dressing room to prepare for the showdown he knew must come.

As he waited for the cast, he tried hard to clear his head. *The Winslow Boy* was finished now, could never be redeemed. But perhaps out of the shambles of the evening he could reestablish his control. He would put it to the membership, in the few minutes between the acts. They could decide, right then, where their interests lay—with the American hack and his stale jokes or with Laurence Luscombe, who'd taught them how to act.

He was still glowering when they came in, but something in their manner put him on his guard. Instead of pouncing on Kelly, Jill Packwood and Jack Whyte were patting him on the back.

"Now look here," said Laurence. "These antics have got to stop. I don't know why you started, but you've ruined half the play."

"Ha!" said Kelly. "Don't know why we started! In case you didn't notice people were walking out."

"There weren't any walkouts. It was Inspector Ouazzani, called away by the police."

"Oh, come off it, Luscombe. The play's a bomb. There was someone snoring in the first row."

"Who was snoring? Just tell me who he was!"

"That old coot Bainbridge," said Whyte. "We could all hear him from the stage."

"Then ignore him, pretend he isn't there. You've got to go back and do it right."

"Damn," said Kelly, "we were making jackasses of ourselves. A few laughs is what this play needs."

"Joe's right," said Jill. "The audience is lapping it up."

"We'll really give it to them in the next act, honey. Let's all try for collisions at the drawing room door."

"Now listen!" shouted Laurence, red in the face. "I'm the director, and I'm laying down the law."

"Oh, hell, Luscombe, we're only having fun. It's a rotten play. Everyone knows it now."

"It's serious—"

"My ass! It's nothing but a crock of shit. You're standing there all cozy in the back, but our asses are on the line. This is my first time on stage in Tangier, and I don't need a bad review. You always wanted me to play Winslow like a fart. Well, I refuse! Your corny West End stuff doesn't go down with me. Your trouble, Luscombe, is that you've been out of it too long. That audience wants to laugh; I say give them what they want."

"I'm with you, Joe," said Whyte.

"Me too, Joe." It was Jessamyn Drear.

Derik Law stuck in his head. "They're filtering back from the lobby, Larry. It's a two-minute call."

But Laurence didn't hear him. He was glaring at Kelly's eyes. "You're doing this because you want to destroy TP. Admit it! That's your game!"

"Oh, puff—" Kelly blew a smoke ring, then stubbed out his cigarette in a cold cream jar. "*I* say let's take a vote. TP's democratic, right?"

"Of course TP's democratic, but you don't vote between the acts. I chose the play. I directed it. It's *got* to be done my way."

"Listen, dear old hack—"

"Don't you dare call me hack, you *swine!*"

Derik Law bobbed in again. "One minute. Everyone in the wings."

"All right. Now stop it, both of you." It was Jill Packwood waving her arms. "We can't settle this now. I'm for a compromise. I say let each actor make his choice. Those who want to do it Larry's way, fine, go ahead. And the ones who want can follow Joe."

"I'll go along with that, sweetheart." Kelly turned and started toward the stage.

"But that won't work," Laurence yelled. "It won't work, I tell you. You can't compromise on acting style."

Jack Whyte turned, came to him, patted him on the back. "Oh, come on, Larry. Get off your high horse. The audience loves it. Who the hell really cares?"

Through the second half he burned with humiliation, quivered with impotence and rage. The whole cast set out to ridicule the play, and at one point, when Kelly turned to the audience and said "Ridiculous, isn't it?" after his most moving speech, Laurence withdrew to the lobby in a fit of coughing and despair. Even there he couldn't escape—the ruined lines came to him only slightly muffled by the walls, and the titters of the audience, the occasional roars, left him unconsoled.

He left before the end, but even outside in the cool, windless night the thunderous final applause only amplified his shame. Drawn by instinct, he went back for the curtain calls and was shocked by the truth of what Whyte had said: Tangier *did* love it, *did* prefer the farce. It was sickening, but there it was. When the applause began to die and the curtains were drawn, Peter Barclay rose to his feet and began another round. The rest of the house followed him, the way the town always did, and so the clapping went on and on.

Finally, when the people streamed out, Laurence listened to their gaiety and suffered even more. Robin Scott gave him a pleasant nod—the review, he was saying, would be good. And Barclay, about to enter Camilla Weltonwhist's Rolls, caught his eye for a moment and smiled. Ouazzani's girlfriend wandered off, followed at a distance by Peter Zvegintzov. Then everyone else drove off, to the consulates or apartments in the town.

Usually on an opening night Laurence would head over to Heidi's Bar to receive congratulations and a few free drinks from friends. But he had no taste for that tonight, couldn't imagine what he'd say. Though the production had been successful, the success did not belong to him. So he left, making his way by the sulfurous street lamps, down the road that led through Dradeb.

He walked everywhere, didn't own a car, couldn't have afforded the petrol if he did. Every day he walked to town to shop and take his daily shower at the flat of Derik Law. People were kind—if they passed him on the road they'd pull over and offer him a lift. But this night the Mountain crowd had rushed off to Barclay's house, and the others went home a different way.

At seventy-five he was still strong, though at times he could feel his energy fade. The drama of the night, all the tension and despair, had suddenly made him feel old. As he walked slowly, watching out for mad stray dogs, he began to dread the coming summer and its heat. How much longer would he be able to make this walk, which was taking so much out of him tonight? Trouble was there was no alternative—he couldn't take taxis, could barely live on his income as it was. He had an inheritance from an aunt, twelve hundred a year, but prices were going up, and the pound seemed to fall lower every day.

He was the only Englishman to live in Dradeb, though he felt no shame about that. Over the years he'd learned Arabic, enough to get him by, and now he had friendships with his neighbors and Moroccans all over town. That was more than anyone on the Mountain could claim—those people didn't know they were in Morocco half the time. He, at least, had some contact with the world, knew Moroccans, shared their struggle to survive.

Better that, he thought, than the easy life, though now he wished he owned more than TP. Why? Why had they turned on him? How could they have been so cruel? They had stood there, supposedly his friends, simply stood there, nodded at Kelly, and acquiesced. He'd been insulted to his face, and not one of them had come to his defense. Were they all so false—Jack Whyte, Jill Packwood, the Drears? Was it true, as Derik had told him, that the Calloways made fun of him behind his back? He couldn't bear the thought—it hurt too much—that his decade in Tangier had added finally up to that.

He was in the middle of Dradeb, lost in the odor of the slum, when suddenly something hit him in the back. The pain was sharp, quick, and instinctively he cried out. Some men sitting in a cafe looked up. He heard laughter and obscene Arabic words. He turned to see a gang of boys, stones in their hands, poised to throw at him again. One of the men said something, there was some shouting back and forth, and then the boys threw down their stones and ran up an alley out of sight.

They had hit him in the shoulder; he could feel the bruise. The man who'd stopped them came over and shook his head. He was old, bearded, a gold tooth in the center of his mouth. Did the foreign gentleman need assistance? Did he need help in getting home?

Laurence thanked him, shook his head, and continued on his way. At least, he thought, the older generation still is decent, though not the Moroccan young. What had just happened would have been unthinkable a year or so before, but now for some strange reason all the young Moroccans were turning mean. It was all those Kung Fu films, he was sure—in Dradeb, often, he saw boys practicing chops and kicks. What did it mean, this anger? Why this hostility toward foreigners when tourism was the bread and butter of the town? Now, lately, more and more he felt this violence in the poorer sections, a vague and generalized rage.

He turned up an alley and entered his house, past the smell of the septic that oozed always near the door. The building wasn't so bad, on the edge of the slum, away from the worst sections, in a quarter that was vaguely middle class. He had two small rooms on the first floor, separated by an archway, ventilated by a window on the street. No hot water, of course, but a clean well around the back; no central heating, not even a fireplace, but he had a butane heater and in winter piled blankets on his bed. There was a toilet, Moroccan style—two cement footprints set into the floor. He didn't mind. And there was electricity, at least, which was a blessing since he liked to read.

He went to his bedroom, hung up his jacket, took off his shirt, inspected his wound. He wasn't cut, though the bruise was tender to the touch. He lay down on the bed that had been a gift from Musica Codd, thought over the evening, and wished that he could sob. But there were no tears left—too many parts lost, too many lovers gone, too many failures, too many disappointments had used them up. Well, it was done, the play was ruined. He would have to discipline Kelly, of course, ban him from the club. But he couldn't do that without a vote, and then the issue would become himself.

What would become of him if he lost TP? Surely his health would begin to fail. It was keeping him alive, the excitement of the club; without it he would hardly have a life. He imagined himself falling with a stroke. How many hours would he lie writhing on the cold cement? They'd find him eventually—people would notice he hadn't been around—and then they'd carry him up to Achar's clinic, or maybe to Dr. Radcliffe's in town. Would the ones who'd turned on him feel sorry then? Would they take up a collection, buy his medicines, bring him books? Or would he die alone, a ruined old actor, come to grief in a slum in Tangier?

It was all too depressing and, he knew, unwise to fall into the self-pity trap. After a few minutes of concentrated misery he made a firm resolve: he would fight Kelly and all he stood for with everything he had, would fight him to save TP, would fight him to save his life.

Peter Barclay
Rethinks His Garden

He opened his eyes, blinked at the sunlight that burst through the slats and striped the room. "Good morning, darling," he moaned, though there was no one else in the bed.

He didn't know why he said it. Out of habit, he supposed. And sometimes there would be someone beside him—some primitive, well-built fellow named Mohammed or Mustapha who would think the greeting was for him. It wasn't; it was something he said only to himself. He'd slept, dreamed, awakened unscathed, and for that a sensuous "Good morning" was the very least that he deserved.

He deserved a lot more, evidently. "A good thrashing" that horrid little note had said. Who could have written the foul thing? Who could have had the nerve?

He rang for his coffee and pondered the problem. Why did the note bother him so? He'd been called worse things in his life—"snob," "poseur"—but "hypocrite," never! The charge simply wasn't true. Others might go to church to see and be seen, but he went only to worship God. It was lonely being pasha of the Mountain, with the whole town scheming to be invited to his house. It amused him to see them jump, but he was human too, and church was one place he could leave the burden of his pashadom outside. God, fortunately, was not fooled like everybody else. When he prayed, Peter Barclay was sincere. *In fact,* he thought, *that may be the only time I am.*

Then there was the business about his sleeping with the boys—something the Philistines always brought out. They hated the vice, for it resided also in them; they reproached him for it because they feared it in themselves. Well—he didn't care, didn't give a damn. He wasn't going to slink around like some poor old Oscar Wilde type. Not for him "the love that dares not speak its name."

In Tangier he could be anything he liked, pasha of the Mountain, king of Tangier queens. But he didn't flaunt it, stayed clear of people's sons, didn't mince or lisp or bitch. The boys he slept with, from the Moroccan working class, were simple lads with tantalizing skins. Street whores mostly—he liked them the best, the darker the better, though it pleased him to make Eton boys out of them if he could. Yes, he could lust after a European boy but resist taking him to bed. He much preferred Moroccan trash, and everybody knew that too.

What was it, then, that had hurt? How had he generated so much rage? He couldn't understand it, was mystified. He'd never meant anybody harm. Of course he'd hurt people. One couldn't live without doing that. If he snubbed someone, or dropped him because he was a bore, it was not to give deliberate injury but to simplify his life. People had no idea how difficult his position was. Everyone was after him; he had no time to suffer fools. The point was to stick to quality—people who were beautiful or rich. The author of the note had proved the point by showing he had no quality at all.

It didn't matter. Nothing people said ever did. *He was Tangier*—everyone knew that; as far as society went he was the top. Others might have more money—people like Patrick Wax with his palace and unlimited stocks of foie gras and champagne—but when word went out that Peter Barclay was giving a party everyone prayed that he'd be asked. His was still the best table, the best house in Tangier. And he didn't go after people—they all came running to him.

His coffee came, he drank it, then washed and dressed and shaved. He walked downstairs, past mirror after mirror, nibbling a croissant as he went. People said that Patrick Wax had more mirrors, but Wax had more wall space and his things were mostly fakes. Peter's mirrors were genuine antiques salvaged from his family's ducal home.

Power! Ha! He had so little really—if people only *knew.* In London he'd be nothing; the place was filled with cousins to dukes. But here in Tangier it was a different world. Here he could be—a *king.*

He'd come down, settled in, built up his garden, made his myth, and now some poor beggar who felt abused was trying to evoke God to frighten him out. He'd have none of it. Life was much too sweet. He had an evening free on the following Tuesday, and he'd give a little dinner to fill it up. A circle of his confidants and closest friends, and a few powerful personalities as well. An intimate sixteen, seated around his big table, to whom he'd hold forth with such a barbed wit that his aphorisms would be repeated for days, even to the amusement of the ones they hurt.

He went to his desk to consult his address book, but there were so many names it was a bore to keep them straight. Better to ring up Camilla Weltonwhist and get her views—she was probably frantic now, waiting for his call.

"Camilla, *darling,*" he crooned. "You must drop everything and help me out. I'm giving a dinner next Tuesday—you're invited, of course, but I need you to help me with the list."

"Tuesday? Tuesday?" Camilla seemed stunned. "Maybe another night would be better, Peter. I think Françoise is giving a party then."

"Well, she didn't invite *me,* darling."

"Or me either, *yet.* But I know she called Percy and Vanessa. A couple of days ago at least."

"If it was a couple of days ago, darling, then we're not going to be asked."

"I suppose not. Do you think she's offended? What could we possibly have done?"

"I'm sure I don't know—we'll have to see about that. Meantime I'll ring up Percy and Vanessa. I guarantee they'll cancel and dine with us."

"It'll ruin her evening."

"Of course, darling. That's the *point*. If she's snubbing us, it'll be just what she deserves. And if she isn't—well, that'll be too bad too."

"She'll find others, I suppose—"

"The Manchesters? Wax?"

Camilla chuckled nastily, though nastiness was not her style. She behaved like a chameleon, altering her moods to blend with his. "You're sure you want to do this Tuesday?" she asked.

"I wouldn't change the date now, not for anything in the world. Come—let's make a list. I'm foggy this morning. You've got to help."

"You could have all the usuals, I suppose. And maybe try out someone new."

"Such as whom, Camilla dear?"

"Maybe Kelly. They say he's a decent chap."

"Kelly! You can't be serious! Face all scarred up, and so underbred. Really, Camilla, whatever goes through your mind?"

"Oh, you're right, Peter. Of course. Now let me think. What about the Lakes?"

"You mean Mr. Null and Mrs. Void?"

A pause then while Camilla collected her thoughts. She meant well, poor thing—he was sure of that—though at times she was awfully dense. She'd make an almost ideal companion, he thought, if she just wasn't so stout and didn't gobble up so many scallions at lunch.

"Hmmm," she said. "There's always Kranker."

"Ugh! Such a toad."

"Sven Lundgren?"

"You mean the dentist? He'll be staring around, looking at all our *teeth*."

"Well, there're the de Hoags, though I find Joop a nasty man."

"He's only got one ball, you know. Claude told me—in confidence, of course."

"One ball! Oh, dear! Can't they fish the other one out?"

"No, darling. Evidently they *can't*." He raised his eyebrows at her naiveté. Sometimes she could be intelligent, but this morning she was not. She'd had a husband once, but she still didn't understand how the male body worked.

"Well," he said, "if Joop is out of town, I could invite Claude and ask her to bring Tassigny. He's Joop's assistant, a terrific-looking boy. He and Claude are having an affair. I watched them playing tennis the other day."

"Hmmm, interesting. But you need some Moroccans too. What about the Governor? You haven't had him in donkeys' years."

"Yes. All right. But that means two tables. His wife doesn't speak any French."

"There's Salah—"

"Good idea! I can put him with Madame Governor and Rachid El Fassi on her right. That way she's covered—she can speak Moroccan, or Hindi if she likes, and I can still use the big table the way I planned. Brilliant, darling. And Salah's such a dear. He gets my things through customs all the time. Now stop—let's take a count. There's you and me, Percy and Vanessa. I'll ask Lester too, plus the Governor, his madame, Rachid, his wife, and Salah make ten. Then there's Claude (if Joop is away), Tassigny, and maybe the Whittles. That's fourteen with six women and eight men. Not bad for Tangier. But we still have to even things up."

They talked on until they'd sketched out the party, balancing the sexes, ending with his maximum, sixteen. It was a wearisome process, and when they finished Peter set down the phone with relief.

He was fifty years old and beginning to feel his age. His hair was iron gray, he walked with a cane. The world was changing too, and he knew his power couldn't last. Nobodies with money had gotten the upper hand every place else, and now he could see the trend beginning in Tangier. It was still the last outpost of a certain style of life, but it was changing, with people like Wax and Henderson Perry, with his millions, challenging the order of aristocratic power.

If only he were *Lord* Barclay—that would indicate his station to all concerned. He considered listing himself that way in the next edition of the Tangier telephone book, but knew someone would tip off the London papers, and then everyone would make a stink. He shrugged. Titles were amusing. As far as Tangier went he might as well be a duke. He had, he thought, as much right as anyone else: Lord Pitt was only a life peer, and Françoise called herself "Countess" though the French monarchy had been dead a hundred years. Anyway, lord or not, he could still make the others jump. He would stop Vanessa Bolton and Percy Bainbridge from going to Françoise de Lauzon's.

Vanessa turned out to be difficult, refused to alter her plans. He was annoyed, put a little X beside her name—it would be a long time before he'd ask *her* again.

"What's kept you?" he demanded when he called up Percy and had to wait for him to be summoned to the phone.

"Matter of fact, Peter, I was in the garage finishing up the prototype of my new papoose."

"Papoose! What will you think of next? Never mind—don't tell me now; we can discuss it at dinner Tuesday night."

A pause then while Percy considered his dilemma: How was he going to extricate himself from his acceptance to dine with Françoise? Peter waited, delighted by the situation—the old inventor was too cowardly to refuse an English peer. Percy's inventiveness, of course, was nothing but a joke. The Australian had written a little book about his discoveries—ways to make soybeans taste like turkey, and lampshades out of old gloves. Poor Percy—he persisted, though his magnetic broom for ironmongers had failed to catch on, and after ten years of development his grapefruit juicer still ran too hot.

"Tuesday would be perfect, Peter. Just had to check my book."

A lie, of course, but touching in a way. Peter, relishing his power, decided to make Percy crawl. "You know, Percy, I've been thinking about you, and I've decided there's something in the house you simply have to change. That ghastly watercolor, the one hanging in the hall—it's time to stash it in the attic for good."

"Hmmm. Do you really think so? I never actually thought of that."

"Well do, dear, *do*. It'll give the hall a cleaner look. Do it this afternoon—you'll see instantly that I'm right."

Percy promised to give it thought, and Peter smiled as he

rang off. The watercolor was one of Percy's best things—Peter would be pleased to own it himself. But it was always necessary to make these little tests, check around and see who still obeyed. If Percy did take the picture down, then that meant things hadn't changed: he was still pasha of the Mountain and the peasants still ran to kiss his feet.

"Oh, dear," he said suddenly, looking up at himself in a gilded mirror. "Peter Barclay: you *are* a nasty pouf!"

The phone rang just as he was staring at himself. It was Vicar Wick, calling about the note.

"I've spoken to Consul General Whittle," he said in his nervous voice. "As the police here refuse to help, we're going to send the note up to Scotland Yard. Not for fingerprints, mind you—they're probably all smudged out. Handwriting analysis—that's the thing. We'll catch the culprit yet."

"Yes," said Peter, somewhat dazzled by the thought. "Sounds perfectly reasonable to me."

"We've thought of everything, Whittle and I, and we've come up with a jolly good plan. At the Consulate they've got a file of old Christmas notes and B&Bs. We'll send the whole batch up to London too, so that hopefully they'll match some writings up."

"Good thinking, Vicar, I must say."

"Thank you. I thought so myself. Also, with your permission I want to bring in Colonel Brown. He's an avid reader of detective novels and would make an excellent sleuth. Plan is for him to give a series of luncheons, invite all the suspects, and try to smoke them out. Watch the eyelashes and all that. I think it's worth a try. Meanwhile next Sunday I shall preach a sermon that'll get our man where he hurts. Just look around church for a pair of burning ears—we may trap him right there."

It all sounded excellent, the Vicar's three-pronged plan, and set Peter to pondering the punishment he'd exact. Ostracism was one possibility. Let everyone know the anonymous author's name, then put him in Coventry until he was driven from Tangier. But the more he thought about it, the more he preferred the opposite course: seduce the villain by sweetness, treat him like his closest friend, and then, when he'd done that, confide how much the note had hurt. He'd offer his fair cheek to those sickening underbred lips, *and then,* he thought, *we shall truly see just what the word "two-faced" means.*

He laughed at the thought, then dismissed it from his mind. While the Vicar, the Colonel, and Scotland Yard worked to break the case, he'd forget about the note and have some fun. If his days as pasha were numbered, he'd do well to enjoy his power now. Eventually, some way, he'd find his enemy out and crush him like a fly.

He wandered into his garden, along its many paths, stroking his day lilies as he walked. The garden was nearly as he wanted it, after a quarter century of work, but still there were problems with the view. There was something wrong there that disturbed him more and more. And as much as he tried, he didn't know how to set it right.

It was Dradeb that bothered him—that damnable, horrid slum. It lay between the Mountain and the city and ruined the whole effect. It wasn't that Dradeb looked so terrible from the Mountain—from high up it appeared as a white cubistic maze. It was just knowing that it was there, knowing what it was and how it reeked, that spoiled his paradise.

But what to do? It would be splendid if he could just wave a wand and make it all go away. Or if, by some magic in the night, it could become transformed into a valley full of Moroccan shepherds playing flutes. That would be marvelous, and then the filthy Jew's River could become a babbling stream. *Or else,* he thought, curling his lip, *those damn people down there could be taught to devour their young.*

But then, suddenly, there came to him a solution, and he wanted to kick himself for not having thought of it before. All he needed were a few fast-growing eucalyptus. Then, in a couple of years, he could screen the Dradeb out.

He became excited and entered the garden again. He walked to the edge of his property, then sadly shook his head. There wasn't enough room, and his shrubs would be ruined by the eucalyptus' invasive roots. But the property just below his, vacant Moroccan-owned land, would make a perfect place for such a grove. He could plant down there and, when the trees reached the proper height, pollard their tops and create a verdant wall.

The problem was to get hold of that land. He couldn't afford to buy it himself. Perhaps Camilla would help—she had old Weltonwhist's fortune and could certainly spare some pounds. Yes—she might do it; it would be a good investment for her too. She'd probably jump at the chance if he handled her right. Yes, that was it, he'd get Camilla to buy the land, then plant the trees and abolish the excrescence from his sight.

He began to dream of how he'd make the Mountain reach Tangier, of the view he'd have: foliage, the city, and the sea.

Kalinka

Whenever Hamid thought about it, he was amazed by how little he knew about Kalinka. It was his habit to plumb a person's depths—he did this every day in his office, interrogating suspects, probing informants, seeking a conception of their characters beyond the information they had to give. But with Kalinka it was different. He hadn't pressed her, and as a result she'd remained mysterious, the mysterious woman who'd floated into his life.

He wondered whether he feared the ruin of an illusion if he came to understand her well. But he did know her, knew every curve, every crevice in her body, knew the texture of her hair, so long and black and thick, the way morning light could gleam off her ivory skin. And her eyes, large and dark, surrounded by disks of glittering hazel—he knew the wide-open softness of them when she awoke, and the rimless Oriental lids that covered them while she slept. Yes, he knew her, but underneath there was something he did not know. Her history. Her past.

He was thinking about this as he sat in his car parked across the street from Peter Zvegintzov's shop, waiting for the customers to leave so he could go inside and confront the Russian with the fact Kalinka had revealed the night before.

They'd just finished dinner, were sipping tea in silence, when suddenly she'd turned to him and spoke.

"He followed me."

"What? Who followed you, Kalinka?"

"Peter," she said. "At a distance. Discreetly. Perhaps fifty yards behind."

"When? When was this?" She'd told him before that she thought Peter followed her, but always when he'd asked her if she was sure, she'd stared down at the floor.

"After the play," she said, "the British play. Remember— you left early with Aziz. Later, when it was over, I walked back here. And he followed me the entire way."

"*What?*" Suddenly his heart stood still.

"Yes. I'm sure of it. When I was safe up here I went out on the terrace and looked down. There he was, standing on the street. He saw me. Our eyes met. Then I stepped back inside."

"I'll close him up, Kalinka. I'll drive him out. I'll expel him from Tangier."

"Oh, no! He's harmless. Please, Hamid. It doesn't mean anything. You mustn't hurt him. Please."

"But it's not right. He can't follow you—"

"He loves me, Hamid. There's no crime—I don't see any crime in that."

No crime. Why couldn't she understand, why couldn't she see that it was intolerable for him that the man people thought was her husband now openly followed her on the street?

Love! he thought—*he has no right to love her anymore.* But then he stopped himself, contained his fury. He would not burden her. He would settle this himself.

So now he was waiting outside the shop for the second time in ten days—the second time in all the months since he and Kalinka had fallen in love and he had brought her here and waited for her to fetch her clothes—and he wondered: *What can I say to him except to warn him that he must never follow her again? What can I say beyond that, since I know nothing of what went on between them all those years?*

For months now, he realized, he'd been resisting his policeman's instincts. The memory of the previous winter, the intense, unspoken way they'd fallen in love, the way they'd discovered their love for one another amidst the chaos of Tangier—he'd treasured that time so much he'd been afraid to tarnish it by exploring what had gone on with her before. And then, after she'd moved in, he didn't want to disrupt the quiet of their lives, the special calm with which she surrounded him, the vagueness which was as much a part of her as the aroma of hashish that forever filled their flat. *Better,* he'd thought, *not to disturb this calm. Kalinka is my refuge. In her stillness I have an oasis in Tangier.*

But there was more than this stillness that he savored and feared to disrupt. There was her passion too, which burst out unpredictably, causing her to grasp him, crush her body against his. And, too, there were those times when they loved each other subtly, when she seemed to lie still and yet moved, caressing him, drawing him in, extending their lovemaking for hours until he became lost in her body, her embrace. At those times she drew him into a world which he explored in an intoxicated state, a dazed sensuality in which he reveled, her strange world of subtlety and dreams.

And yet, more and more often lately, he'd asked himself how long this magic of theirs could last. It worried him, for he could see no end to her dreaminess, could find no fixed points by which he could relate her to Tangier. And he knew too that the disconnection between their love and his public life must, somehow, be resolved.

He'd begun to ask her questions, but the more he asked, sensitive to her resistance, her unwillingness to talk and to reveal, the more he found himself disturbed by her refusal to respond with facts. She would turn away, busy herself with sketching or cooking or housework, rearrange flowers in a bowl, water the plants she was growing on the balcony, fold laundry, or else take his hand, bring it to her lips, stare back at him with her large, glazed eyes, smiling as if to tell him that she did not want to doubt his love, and then shake her head and dismiss his query from her mind.

What could he do in the face of that? He was not a man accustomed to being evaded. Could there be something terrible hidden behind her smile, something criminal, some awful crime? He knew so little about her, had such a sketchy notion of her life. He knew only that she'd been born in Hanoi and orphaned at a young age, and that Peter Zvegintzov had adopted her, taken her to Poland to escape some cataclysm of Asian politics, and then finally to Tangier where he'd imposed the pretense that she act as if she were his wife.

She was adamant on one point: that she and Peter had never been married; that Peter had never touched her as a man might touch a wife. And yet, despite her assurances, the thought of Zvegintzov living with her so many years, in some strange relationship he could neither define nor understand, preyed upon Hamid. The thought of this obsequious man, this second-rate, tattered little man with his vague past and his frayed cuffs and his formless, odorous suits, whose face announced to the world that he was ready to be trampled upon and used, that this awful man had invented the pretense that he'd been a husband to Kalinka, had slept with her—he could hardly bear the thought. It was almost worse than if Peter's claim had been true, for there was no logic to it and something disgusting, something awful, that made his stomach turn. Now all his work at the Sûreté, his confrontations with smugglers and drunkards and men who'd come to Tangier to misbehave—all of that seemed meaningless in the face of the mystery of Peter and Kalinka and their past.

He thought about it all the time now, tried to recall details, hints from Kalinka, little things Zvegintzov might once have said. He realized, thinking back, that he'd never actually heard Peter say that Kalinka was his wife, not in all the years he had frequented the shop, seen Kalinka there, hardly noticed her, thought of her as a fixture or a pet. Yet everyone in Tangier *knew* that they were married—it was something that had always been assumed. And then there had come that strange night the previous January when the hailstones had rained down upon a cold and damp Tangier, that night when Zvegintzov had come to his flat on Rue Dante with a riding crop hidden in his sleeve and said: "My wife tells me she's leaving. I am the husband. I have certain rights." It was only then, that one time, that Hamid had actually heard Zvegintzov make the claim. And the next day, when Hamid met her at Farid's shop, when they'd kissed and touched and held each other for the first time—that day she'd looked steadily into his eyes, told him that she loved him, and swore to him she had never been married to Zvegintzov, had never been his wife.

He'd accepted that—another mystery, he'd thought—and yet he knew now he would never have accepted such a statement from any person he suspected of a crime. He would have probed the claim, asked questions, cross-examined, insisted on dates and facts. But after she moved in with him it didn't seem to matter—though, if he were to marry her, it would matter very much.

But now he wondered, waiting outside Zvegintzov's shop, trying to formulate what he would say to him, the cold words which must not reveal the heat of his fury, the warning which would leave no doubt in Peter's mind that he must never follow her again. Yes, now he wondered: Who was she? What mystery lay behind her smile? What strange childhood had she had? Why had Zvegintzov brought her to Tangier?

Her passport told him so little, her old Polish passport, listing the name of her mother, someone called Pham Thi Nha, her father "unknown," and the fact that she'd been born in Hanoi in November 1943. Were there other documents? Adoption papers? Certificates from schools? When he'd asked her she'd shaken her head, perhaps to say she didn't know, or that Peter had them and would never give them up.

Now he would have to find out, no matter how great the risk. If she could not give information like other people, if she was able to communicate with him only by signs and gestures and nods and looks, then he would have to learn to decode these signals too. He thought about her then, the way she watered a plant and fried a fish, the way she undressed, cast aside her clothes, the way she smiled, turned when he called her, kissed him, or lay slightly curled on their bed waiting for him to come home with the late afternoon light, the intense blue light of a Tangier afternoon cutting through the blinds on their bedroom window, striping her body with diagonals, and her hashish pipe set on the bedside table, perfectly angled as if for a photograph in a book about the mysteries of the East—just the thought of her like that stabbed at him with love.

Yes, he loved her, adored her, could not imagine life without her now, and yet he could not help himself, could not hold himself back any longer, even at the risk of destroying this spell of hers, this sense of refuge by which she held him in such thrall.

He looked back into La Colombe. There still were customers inside and he could see Peter too, in silhouette, making those too hasty movements by which he brought requested merchandise to the counter, or used the long stick with the pincers at its end to extract large boxes from the shelves above his reach, and he thought: *I can't go in there now and threaten him, tell him not to follow Kalinka on the street. I'll become too angry, ask too many questions, appear too jealous, and lose my dignity as an inspector of police.*

He shook his head then and started up his car. He would not go in, and he was amazed at himself for that—that he, Hamid Ouazzani, a chief of section at the Tangier Sûreté, so cool in his dealings with foreigners, so dignified, such a smooth practitioner of an inspector's manner, that he could not now find the words or the poise to deal with a man who, he knew, could only gape at him in fear.

Driving back toward his apartment through the main street of Dradeb, he thought of the words of Mohammed Achar when he'd come to him with his worries the afternoon before.

"I don't think I can help you, Hamid. I'm a surgeon—not a psychiatrist. But I think maybe this is good for you, to have something in your life you can't easily understand. You look for rationality in foreigners where only irrationality exists. What harm is there in just living with Kalinka, accepting her as she is? You must learn to live with mystery and ambiguity, put aside your compulsion to analyze. . . ."

Achar had brushed his thick fingers across his mustache and had smiled at Hamid. It was an old issue between them; Hamid's hope that he would someday come to understand the foreigners, and Achar's insistence that there was no logic to their acts. And it amused him to hear Achar promote the virtues of mystery and ambiguity, since he was a man who prided himself on the rigor of his analysis of justice and politics and power. Still, after their conversation, he'd asked himself: *Why can't I just accept her as she is?*

He knew now why he could not. He loved her too much, wanted to marry her, and yet could not marry a woman he did not understand. It was his life's work to understand people, had been since he'd been a boy and become infatuated with the foreigners who owned and ruled Tangier—those rich men with the fine villas and automobiles whose women went about with uncovered faces and lay nearly naked on the beach. Boulevard Pasteur had been their street then—the medina belonged to the Moroccans, but the European city and the Mountain belonged to the people with the golden hair. They were the ones who bought the bodies of his friends, who'd corrupted Farid, the brother he loved but on whose behalf he'd felt such shame. (He had not been ashamed *of* Farid, but *for* him.) And when the time had come for him to decide what he would do, the old cherif who'd coached him so he could enter the Lycée Regnault had talked to him, after Achar had gone off to Cairo to study medicine, and suggested that since he was so interested in people's motives he take the examination for the police.

He'd liked the idea of that, especially when he foresaw the possibility of policing the foreigners of Tangier. Understanding them had become his work, and now, many years later, he was living with Kalinka, a foreigner, who contained all the mystery of all the foreigners he'd stared at and wondered about so long. He lived with her, but holding her in his arms, covering her with his body, kissing her and being kissed by her, loving her and being loved by her, he felt in her the mystery of all of them, close to him, closer than any foreigner had ever been to him, yet apart from him, illogical, incomprehensible—foreign.

It's because of that, he thought, parking his car, walking into his building on Ramon y Cahal, *that I must finally understand who and what she is. For if I can unravel her, I shall come to understand them all, their whole world, which has baffled me and repelled me and attracted me so long. And then the mystery will be solved. I will be free of it. I will marry Kalinka. We will be happy. I will be a happy man.*

He rode the elevator to his floor, stepped out, walked the

corridor to the doorway of his flat. He paused outside, knowing that in a few seconds he would find her waiting for him, lying on the bed, the afternoon light painting her curled body, her pipe set at an angle on the table, a cloud of smoke above her head.

Robin

Harsh, insistent knocking woke Robin from his dream—of a boy flying a kite in a meadow, of dazzling sunlight catching his gray woolen shorts, causing them to glow like lustrous pewter.

"*Entrez,*" he growled, semicomatose. "Come in, whoever you are."

The form of a man appeared at the door. Robin recognized the catlike step. "Inspector Ouazzani. Come in. Come in." He brushed some newspapers off the stool by his bed.

The Inspector advanced through the gloom, then stopped. A moment later he was at the window throwing open the shutters.

"Christ, no, Hamid! You'll wake me up!"

"Can't stand the smell of hash."

He came then and sat down, his black leather jacket gleaming in the light.

"You don't usually call so early. I hope there's nothing wrong."

"There's always something wrong, Robin. You ought to know that." He put his feet up against the side of the bed.

"This morning, fortunately, it doesn't have to do with you."

"Well, I'm glad of that." Robin sighed, then pulled up his naked body and arranged a decaying pillow behind his head.

"How can you live in such filth? The poorest Moroccan wouldn't put up with this."

They both gazed around at the mess. Suitcases were piled into a teetering tower, books were scattered everywhere, along with boxes of newspapers and other trash. Broken phonograph records and unwashed laundry littered the floor, ashtrays overflowed, and the little table where Robin worked was piled with dishes and a typewriter covered with dust.

"This place is disgusting—absolutely foul. Even your sheets are filthy. What a hole!"

"It's my lair, Hamid. All my treasures are here."

"At least you could change your sheets."

"I will. Today is washday. On my way to breakfast I'll take them out."

"I smell something. Do you keep a cat?"

"They come and go—come and go."

"Well, I'm disgusted. You live like a pig!"

"This is just my little niche in Tangier."

Hamid offered him a cigarette.

"No thanks. My throat's still raw."

Hamid shrugged and lit up. "Why don't you get an apartment somewhere, get out of this stinking hotel?"

"I should. I keep telling myself that. But I like living day to day. Also, it's nice to have the Socco Chico downstairs. It makes a good salon."

Hamid shook his head. "You're lazy. You need a good kick in the ass."

Robin brushed some crumbs out of his bed—he'd had a picnic the night before. There were some kif seeds too, where his body depressed the mattress. He rolled over and swept them out.

"Ugh!"

"All right, Hamid. Enough about my habits. Please tell me what you want."

"Nazis," the Inspector said.

"Nazis?"

"Ex-Nazis—you know what I mean."

"You mean former Nazis who might be living in Tangier?"

"Yes. That's it."

"Well—what about them?"

"I want their names."

Robin shrugged.

"There aren't any since Dr. Keitel left."

"Keitel?"

"Awful little man. He's in Liberia now."

"Well, there must be others. Tangier's filled with scum."

Robin shook his head. "There're plenty of old collaborators. Lanier, the surgeon. Princess Leontieff—they say she had an affair with Von Stuelpnagel. For that matter there's Madame Diplomante, but she was more of a Fascist type. Plenty of those left, but not the real thing. I guess there were a few in the international days."

"Some of them must still be around."

"Of course, Hamid, if you insist."

"Damn it, Robin, think. You know all the seamy types."

Robin shrugged. "There's a German boy who lives in the Casbah, but he must have been an infant during the war. He's writing a book about Himmler, who was 'vastly underrated' he says. I don't know him very well."

Hamid shook his head. "That's not what I mean."

"I'm sorry. I can't help you."

"All right." The Inspector stood up. "Call me if you think of anyone else. And clean this damn place out."

"Ha!"

When Hamid was gone, Robin slumped back in his bed. He scratched his chest and then a sore on his rump. The Inspector had looked tired, as if he wasn't getting sufficient sleep. What did he mean—he couldn't stand the smell of hash? With Kalinka he lived in it all the time. Everyone knew she was stoned to the ears.

He pulled himself up, limped over to the mirror above his wash basin, and inspected his unshaven face. His hair was a mess, a halo of tight red curls. He needed a bath and a good combing out. He splashed on some water and scratched at his rear again. Suddenly a burst of laughter spilled into the room. He turned to the window and saw two little Moroccan girls watching from a roof across the way. They were giggling at his nudity, their hands covering their mouths. He made a threatening gesture and slammed the shutters closed.

Oh, the medina, he thought, *how I adore this stinking place.* There wasn't any privacy, and the Oriental Hotel was one of the seediest around, but at least there was life in the medina, not the sterility of the European town. He cupped his balls and bounced them several times. *Good exercise,* he thought. He tore a comb through his hair with no result, then brought it to his nose and shrugged.

He struggled into a pair of jeans, pulled on a red turtleneck, and stooped to tie his sneakers. Still bent, he gathered up his laundry: socks, underwear, numerous shirts and pants. When he had everything together he ripped the sheets off the bed and stuffed the whole lot into a burlap sack. He loved this sack, for it was stenciled with a pair of shaking hands and the slogan "A Gift from the People of the United States." He had a scheme to buy up a truckload, then have the sacks converted into hippie clothes. He was sure he'd make a killing if he ever got around to it, and equally sure he never would.

He was a flight and a half from the lobby, the sack on his shoulder and an unlit cigar dangling from his lips, when he remembered it was Thursday, the day his column was due. He'd have to get it in by noon or face his editor's wrath. *Damn,* he thought. He didn't feel like work.

Out on the street he paused, wondering which way to turn. He'd given up trying to find an honest laundry—whichever one he came to would have to do. All of them stole, either socks or underpants—the Moroccans were short of both, it seemed. But though they all charged outrageous fees, they were far better than the hotel. He'd had a terrible row there the year before, when the maid had taken all his clothes and washed them without his consent. Furious over that and the outlandish bill, he'd gone to the desk to complain.

"Your things have been washed," said the manager, "so you have to pay."

"But the point," Robin protested, "is that I didn't *ask* that they be washed. I prefer to take my washing out."

"Take it out. By all means take it out. But pay this time, or we'll dirty your clothes before we give them back."

"Dirty them? How will you dirty them?"

"Use them as dust rags, I expect."

It was absurd and hilarious—a typical situation with the people of Tangier. They'd do anything for money, anything to cheat, but later they'd want to discuss existentialism over sweet mint tea. Robin loved them, and hated them too. Though frequently they drove him to despair, he found them irresistible. What can you do with people, he often wondered, who throw up their hands and say "God's will" no matter what miserable thing happens in their lives? Their submission to destiny made them passive about everything but money—the one subject about which they were impossible all the time. They'd steal most cleverly, but not blame themselves if they were caught. It was always God's will— *Imchalah,* as they said, until Robin swore he'd scream the next time he heard that word. Their religion had most certainly destroyed them, but had also made them great. It had set them back centuries, if one counted up all the months they'd lost during their annual Ramadan fast, but it had given them a kind of grandeur—there was nobility in their helplessness in the face of fate. He much preferred their style to the North American one he'd left, but he never failed to be amazed when he gave a few francs to a beggar, then watched the man stare at him and thank Allah instead.

After depositing his sack at a laundry, where it was weighed on a crooked scale, he walked back to the Socco Chico and slid into a table at the Centrale. He loved this dilapidated cafe, which abounded with hustlers day and night. People constantly passed by—Moroccans on their errands, young Europeans in walking shorts lost in the medina maze. Here, for the price of a glass of tea, he could sit for hours and admire all their legs. Boys or girls, it didn't matter—smooth, tanned skin was his delight.

He ordered a coffee and lit his cigar. Two girls with stringy hair sat a table away, their eyes blue and empty from a night of kif and sex.

The season, he thought, is beginning—the parade of the sensuous young. They came, girls like that, proud, independent, with their bedrolls and their cash. Tangier welcomed them and gave them everything they sought: drugs, rape in their hotel rooms, unspeakable penetrations on the beach at night. When they left it would be without regrets, though later, back in Stockholm or Montreal, at the universities where they prepared themselves for wholesome competitive careers, they might find cause to worry about venereal disease.

Oh, he thought, *to be young again, tanned and strong and smooth. To have a virgin asshole and be full of hope. To smoke my first pipe of Moroccan kif.* He sipped at his coffee and stared out at the street. No cars allowed in the medina—just people walking back and forth. He knew all the regulars—the hustlers, rug merchants, bazaar keepers, and whores.

"Hello, Robin."

"Good morning, Robin."

"Hey, Robin—hi!"

He'd been in Tangier a decade, and his face was part of the scene. He was one of the fixtures around the place, like the one-legged fellow who guarded cars in the Casbah or Mustapha, the mailman, who worked the Mountain Road. Everyone read his column too, though he couldn't imagine why. They loved his gossip, though it was about people they didn't know, lives that had nothing to do with theirs.

Pumpkin Pie walked by, pacing the little square like a high-stepping Harlem dude.

"Hello, Robin. Where you been?"

"Around, Pie. Around."

"Yeah. Around. Always around. Good to see you, Robin babe."

And then he was gone, disappearing into the crowd. A beautiful specimen, Robin thought, though beginning to lose his looks. Yes, he'd been here ten years—ten years of nothing, he sometimes thought. But he never wanted to exchange that time for a decade anyplace else.

A boy in a faded jeans jacket sat down with the girls, setting his backpack on the terrace floor. Robin closed his eyes and listened to their dialogue, mellifluous counterpoint to the guttural Arabic spoken around.

"Didn't I see you last night?"

"Did we see him, Carol?"

"I don't know. Where *was* he last night?"

Good, he thought. *A classic ritualistic beginning.* He'd tried to capture that idiotic tempo once, in a long poem he'd called "Medina Voices."

"Hey, where do you get your stuff?"

"Don't tell him, Cynthia."

"What's the matter with her?"

"She's a slut."

"Now, look, Carol. I told you not to say that—"

"Who cares anyway."

"You're *really nasty* this morning."

"Shit—why don't the three of us get stoned?"

"Hey—wow!"

"We don't know this creep."

After a while Robin turned off—he'd heard *that* conversation a thousand times. The same petty insults, the same probing around, and all it ever came to was a lumpy mattress in a fleabag hotel and a third-rate screw. Still it was life, and there was something to be said for that. *Or,* he asked himself, *is it really a kind of death?*

He watched the threesome firming up their deal. In a few minutes they'd be pooling their cash and then the hustlers would crowd around. Someone would have some "special stuff" to sell; someone else would offer a "terrific freaky room." It was all marvelously degrading, but that was what he loved about the town—the crumbling buildings, the seediness, made a perfect backdrop for bringing fantasies to life.

He loved the medina and the Casbah, especially at night, loved to roam the littered streets, loved the stink of excrement, the quarrels, and the slops that were constantly being emptied from windows overhead. The medina had an intricate rhythm, was a slum, but not a serious one, nothing like Dradeb. The same rats, of course, the same ooze and fights and overcrowded Arab life, but with a sort of grim humor that redeemed it in the end. The people of the medina had a cosmopolitan style. They were poor, but they didn't starve. In Dradeb, on the other hand, life was all despair.

Well, he thought, *it's time to go to work.* He left a coin for the waiter, pocketed some sugar cubes, and nodded to the three Americans, who glanced back curiously at him. Perhaps someone had told them he was a man to see. But long ago he'd decided to deal only to his friends.

At the Oriental he began scrupulously to clean his desk. When everything was dusted off, he stared down at his battered Olivetti and wondered what to write. It hadn't been much of a week, though he had enough material for a column. He rolled in a piece of paper and began to type.

ABOUT TANGIER
by Robin Scott

PEOPLE ARE TALKING ABOUT two parties on the Mountain Tuesday night, at Peter Barclay's and Françoise de Lauzon's. The rivalry between these two hosts has reached the point where their friends don't know what to do. Our informants tell us that at least one of Barclay's guests accepted with Françoise first. Was he right? We hear that Françoise gave a better time. Champagne flowed, and Mr. Patrick Wax gave an imitation of Barclay saying "Hello." Then Inigo, our Paraguayan genius, drew OBSCENE pictures with lipstick on the Countess's lavatory mirrors, and the Mesdames Drear, also in attendance, pleased everyone with a dance. At Barclay's the usual crowd, plus the Governor and our esteemed chief of customs, Omar Salah. Madame Joop de Hoag was accompanied by Monsieur de Hoag's confidential assistant, young Jean Tassigny, whose good looks have taken Tangier by storm. Camilla Weltonwhist complained to Mr. Salah about the shortage in town of Camembert cheese. The talk then turned to the price of aubergines, and the quality of grapefruit and courgettes. General Bresson complained to the Governor about his difficulties with his telephone. The Governor replied that he'd look into the matter the next time he had a chance.

THE NOTE: Much talk this week about *the note* delivered on the collection plate at St. Thomas Church. No one knows who wrote it yet, but rumors are all over town. Will our amateur sleuth, Colonel Lester Brown, be able to smoke the villain out? He's an avid reader of detective novels, we hear. The Vicar's up to something too. The service this Sunday may be the ecclesiastical event of the year.

OTHER SCANDALS: Sad scene at the airport a week ago Monday night. Members of a certain British ballet company were escorted to the London plane in handcuffs by Tangier police. Tourists gawked and flashbulbs popped. What was it the *dear* boys did?

TANGIER PLAYERS: Fever over at TP has gone up another ten degrees. Larry Luscombe, the club's founder and president, has told this column he won't resign. "Not under any circumstances," he said, and we take him at his word. If worse comes to worst, and the AMERICAN powerplay does succeed, Larry has promised he'll start another group.

DIPLOMATICALLY SPEAKING: The Foster Knowles' out the other night at Heidi's Bar, along with the Willard Manchesters and the Ashton Codds. The young Knowles' are becoming quite popular, we hear. A number of our older fellow Tangerenes have joined their early morning jogging group.

BY THE WAY, speaking of Heidi's, we wonder how they liked the food. We were poisoned there, ourselves, last week, by some overpungent ratatouille!

DIPLOMATICALLY TOO: The Dan Lakes have been seen socially with Peter Zvegintzov. Just shows that détente works, even in Tangier.

BITS AND PIECES: Tessa and David Hawkins back from Dublin, where they bought an Irish jumper. This brother and sister horsebackriding act, which has won every prize in Tangier, will be heading down to Rabat soon to take on the Royal Equitation Team.

ON THE LITERARY FRONT: Kranker, Klein, and Doyle back from Marrakech, where the three literary lions held forth at the Glacière. The fourth member of the old quartet, Martin Townes, has been in deep seclusion for a month. We don't know what he's cooking up, but there are rumors that CERTAIN TANGIER PERSONALITIES may find themselves in his forthcoming book.

PEOPLE COMING: Pierre St. Carlton will be at "Capulet" by June 15. Our dapper Indonesian friend Jimmy Sohario is also expected soon. Dolores Faye spent the spring in Nepal and will come here after a stopover in Jaipur. No word yet on Henderson Perry, but his yacht has been spotted off Iran. When he gets here the real parties will start, and the talk won't be about the price of aubergines either.

FINALLY this from the Beaumonts (younger generation): a valuable pre-Colombian *objet* is missing from Villa Chapultepec. Would whoever took the thing, INADVERTENTLY, OF COURSE, please leave it with the gatekeeper? We promise not to report his name.

Robin pulled the last page out of his typewriter, sat back and gasped. He'd written the entire column in ten minutes, without stopping to choose his words. He lit up a pipe of kif and inhaled. Then he read the column through.

Poetry it wasn't. He folded the pages neatly, sealed them in an envelope, and threw himself down on his bed. His dream of making his name with serious verse had fled him years before, and now he didn't care anymore—life in Tangier was much too gay. There were still too many marvelous characters to meet, too many fine young bodies to screw. Hustler. Police informer. Dope dealer. Gossip. Robin, the redheaded weasel with the barbed tongue. He was all of these things, and had found himself a town that matched his seedy vision of his soul.

A little before noon he gathered himself up, walked out of the medina to the offices of the *Dépêche de Tanger*. He left his column under the door; he had no wish to see his Moroccan editor or hear a lecture on the dangers of submitting material late. Besides, he wasn't owed any money—he'd borrowed a month's salary in advance.

An hour later he was at the base of the Mountain, having walked across the city and through the valley of Dradeb. The Jew's River was marshy, full of debris. Women, washing clothes there, had spread sheets on the banks to dry. As he hiked by La Colombe, he saw Peter Zvegintzov closing up for lunch. The Russian was wrestling with his iron grill, but Robin didn't stop to help. Zvegintzov was like a tailor, he thought, with a little bedroom tucked away behind his shop. There he sat, glasses glinting, worrying over his accounts.

At Villa Chapultepec he rang the bell, then waited before the iron gate. Finally a servant opened up and led him through the house. It was a rambling old Moorish palace where the younger Beaumonts, all in their twenties, sat about wasting time. Their parents were in Paris fighting off litigations that had followed the collapse of the family's bank.

Robin was led down long, damp corridors and finally into a great salon. Here he was greeted by Hervé Beaumont, a dark, brooding young man of twenty-five. His two younger sisters, Guyslene and Florence, came up too, and Robin slipped them a kilo of kif. Hervé handed him some soiled banknotes, and Florence grasped his hand.

"Oh, Robin," she said, kissing both his cheeks, "you're just in time to see our film."

She led him around to greet the other guests—all people

he knew. They were sprawled on sofas yards apart, and he had the impression of an inanimate group. There was Patrick Wax, who raised his little pony whip in salute, Inigo in a white suede vest worn over a black shirt, the Hawkins' in riding clothes, Madame de Hoag with Jean Tassigny, and Martin Townes.

Townes was perched on a huge white Marrakech hassock, his blue-tinted glasses cocked warily on his nose. Robin sat next to him—though he didn't know the writer well he liked his looks and saw a plate of hors d'oeuvres nearby. The Beaumonts and Inigo were smoking kif. Wax was sipping champagne, the Hawkins' were drinking vodka, Claude de Hoag a pastis, and Townes a bottle of beer.

"You know," Robin said, "it's amazing to find you all here. I just finished writing my column, and there's not one of you I didn't name."

"You write nasty stuff, lad," said Wax, hissing through his teeth. "But I love it anyway."

"What did you say about us, Robin?" Hervé passed Florence his pipe.

Robin brought a finger to his lips. "They're sealed," he said. "Anyway, you can read it yourselves Saturday morning. Nothing juicy, I assure you, though I mentioned your missing statuette. Oh, yes—I did take a few swipes at the conversation at Barclay's Tuesday night."

"Good for you," said Wax. "He's got it coming to him, the bloody snob. So grand he is, and so awfully dull. I'd love to know who wrote that note."

"You're a prime suspect," Robin said.

Wax laughed. "Unfortunately I don't go to his dreadful little church. They're all such phonies there, and the Vicar's liturgy stinks. But I'll be there Sunday—to hear the sermon, though not, I assure you, to pray." He brought down his little whip hard on the arm of the couch. The smokers were too stoned to turn, and the Hawkins' so drunk they didn't hear.

"I doubt," said Townes, fixing Robin with a stare, "that you could have said very much about me. We rarely see each other, and everyone knows I don't go out."

"That's just what I wrote. I suggested you were up to something. Scribbling something nasty in that windowed tower of yours."

"You speculated, then?"

"If you want to put it that way."

Townes looked at him closely, then turned back to his beer. Robin lit his own pipe and watched Hervé set the projector up.

"Listen, everybody," said Florence. "We're going to show the film. It's just a home movie—nothing dirty. Move your chairs around. We'll project it on the wall."

"Guyslene will do the commentary," said Hervé.

"No," said Guyslene. "Florence."

"I think Florence might do better," said Patrick Wax. "She's a little less badly stoned."

"All right. Now someone draw the curtains." When no one did, Florence drew them herself.

A minute later the film was on, a flickering study, Robin thought, of a family in decline. Florence's voice-over was full of giggles and breathy gasps.

"See—there's Hervé in his Maserati! Just like James Bond! And there he is leaving the hospital. After his heroin deintoxication in Suisse."

A cut then from Hervé walking out the hospital door to shots of Mexican women dressed in black sitting on mules.

"This is Acapulco, I think. We had Christmas there last year."

Florence was seen jumping topless into a pool, while a pair of panting Afghans eyed her from the side.

"You're fatter now," said Claude de Hoag.

"Hmmm. Maybe. There's papa leaving court! See all the photographers. And the mob!"

"The stockholders put them up to that," said Hervé. Robin watched a pan of angry faces—people who'd lost their savings in the Beaumont bank.

"Look! Here we are skiing. That's Jamie Townsend, Guyslene's fiancé last year."

The images went on, shakier and more blurred. There were scenes of the Beaumonts sitting around smoking hash, and barely legible footage of a Djillala party they'd organized the previous summer on the beach at Cap Spartel. They all looked young and rich, and vulnerable too, beneath their smiles. There was a sense of doom in the background—people playing while their fortunes turned unseen. Gone now were the Maserati, the Christmas vacations in Acapulco, the ski chalet in Klosters. Robin had heard that the elder Beaumonts were living on credit in a commercial right-bank hotel, and that their legal fees had mounted to more than a million francs.

Once, when the film broke and Hervé worked to splice it up, Martin Townes wandered out of the salon. Robin thought he'd gone to the toilet, but after a while, when he didn't return, Robin excused himself and went out to look. He found Townes, finally, sitting in the garden stretched out on a wicker chaise lounge.

"Couldn't stand it, huh?" Robin asked.

"I got the idea pretty quick."

"Disgusted?"

"Not really. These people are fascinating, in a macabre sort of way."

"Why do you think?"

"Their emptiness, their superficiality. In some strange way that film shows them as they are."

"It'll be over for them soon, you know. This house is on the market. Not that anyone in his right mind would want to buy it, of course."

"I'm a great admirer of your column," said Townes, looking suddenly into Robin's eyes.

"Well, thank you very much. I wouldn't have thought you'd like it much."

"Actually I do. Gossip is what the novel is all about. Men and women, society, news. But there's something special about your work that's attracted me a long time. You don't write particularly well, and most of it's crap, but still, beneath it, there's a voice. A distinct one, I think."

Robin was caught off guard. He knew his column was "crap," but he wasn't particularly happy to be told so to his face. "Oh?" he said. "Please tell me more. Just what is this voice you hear?"

"It's the voice of a young man weary with life, and also fascinated by his own despair. He loathes what he does, and revels in it at the same time. The Robin Scott that emerges from a year or so of reading 'About Tangier' is a soul who's found grandeur wallowing in the abyss. He leads a perfectly pointless life, but somehow, despite that, he achieves a kind of sainthood in the end."

"Like Jean Genet?"

"No. Genet is a thief. Robin Scott is not a criminal, except perhaps in a broader sense. But certainly he's an existential character living on the edge, striding through Tangier's filth with an angelic smile on his face. People say terrible things about you, Robin. They say you inform for the police."

"That's rubbish, of course."

"Of course. Anyway, the point is that people apprehend you as a diabolical character. You're sinister in their eyes, and they can't reconcile that with all the fun you seem to have. There must be envy in it too. Everyone, at times, wishes he could embrace immorality."

"So, I'm an immoralist. What else do people say?"

"Oh, the usual things. Faggot. Pimp. Heroin racketeer. What is this business about putting young boys in woolen shorts?"

Robin blushed. "It's something I've wanted to do."

"Tell me about it."

"I'd rather not."

"Come on, Robin. It's all the same to me. Besides, I've read your poems."

"You have? How on earth did you find them?"

"Doyle showed me some things, in a little magazine."

"What did you think?"

"There were some lines. I remember a pair: 'His face is the triangle of a Berber horse / He has the burning eyes of Moroccan dice.' Something like that. Anyway, what comes through is the voice of a man who has a passion to confess."

"Perhaps I do, but my woolen shorts fetish is something I don't talk about anymore."

Townes shrugged. "As you like, Robin. But please tell me the story about your being nearly castrated last year. I've heard several versions, but not the true saga from the authoritative source."

"Ah! That was *something!* I was asleep in my room, my grubby little hole as everyone calls it, when this Moroccan boy I know—not a boy, exactly; he's over twenty—stole in and got into my bed. I didn't lock the door in those days, though I sure as hell do now. Anyway, he snuggled down next to me, and I was quite happy about that until I suddenly felt this rather sharp, cold piece of steel just beneath my balls. Christ, he had a knife down there. He told me not to move or he'd cut the damn things off. Then it began, his tirade, two hours in broken English, French, and then Arabic—so fast I couldn't make much of it out. It was all about Vietnam and U.S. imperialism, and when I protested that I was Canadian he brought the blade up a little tighter and told me to shut my trap. He went on and on then, pouring out his poor, young, angry heart, and I lay there terrified, afraid to say a word, wondering if I was going to be unmanned to expiate America's sins. Finally he grew tired, pulled the knife away, and gave my cock (totally retracted by then) a few smart fondles, which did *not* bring it back to life. He snitched my wallet, my coins, my watch, even my wretched stamps, and stole back out into the dark. I lay there the rest of the night shaking with fear, and in the morning, when I'd more or less recovered my senses, I thought about going to the police. Anyway, I thought better of it, decided the whole business was a crude but important experience, and so I kept quiet until, a few days later, I ran into him again."

"How was that?"

"He was simply sitting, sweet as you please, at a front table in the Cafe de Paris. I went up to him, we shook hands, then I sat down and we began to talk. He wasn't wearing my watch, and he said nothing about what he'd done. We chatted about this and that, and he was absolutely normal—as I'd thought he was before. We had such a good time we went out to a couscous joint and continued chatting there. Then, afterward, we shook hands, and he went back to his place and I returned to mine. Why didn't I ask him about it? Or at least ask him to return my things? I don't know. It was very odd, and he was so correct, so charming, that I wondered if I'd dreamed the whole thing up. But there was this thin red line where he'd pressed the blade beneath my balls, and I knew I hadn't done that to myself. Later I told a few people—it was such an extraordinary experience, perhaps the most terrifying and extraordinary of my life."

"And you never went to the police?"

"No."

"Did you ever see your things again?"

Robin shook his head. "Lost. Completely lost. A few weeks later I bought myself a cheap Japanese watch."

"Was this boy a political type?"

"No. That's the point. None of his political talk made any sense. I think he was just filled with rage—the rage they all have against us every now and then—and he simply expressed it in this strange dual way, the knife (which is pure Moroccan) and this crazy rhetoric he'd heard and half understood from Europeans he'd met around the Socco."

"Fascinating! I'd like to meet him if that's possible."

"You know him already, I think."

"I do?"

"Sure. He's around Inigo all the time now. The queens all call him Pumpkin Pie."

Townes nodded and the two of them fell into silence. A few minutes later the others drifted out. They assembled on the lawn furniture, drinks and pipes in hand, while a servant passed bowls of olives and dates, and the conversation, which was intermittent, lapsed slowly with the afternoon.

"Soon," said Wax, "the summer will come, and we'll not be able to bear the heat."

"Parties," said Florence. "Parties. Parties. I wish it were summer now."

No further talk about the movie they'd seen, but it had induced a feeling of malaise. The Beaumonts sensed this too and sat curled, brooding with their pipes. After a while Hervé got up to take a long walk along the cliffs above the sea.

At four o'clock Townes and Inigo excused themselves—they both, they said, had to return to work. Townes looked at him warmly as they shook hands. Robin decided to seek him out and talk to him again. As they left he was filled with the feeling that they were serious people and he was not. He had no doubt they were much more talented than himself—Inigo was probably a genius and Townes' books were good—but talent wasn't the point so much as waste: he knew that if he still had something to say he wasn't bothering to say it anymore.

He stayed until everyone had left—Wax off to Madame Porte's for his daily tranche of pâté de foie gras, the Hawkins' for their afternoon ride, Claude de Hoag and Jean Tassigny to the Emsallah Tennis Club, where their matches were said to be a disguised erotic dance. Finally, when the Beaumonts had become impossibly uncommunicative, Robin decided it was time to leave himself. There was nothing to say to them anymore, not even any gossip to pick up. So he loaded his pockets from the bowls of food and made his way, against the sunset, down the Mountain to Tangier.

Eleven o'clock. He was sitting in the Centrale surveying the scene. The small-time hustlers, the ones who sold fake watches and third-rate hash, had long since disappeared. Now the big-time dudes were out, and a hard core of Anglo-American queers inspected the meat rack as it passed.

Darryl Kranker was sitting with a boy whom Robin had once known well. He was a dancer now—a teenage beauty who put on makeup, danced with a tray of candles on his head, and made passes at men sitting in the nightclubs on Avenue d'Espagne. Robin had known him when the boy was thirteen years old. He was the last of the ones he'd dressed in woolen shorts.

He had no idea where he'd acquired that obsession: perhaps at his Canadian boarding school, a strict, cold, damp, unhappy place. Somehow the image had infected his brain—sunlight glittering off shorts of the purest wool, worn by pre-pubescent boys whose leg hairs still were fair. He'd never been able to shake it off, and when he'd moved to Tangier he'd brought the dream to life. One winter he'd grubbed his way to London on a cheap charter out of Gib and bought a dozen pairs. These he'd put on his favorite boys—made them wear them when they were in his room. When he was alone he kept them tucked in the closet, to be brought out when he needed inspiration for his work. The habit was so odd he spent much time trying to analyze it—more, in fact, than he spent composing verse. In the end he gave up the boys—there'd been too many close calls with Hamid. The Inspector, he knew, would not hesitate to throw him out; despite their friendship it was the one vice he despised. And soon after that he got rid of the shorts too, sold them in the flea market for a few measly francs. He'd hoped that some Moroccan mother might buy them for her son, and then, at least, he'd have the pleasure of seeing them catch the sunlight around Tangier. It was a gamble that didn't pay off: he never saw the shorts again.

Still the image haunted him, no matter how hard he fought it off. It was sick, he knew, and he was afraid to yield to it again, fearing a fall so deep he'd never find his way out of the abyss. He'd decided to draw the line, and kept to his resolve, for it was one thing to revel in degradation and quite another to yield so completely that he'd be addicted the remainder of his life. This way, guarding it as a fantasy, he could maintain the balance of his mind. And he recognized that he sublimated in many ways, absorbing himself in gossip, becoming a raconteur.

Boys—mere children: though he lusted after them terribly, he repressed that desire now too. Better to imagine a young man as a boy, hold him in his arms and transform him in his mind, than to corrupt a child who deserved something better than to be used as a receptacle for a sick man's lust. Still it was difficult—he suffered over his fantasies and accumulated guilt.

He looked over at Kranker, seated at his table, his piercing eyes focused on the boy. Suddenly Robin was filled with envy. Kranker did what he wanted and never suffered a pang. Why couldn't he do the same? It was so hard to fight off desires, to immerse himself in the foolish gossip of Tangier, to care what Peter Barclay thought, or about the absurd antics of Patrick Wax. *Sainthood!* Martin Townes had been wrong about that, but Robin wished he'd been right. If only he could pass through the barrier that kept good and evil apart, become a true immoralist and leave the guilt, like a whiff of smoke, trailing behind him in the breeze. Then he could turn evil into a festival of joy and revel in the dirt.

Suddenly he hated Kranker, sitting there so guiltless, so steely and cold. He was an unattractive man who'd always had to pay his boys. He was horrible, a man who'd never known love and never would.

All of us in Tangier, he thought, *live in our grubby little holes.*

At that he stood up, stretched and yawned, then walked back to the Oriental, where he mounted the stairs, entered his shabby room, flung himself down on his bed, lit up a pipe of kif, and dreamed, dreamed of a boy flying a kite in a meadow, his woolen shorts glowing in the light.

The End of
Spring

On the last Sunday in May the weather in Tangier began to change. Gone were the chilly nights and the sparse rains of spring. The wind was finished for a while, and the sky, which had been blue since the previous autumn, began to haze. Summer was coming to the city. The proprietors of the restaurants that fringed the town beach prepared to open up, and all the seats in the cafes on the Boulevard were filled.

On the west side of Tangier, on the Mountain, in the light-filled studio of his house, Inigo, the Paraguayan, was staring at a canvas he'd been working on for over a month. It was of Pumpkin Pie in Moroccan pantaloons, bare above the waist, his feet spread and planted firmly on the floor, looking directly out from a background of the sea. Inigo had put more into this canvas than into any he'd painted before. He'd been working frantically, from dawn to dusk every day, striving to make a statement of his feelings about Tangier.

He wanted to paint the boy as an archetypal hustler, strong, savage, willing to please. But there had to be a measure of vulnerability too—a haunted fear of poverty in the eyes. This, he thought, was the key to the portrait—a Nietzschean savagery, a powerful contempt, softened, even bankrupted, by a storekeeper's greed. He'd set himself the task of catching these two elements at once. If he succeeded he had no doubt the painting would fetch a fortune in New York.

But it was even more complicated than that—there was a third quality he wanted too: a decayed sensuality, a barely putrefied eroticism, the allure of vigorous young flesh slightly used, soiled, worn out. It was like painting the *Mona Lisa,* he thought—so many levels, so much complexity: he needed to peer with great depth into a personality in constant flux.

It was a difficult project, and Pumpkin Pie, as expected, gave him little help. The boy was restless all the time, bored with his model's role. Often he relaxed his pose or simply wandered outside, where he gunned his motorcycle, knowing that Inigo detested the noise. Several times he simply vanished, flew off to town without a word, disappeared for hours and then returned with torn clothes and disheveled hair.

Inigo knew better than to ask where he'd been—he was tired of his supplicating voice, and of Pumpkin Pie's cunning lies. By now he was inured to the boy and simply accepted him for what he was. He carried on as best he could, continuing work from his preliminary sketches and from the image he carried in his mind.

On this particular Sunday morning the boy sent word by a servant that he was resting in bed, fatigued and indisposed. *He's probably masturbating,* Inigo thought. Then he shrugged and returned to work. He'd been filling in the background, searching for a perfect clash of shades where the sea would meet the sky. But as he paused and contemplated the half-completed face, he decided to work more on the lips. He wanted to combine charm and arrogance there, catch the two qualities at once.

The painting had come to obsess him. One part of him wanted to finish it quickly, and another to work on it for months. He was repelled by it, and fascinated. Often, not against his will, he found it drawing him into the amoral twilight world of his friend.

Laurence Luscombe walked to town early, his empty shopping basket swinging from his arm. He knew he'd find himself a lift if he waited until the Mountain people left for church, but he had no desire to see them—their questions and glances disturbed his mood.

He'd spent the last weeks keeping to himself. All people did anyway was ask him about the feud—the talk of the Mountain, it seemed, fanned by frequent mentions in Robin's columns. One time when he did accept a ride in Camilla Weltonwhist's Rolls—he couldn't refuse; her driver had pulled right up to him—she talked the whole way of how much "fun" TP was getting to be now that it had "come of age." He knew damn well what she meant: that he was too serious, and that Kelly's vulgar humor made good relief.

This particular Sunday he walked early to the Socco, bought himself fruit and a quarter kilo of fish, then trudged over to Derik Law's flat, a cozy place on Campo-Amor.

Derik, off from his travel agency, met him at the door. "Bathroom's all ready, Larry. Dry towel and fresh bar of soap."

It was kind of Derik to let him use the shower. He'd given Laurence a set of keys to the flat so he could use it whenever he liked, but Sunday was best, since Derik was at home and after the shower the two of them could talk.

"You going to church?" Derik asked, as Laurence emerged from the bathroom combing his hair.

He shook his head. "I've no particular desire to see Peter Barclay in his glory. I've got enough problems of my own."

Derik nodded. "What're you going to do, Larry? Call a special meeting and read Kelly out?"

"Not sure yet. Still have some thinking to do. Be stupid of me to go through with that if I didn't have the votes."

"I know Kelly's got the Calloways and Whyte. David Packwood doesn't like him, though—he and Jill would probably split."

"What about the Drears?"

"Jessamyn's sold on the Yank, but Jessica's still up in the air. What you've got to do is bring in the patrons. They're entitled to vote, and if enough of them show up you'll win."

"I know. But I don't want to win that way. It would be a Pyrrhic victory and would split the group. I have to think beyond Kelly, to the seasons ahead. If we read him out, with the patrons throwing their weight behind me, we alienate the active members, and when Kelly cries in his coffee they'll all go off with him. The Drears, the Calloways, and the Packwoods are the hard core. That's the problem—what happens *after* Kelly's out?"

"Well—maybe the best course would be to let everything cool down. Don't call any meetings and forget the summer production. In the meantime you and Kelly could try to work things out."

"Never!" said Laurence, pounding the arm of his chair. "Not after he called me 'dear old hack.' "

"Oh, forget that. He didn't mean it. Suppose Kelly apologized—would that make things all right?"

"He won't do it. Man doesn't have a decent bone in his body."

"But suppose he *did*? Suppose some of us went to him, told him how we felt, and tried to patch things up? Neither of you wants to see TP go down the drain."

"Kelly doesn't care a fig about TP."

"But suppose he agreed to split productions with you? Each of you would do two a year, and the rest of the time you'd stay out of each other's way. What would you think of that?"

Laurence sat up straight.

"Have you been talking to Kelly behind my back?"

"Oh, come off it, Larry. You know me better than that. It's just the only way I see. Each of you has to come halfway."

"I founded TP, damn it! Now you ask me to give half of it to a man I don't respect."

Laurence wondered then whether to confide his calculations or wait until later when he was sure. A glance at Derik's sympathetic face convinced him to confide. "I've been thinking about this a lot lately," he said, "and I've a few ideas in mind. Maybe TP *is* getting stodgy. Maybe we *ought* to bring in new blood." He paused, gave a little smile. "Not at the top, necessarily, but among the actors. The way I figure it, if I go out and recruit new people it'll throw the old hard core off. I mean they might forget about Kelly and start worrying about their own hides for a while. They all think they're indispensable, but if I brought in Mr. Fufu, for instance, and, say, launched him in *Emperor Jones,* or the Knowles'—damn at-

tractive couple; they could do situation comedy for sure—
then you might see Jack Whyte's hackles rise, and a jealous
pout on Jill Packwood's face. See what I mean, Derik—put
them on the defensive, make *them* feel insecure. Then you
can bet they'd forget about Kelly and be around to curry favor
with me."

Derik thought a while before he replied. "It might work,
Larry," he said. "And then again it might not."

Robin Scott came early to St. Thomas—he wanted a good
seat for what he'd billed in his column as "the ecclesiastical
event of the year." After Camilla Weltonwhist showed him to
a rear pew, he began to jot down notes on the personages filling up the church.

> *The Foster Knowles':* elastic bodies—lanky minds
> *The Ashton Codds:* out-of-date clothing; a last hurrah
> *Patrick Wax:* cold, flawed steel
> *Dr. Sedgewick Radcliffe:* wrinkled neck
> *The Willard Manchesters:* sloppy socks
> *The Clive Whittles:* imperious airs
> *Deborah Gates:* squishy wench
> *Darryl Kranker:* malformed queer
> *Percy Bainbridge:* fragile pride
> *Lester Brown:* barracks buttermilk
> *The Drears:* God help us!
> *Vincent Doyle:* old literary lion nibbling on
>   his own claws
> *Lord and Lady Pitt:* wrinkled parchment
> *Heidi Steigmüller:* cigarettes-and-whiskey voice

After a while Robin gave up—too many people were
thronging in. Tessa and David Hawkins appeared in riding
garb, their crops stuck into their boots.

In the last minutes before the service began there was a fe-
verish rush for seats. There was suspense too—the sort one
might expect at an arena just before someone is due to be
thrown to a lion.

When Peter Barclay walked in, late as usual, all heads
craned. He went to the front pew, cool as anything, Robin
thought, head held high, upper lip stiff, stabbing methodi-

cally at the floor with his cane. Some dastard in the church had done him a nasty deed, but Robin could read nothing on his face but a decadent aristocrat's pride.

Soon the overcrowding and the pleasant weather outside began to build up the heat. People's foreheads gleamed, and by the reading of the first psalm Robin felt wet patches growing beneath his arms. He'd worn a ratty tweed jacket, and cursed himself for the mistake.

He hadn't been in a church in fifteen years, but it seemed to him the service was running much too long. It was as if Vicar Wick, enthralled by his captive audience, wanted to unleash every bit of hocus-pocus in his Anglican bag of tricks.

Robin was disappointed at the sermon. Taking Christ's Golden Rule as his theme, the Vicar preached a full ten minutes on the virtues of loving one's neighbor as oneself. Robin was lulled and about to doze, believing his excitement had been falsely aroused, when suddenly, after the reciting of the Lord's Prayer, the Vicar stepped to the middle of the transept and made a gesture with his hands. He'd been holding them together, fingers touching at the tips, with the meekness of a pastor ministering to a patient flock. But then, without any warning, he clasped them smartly behind his back. That moment his eyes became flinty, and he resembled a sergeant addressing raw recruits.

"Members of St. Thomas," he began, in a new, brusque tone of voice, "I have the sad duty to report to you this morning on an occurrence that has taken place within these walls. Someone, some member of our flock, has seen fit to use our little church as the launching pad for a personal attack. In an act of craven cowardness unworthy of a Christian, this person, behind an anonymous cloak, used our collection plate to deliver a slanderous attack upon the gentlest, kindest, most noble-hearted man to have ever graced our community in Tangier. It saddens me to say this, but in all my years as a vicar I have never before heard of such an act. I do not know whose twisted mind is responsible for this sin. Nor do I care to know his name. Since the act was clearly premeditated, the heat of anger cannot be an excuse. It is sad for us to know that there is such a creature in our midst, someone so evil, so vile, so lacking in grace and tact as to perpetrate such a deed. This person has defiled this holy place, but our church is strong and cannot be hurt. And the man who was attacked is also too strong and good—yes, I say good, and honorable too—to allow this injury to fester long. I conferred with him today, before the service, and he told me that he has forgiven the transgressor in his heart. He has, in Christ's own way, turned the other cheek. Now it remains for us to do the same. I ask you all now to join me in a prayer. May God forgive this poor creature for what he's done. May He show him the way to confession and repentance. And may this creature, so long as he does not repent, wander godless, without grace, lonely and scorned, until he must face his Maker and be judged."

There was such exquisite silence as the Vicar spoke that even Robin restrained a burp. When he finished the Vicar bowed his head, and everyone else did the same. Then, for a full minute, there was silence while the entire congregation prayed. Finally, when the Vicar said "Amen," the organ burst forth with "Jerusalem," and while Peter Barclay passed the plate everyone stood solidly and sang.

By far the best touch of the morning, Robin thought, was the way he and everyone else were scrutinized as they left. Wick stationed himself just outside the door, with Colonel Brown on one side and Barclay on the other. Since Robin had sat in the back, he was among the first to run this gantlet, receiving a stiff "Good morning" from the Vicar while the Colonel, short, bull-necked, his bald head gleaming in the sun, peered searchingly into his eyes, and Peter Barclay looked him over with a grin.

After he was through (found innocent, he hoped), he watched the others endure the same scrutiny. When, finally, all had passed, he watched them form themselves into muttering groups.

Ah, the English, the poor, antiseptic English, he thought as he wandered back to the Socco for a beer.

It was only later, at six that afternoon, that he heard what happened next. He was with Hervé Beaumont, prowling the medina, when they ran into Kranker, who stopped to report the news.

"Everyone," he said, "thought old Wick put on a damn fine show, and that would be that until Scotland Yard and the Colonel cracked the case. Barclay sauntered back into church to count the money, and then, a few minutes later, we heard a scream."

"What happened?" Robin's eyes gleamed with excitement.

"Well, my dear, it was *something!* A piece of writing paper, the same as was used for the infamous note, was pierced by a steel needle. Something moist and squishy was pinned inside. Peter took it apart, and, lo and behold, he found a freshly killed sheep's eye streaming with blood."

"A sheep's eye! That's Moroccan voodoo!"

"So it seems. One can apparently buy such things from a man who sells spells a little ways down from the church. Lester Brown hurried over to him, steaming with rage, but the Moroccans shooed him away. The medicine man's a mystic and a cherif, and he wasn't about to answer a lot of silly questions from an angry infidel. No one knows who did it, of course, but we seem to have a maniac in our midst."

On Sundays Peter Zvegintzov opened La Colombe at twelve to catch the Mountain crowd as they made their way home from church. Lake knew this (he'd become a regular customer and close observer of the shop), and also knew that Peter kept irregular hours on Sunday afternoon, closing sometimes at two, sometimes as late as four, depending on his sense of the needs of his clientele. In the few weeks that Lake had been frequenting the shop he'd tried, as often as he could, to come in just as Peter was closing up. He felt there was some advantage in being the last customer—opportunities to ask Peter how his business day had gone and to project himself as a sympathetic friend.

Thus on the last Sunday in May he waited nervously in his office in the deserted Consulate, anxiously calculating the best time to arrive. These planned intersections with Z had become a game. Lake had never willed himself into a friendship before, but he found the process exhilarating, a distraction from the frustrations of his work.

On his way over to La Colombe, driving through Dradeb, he asked himself why he was doing this, what goal he was hoping to achieve. He wasn't clear about it, had only the vaguest sort of idea. It had something to do with the forging of a link, creating a relationship with a man who seemed very different from himself, and yet with whom he felt a bond.

He was delighted to find the shop still open and only Colonel Brown's dusty Plymouth parked outside. He walked in, nodded to Peter, then inspected a rack of spy novels while observing the transaction taking place in front.

"Bunch of damn baboons," the Colonel was saying, "that's what these Moroccans are. Still swinging from the trees as far as I'm concerned."

He purchased an oversized bottle of soy sauce and a pair of gardening gloves. "It's not just Barclay," he muttered as he paid. "It's all of us now—the whole British community under attack."

He rushed off then, the door slamming behind him. Lake emerged from behind the book rack and approached Peter with a smile.

"I know," he said, "Katie Manchester called Janet the minute she got home from church. Guess you've got some ideas about that, Peter. Who do you think it is?"

Zvegintzov squinted through his spectacles. "If I've learned one thing," he said, "it's not to speculate about the British."

"Very good," Lake laughed. "Well put, Peter. So—have you had a good business day?"

"So so," said Zvegintzov. "I sold a chess set and an Arabic-Spanish dictionary, along with the usual decks of cards. Lots of blueberry jam too. There's been a run on that. I have to order another case." He wrote something on a pad he kept on the counter, a reminder to himself about the jam, Lake guessed, though he wasn't sure, because Peter wrote it in Cyrillic script.

"You know, Peter," he said. "You've got a terrific little business here. Wonderful location. You catch them both ways I bet."

"Catch them? Oh—I see. You mean the Mountain people. Yes, I do."

"Sure. Mountain crowd's your clientele. You got a real sweet setup here."

Peter sat down on a hassock, his thick glasses perched upon his nose. One of the reasons Lake liked to come in at the end of the day was that he could count on finding Peter weary and, he thought, less on guard.

"Yes," said Peter, "but they come from all over the city too. I'm still the only one in Tangier who imports real Stilton cheese."

Lake nodded. "Quite the capitalist."

They both laughed then, a little awkwardly, Lake thought. "You know, Peter," he said, "maybe you ought to give a harder sell."

"Hmmm. What do you mean?"

"Well, for instance—" Lake moved to the center. "You could move the freezer over here against the wall. That way when someone comes in with a bunch of kids they go straight for the ice cream before the parents have time to object."

"Yes. I see. But I keep the records over there."

"Well—move them. Make a little display. Keep the hot stuff in front, the rock and roll, and the ones that don't sell too fast, the classical ones—stack them behind on the shelves."

"Hmmm—"

"You've got to start thinking in terms of packaging. Catch the eye. Grab the public. Give people the feeling they're in an attractive environment, and put them in the mood to buy."

"Yes—"

"That's the problem with Russia, you see. Those drab state-owned stores. Rude clerks. People waiting in line. Everything out of stock. Three thousand size-twelve shoes, but they only fit your left foot. If you started thinking in business terms, you could make some real dough." Lake bit into his lower lip. "Yeah—a gold mine. You could have a real gold mine here."

"I don't do so badly now," said Peter. "My clients seem pleased enough."

"Of course. Of course they are. I didn't mean that. You're doing a hell of a job. But what happens when they put in this new road? Then the Mountain people won't be coming by here every day. Course you could move the shop, but you'd probably lose momentum if you did. I personally think you should stay here, brighten the place up, regulate the inventory, and make it worth a special trip." He paused. "Listen, I got to get going. Janet'll kill me if I'm late. Reason I came by was to invite you to dinner. We're having some Moroccans, official types, over Wednesday night. Wondered if you'd be free."

"Yes, yes. Thank you. Thank you very much."

"Good. Wednesday then. Eight-fifteen. So long, Peter. And think about what I said."

It had been a curious exchange, Lake realized, as he paused outside the shop, watching Peter struggle with his iron security grill. There was an awkward moment then as Peter locked the door, and they grinned at each other through the glass. Lake waved, Peter waved back, then turned off the fluorescent lights.

Lake waited until he'd disappeared into his little bedroom in the back. Was Peter intrigued, he wondered, about why the ranking American official in Tangier was taking such an interest in his shop? Impossible to know. His face was opaque. He revealed nothing, nothing at all.

Hamid Ouazzani was thinking of the summer as he stood on his balcony late that Sunday afternoon. The sun was above the Mountain, just about to set, and to the east he could see Djebel Ben Moussa shrouded in a darkening mist. Soon, he knew, mobs of tourists would descend upon Tangier, and with them all sorts of petty crimes. He could look forward to three months of hard work, new assistants in his office, foreigners haranguing him in European tongues, kif arrests, pickpocketings, fights in bars, rapes, cat burglaries, and trouble on the beach. He could count too, he knew, on one murder at least.

Kalinka was sitting on the banquette in their salon bent over her sketchbook, intent, working with her crayons. Hamid was pleased as he watched her draw. He'd been encouraging her the entire day. "Draw your memories," he'd said. "Draw your mother, your childhood home." And she'd surprised him—she'd agreed.

Perhaps, he thought, it was language that was the barrier,

that made it impossible for her to answer his verbal probes. He didn't know, but now, watching her, he congratulated himself for suggesting that she draw. She was so talented, her sketches were always so fine, so beautifully crafted, executed with such delicate, patient strokes, and now it seemed that through them she might be able to tell him things which she could not or would not reveal to him in words.

He left the balcony, walked over to her side, peered down at her work.

She looked up at him and smiled. "Just as you said, Hamid. Pictures of the past."

She flipped through the pages, showed him what she'd done. He was fascinated, sat down beside her, looked carefully at every sketch.

The figures in them were clear and quickly drawn, all enveloped in a moody haze. There was a sketch of a petite Oriental woman ("My mother," she said) standing beside a bicycle with a conical straw hat in one hand, her other arm raised to wave. There was a picture of a heavy-set man holding a little girl by the hand and walking with her beside a lake. There were several views of streets jammed with people, all wearing conical hats, running, escaping from a storm of slashing rain. There were pictures of stoop-shouldered men dressed in black, carrying guns, slinking among trees, and a sketch of a column of upright soldiers marching behind an officer wearing a kepi.

"With my mother in a cyclo," she said, pointing to her sketch of a little girl beside a woman with the same conical hat upon her lap, the two of them sitting in a contraption attached to the front of a bicycle pedaled by a bare-legged man. Finally she had drawn a low-angle view through a doorway. In a room beyond, Hamid could see a person's back.

"That's Peter," Kalinka said. "Peter in his store serving his customers. I am behind, in the back room, looking out from the dark."

"Go on!" he said, excited now, feeling that at last a curtain was being raised. "Tell me stories about them. Talk, Kalinka! Talk!"

"They are only the past, Hamid. You asked me to draw them, and now I have."

At that she began to sign the sketches, compressing the letters of her name so they formed a seal. He looked at her—she'd surprised him again. It was the smoke, he was certain, the smoke of her hashish which she'd sucked into her lungs for so many years and which now was working its way out through her fingers, her crayons. But still she was vague. He looked at the pictures again. A beginning, he thought, a breakthrough, an access to the mysteries locked inside her brain.

Late that evening he took a walk. From his apartment on Ramon y Cahal he made his way by a circuitous route (Rue d'Istamboul, Rue Leonardo Da Vinci, then Rue Mordecai Bengio through the Jewish quarter) to the steep west Casbah gate. Once inside the old fortified section, he began to wander through a labyrinth of ancient, narrow streets, alleys really, not wide enough for two people to walk abreast, with high, straight walls on either side and small, narrow barred windows overhead.

He walked aimlessly, losing himself in the maze, wandering from time to time into dim culs-de-sac. It was intentional, this becoming lost—he knew the alleys of the Casbah well, but he was deliberately trying to forget his way, lose himself, as if he were a tourist or a man gone blind. It was a game he was playing. He was practicing being a detective the way a cat practices hunting on a rug. He wanted to see if he could find his way by sound alone, listening for water flowing in the sewers beneath the streets, without looking up to search out landmarks in the night.

The echoes helped him more than the sewers did, and eventually, with less difficulty than he might have thought, he emerged by the old wall on Ben Abbou, the back wall of the Casbah, separating it from the medina below. He walked swiftly then by the Casbah mosque until he reached the giant square, emerging at the far end of it, the side away from the cliffs and sea.

There was no one about except the one-legged man who watched the cars. Hamid strode across the old stones, hearing the echoes of his footsteps as he walked, until he reached the overlook where he'd encountered Kalinka one night so many months before. Here he lit a cigarette and stared down at the beach and bay, feeling the east wind blow gently across his face. There was a yacht anchored off the mole. He could see people aboard her, could make out their silhouettes. They were Europeans, moving, dancing. He could hear faint music, something romantic, out of date.

He stood for a time staring out, thinking of Kalinka's drawings, the ones she'd made that afternoon. He'd been tremendously excited by them, but still he wondered: *Who were those people? What were they doing? What were their passions, their struggles, the meaning of their guns?*

He would find out. He was a policeman, a detective. He would investigate the matter as if Kalinka were a suspect in a case. He would start a dossier, write her name on the cover. He would file the drawings there, and any others she might make, and his notes on their conversations, everything she said. He would find his way through the maze of her mind just as he had moved through the labyrinth of the Casbah, feeling his way, all his senses alert. Yes, he would discover her, solve the mystery of who she was, and when he was clear with her, when all her past was finally laid out and her foreignness revealed, then he would be free to bind himself to her, make her his wife.

II.

By the middle of June our town had undergone its annual transformation from sleepy Moroccan village to thriving international resort. Boats and jets disgorged tourists, and the town beach, at noon, became a carnival of reddening flesh. At night the Boulevard, closed to traffic, became the ground for a great passeo, while on the Mountain the warm nocturnal air brought our damas de noche into bloom.

Certain incidents those early summer weeks, though quite small, even insignificant in themselves, and later overshadowed by more vivid events, seem in restrospect to suggest the tensions that were then building up in certain quarters of our town.

The stones that had hit Laurence Luscombe one May evening became more than an odd occurrence to those of us who drove daily through Dradeb. Sometimes we felt we were run-

ning a gantlet as teenage boys shot rocks at us from vantage points on the roofs. For a while it became an adventure to drive through at night. We'd close our windows, hold our breaths, and sigh relief when we reached the Jew's River unscathed. But after a while the fun wore off. Camilla Weltonwhist, on her way home from a party at the British Consulate, received a nasty gash on her forehead when a stone shattered the window of her Rolls. We felt anger on her behalf but were reconciled soon enough. We learned to accept these bombardments, as we did the Socco pickpockets, as part of the price we paid for living in Tangier. . . .

Achar

Mohammed Achar's clinic, a subsection of the Ministry of Public Health, was known in Dradeb simply as "Dr. Achar's." It was a maze of tiny rooms linked by passageways that were narrow and damp. When the wind blew, which was often in Tangier, the place was a symphony of slamming doors.

Achar prowled about the corridors like a bear. Burly and strong, he moved like a man with too much to do and insufficient time. One Saturday in the middle of June he was everywhere at once, dropping into the tiny treatment rooms, assisting doctors who needed his advice, holding hurried consultations in the hall on the cases that kept pouring in. From time to time he'd disappear into his refuge, a cluttered, book-lined office in the back. Here, at a desk heaped with X-rays and reports, he puffed on cigarettes, sipped mint tea, and shouted furiously over the phone. His heavy bass voice boomed down the hall to the waiting room at its other end—a signal to the people thronged there that someone in Dradeb cared.

On this particular Saturday there was a small operation to be performed. Early in the afternoon Achar went to the scrub room, washed his hands, then extended his arms so that his nurse could help him with his gown and gloves.

The patient was a boy with a hernia near his groin, so small it took the doctor more than twenty minutes to find. Achar took no notice of the time, was too involved with his work. He liked surgery, enjoyed patching people up. His hands, he thought, were skillful though hardly great. It embarrassed him that there were rumors they were magical and blessed by God.

Had his staff started that? He hoped not, though he knew they loved him as much as he loved them. He was a benevolent dictator who shouted orders in crises. But when there was time he always asked their views. "If any of you ever thinks I'm wrong," he told them, "tell me right away. Even if I don't take your advice I still want you to talk. And if I seem to be acquiring a complex, you must tell me that too. I detest the myth of the master physician, the all-knowing doctor-saint." He meant it, and hoped they understood the dangers of being corrupted by the healer's power. When he passed through the waiting room and poor people leaned to touch his hands, he turned away with shame.

It was difficult to work in Dradeb, but Achar had no desire for a private practice on Boulevard Pasteur. He was always short of antibiotics and blood, and had constantly to worry about keeping his reservoir filled and maintaining his generator in case the electricity should fail. Still he persisted, and now, after some years of effort, he'd managed to assemble a devoted staff who shared his notion that there was too much disease to allow oneself to rest.

Probably, he thought, he was a better administrator than anything else, with the gift of motivation, of getting people to work. But it took so much energy to enliven others, to give and give while taking nothing in return. Surgery was his diversion from that, an abstract game he played. Looking down at the exposed tissues of the boy, he thought of the body as a puzzle. But afterward, when he'd closed the wound and sewed it up, he felt a rush of exhaustion, a need to rest and close his eyes. It came upon him always after an operation—his bones ached from standing, his eyes from so much strain. And, too, he wondered about usefulness—whether these little operations, these little patchings-up, were really the answer to human pain.

When he returned to his office, hoping for a quarter hour's rest, he found a young man named Driss Bennani sitting before his desk. "Fischer's dead," Driss announced. "He died in California ten days ago."

Achar lit a cigarette. "His heart?"

"I suppose so. His son didn't say. Just a note to tell me that he was dead and that he thought I ought to know."

"Well," said Achar, thinking back to the last time he'd examined Fischer in Tangier, "I'm very sorry to hear this, Driss. He was the only American I ever liked."

"He was a great man, Achar. I learned more about architecture in my year with him than from all the professors I ever had. He was a visionary. He knew that buildings were for people. An obvious truth, but not many people see it here."

Achar nodded. "Yes," he said, "Fischer had great plans for us. He was going to build us a great hospital, the best equipment, a place where we could really work. I suppose all that's out the window now—they're going to tear us down, I hear, and put up skyscrapers in our place."

"Not quite yet," said Driss. "The redevelopment of Dradeb has been postponed. They've got a different project now. They're going to use the money for a road."

"I see, though I'm not sure where they'll put it. There're buildings to the edges of the road we have now."

"No, Achar. You don't understand. Not a new road through here. A road to go around."

"Oh, yes, I see." He didn't, though—was too tired to concentrate on what the boy was trying to say.

Driss noticed his lack of attention and began to raise his voice. "A new access to the Mountain. The Governor doesn't like driving through here, and also there's the King. Not that he ever comes to Tangier—I don't think he's been here in three or four years—but in case he does come he'll have a more pleasant access to the hill. So the plan is to build a road up the Mountain from the other side. That way the people who live up there won't have to drive through here anymore."

"A blessing, I suppose."

"But don't you see?" Driss was angry. He stood and began to pace around the little room. His bitterness caught Achar by surprise. "There'll never be a rehabilitation. The whole project was a charade. They just wanted to cosmetize the place, put up some high rises to make the street look good. Fischer's idea, to make a new village here, never had a chance."

Achar watched him carefully. "Sit down, Driss," he said. "You don't have to shout in here. And stop talking like an idealist. It's foolish and boring too. If Fischer's plan had been approved, two-thirds of the money would have been stolen before they laid a brick. Fancy designs, big talk—that sort of thing always conceals a sham. The only way you ever change conditions is to get the people to change them for themselves. Fischer didn't understand that, but he was a foreigner. You were born here. You don't have that excuse."

"Yes. Yes." The boy seemed dejected. "I know all that, of course."

"Good! Then you can start doing something instead of talking about how bad things are. Get them to put up some lights. Stop the traffic every few minutes so people can cross. Get some damn water in here—dig up those rusted pipes, or whatever is wrong, and put in some new ones so we can drink. Look at this clinic. It's falling apart. It leaks when it rains, and in winter it's like ice. But we function here, Driss. We make it work."

After a silence Driss leaned forward, spoke angrily between his teeth. "Let me tell you, doctor, why there's no water here—the real reason. It's not the pipes. The golf course on the south flank of the Mountain has to be watered all day long, and since there's a shortage now, they're drawing on the reservoir that feeds Dradeb." He shook his head. "I don't want to build anymore," he whispered. "I want to tear things down."

Achar looked at him. He had to be careful now. But the young architect seemed sincere, with an anger he thought he could use. "All right," he said finally, "that's very nice. You want to tear things down. But not old buildings. Something else."

"Yes," said Driss. "You know exactly what I mean."

Achar lit another cigarette. "Why have you come to me?"

"People tell me you're a man who understands the future. That's why I came. But not just to talk."

"But you *do* talk about these things?"

"Sometimes—with people I can trust."

"It's dangerous to be a dissenter, Driss. There're a lot of people who make their living turning other people in."

The young architect nodded.

Achar leaned back. "So," he said, "you want to see things changed."

"Yes."

"Well—we'll see. I'll mention your enthusiasm to some of my friends. Perhaps one of them will get in touch. Excuse me now. I need to rest. Then there're patients I have to see."

After Bennani left, Achar closed his eyes. Now, thirty-eight years old, he believed in ideas but no longer in men. When he'd been a medical student, at Cairo University, Gamal Abdel Nasser had been his god. He still kept the man's photo on his office wall, but he'd decided years before that Nasser had been weak and failed. All the talk about pan-Arabism, a great new era, a new place in the world for the backward peoples of Islam—all that had been rhetoric for the masses, without any result. Nasser had plunged into the anti-Zionist cause while his regime became corrupt and his power was misused. While he became a world figure, rushing to conferences here and there, to Washington and to Moscow for aid, he neglected the real issue, which was misery, the misery in which people lived. He became corrupted by his glory and lacked the courage to take away the privileges of his friends.

Now Morocco was miserable, it seemed to Achar, and the King, a clever man, was working ruthlessly to preserve his power. He'd nationalized the foreign banks, confiscated the foreign-owned plantations, but the only difference that had made was a few favored Moroccans had become rich. Achar didn't like foreigners much, but his dislike of them was nothing compared with his hatred for the Moroccan ruling class. Not just for the King (who symbolized everything that was wrong) but for the whole rotten system, the payoffs and favors, the entrenchment of powerful families, the shallow self-seeking of commercial people on the rise. The country was going under while they played games in Rabat—a modern Versailles, he thought, where the King distracts his rivals with golf tournaments, luxuries, and intrigues.

Now the system was starting to bend beneath the pressure. Achar, with other men, wanted to be sure that it finally cracked. He'd decided to devote his life to that—it seemed a logical extension of his work. What was the point of treating symptoms when the problem was the disease? He wasn't interested in a military coup. Monarchy or dictatorship—the repression would be the same. He wanted radical change, an austere socialist regime, first of all a program to break the psychological power of Islam. As long as Moroccans could shrug and say "It's God's will" before their miseries, it was hopeless to try to improve their lot. As a surgeon he'd shown people that the ills of the body could be attacked with a knife. Now he wanted to show them that the system that oppressed them must be attacked the same way.

Yes, he thought, *Driss Bennani might be one to help.* He could join the cadre that met in the clinic in the night, discussing ways to build a new Morocco, making plans to tear the old Morocco down.

Several hours later he was passing through the waiting room when a familiar face caught his eye. It was Kalinka Zvegintzov seated among veiled Moroccans on one of the hard benches that filled the room.

"Kalinka." He came up to her. "Are you waiting to see me?"

When she nodded he motioned for her to follow, leading her to an examination cubicle in the back.

"How are you?" he asked. "And how is Hamid? I haven't seen him in weeks."

"He's been very busy, I think."

"Good. I was worried he'd forgotten us. It happens so often when people leave Dradeb."

"He's working all the time," she said. "Sometimes he doesn't even sleep. When he thinks I've fallen off he slips out to the other room. Then he sits in the dark smoking cigarettes."

"Thinking about something?"

"That's what he says. But he doesn't talk about his work. I think he's healthy, though. Otherwise he'd come to you."

Achar laughed. "Oh, Kalinka. Hamid can come here anytime, whether he's sick or not. I've known him all my life. We were born within a hundred yards of this place."

She nodded, and as always Achar felt a certain strangeness in her manner, a retreating inside, a distancing from events.

"Now what brings you here, Kalinka? Your spring cold's all gone, I think."

"I don't know," she said. "Sometimes I feel weak. My chest hurts. I'm tired all the time."

"Well, I'll have a look at you. Come on then. Take off your dress."

She looked up at him and hesitated. He excused himself to fetch his stethoscope, and when he returned he found her sitting on the examination table in white silk trousers and brassiere. Her dress, an Oriental floral print, was hanging from the hook. He looked at her carefully—her skin was pale and so translucent he felt he could see deep within, even past the network of blue veins.

"You're so very thin, Kalinka. Perhaps you don't eat enough."

She shook her head. "I'm not very hungry," she said.

He began to examine her, listen to her heart, then thump his forefinger on her chest and back. She seemed fragile to him, perfectly proportioned and yet petite, her rib bones so delicate he felt they'd break if he touched too hard. It seemed improper for him to lay his thick, hairy fingers on such a fragile creature, and yet, thinking that, he suddenly understood her attraction for Hamid.

When he was finished with her torso he stared down her throat and then, with his magnifying flashlight, deep into her eyes. The whites were a little jaundiced, he thought. Bent over, so close to her face, he felt suddenly that his head was twice as big as hers.

"You still smoke, Kalinka?"

She nodded and looked down.

"I told you last time you'd have to stop."

"I try," she said in her funny sing-song French. "But there is nothing else for me to do."

⟨ 139 ⟩

"Don't be ridiculous. Tangier is full of things. You like to draw. Why don't you do that?"

She shrugged.

"Learn Arabic then. It's the least you can do."

"Hamid is unhappy with me." She blurted out the words so quickly they caught him off his guard. Then, immediately, she raised her hand to cover up her mouth.

He sat back, looked at her, thought a few moments, then spoke. "Why, Kalinka? Why is he unhappy? What makes you think he is? Tell me what's wrong."

"I don't know," she said, shaking her head. "Sometimes he looks at me so strangely, and I feel he's about to speak. Then he turns away. He questions me. I try to answer but I can't. He asks me to draw pictures and tell him stories. I try my best but he's not satisfied." There were tears forming in her eyes.

"You're not unhappy with him?"

"Oh, no! I love him. He's the only thing I care about here."

"What are these questions? What does he want to know?"

"Everything. He wants to know about the past. About Peter and Hanoi. My life. He asks me questions about my life."

"Surely you can answer him."

"No," she said. "I try. But I cannot. It's all so vague to me. Like a dream."

He didn't know what to say. Here was a woman who lived with his boyhood friend, a strange Oriental woman who said her past had fled her memory. It was hard enough to be a doctor, to diagnose illnesses, to examine the exteriors of patients and from them divine the processes beneath. But to diagnose a woman's heart—that was beyond his skill.

"You must stop smoking. I insist on that. The hashish makes everybody mad. It's an opiate here—the fog in which Moroccans sleep. People who smoke it turn inward, confused, and can no longer see the world. It's very bad for you. It makes you dream. It dulls your senses. It clouds your sight. You must give it up, Kalinka—right now, right away. Take walks. Grow plants on your balcony. Draw pictures. Listen to music. But stop smoking. That's why your chest aches. That's why you feel weak, tired all the time. It's the hashish that has made you forget."

He was surprised at the force with which he delivered his little speech—it was not like him to lecture a patient that way. He thought back upon what he knew of her life—her reputation as a femme fatale. This tiny creature had broken the spirit of the Russian, then ensnared Hamid. Achar did not believe the talk about her casting spells, but when Hamid had fallen in love with her he'd acted like a fool. What was it about her? What was the source of her power? He looked at her carefully again and for a moment, a splinter of a second, saw something that made him feel weak. It was something ancient, veiled—a whole history that showed on the smooth, blank features of her face. It was as if all the mystery of the Far East showed there, all the centuries of struggle and bloodshed, strange rites, formal rituals, something placid, hieratic, deep. It was so compelling that, for a minute, he could not tear his eyes away. But finally she grinned and broke the spell.

"Yes," she said, "the hashish. I will try. I promise I will try to stop."

At twilight Achar went out to walk. It had been a busy day at the clinic, and still there were people waiting to be helped. But he needed to breathe, to get out of those narrow rooms, to feel the cool air that rolled across the valley from the sea. The taps were not yet turned on, but children were waiting near the pumps. Dradeb was a beehive, pulsing with misery and life.

Most of its houses were constructed out of discarded bricks mortared in haphazard ways. The roofs were sheet metal, kept in place by stones on top; otherwise, when the wind blew the roofs might fly away. There were large portions of Dradeb where the houses were not so good, shacks made of discarded pieces of cars and bamboo culms with only a blanket for a door. There were shanties that had been erected on top of an old Jewish cemetery—the gravestones, poking up in the middle of the rooms, served as tables or even beds. *Such rot,* he thought, *such a rotting place.* Dradeb stank of overflowing septics. Its little lanes were filled with rubble and discarded blackened greens.

Achar thought of Fischer then, walking these alleys with

Driss Bennani months before, such an improbable combination, he'd thought so many times, the young Moroccan with the old American Jew. He'd liked Fischer, missed him, was sorry now that he was dead. The man had been a builder and a dreamer. Now Driss wanted to tear things down.

Achar passed a carpentry shop, waved to the men inside. Walking up an alley by the mosque, he could hear the machine in the miller's shop grinding flour out of wheat. He walked up Rue de Persil, moving to the side to avoid a rat. It lay dead in ooze that trickled down from an outhouse. There were dogs standing in the alleyway, thin, bony mongrels with supplicating eyes. A week or so before, the police had come while men demolished shanties that encroached on private land. Then the trucks took people and their possessions to another quarter, and the uncomprehending dogs were left behind. They seemed to Achar to be getting thinner every day. *Soon they must find a source of garbage,* he thought, *or else they will become savages or die.*

Finally, at the top of the hill, he turned and looked back down. There it was, Dradeb, the slum, and his clinic, a compound of shanties too. The place needed schools, water, most of all a passion to change. Only yards away, across the river on the Mountain, one could buy Cuban cigars and English marmalade.

It was foolish, he knew, to agonize over injustice. Fischer had done that. He'd been naive. Achar knew the world was full of inequalities, always had been, always would be. But Dradeb was so unnecessary. Morocco was not poor. There were huge deposits of phosphates in the south, and tourism earned a fortune in foreign exchange. There was money, it flowed in, not to the people who needed it, but to the coffers of the King and his friends.

Let them be rich, he thought. *Let them play golf and live in palaces and eat great banquets and dress in haute couture.* They could have all that if only they would share. But they shared nothing, and even took from those who had so much less. They watered their golf course from the reservoir of Dradeb, so that even to drink was now a luxury in the slum.

He looked up at the Mountain, the glittering villas, hanging in terraced gardens so high above.

The Hunter

By the middle of June Hamid Ouazzani began to notice certain things that reminded him of other, less unhappy summers in Tangier. In the early evening a huge moon hung full and low above the city while the wind blew wisps of clouds slowly across its face. There was a smell of overflowing sewers in the Casbah, the screams of cats on the roofs at night, and, as he prowled the Moroccan quarters of the town, he felt an anger familiar from the past. The city was short of water. There was garbage on the beach. At noon the crowds of petitioners were thick around the Sûreté. Demonologists stalked the streets offering to rid homes and shops of unwanted spells.

Sometimes Hamid would stop his car at an irregularly shaped rubble-strewn lot. Then he'd get out, lean against his fender, and watch boys playing soccer in the dust. He had played himself at this place when he was young, had run for hours in tattered shorts, his stomach distended by worms. After the games he and his friends had shared their bread, then hiked to the beach to wash. He longed at times to relive those simpler days, the joy of kicking at a battered, misshapen ball. But now his life was being written in another way. He was embroiled in the unsavory affairs of men.

Already his desk was piled with dossiers, and the summer had just begun. Even with extra summer help he was having difficulty keeping up. An English girl drowned at the beach. He talked to her weeping mother on a bad connection to Liverpool. A few minutes later he interrogated a Dane arrested for cavorting naked in the fountain at Place de France. There were complicated automobile accidents involving foreigners' cars. How many times would he have to explain to German tourists that their insurance forms were meaningless when they killed a peasant's sheep?

Then there was a tempest on the Mountain over mishandled deliveries of manure. Patrick Wax was the latest in a chain of victims to find a truckload of goat pellets dumped unceremoniously on his lawn. Hamid investigated. The manure dealer claimed he'd received precise instructions on the phone. He proclaimed his innocence. Hamid believed him. They looked up at the Mountain, faced each other, and shrugged.

Later Hamid drove up the Mountain to see the damage for himself.

"Now look here, Inspector," said Wax, pointing at the pellets, covering his nose with a perfumed scarf, "this has got to be a deliberate thing. The pellets were dumped at the very spot where I erect my summer party tent."

"Could have been an honest mistake," said Hamid. "Perhaps the manure man got his addresses mixed."

"Impossible! The same thing happened to Countess de Lauzon. Someone's calling up and ordering the stuff, then telling the deliveryman to dump it in just the places where it hurts."

"But who, Mr. Wax? Whom do you suspect?"

Wax looked at him, narrowed his eyes. "Bainbridge," he said. "Couldn't be anyone else. He's cross with me, and also with Françoise, because neither of us will have him in our house. This whole thing smacks of Percy's style—just his sort of revenge."

Hamid wanted to laugh, but he listened solemnly as Wax elaborated on his complaint. He took notes and, when Wax

was finished, suggested the pellets be raked around to fertil-
ize his flowers.

"Of course," Wax exclaimed, "that's just what I intended
to do. But I wanted you to see this first. This pile of shit is the
only evidence I have."

Could it be, Hamid asked himself, driving back to town,
that police in other countries trouble themselves with matters
such as this? The Europeans were crazy, ordered manure
dumped on each other's lawns. What did it mean? What was
the pattern of their dance?

Later, back at his office, he paced around his desk. The
"Manure Affair" was a comic operetta, but there was a victim, the manure dealer, who'd acted in good faith and now
would not be paid. The trouble with police work, he thought,
was that it was so inexact. Cases overlapped, dragged on
unresolved, everything was a mixture of half-truths and lies,
the city was a web of interlocking snares. He felt frustrated,
longed for clarity. Even his feelings about Kalinka were
murky: love for her and troubling questions about her past
were inextricably mixed.

A few days later his head was temporarily cleared. He was
sitting in his car outside La Colombe, waiting for Aziz. The
two of them had been making the usual rounds, checking in
with their informants. When they'd arrived at the shop
Hamid had asked Aziz to go in alone. He'd seen Zvegintzov
several times since May, but he found their meetings difficult, fraught with excessive strain.

When Aziz came out Hamid started up the car. Aziz slid
into the passenger seat, then laid his hand on Hamid's arm.
"He wants to see you."

"Any idea why?"

Aziz shook his head. "I told him you were busy, but he insisted it would be worth your time."

Hamid thought a moment, then nodded and turned the ignition off. As he walked into La Colombe he dreaded another
scene, another request to see Kalinka. But he was determined, no matter what Zvegintzov said, to remain cool and
aloof.

Peter was waiting for him, both hands face down on the
counter. His shirt was wet beneath the arms.

"You asked to see me?"

"I have information."

Hamid nodded.

"This is valuable information. Possibly worth a great deal."

"You know I'm not going to pay you, Peter. We needn't go through that charade."

"I don't want money, Inspector. I simply ask that you recognize the fact that I'm about to give you something you can obtain from no one else."

"If that's true I'll recognize it."

Peter looked at him. "I want more than that."

"Tell me what you want."

"When I have told you this I want your good regard."

Zvegintzov ran his tongue across his upper lip. He turned slightly, until his thick glasses caught the light.

"I've always had high regard for you, Peter."

"But you haven't had respect."

"All right." Hamid was impatient. "What is this about?"

"Last week Aziz asked if I knew of any Nazis in Tangier. I can tell you now that I do."

"I'm listening."

"You're surprised, Hamid. You didn't expect to receive such information today. Admit it. You really do respect me a little now."

Zvegintzov grinned, displaying a row of stained and crooked teeth. Hamid stared at him, tense, annoyed.

"Admit it. At least admit that you're surprised."

Hamid exhaled. "Yes, Peter, I'm surprised. Does that satisfy you? You've made your point."

"You really do respect me now?"

"I respect you more and more as each second passes by."

"Thank you." His hands, Hamid noticed, were now loosely curled into fists. His face betrayed a child's pleasure—he'd won himself a trivial point. "There is only one case that I know of undiscovered Nazis in Tangier. These people have gone to great lengths to disguise themselves. I believe I'm the only person here who knows who they really are. When I tell you their names you'll kick yourself for not having thought of them. You'll know instantly that I'm right, and you'll gladly acknowledge that I have formidable abilities which you've underrated much too long."

"In a minute, Peter, I'm going to walk out of here—"

"Yes, yes. You're busy. I know. The Freys. You know their house, of course. Their collections. Their paintings and antiques. You know they raise Alsatian dogs. But did you know too that there are indictments against them in Belgium? That there are people in several countries who would give a great deal to know that they are here?"

"How do you know this?"

"I've known for a long time."

"*How*?"

"I've heard certain things. And I've discovered others on my own."

"You have proof?"

"I'm not a judge, Hamid."

"Who are they?"

"So! You believe me. Good!" He leaned forward, toward Hamid's ear, and spoke rapidly in a hoarse whisper, turning away every so often to clear his throat and cough. "They are notorious. The Beckers. Kurt and Inge Becker. Same first names, you see. During the war they ran a confidence ring, pretended they could help prominent Jews escape. They doublecrossed them, stole everything they had, murdered them after they'd signed over everything and placed themselves in their hands. They amassed a great fortune which they somehow managed to have transferred here. You can read about them in books, I expect, and also in Israeli files. Ha!"

He pulled Hamid by his sleeve over to the window, then pointed up at a palace that hung precipitously above the ravine. "Now they live quietly in their big house on the Mountain. That place is impenetrable as a fort. Walls, wire fences, dogs, electric gates. The Freys are courteous people, always dignified and correct. They give money to the local charities, and their servants report that they are kind. There is a rumor around that they are under royal protection. There's nothing more that I can tell you, except that everything I've said is true. They're excellent customers, by the way. Tell me what you'll do."

"You give information to me, Peter. I don't give it to you. But for what you've just told me I certainly hold you in regard."

He was pleased, walking back to the car. Though he knew he couldn't always trust Zvegintzov, this time intuition told him that he should. He had performed, he thought, a marvel of detective work, forming a theory that would explain the presence of an Israeli agent in Tangier, then uncovering information that suggested his theory was correct.

But later, that afternoon, he thought about Zvegintzov and the curious price he'd extracted for the Beckers' names. *Why does Peter want my respect? What possible good could it do him now?*

He was disturbed the next morning by something he saw on his way to work—a girl, no older than twelve, swinging a cat by its tail against a telephone pole on Rue de Belgique. He stopped his car, called out. The girl glared at him, heaved the cat away, and ran off down the street. The cat was dead. Hamid wrapped the carcass in a newspaper and deposited it in the trash.

Arriving at his office, he felt depressed. A great number of new cases had accumulated during the night. Aziz had arranged the dossiers in order of importance on his desk. Hamid looked at them, groaned, then set to work. By eleven he was finished, and exhausted from the task.

"About Lake," he said to Aziz. "Any idea why he's hanging around La Colombe?"

"We don't have anything on that, Hamid, except that he and Zvegintzov are friends. Lake's had him to the Consulate several times. The Russian takes part in the conversation, sometimes drinks too much and runs off about his clients. Lake's chauffeur says the Consul drives over there nearly every day, and that Zvegintzov gives Lake cigars."

Someone blew a whistle outside. Hamid walked to the window. Two cops were tussling with a boy in front of the building. A small crowd had gathered. A man in a bloodstained butcher's apron was waving his fist. A police jeep was parked by the curb.

"I've never known Peter to give anything away."

Aziz bent forward. "What do you think, Hamid?"

"Nothing. I don't think anything. I wish I were home in bed."

At noon he picked up his brother, then drove out to a fish

restaurant on the Atlantic beach. They ordered seafood *tapas,* dishes of tiny eels and clams and squids, which they ate with bits of Arab bread.

"I'm worried about Kalinka."

He spoke rapidly, after a silence. Farid looked up and wiped his mouth.

"She's very strange lately. She's stopped smoking—Achar convinced her, but in a way that's made things worse. Now she draws and broods. I come home and find her sitting by the window. When I ask her what she's done, she looks at me and I feel her eyes drilling to my heart. I ask about the pictures. She shows them to me—strange, shadowy scenes. I ask her what they mean. She blinks at me and smiles."

"Well, Hamid, you have to take her to a doctor."

"She's been to Achar. Radcliffe too. They tell me she's just a little nervous, and I shouldn't allow myself to become upset."

"Maybe a psychiatrist—"

"In Tangier? Our so-called psychiatrists are madhouse attendants. Anyway, how can I send her to one of them? I'm an inspector of police. Soon everyone will be saying she's sick in her head. People will use that against me. I don't care, but those pitying looks, those suggestions that I throw her out. Ah!"

He swirled his fork among the eels. Farid pushed back his chair. His face was like Hamid's, but less Berber, prettier.

"She's always been strange, Hamid."

"I know. At first I thought it didn't matter. She was what she was, I loved her, and that was enough. But now I feel I must understand her. She suffers. Perhaps she longs for something. Some loss. Torment. I don't know."

Then, sensitive to the fact that he was making his brother uneasy, Hamid switched the subject. "Have you ever sold anything to the Freys?"

Farid shook his head. "They don't collect Moroccan things. They like signed French furniture. Impressionists. Roman coins."

"You've seen all that?"

"One time. With Wax. He was after them for a while. When he smells money on people he warms up to them, and he smelled it on the Freys. He's drawn to rich people. When he finds them the first thing he does is think up a swindle. There was a jade scepter they had, and he wanted it. He had in mind a trade, a pair of short obelisks which he claimed were ancient pieces from Luxor, though I happen to know he had them made by the man who makes gravestones on Avenue Hassan II. Anyway, we went up to the Freys'. This was during the time that Patrick was teaching me interior decoration and good taste."

Hamid laughed, though his memory of that time was sad. He'd felt such shame for his brother then, the "bought boy" of Patrick Wax.

"He taught me a lot, you know. Took me to Europe. Showed me the museums. Enough so I could tell that the things up at the Freys' were good. They have an excellent Renoir and some wonderful bibelots."

"Did you like the Freys?"

"Are they involved in something, Hamid?"

"Perhaps. I can't tell you more than that."

"Well, all I can say is that they were pleasant enough, though not especially refined. There they were, living amidst all that splendor, but there was something ordinary, peasant-like about them too."

"Did Wax get his scepter?"

"No. They were shrewd. They saw through him. They sensed he was a charlatan. But they didn't let on. They just smiled and shook their heads."

As they drove back to the city, Hamid marveled at how much his brother had been changed by the three or four years he'd spent with Patrick Wax. He'd been taken into palaces and chateaux, taught about precious materials—marble, silver, bronze. Now he had his own shop, where he sold rugs and Berber jewelry. He designed candelabra, based vaguely on Moroccan models, which he sold to European decorators at many times their worth.

"It's funny, isn't it?" he said as they were passing through Place de France. "I became a policeman, and you became an *antiquaire*. Can you remember, fifteen years ago, the two of us kicking around a soccer ball in the dust?"

He stopped to let Farid off at his store. Farid opened the car door, hesitated, then shut it again.

"About Kalinka, Hamid—"

"Yes."

"I can talk to her if you like."

"Well—"

"We've always gotten on. Perhaps she needs a confidant. I'd be happy to talk with her if you agree."

"Thank you, Farid, but I don't know—"

"Well, anyway—let me know if I can help."

He was grateful to Farid for that, but thinking about it through the afternoon, he decided he must continue to try with her himself. But differently than before, along another line.

That evening he waited until they were finished eating dinner and were reclining on banquettes with their cups of tea. Kalinka always prepared Oriental tea, rather than the sweet mint kind that usually followed a Moroccan meal. He'd become used to it, now preferred it, and liked the little wicker basket she'd made, based on a Vietnamese idea, molded inside with silk-covered stuffing so that the pot fit snugly and the tea stayed warm for hours.

"I saw Peter yesterday," he said.

"Oh—" She didn't seem surprised.

"An interesting meeting, Kalinka. He told me a secret about Tangier."

She smiled. "Secrets. Secrets. He has so many secrets. Poor Peter, so many secrets in his head."

"He doesn't follow you anymore, I hope."

"I'm sorry I told you that."

"You *had* to tell me."

"No, Hamid. You become too angry. Peter's harmless. He follows me, but it isn't what you think."

"What is it then? Tell me. Explain it to me. *Please.*"

A silence. She put down her cup, then placed her hands together on her lap. "We were never married. I told you that. He brought me up. He took care of me. He brought me here to live."

"Yes, you've told me, but you've never told me why. *Why* did he introduce you as his wife? *Why* did he pretend?"

"He thought—I don't know. He did it—that's all. When I came here from Poland he just did it. He said something then, but I don't remember. So many years ago. Something—

he said that it would be easier that way. I would have more protection. He wanted to protect me. It was so difficult for him to bring me here."

"So people thought—"

"Yes. That was it. He wanted them to think I was his wife. There was his name on my passport. Kalinka Zvegintzov. He arranged that. It was difficult to do. The same name—he showed me that. Put the two passports together, showed me the name was the same. 'We're married now, Kalinka,' he said. I remember now. He laughed. 'That's our secret, Kalinka. That's how we'll protect ourselves.' "

"And you accepted that?"

"Oh, yes. It didn't make any difference. I was only a girl then. When we were alone together he treated me the same. Don't think anything bad, Hamid. Nothing happened in all those years. We slept together in the back room of the shop, in our separate beds on opposite sides of the room. He only touched me as a father would. Kissed me as if I were his child. But he liked the secret. He would become very gay whenever he mentioned it. 'They think you're my wife,' he'd say, laughing, nodding his head. 'Such fools. It's good to have secrets from people, Kalinka. A man should always have secrets. It's a fine feeling when people are fooled.' "

It was so strange. Hamid felt no anger anymore, but lost, lost in a mysterious plot. He'd seen her passport, had examined it many times. It documented a marriage which she claimed did not exist. But why? Why these secrets? What had Peter's motives been?

"Is Peter your father?" he asked, immediately regretting the question, for it had been direct questions such as this which had always made her turn away.

"No," she said. "But he was my father's friend. He took care of mother and me. He loved my mother—I'm sure of that—though they were comrades, nothing more."

"And your real father—do you remember him?"

"I never saw him."

"But Peter told you?"

"Yes."

It occurred to him then that since Peter was so fond of secrets, he might have lied to Kalinka about her father too. "On your passport it says 'Father's name: unknown.' "

"That's not true," she said. "I know my father's name."

"What is it, Kalinka? Why haven't you told me this before?"

"His name was Stephen Zhukovsky. I didn't tell you because I forgot."

"But how could you forget a thing like that?"

"I never knew this man. He died soon after I was born."

"But Peter knew him?"

"Knew him very well. He and Peter were best friends in Hanoi. Peter told me that, and how my father died."

"Tell me."

"It was terrible," she said. Tears formed in her eyes. "In jail. In Hanoi jail. He was tortured by the Japanese. They tortured him—to death."

"Peter told you that?"

"He was there. He told me he was there. Nearby. In a cell nearby. And he heard my father's screams. They tortured him too, he told me, but not so much. My father was a great hero, he told me. And my mother—she was a great heroine too."

She was crying now and trying to smile through her tears. Hamid moved close to her, held her, kissed her, stroked her hair. In the six months he had lived with her she had never told him so much. He knew that now that she'd begun to talk he must press her to tell him more.

"Your mother—tell me about her."

She thought a moment, then she smiled. "Like Achar," she said. "Mama was like Achar."

"But that's ridiculous—"

"No, Hamid. Of course, she didn't look like Achar." She laughed. "Achar is big and hairy. No—mama didn't have a mustache. But she was like him another way. She worried about people, cared for people and the way they hurt. She hated injustice and worked to set things right."

"So you know Achar is interested in that?"

"Oh, yes. I can see it in his face. That's the thing I remember best about mama—her eyes, her concern. She would have loved Achar."

What a curious thing to say, he thought, and he was surprised that she understood Achar so well. It was uncanny the way she grasped the essence of people. She understood them by intuition. His own mind did not work that way. "Tell me more about her, what sort of things she did."

"She was a spy. She and Peter—together they spied upon the French."

"You're not serious."

"Of course I am."

"But how did you know?"

"They talked about it all the time. You see, Peter had a shop in Hanoi, a shop just like La Colombe. And it was filled with French people, officers and their wives. He sold them things, found them servants, stood in line for them with their letters at the Poste. They talked among themselves, and he asked them questions about their lives. Then he would tell mama—they would discuss these people for hours. They would put together what they knew and overheard—things having to do with transfers, movements of troops, boats that might arrive, airplanes, politics. They talked about all that, and then mama would carry the information someplace else. It was dangerous, I know. Peter was always worried when she left. Sometimes she was gone for six or seven days. We were always so happy when she returned."

"Were they married?"

"No, but people thought they were. Like Peter and me, you see. He pretended my mother was his wife. People called her 'Madame Zvegintzov.' We lived with him behind the shop. Mama and I slept in one bed and Peter in another. There was a curtain down the center of the room. Peter pulled it closed when it was time to go to sleep."

She locked her hands together then and threw them, like a lasso, around his neck. Then she lay back upon the banquette, pulled him down upon her, and buried her face against his chest. Later, in bed, they made love in that special way of hers, that strange Asian way which gave him such delight—lying nearly still, barely touching, changing their rhythm again and again, extending their pleasure to the limits of their ability to prolong it, then joining in a climax that left their bodies shuddering from head to toe.

The next day was busy, monotonous. A gang of Moroccan toughs had burglarized the auto camping grounds. Light-bulbs and plastic lenses were missing from all the cars. In the middle of the morning Foster Knowles turned up with a set of worried American parents whose runaway daughter had sent them an enigmatic postcard from Tangier. They showed Hamid photographs and beseeched him to help. He nodded, stared at the photographs. The girl looked lost and innocent. He tried to memorize her features but they blurred before his eyes.

Late in the afternoon he went to see the Prefect. He told him what he'd found out about the Freys and suggested he put a watch around their house. "It's a long shot, of course," he said, "but I can't think of what else would interest an Israeli in Tangier."

It was six-thirty when he left the Prefecture, a good time, he thought, to drop in at La Colombe. He became snarled in a traffic jam in the middle of Dradeb, caused by two huge tourist buses trying to pass one another at the narrowest portion of the road. It was ten to seven by the time he reached the shop. There were no European cars parked in front.

"Ah—it's you, Inspector." Peter was in a jovial mood. "Just like old times. Now we see each other every day."

The Russian was busy straightening up his cigars. Hamid wondered how many hours he wasted arranging and rearranging things, how often he clicked the keys of his old French cash register to ring up a purchase or just to hear the little bell.

"If you're back about that matter we discussed the other morning, I told you everything I know."

"No, Peter, I'm not back about that. I'm here about something else. I want to know what you think you're doing, following Kalinka on the street."

Peter stopped fidgeting with the cigars. For a moment he seemed to freeze. Then he picked up a feather duster and began to move rapidly around the shop, flicking dust off the book racks and the counters covered with games and imported jams and cheese. Hamid stood in the center watching him, waiting for his reply.

"Well," he said finally, "have I embarrassed you? Are you going to answer my question or not?"

"I don't know what you're talking about. Your question doesn't make any sense."

"All right, Peter. Forget I asked. But don't let me hear

you've followed her again. I'm warning you. Every policeman in this country will stand beside a colleague when his honor is at stake."

Peter was still waving his duster, even more frantically than before.

"Why did you lie, Peter?" Hamid asked. "Why did you pretend Kalinka was your wife?"

Peter suddenly stood still. Then he lowered his head. "Please," he said, "I so want your respect."

He raised his head again, showed his face, so that Hamid could see the moisture glistening in his eyes. For a moment Hamid felt ashamed that he'd been so harsh, but then he wondered if these tears were only another one of Peter's tricks. Kalinka said he liked to play with people, keep secrets from them, then laugh at them and call them fools behind their backs.

"Who is Stephen Zhukovsky?" he asked, as gently as he could.

"Oh, my God! Don't ask me questions. You have her now. Isn't that enough?"

Hamid moved close, grasped his shoulders, forced him to look into his eyes. "I'm not trying to hurt you, Peter. I don't wish you harm in any way. But I must know. I have to know what this is all about. These pretended marriages. These secrets. You must tell me everything now."

Peter's eyes were squeezed shut, tight behind the lenses that magnified his tired lines. Hamid let go of him and stepped back. Just then he heard the bell that rang whenever a person entered the shop. He turned. The American Consul, Daniel Lake, was there, staring at them from the door.

"Excuse me," said Lake. "I didn't mean to—"

Peter rushed to him, shook his hand, then took hold of his arm and faced Hamid. "You know Inspector Ouazzani, Dan."

"Yes. Of course."

Hamid nodded. The three of them stood awkwardly, staring at one another with simulated smiles.

"Actually, Peter, I saw the light and—"

"Yes, yes, Dan. The Inspector was about to leave."

Hamid started toward the door. Lake mumbled something,

then followed him into the street. "Nice night," he said. "Warmer now. Good for the gardens, I understand."

Hamid nodded. He wanted to get into his car, but the American, edging in front of it, had blocked his way.

"Thank you, Inspector, for being so kind this morning—with the couple Foster brought around. He told me you were very patient with them. It's so sad about these runaways."

"We rarely find them. They go south, to the desert, or the beaches west of Marrakech."

"Well, we're appreciative just the same. I want you to know that. Foster's impressed with the way you handle things, even though you had him in a sweat a few weeks ago."

Hamid felt the American's hand slap down upon his shoulder. The gesture annoyed him. He moved back a step.

"Come on, Inspector. Surely you recall." Lake was grinning. "You told him you'd been watching him. You asked him what he was doing around a certain shop. He was pretty upset, I can tell you. He came to me. Asked me what to do."

"Oh? What did you tell him?"

"I reminded him of his diplomatic status here. I told him he wasn't under the control of the local police, that he didn't have to account for his actions to anyone but me."

"Very good advice, Mr. Lake."

"Yes, I think it was. But what I'm getting at is the remarkable way you do your job. Foster and I are both impressed by that. You'd observed him. You knew what he was doing. I'm told nothing happens in Tangier that you don't find out about pretty quick."

Hamid looked at Lake closely. He wasn't sure whether the Consul General was trying to fence with him or whether this curious turn in their conversation had been contrived to make some point. Perhaps Lake suspected he was being watched. Perhaps Zvegintzov had told him that he was.

"And Kalinka?" asked Lake suddenly. "Tell me—how is she?"

"I didn't know you knew her."

"We've never been introduced, actually, but she's been pointed out to me as one of the beauties of the town."

Suddenly Hamid was angry. "Perhaps, Mr. Lake," he said

in a fierce whisper, "perhaps you've been gossiping too much with your Russian friend."

"Ah—you see!" Lake grinned. "Just as I told you. You *do* know everything, just as people say."

Lake turned away then, flushed with bravado. Hamid watched him chuckle to himself, then slip into his car. He was puzzled. The man had baited him. But why? What had he meant by it? Lake was not stupid, despite the odd way he babbled on, but there was something off center about him, something strange.

Hamid worked late that night shuffling through a stack of dossiers. He sorted out his cases, searching for coherence, but he could find nothing, no pattern, no sense of order in the town. A Nazi couple on the Mountain—Farid said they owned a Renoir. An American Consul General who leered at him like a fox. A Russian shopkeeper who begged him for respect. The streets were full of confusion. The summer was dry and hot. He was living with a woman, a foreigner, a cipher, whom he loved but could not understand.

Driving home very late, he noticed a car parked outside Heidi's Bar. Passing it, he had a quick look at a man inside— Inigo, the painter, shaking with laughter or perhaps in tears. As he drove farther, his headlights caught a pack of wild dogs running the deserted alleys near his street. In the flat he found Kalinka in bed, breathing gently, eyelids fluttering, safe in dreams and sleep. He stepped out onto his terrace and surveyed Tangier, listening to the clash of radios, each set to a different station, rebounding from the rooming houses all around. Dogs barked. The wind blew. Nothing was clear. The city was a labyrinth, a maze of pain and rage. He thought of people rotting away in decaying buildings, foreigners filled with violent passions, Moroccan children beating animals to death.

The Picnic

Robin ran his hands over his stomach and chest. His whole body was bathed in sweat. He sniffed around—there was a pungent odor in the room. Old cat piss, he thought, brought to life out of his soiled rug by the terrific Tangier heat.

He stumbled to his sink, grabbed a towel, flopped back onto his bed, and mopped off. The heat was terrible, had closed Tangier in. He couldn't see Spain anymore from the roof of the Oriental, and the Rif mountains were lost in haze. All the rogue cats of the medina seemed to be in heat. At night their cries echoed in the alleyways, reminding him of sex and love and pain.

He'd been miserable for two weeks because of the heat, and bored too with the town. There'd been nothing, not a glimmer of a scandal, no material for his column at all. This was a recurring problem, and Robin knew what he had to do: stir up Tangier, force the city to act itself.

A *picnic*. He'd give a picnic and see what material developed out of that. He owed everybody anyway. A picnic would be a good, cheap way to pay them back.

He snatched up a pencil and began to make a list. Barclay,

of course—he put down his name first. He didn't like Barclay but felt he had no choice—the man, for all his faults, would give his picnic cachet. But to make some trouble he listed Patrick Wax and Inigo, whom Barclay despised, then added Darryl Kranker because he was devious and sly, and Larry Luscombe, who'd been in a deep depression since his humiliation in May. He could have Joe Kelly too, he thought—that would annoy everybody, because Kelly was so awful and low—but he rejected that idea and crossed off Luscombe's name as well, afraid that when the others saw these two they'd make excuses and leave. He put down Bainbridge, so that Barclay would have an ally, and Sven Lundgren because the dentist was close to St. Carlton, and he wanted to be remembered when the couturier came to town. He thought a while longer, dabbing at his pencil with his tongue, then added the writer Vincent Doyle and Hervé Beaumont, who'd recently confided that he was thinking of turning queer.

The next thing was to draw the invitation—something Barclay and Wax couldn't resist. He set to work, revising to achieve the proper effect. When he was finished he read his draft aloud:

> Robin Scott most cordially invites you to a picnic to celebrate the summer solstice. Date: June 21. Time: 1:00 P.M. Place: By the rocks near Robinson Plage. Bring a salad and a Moroccan "friend." *Everything* will be shared!

That, he decided, was irresistible. It was a stroke of genius to ask them to bring their bumboys. Before he went out to breakfast he scrounged up paper and envelopes and in an elaborate script wrote the invitations out.

He spent the morning delivering them, trudging up the Mountain in the heat. His last stop was Villa Chapultepec, where he also delivered a kilo of kif and persuaded Hervé Beaumont to loan him glasses, skewers, and a tent.

That evening Patrick Wax stopped by his table at the Centrale.

"All chickenhawks, Robin?"

"With chickens too."

Patrick was delighted and blew him a kiss. Kranker came

by a few minutes later and said he'd be there with his latest, Nordeen.

Over the next few days the others accepted—everyone except Barclay, but that, Robin knew, was his game. Barclay liked to create anxiety by being unpredictable, accepting and then not showing up, or not accepting and then arriving by surprise. He was the only man in town who could get away with that—the fault of the rest of us, Robin thought. Still, as much as he disliked him he desperately needed him to come, so he rang him up determined to get him and quite prepared to kiss his ass.

"Are you coming to my picnic, Peter?" he asked in an appropriately humble voice.

"Who's going to be there, darling? I know it's rude, but—"

"Everyone, Peter."

"*Everyone?*"

"Friends *and* enemies. That's the fun."

"With Mustapha too, you mean?"

"Of course, Peter. Of course."

"I'll think about it, dear, but forgive me if I don't turn up. I get headaches on the beach."

Robin thought then that he'd hooked him, but just to make sure he threw him another bone. "I really hope you bring Mustapha, Peter. It's so amusing the way Wax turns envious when he sees that boy with you."

Peter muttered something and rang off. Robin felt he'd escaped with his dignity intact, and without the gouged scar that was Barclay's usual price.

He was thinking hard then about saving money on the food. He considered buying horsemeat for the kebabs, but he knew the Moroccan boys would recognize it no matter how much salt and cumin he packed on. He decided against it, since one of them would surely tell, and then his more fastidious guests would retch.

He only wished he could invite his real friends—Jean Tassigny, the Beaumont girls, the Hawkins', Vanessa Bolton, Martin Townes. But his picnic was strictly confined to queens. The Moroccan boys would be prancing around in their skimpy shorts, and he expected biting insults and nasty repartee from his European guests. A mean and nasty social life was indispensable to his profession—a flaw, he knew, in his hugely flawed character, part of the aura of corruption he was trying to cultivate about his name.

On the morning of the solstice Hervé Beaumont came by to pick him up. They stopped at a cheap butcher shop, picked up wine and bottled water, then drove out to Robinson's beach. It was such a searing day that they immediately took a swim, then worked to set up the tent. Robin was clumsy with the pegs and stakes, and finally, after everything collapsed, Hervé erected it himself. Robin lay in the sun for an hour in a pair of cutoff jeans. He knew his guests would be late, vying to make spectacular entrances, so he waited patiently and with a hopeful heart.

Percy Bainbridge was first. The Australian inventor brought an English boy, an ordinary tourist he'd picked up at a bar. This boy, he said, ran a poodle-clipping service in Liverpool, which fascinated Percy, who had the notion of turning dog's fleece into yarn. "That way, you see," he explained, "a master could have a sweater knitted from the hair of his very own dog. Think of it—master and dog in matching coats. It's just the sort of thing that could catch on."

Robin was irritated when Vincent Doyle arrived alone. The old exemplar, the literary lion, gaunt and bony, his hair shaved nearly to his skull, explained that his friend Achmed was indisposed. Doyle was excessively polite, but Robin sensed he was on edge. He settled on a rock and immediately lit up a pipe of kif.

Doyle always carried his manuscript with him, packed in a burlap sack. He was known for his paranoia, his fear of Moroccans, particularly servants and police, and his belief that a revolution might break out at any moment, making it necessary for him to leave the country without his work. Doyle was almost as well known as Ashton Codd, but he hadn't published anything in years. The manuscript he carried was to be his swan song, a huge novel into which he was pouring everything he knew and by which he hoped to remind the world that he was still alive.

Robin offered to store the sack in the tent, and actually had his hands on it when Doyle suddenly grabbed it back.

"Christ's sake, Vincent. What's the matter? This thing's as heavy as bricks."

Doyle, upset, stashed the sack beneath his knees. "I'm most particular about my manuscript," he said. "I'm a mother you see. I must keep my baby in my sight."

"Yes, of course." Robin nodded, though it saddened him that Doyle, once such a famous hipster, had become an old lady about his goods.

Sven Lundgren arrived next, with his Mohammed, *thank God*. Immediately they stripped to bikinis and ran hand in hand into the surf. Mohammed was delicate as a willow branch, his smooth, bronze flesh marred by adolescent pimples along his jaw. Robin was entranced, for he was truly a chicken, his innocence set off by contrast with the dentist, whose torso was covered with a pelt of thick blond hair.

Kranker arrived then with Nordeen, a sulky boy whom Robin knew from around the Socco. Kranker liked professional hustlers; he had no interest in finding and courting a lover, preferring to pay for sex and keep himself detached. This had its advantages, and dangers too, since most of the hustlers Robin had known were capable of exhibiting psychotic rage. Kranker, Robin thought, must be excited by the danger, the possibility of being suddenly turned upon with fists and knife. He lay down beside Doyle, leaving Nordeen to his own devices. The boy drifted down to the tidewater and began to build a castle in the sand.

So far the picnic was shaping up with a lot less style than Robin had hoped. Hervé was literally sulking in his tent, Lundgren was in the ocean, Bainbridge and the poodle clipper were lying in the sun, and Doyle and Kranker were whispering together by the rocks. But then suddenly and simultaneously Inigo and Patrick Wax appeared, and at the sight of them Robin knew everything would be all right.

Inigo, wearing nothing but a white panama hat and green silk slacks, walked across the sand with the panache of a South American millionaire, stalked by Pumpkin Pie bearing a great plate of salad, with Inigo's sketching kit strapped across his back.

Wax arrived from the opposite direction in a flowing white djellaba and gold-trimmed Arabian headdress, his riding crop in his hand. His Kalem followed, bearing salad and a folding beach chair—a marvelous, tough-looking Arab boy, Robin thought, with bulging muscles and a cruel face. This Kalem was only the latest in a long line of chickens whom Wax had ferreted out, instructed in interior decoration, introduced into society, then dropped when the youths became twenty years old.

"Oh, Patrick," Robin yelled. "You look just like T. E. Lawrence."

"*Florence* of Arabia, dear boy," Wax replied. "I see Mother Barclay hasn't arrived."

"She will," said Bainbridge.

"He'd better," said Wax. "I want to arrange a wrestling match between his Mustapha and my Kalem." Then, *sotto voce:* "I've been teaching this beauty the manly art of self-defense. He'll pin Barclay's chicken in the dirt."

Robin was elated. This was just the sort of thing he'd hoped to see. He helped Wax arrange himself, then hurried to Inigo on the other side.

"My salad and my friend," the artist said, snapping his fingers at Pumpkin Pie. "You must come see his portrait before I ship it off to New York."

Pumpkin Pie grinned.

"Oh, he's very pleased," said Inigo. "I've flattered him a lot. He's being good to me this week—I've promised to take him to Madrid. Well—first we're going to swim, and then we're going to draw."

"Come say hello—"

"No thanks, Robin. I detest homosexuals. Wait—isn't that my dentist in the sea?"

"If you're such a snob, Inigo, you can swim farther down the beach."

"Yes. That's what we'll do." He snapped his fingers at the boy. "Come!"

Pumpkin Pie handed Robin the salad and sketching pack and followed Inigo across the sand. A few minutes later, when Robin came out of the tent, Patrick Wax beckoned with his crop.

"Look," he said. "Do you see Doyle? Now why do you suppose he doesn't undress?"

"The sun's hot today—"

"Rubbish, Robin!" Wax switched him gently around the navel. "There're black-and-blue marks all over him. That

Achmed of his beats him up, and of course the man's ashamed."

Now that was something Robin didn't know, and wasn't about to concede. Wax was a marvelous character but he lied all the time and was the most evil man in all Tangier. Though he lived in a palace on the Mountain, he kept a flat for assignations in town, a deteriorating place that Robin had once seen, filled with dusty, rusted mirrors and scores of crucifixes on the walls. The crucifixes, Wax claimed, were part of a valuable collection he'd inherited from his mentor, a Polish cardinal or a Bavarian bishop, depending on which version he was telling at the time. They had, he said, a two-fold usage: as religious paraphernalia, and to ream boys in the ass.

Inigo came out of the sea, fetched his sketch pad, then went back to the sand to draw Kranker's Nordeen. Kranker watched with Doyle, a twisted smile on his face, which Pumpkin Pie tried to catch in a crude drawing of his own.

"You see," said Robin to Hervé, whom he'd finally enticed out of the tent, "all the boys are learning from their mentors. Wax is teaching Kalem interior decoration, and Inigo's teaching Pumpkin Pie how to draw. Doyle's got Achmed writing verse, and Barclay's Mustapha is learning how to entertain. We expatriates leave a magnificent heritage. Look at Farid Ouazzani, the Inspector's brother. Wax taught him about antiques, and now he has a shop on the Boulevard."

"Bazaar Marhaba—is that the place?" The poodle clipper had been listening in.

"Yes," said Robin. "Been in there?"

"Uh huh. The other day." He pulled off his T-shirt, exposing a pale, fragile chest. "The young man showed me everything, and then we went upstairs to look at rugs. As soon as we were alone he took my arm and asked if I felt like making love."

"Ha!" said Wax. "That's Farid!"

"Did you do it?"

"Certainly not. I didn't know him, and besides, I didn't come down here to catch a disease. I bought a little bracelet from him, though, so he wouldn't feel hurt." He flashed his wrist. "Sort of cute, don't you think?"

Robin was beginning to take a dislike to this nelly queen, who seemed so ordinary among his Tangier friends. He was about to say something nasty when Wax guffawed.

"Ho, ho! Look who's there. I believe Mother Barclay has arrived."

Barclay had managed to come last, but his entrance, Robin thought, was not the best. He and his Mustapha trudged across the sand, giving identical little waves of the hand. Barclay's hair showed silver in the sun, matching the handle of his cane.

"Hello. Hello. Hello, dear. Vincent. Percy. Robin. Hello."

Barclay waved especially vehemently toward the Moroccans, all helping Nordeen now with his castle in the sand. While Robin assisted him with his towels, Barclay gave instructions to his boy. "Mustapha, look there! What a lovely bit of sandcraft that is! Go on down there and play with the others. Show them how to build!"

When the boy was gone Barclay sat down a decent distance from Patrick Wax. "I feel just like a scout master," he said to Robin, then turned to peer at the sketch of Nordeen that Inigo was passing around.

"I'd like to own that," said Kranker.

"Oh," muttered Wax. "How I bet he would."

"It's yours," said Inigo. "But you must pay my price."

"Certainly," said Kranker. "How much would that be?"

"Oh—a thousand pounds."

Kranker scowled.

"I adore Inigo," whispered Wax. "He knows his worth."

"Yes," said the artist, sitting between him and Barclay. "I think that's an important thing. I'm looking forward to my forties—I see myself becoming very 'Rolls Royce.'"

Robin brought wine to Kranker, but Doyle declined, pointing to his pipe.

"I was just telling Darryl," he said, "I think your column is rather Proustian."

"That's very complimentary, Vincent—"

"Oh, I don't mean in quality. In its aggregate, you understand. One can follow all sorts of little stories through the years. If you'd just paste your columns together you'd have some kind of chronicle. Perhaps a book."

"I don't like that Inigo," said Kranker, still annoyed.

"He's very talented," said Robin. "Closest thing we have to a genius in Tangier."

"Genius! Don't be absurd. We have Doyle and our poet, Codd. Anyway, his paintings are too stylish. Too superficial and slick. If Picasso were alive I know precisely what he'd say. 'You draw very well, *mon petit*. But your paintings are only decoration.'"

"I think that's unfair."

"What's the point in being fair? He has a bloody nerve asking a thousand pounds for a sixty-second sketch of a five-dirhan street whore."

"Well," said Doyle, embarrassed by all this, "I think I'll take a walk."

He gathered up his manuscript sack and started down the beach. Robin and Kranker moved to join the others, now polarized into separate groups around Barclay and Wax.

"I'm *devoted* to the Sultan," Wax was saying to the poodle clipper. "And he, of course, is *devoted* to me—"

Barclay had brought out a pair of opera glasses, encased in mother of pearl, and was training them on the Moroccan boys. "You know," he said, "I think Pumpkin Pie just goosed my Mustapha. What the hell is the dentist doing down there?"

"I like Moroccan bodies," said Bainbridge, "but they have such gorillas' heads."

"I love their faces," said Inigo. "Their bodies strike me as Japanese." He got up then, asked Robin for more wine, and followed him into the tent. "Your friends are all so witty," he said. "I'm at a disadvantage. I'm a visual man."

"Nonsense, Inigo. Your English is very good."

"It's difficult. I'm always getting mixed up. In English, it seems, an asp in the grass is a snake. But a grasp in the ass is something called a goose."

Hervé was pumping a bellows at the fire he'd built to grill the kebabs. Robin helped him, showed himself clumsy again, and retired when Hervé gave him a mocking look. Returning to the group before the tent, he nearly collided with Sven Lundgren, who'd left the Moroccan boys and had flopped down on the sand to everyone's barely concealed distaste.

"They're building such a castle down there," he said. "Tunnels, alleyways—you ought to see."

"Sounds like the Casbah."

"Yes," said Kranker. "Unconscious replication. It's in their blood. The little beasts are prisoners of the collective unconscious of their nasty, backward race."

"I wonder if it isn't time," said Barclay, "for our little chickens to come home to roost."

"Oh, let's leave them where they are," Robin said. "They're getting acquainted. We'll be eating soon. Anyone seen Doyle?"

"He took a long walk down the beach. I think I see him far away."

"In a minute he'll lie down and let the flies descend upon him. Then he'll count them. He does things like that."

"Strange man," said Robin. "And that sack of his is heavy. I tried to help him with it, but he wouldn't let me. It weighs a ton."

"I'll tell you something about that sack," said Kranker. "But you must all promise you won't tell anybody else."

They all nodded except for Robin, who made a practice of never agreeing when people asked him not to repeat confidential things.

"You too, Robin. I don't want to see this in your column."

"All right, damn it. Go ahead."

Kranker smiled, looked around. "He has a manuscript in there, you can be sure, but it's light and it's very thin. The weight you felt was his silverware. He hauls it around with him because he's afraid to leave it in his flat."

"My God," said Barclay. "The man must be cuckoo mad. How did you find that out?"

"Achmed told me. It's a game they play. Achmed tries to steal the silverware, and Doyle tries to keep it safe. A year or so ago Achmed got hold of some spoons which he immediately sold in the flea market. Doyle never said a word, pretended it didn't happen. That's their relationship. They play psychological chess."

"Is it true that Achmed beats him up?"

Kranker shook his head. "No. They torture each other mentally. That's the trouble with Vincent Doyle—he'd like to be a physical masochist but he has too low a threshold for pain."

Robin looked hard at Kranker, so gleefully attacking his friend. *Never trust a writer,* he thought. *Sooner or later he'll sell you out.*

When the kebabs were ready Robin called everyone to lunch. Doyle came back from his walk, and all the Moroccan boys returned from the sand. They sat in their bikinis in an inner circle chatting in Arabic about sports, while their benefactors lounged behind them on beach chairs speaking of the Tangier demimonde. Robin served the skewers and passed the salads. Fortunately Inigo and Wax had brought lavish ones, since Barclay had brought nothing except Mustapha, his towels, and himself.

"How's everything at the church these days, Peter? Your investigations getting anyplace?"

"We have our suspects." Barclay laughed. "We're narrowing down the field."

"None of us, I hope."

"Oh—maybe. You'll have to ask the Colonel about that."

"But surely you don't expect him to solve the thing?"

"Why not?" said Robin. "He's got nothing else to do."

"But *really,*" said Wax. "Horticulturalist, genealogist, and now amateur sleuth. Old Lester is good at things like checking up on a story. If someone claims his uncle was an earl, old Lester will find him out. But he's no detective. He's too lazy and stupid for that."

"Don't underrate him," said Bainbridge. "He's got a passion to get to the bottom of this thing and I wager his stick-to-itiveness will out."

"You certainly have plenty of that yourself, Mother Bainbridge. By God, you've stuck to that grapefruit juicer of yours."

Everyone laughed a little, and Bainbridge wilted. Robin felt sorry for him. For years his inventions had been a joke, but recently people had begun to make fun of him to his face. Barclay, who pretended to be his friend, never came to his defense and scornfully called him "my lady-in-waiting" when talking about him behind his back.

Wax must have felt sorry for him too, for he immediately

launched into an irrelevant story. Robin had heard it before, but Wax's gestures were so theatrical, and his voice so compelling, that he found himself falling under the old man's spell.

"Oh, about 1938 I met Bosie Douglas in Florence. He was old then, a ruin, but still a magnificent-looking man. I told him how awed I was to actually meet such a legend—how I'd read all about him as a boy. We became rather close, and of course I asked him about Oscar Wilde. He told me the most incredible thing—that he and Wilde had never screwed. I couldn't believe it, but he insisted. Wilde, he said, was after him for years, but Bosie always resisted him, and the most that ever happened was that occasionally he'd let old Oscar suck him off. This suggests a theory about the idea behind *Dorian Gray*—imbibing the life juices of a younger man in order to stay young oneself. Anyway, I said to him: 'If you weren't that way, Lord Douglas, why did you go around with Wilde all the time?' 'Simple,' he answered. 'Wilde was the most brilliant companion a man could have. And it annoyed my father, whom I loathed.' Fascinating! The funny thing about Bosie was that he was interested in girls—young ones too, twelve and thirteen years old. He'd follow them around Florence like a rake. I told him he'd better be careful about that, but he laughed me off. 'There's not a court in the world,' he said, 'that will ever believe that Bosie Douglas is a dyke!' "

In a way, Robin thought, it was a precious story, and he was annoyed when Barclay tried to eclipse it with one of his own. He told a boring anecdote about an English actor he'd once slept with who'd used his appendix scar as the centerpiece for a butterfly tattooed above his loins.

When he was finished Wax baited him by suggesting that Kalem and Mustapha fight.

"Won't allow it," Barclay said. "I know you sent your boy to karate school. I've been coaching Mustapha in something else."

"Oh? What's that?"

"To speak like an Eton boy. A hopeless cause, of course."

Inigo excused himself, gesturing for Pumpkin Pie to follow him into the sea. Doyle went off in another direction, Bainbridge and the poodle clipper went to sun themselves on the rocks, and Lundgren and the Moroccan boys began to play soccer on the beach. This left Robin with Barclay, Kranker, and Wax, and a discussion of the "Mohammed problem" upon which they were all quite eloquent, he thought.

"Oh, they make us suffer," Barclay said. "They love to do that. Look at Inigo. The terrible things he has to take from that Pumpkin Pie. We teach them, introduce them around, show them how to use a knife and fork. And what do they do? Steal, chase after girls, and feel no gratitude for all the love we lavish so generously upon their wretched souls. They're in it for the money and the comfort. Certainly not the love. And we can do nothing to change them. We can only acquiesce."

"That," said Kranker, "is why I stick to the Socco. They're good for sex and nothing else. I wouldn't live with one if he paid me. I don't have time to suffer on their account."

"But it's marvelous to suffer," Wax put in. "Don't you think, Robin? Oh—but you're too poor! To really suffer you have to be rich like me, and offer them ways to become corrupt. Look at them over there." He pointed to the soccer game. "Look at them, preening around like little cock dandies. They're animals, that's all, and they don't care a hang about us. Except for what they can get—food, clothes, a warm bed. Thing to do is trick 'em. Make 'em think they'll be remembered in our wills. Kalem, like the rest of them, is in for a big surprise. I promise him things, tasty little *objets d'art*. 'This necklace will be yours someday, dear.' 'Someday you'll have my crucifixes, my furs, my robes.' Ha! He won't get a cent. I'm leaving everything to my sister in Sussex."

"Oh, come, Patrick," Robin said. "What you say is cruel—to corrupt them with all your stuff and then throw them back on the dungheap when you're done."

"Not cruel at all, my boy. The dungheap's precisely where they belong. It's good for them to be there. Builds their characters, you see. Anyway, they can study me, and when I'm done with them they can sink or swim on their bloody own. If they don't learn how to hustle from me, they certainly don't deserve to survive. Tangier's a cruel town, and I'm no exception. Let's face it—it's the boys who brought us here. And we pay a hell of a lot for that."

"One pays for everything," Barclay said.

"That's right. So why be sentimental? But you are, Peter. You have a nauseating sentimental streak. What's this I hear about Camilla Weltonwhist giving a birthday party for Mustapha?"

"She is, next week. Nice of her too."

"She's secretly in love with you, Barclay. It's her poor, sad way of ingratiating herself."

Barclay shrugged. "Fine. Let her ingratiate. She's been a good deal more successful at it than you."

"Look at Sven there," said Wax, pretending he hadn't heard. "He's a terrible dentist. Probably the worst dentist in the world. Yet the poor idiot keeps at it, because he doesn't know how to hustle any other way. He's slept with St. Carlton on and off for years, and all he ever got out of it was a closetful of St. Carlton-designed ties."

"I don't get your point," Robin said.

"Well, I'm sorry about that, dear boy. Let me try to make it clear. My point is that the world's divided between those who hustle, those who squeeze the ripe fruit of life and suck out of it all the juices therein, and the rest of humanity, the poor working bastards who are hustled and squeezed to death. Now which is better—to be a squeezer or one of the squeezed? Do you see? That's the one thing I've learned in life, the one thing I have to pass on. You've been living in Tangier for ten years, you're getting a belly, and you're losing your looks. You live in a pigsty, sell dope, make shabby little deals, and write your delicious column. Well, what have you got to show for it? You should have done like me, latched onto a rich old man when you were eighteen or twenty, learned all his tricks, ingratiated yourself, gotten yourself into his will. Course you're redheaded, and redheads don't usually succeed.

"I was lucky. I found a prince. Not a temporal prince, mind you—a prince of the church. He was rich too, had vast inherited lands. We spent ten years together, and I got everything in the end. Most of it I lost in the war, but I'd learned to hustle and was able to make another pile on my own. How? Selling things, trading, hustling furniture and art. The point is that I had a métier. So here I am, in decadent Tangier, rich as Croesus, with a beautiful chicken who obeys me like a dog. I don't envy anyone. I wouldn't change places with blue-blooded Barclay here for anything in the world. I was born the son of a chimney sweep, but I squeezed the fruit of life and sucked out everything that was there. The trouble with you, Robin, is that you skip around too much. You've got good instincts, but you don't go for the kill."

"Thank you, Patrick," Robin solemnly replied. "I appreciate your analysis. Everything you say is true. Now I shall go into the tent and weep."

"Don't weep, boy," Wax called after him. "You're adorable. We love you, you know."

Robin turned, smiled, waved his hand, then retired to the tent to rest.

Inigo was the first to leave. There were still many hours left of light, and he wanted to go home and paint. Then Doyle left too, dragging his sack, to drive back with Kranker and Nordeen. Lundgren and his Mohammed hitched a ride with Wax and Kalem. Barclay took a dip, put his arm around Mustapha, and came to sit by Robin while he dried off.

"Now, Robin," he said, "we've had our differences. But I like you, so I must give you some good advice. Stay clear of Patrick Wax. He's a nasty piece of work."

"I think he's quite amusing, Peter—"

"Awful person. Phony. A thief. Everything out of his mouth is a lie. That absurd story about Bosie Douglas—and how he loves to say 'Lord Alfred Douglas'! I happen to know Bosie wasn't anywhere near Florence in thirty-eight. He was in London, sick with pneumonia. We were cousins, you see."

"Yes, yes, but what difference does it make? Everyone lies in Tangier."

"There are degrees, Robin. *Degrees.* People like Wax go in for homosexuality because of the social mobility involved. Wax would be a chimney sweep like his father if he hadn't gotten smart and become a pouf."

"What are you saying? That he's not a pouf? That it's nothing but an act?"

"You said it—not me. But it's true. He's false, from A to Zed. He became gay just to get in with his betters, and because it allowed him to enter circles where it was easier to steal. Beware of him, Robin. He really shouldn't have been here. This was to be a chickenhawk and bumboy party. *He didn't belong!*"

He left then, abruptly, and Robin looked after him amazed: Barclay condemning Patrick Wax for pretending to be a homosexual because he couldn't condemn him for pretending to be a lord. Wax made no bones about his background. He loved to tell people he was a chimney sweep's son and played the role of imposter to the hilt. Now Barclay accused him of being a heterosexual in disguise. It was the most absurd thing Robin had ever heard.

Bainbridge and the poodle clipper were the last to go, and Robin was not displeased. Percy said he was working on a new invention, something extraordinary, a "three-cornered kiss."

"It will revolutionize group sex, bring coherence to carnality," he said in his Australian whine. "It's not an invention so much as a technique. I won't be able to patent it, but I do hope people give me credit. I want them always to refer to it as 'the Bainbridge kiss.' "

When they were gone Robin put on his shirt, then lay out in the dying sun. Hervé was down by the sea washing the glasses and plates. Robin watched him, a silhouette against the Atlantic. The sea was smooth, a great expanse broken only by an oil tanker moving slowly out of the distance toward the Straits.

"Shall we take down the tent and drive back?" Hervé asked. He'd packed the skewers and glasses in a basket.

"I don't know," said Robin. "Why don't we sleep out here tonight?"

Hervé agreed, and so the two of them sat together on the sand waiting hours for the sun to set. Robin had taken in too much of it. He felt a fever rising to his forehead as if all the heat he'd absorbed in the afternoon was breaking out now in the cool of the dusk.

Later, feeling better, lying before the tent with Hervé Beaumont by his side, Robin remembered that this was the night of the summer solstice, the shortest night of the longest day of the year. In three months the autumnal equinox would come, then the winter solstice and circles more of changing seasons after that. As he pondered these cosmic matters, the antics of the afternoon began to take on a new perspective in his thoughts.

He felt let down by his picnic, bitter and angry too. He didn't know why, since everyone had been nasty as he'd hoped, and he'd heard some good stories, even picked up some tidbits for his column. Perhaps it was the predictability of the nastiness that bothered him, the way they'd all tattled on one another, the foul perfume of their gossip and lies. It seemed more pathetic than amusing that Vincent Doyle lugged around his silverware. There was pathos in Barclay trying to make an Eton boy out of Mustapha, and in Inigo, a great artist, suffering over Pumpkin Pie. Bainbridge and his absurd inventions. Lundgren, the incompetent dentist. Kranker, so filled with bitterness and spite. He even felt sorry for Wax and his pretensions, his "Florence of Arabia" act. They all seemed so absurd, cruel, self-deceiving fools mingling on the sand, specks on a speck in an indifferent universe, so flawed, so powerless in the face of the burning sun.

Should he leave Tangier? Would things be better for him somewhere else? He doubted it, and at the thought felt disgusted by his life. How pathetic he was, keeping so tight a grasp upon his column, like a clerk in a post office holding on to a tiny power.

Then he thought, how strange to lie here and feel metaphysical distress. He'd organized the picnic, orchestrated it for his amusement. It was just something he'd done to pass an empty afternoon.

But this day was the solstice, a mark on the calendar of life. *How many more seasons,* he wondered, *how many more are there left for me to kill?*

The Foster Knowles'
Entertain

Much later, when Lake looked back, he wondered if that wasn't the night when everything started to go wrong.

It began, innocently, with a dinner invitation from the Foster Knowles'. Lake was not particularly keen about the Knowles'—their sophomoric expressions and youth-culture mannerisms disgusted him no end. And the fact that other people in Tangier seemed to like them only added to his despair. They'd made friends on account of their jogging group and now were on the make, penetrating the society of the Mountain, even rating a tryout at Barclay's house for lunch.

Lake couldn't understand it. They were a pair of straw-haired bumpkins as far as he could see. Jackie Knowles and her gymnastics classes, Foster and his antipathy for meat—perhaps, he thought, it was their wholesomeness that was so attractive in this town where everyone else was either mad or queer. He didn't know, but it annoyed him all the same. The Knowles' were more popular than Janet and himself, though he was Consul General and Tangier was Foster's premier post.

Lake and his wife pulled up to the Knowles' building just as Willard and Katie Manchester were locking up their car. They all embraced on the street, then walked inside. There wasn't room in the elevator for the four of them, so Lake volunteered to take the stairs. By the third landing he was sorry—the Knowles' lived on the sixth floor. He was breathing hard and growing furious at his exhaustion when he heard Jackie greet the others at the apartment door.

"Hi!" she said. "Where's the Consul?" Her shrill voice ricocheted to him on the stairs.

"He's climbing slowly," Janet said. "Dan's not much of an athlete, you know."

"Well, good for him anyway. I think exercise is great!"

Lake swore as he assaulted the final flight. The evening, he knew, was going to be bad.

Foster greeted him. "Hey, Dan!"

Lake didn't know what all the fuss was about, since they'd been working together the entire day.

"Helluva a climb, right? Better have a drink." Jackie glided up and bussed his cheek. Foster handed him a scotch.

Fufu, the UN delegate from Uganda, was on the couch beside his wife. Lake always felt awkward around this man, since he didn't seem to have a first name. When one met him one called him "Mr. Fufu," and then just plain "Fufu" when acquaintanceship became close. He had tribal marks, diagonal slashes cut into his cheeks, and was fond of giving lectures on the destiny of Africa, lectures which he'd enunciate with increasing volume as one tried to wriggle away. Lake shook hands and sat beside Mrs. Fufu, who reminded him of a picture on a package of pancake mix. Big, huge-breasted, full-cheeked, she sat next to her husband like a squaw.

Lake gulped half his drink, then listened to Katie Manchester holding forth across the room.

"Yes, dears, it's *true*. We're really going to *leave*. End of the summer *probably*. Willard was just over in Fort Lauderdale talking to the condominium people. He made the downpayment and interviewed a *maid*. Course it's more expensive than Tangier, but we like the *amenities*. Pool. Shuffleboard. Golf. If it were up to me we'd live in Wisconsin, but Willard's pension's better suited for southern climes."

Christ, what shit!

Originally Lake had liked the Manchesters, but now he found them stultifying, garrulous fools. In the mornings, when he watched them through his binoculars, he was chilled by a vision of himself, retired, with Janet, killing time in some second-rate resort. Would he prattle on like Willard about the deal he was getting on his Buick? Would Janet send out Christmas cards like Katie—four-page newsletters full of emptiness and transparent cheer? There had to be more to look forward to than a condominium in Fort Lauderdale. Lake felt desperate around the Manchesters, for they reminded him of failure; but there sat the Knowles', regarding them as role models, listening attentively to every word they said.

He was just finishing up his second drink when the Ashton Codds came in. They seemed to waltz across the room with a stylish antique gait, Ashton in dinner jacket with Legion of Honor rosette in his lapel, Musica in an expensive caftan, the two of them absurdly overdressed. They were outfitted for a party on the Mountain, not for a dinner with a junior diplomat in town. But the anomaly did not seem to bother anyone else; the Codds made their entrance, then lavishly embraced the Knowles'.

At their arrival the conversation turned to "Tangier," the sort of gibberish that had been maddening Lake for months. Prices at the market, crisis in the theater club, scandal at the British church. All he wanted was to lie back and drink himself to sleep, but the talk buzzed around him like tormenting mosquitoes in the night.

"Poor old Luscombe," Musica was saying. "They've broken his spirit, you know. Ran into him on the Boulevard the other day. He was talking to himself, twitching as he walked."

Ashton Codd was entertaining Jackie Knowles, his wrinkles dancing as he chattered away. "The Moroccans are so damn *stupid,* my dear. I don't know why we writers choose to live in such a place. They're afraid of books here. Can you imagine? I heard a good one the other day. Seems they seized a chess book at the customs. It was the title that got them: *New Ways to Attack the King!*"

"Ha! Ha!" It was Fufu, doubled over with mirth. In his

country they shot people for criticizing the regime, but Lake restrained himself from mentioning that. Across the room he heard Musica Codd say that Vicar Wick was losing his grip. Termites were at work on the beams of St. Thomas, and considering all its other troubles, she was wondering whether the British community could survive.

"*A table! Dîner est servi!*" Jackie called to them in unaccented foreign-service French.

Lake finished off his third drink, then stood up too fast. He felt dazed, reeled, wondered if he'd make it through dessert. There was an awkward moment after they sat down when Jackie reminded her guests that she and Foster didn't eat meat. They were regenerate health nuts and had moral reservations as well, but she said she thought the deprivation might do the rest of them some good.

Actually, Lake thought, the food wasn't bad—crisp vegetables, a mushroom salad, a Moroccan stew of greens. But the whole business annoyed him, and he suffered through the meal, listening to Jackie chatter on about exercise and diets while she filled and refilled his wine glass half a dozen times. The Knowles', he decided, were impossible, patronizing and sanctimonious, but looking around he could see that the others liked them very much.

Right after dinner he shot back a double cognac, and this time the drink hit him hard. It had been a while since he'd tied one on, but if ever he had an excuse for serious drinking, this, he felt, was the night. The conversation drifted around him, and he began to chuckle to himself. He got the idea into his head that Fufu was a baboon and felt an urge to stand up, strip a banana, and jam it into the Ugandan's mouth. Mrs. Fufu looked like she needed a good fucking, but he wondered if he'd have the will to take her on. "Moo moo," she would moan, just like the cow that she was. When she and Fufu were in bed together she'd cry out, "Foo foo moo moo."

He looked around for Janet, saw her with the Codds. The flabby flesh of those old curmudgeons bounced about their brittle facial bones. The noise level rose and Lake felt flushed. He might have passed out a while, for the next thing he knew everyone was quiet, listening to Foster address them as a group.

⟨ 179 ⟩

He had a new recording of the Bach B-minor Mass, he said, which he wanted to play for them without waking the building up. Suddenly an apparatus was set upon the coffee table, and the floor was running with wires. Knowles brought out a tangle of headsets he'd snitched from various airlines. Jackie distributed them off a tray.

She handed one to Lake. He handed it back.

"I pass," he said. "No thanks."

"Oh, *please*, Mr. Lake. It's really good."

He gestured thumbs-down, mumbled an excuse, and headed out to find the john. Once inside he tried to refocus. He was drunk—no question about it. He hiccupped, splashed cold water on his face. On a whim he opened the medicine cabinet and was flabbergasted by what he saw. The Knowles' had two of everything: matching "his" and "hers" deodorants; men's electric razor for the beard and women's for the legs; matching toothbrushes, one pink, the other blue; a big toenail clipper and a little one for fingernails; anal *and* oral thermometers; an unopened sixpack of condoms; and a powdered pessary in a plastic case.

Jesus—they don't take any chances. He shut the cabinet door.

On his way back to the living room he stopped at the hall closet, paused, scratched his head, and opened it up. The closet had a peculiar smell—a mixture of deodorant and a girls' gym. Immediately he understood. The Knowles' sweatsuits were hanging on opposing hooks. He peeked behind one of them, saw Foster's jockstrap hanging limp. He poked at it with his finger. *Ugh!* He was curious to see what size it was, but couldn't bear to touch it again. Then, on a hunch, he looked under the other suit. There was only a bikini bottom there. He studied it a while, felt a strange desire to sniff it, and felt an erection sprouting up.

What's wrong with me tonight?

He was about to slam the closet door when he heard a sound behind. He jumped and turned. It was Jackie, staring at him through big blue eyes.

"Looking for something?"

Even as he grabbed her, moved in for the kiss, he knew he was behaving like an ass. They clinched; he felt her strong gymnast's hands grab his shoulders tight, and then a sharp pain as she pushed him back.

"Mr. Lake!"

"Sorry," he muttered. "I was looking for the john."

"Oh," she said. "I see. Oh, dear. It's over there."

She took his hand and led him back to the lavatory. He had a glimpse of her grinning as he shut the door. He bolted it, sat down on the toilet. He felt dizzy.

I've just kissed Jackie Knowles!

For a moment he couldn't believe he'd done it, and began to fantasize his disgrace. Foster would go to Rabat and complain to the Ambassador. There'd be an inquiry, Janet would hear of it, and, confronted, he'd sob and confess. She'd leave him, take away the boys. He'd lose his job, his pension, his privileges at the PX. There was only one way, he knew, to save the situation. He'd have to go back into the living room, go straight to Jackie, and apologize.

He stumbled in expecting to find the others staring at him with hate. But no one paid the slightest attention. All except Jackie were encased in earphones. Foster and Katie Manchester were conducting with their hands, but curiously, he noted, to a different beat.

This is a madhouse!

He sat beside Jackie on the couch. She looked at him, giggled, placed her headset on his lap.

"I owe you an apology," he whispered. "I guess I drank too much."

"It's OK, Mr. Lake. I thought you were kind of cute."

"Shhh," he begged her, but she giggled again.

"Don't worry. We can talk. None of them can hear us. They're into Bach."

"You're not angry—"

"Oh, no." She smiled. "I like impulsive men."

"Jackie—"

"Look at him." She gestured toward Foster, now conducting along with Ashton Codd. "Oooo, what a jerk. In bed he's a stick. I wish *he* knew how to kiss."

"I thought you two were so—"

She slid her hand along his thigh. "I often ask myself why I ever married Foster. We both like sports. We were both on the track team at college. Tell me, Mr. Lake—do you really think that's enough?"

He looked at her, saw a sulky discontent. "I suppose not," he mumbled, edging away.

Suddenly she pushed her mouth against his ear. "After you and Janet leave, drop her at the Consulate and double back. Park at the traffic circle at the end of the street. After everyone's gone I'll tell Foster I'm going out for a jog. Then I'll meet you, and we'll talk."

Even as he nodded he knew he was making a mistake. But something about her, something aroused and voracious, had suddenly jerked his lust. She wiggled her nose and patted his knee. He stood up, went around to Janet, and motioned that it was time to go.

Janet ripped off her earphones. "I thought you'd never ask."

"Sorry to break things up, Foster. But we've got to be getting back."

The others rapidly stripped off their headsets, grateful for the chance to get away.

"But—but it's not over yet." Foster pointed at the turntable.

Now they were all on their feet. "Good-by." "Good night." "Thanks."

"But there's more—the whole second side."

They were all tearing toward the door.

Driving back to the Consulate, Lake banged his fist against the wheel. "What an evening! Glad to be out of there." He glanced at Janet. "Have you ever felt so trapped?"

"Gosh, you're critical, Dan. I thought you liked Willard and Katie at least."

"Not anymore I don't. I'm sick of them. All that crap about Fort Lauderdale—you'd think it's Eden over there."

Janet sighed. "Sometimes I just don't understand you, Dan."

Well, that was something—he didn't understand himself.

He dropped her at the residence gate, told her not to wait up. He was going to his office to plow through a stack of paperwork. She left him without looking back.

He pulled around to the side of the building, waited until their bedroom light went on. Then he drove slowly through town to kill some time before his rendezvous with Jackie Knowles. It was only a little after eleven, but the Boulevard was empty, just a few straggling tourists in the cafes. He knew the action at this hour was down in the medina, but he felt depressed by the emptiness, the flashing neon, the Arabic banners he couldn't read. One of their damn holidays again, he thought. There was always something going on— King's birthday, anniversary of his coronation, Arab Unity Week. He turned left and drove along the beach, listening for the faint music of bellydancer bands playing in the nightclubs of the big hotels.

Back in the suburbs he slowed as he passed the Knowles', then drove on to the traffic circle and parked. He turned off his headlights and lit a cigarette. There was no one about.

It was another twenty minutes before she appeared, jogging around the corner at a rapid pace, the white stripe of her sweatsuit flashing light from the dim street lamps. She loped around the circle, waved at him as she passed, then raised three fingers and started around again—meaning, he supposed, that she was going to run the circle thrice.

He watched, becoming dizzy as he followed her with his eyes. On her third pass she suddenly stopped, then leaped beside him into the car.

"Hi!" She smiled, leaned forward, planted a long, wet kiss on his lips. Her forehead was sweaty and so was the rest of her—he could feel the moistness as they embraced.

"Can I call you Dan, Mr. Lake?"

"Sure, Jackie. Sure."

"Well, *Dan—*"

She reached for his tie, loosened it, unbuttoned his shirt at the neck. Then with a single stroke she unzipped the front of her sweatshirt. Her breasts popped out. She was naked underneath.

"I'm horny, Dan. It's not healthy to keep urges bottled up."

She placed her hand on his crotch. He couldn't believe it. She started fumbling with his fly.

"Jackie—"

"Shhh!"

"Jackie!"

"Don't talk, Dan. We've only got a few minutes. Foster will

worry if I'm gone too long." She kissed him again, struggling with his zipper. "I want you, Dan. I want you inside of me. But not tonight. It's really impossible to ball in a car." She got the zipper open then and started to fondle him through his shorts. "Drop them, Dan. I want to suck."

She mopped her forehead on her sleeve, then lay her head across his lap. She was sucking him, humming while she did it, the vibrations of her clinging lips bringing him alive.

He felt frightened at first, then hopelessly aroused, the object of fellatio in a diplomatic car. It was crazy the way she lay across him like a vixen, body contorted, straw hair strewn across his lap. But suddenly he was delighted by the danger, and slipped down in his seat. He forced her head against the steering post, and with terrifying spasms shot off in her mouth.

The whole thing had taken less than a minute. When he opened his eyes he saw her making obscene swallowing motions with her throat.

"God! What if someone saw?"

"Never mind, Dan. It's over now."

She sat up and cupped her breasts. There was a radiant, triumphant expression on her face. He reached for her, but she pulled back.

"No, Dan. Not now. Next time you'll have *me*. I'll call you tomorrow as soon as Foster leaves for work."

She zipped up her sweatshirt and backed out of the car. From outside she blew him a kiss, then jogged around the circle and disappeared. He sat alone then, his limp cock oozing onto the plastic seat.

What, my God, have I done?

For a while he drove around the city, losing all track of time. He drove the Boulevard again, and Avenue d'Espagne, then turned and twisted through the maze of narrow streets that ran between the Grand Socco and the beach. He drove up through the old Jewish quarter and into the Casbah, madly honking his horn. He passed beneath the arches, the narrow street along the walls, until he arrived at the Place de Casbah and pulled to a screeching halt.

He looked about. The great square was deserted. He got out, walked to the battlements, stared down the cliffs at the moonlit bay.

What's happening?

He knew now he'd never get to sleep. His head was on fire, though he was sure he was no longer drunk. The encounter with Jackie had taken care of that, and now he felt caught up by something, some passionate force that had seized hold, and to which he'd relinquished all control.

Am I going to snap? Is this the night I'm going to break?

He didn't think so. Despite all that had happened he felt a new, clear vision taking hold. He was a man of the night, a man who acted while others slept. There was a destiny for him in Tangier. Z! Z was the quarry, the man he must begin to hunt.

In Dradeb there were still people in the streets, but he felt no fear of them as he drove through. He'd heard much lately of their vicious taunts and flying rocks, but tonight he felt invincible, the master of Tangier.

After he crossed the Jew's River he slowed down, searching for Zvegintzov's car. He saw it, a rusting old Peugeot. He parked behind it and looked about. The shop was closed. The grill was down, but he could see light coming from a window off the side. He'd never been in there, the room behind the store. He knew it was where Peter slept.

He locked the car, crossed the street, then moved carefully, pressing against the side of Zvegintzov's house. There was a window ahead that cast out light. He stooped beneath it, rose slowly, and peered in through the glass.

He saw Peter then, sitting on his bed not a dozen feet away. He was talking—Lake could hear the sound, though he couldn't make out a single word. He ducked, fearing he might be seen, then realized he was in darkness, invisible to those inside. He backed off a bit, then rose again. He had to see who else was there.

It was the girl, the one living with Ouazzani, Kalinka, Zvegintzov's wife. She was standing, facing Z, at the opposite end of the room, the two of them in profile, faces illuminated by a frayed old lamp. They seemed excited—he could see that in their gestures. Listening carefully, he realized they were speaking Vietnamese.

Suddenly he felt powerful, full of the power that comes to those who spy on others unseen. People said this woman never saw Z anymore. What luck to catch them together, and, too, it fit in with his theory that she was Peter's link with the police. He recalled his encounter with Ouazzani the other evening, coming upon him in the shop, finding Peter in the midst of tears. Later, outside, he'd aroused the Inspector's anger by asking him about his girl. Clever, the way he'd drawn that anger out. Now he wondered who was controlling whom. Blackmail, perhaps, with Ouazzani pulling the strings. Or did Peter have the Inspector in his grip? He didn't know. It was all too complicated; he hadn't sufficient information yet. Now he only wished he had a Minox—one of those miniaturized spy jobs with a superfast lens. He'd snap a picture of the girl and Z, post it anonymously to the police. What would the Inspector do? How would his superiors react?

As he stared at them, however, he became aware of something else. There was something going on in the room, something desperate. He could sense it in their tones as they mouthed their tortured words. Were they arguing? Z seemed tense, and the girl, standing before him, so straight, tiny, thin before his hulk, she, he could tell, was the cause. Was Z sobbing? Lake wasn't sure. Yet her sounds, high-pitched Oriental chirps that cut to him through the glass, were answered by Peter's heavy moans that made the window rumble beneath his palm. Lake was fascinated. All his senses sprang alert. A drama was being played which he, a secret observer, shared.

None of this fit with his image of Zvegintzov the ruthless agent. There the Russian sat, slumped upon his bed, lines in his face gouged deep, wiping at his eyes.

Silence. The confrontation was at an end. The girl stared at Z, who returned her gaze, then dropped his head upon his chest. What had they been saying? What dark Oriental exchange? Lake felt bewildered standing outside, accidental witness to some inexplicable event.

There was movement then. Peter stood as she moved toward the door. It let out, Lake realized, onto the other side of the house. He could hear an exchange, most probably their good-bys, saw the girl disappear, then watched as Z stood alone staring at the floor.

A moment later he heard the ignition of a motorbike. He

darted back to the street just in time to see the girl ride away. He ran to his car, drove rapidly, was halfway through Dradeb before he saw her scooter again. He slowed, dimmed his headlights, followed her to an old building where the Marshan Road intersected with Ramon y Cahal. He waited, watched, saw her enter the elevator from the street. She'd pushed a minute-long night light when she'd gone in, and now it illuminated a cagelike shaft. He watched as she rose slowly out of sight. No choice now. He knew he must follow her up.

Again he carefully locked his car. Inside he peered up the shaft. The elevator was poised at the top. He looked at the lobby mailboxes, saw the name "Ouazzani" beside a number on the penthouse floor. He paused a moment, deciding what to do. There was risk, he knew, in going further, but he felt he had to take the chance. He called the elevator back, stepped inside, pushed the button, held his breath.

He was horrified by the sound. This was not a machine like the sleek, silent elevator in the Consulate. This was a noisy old thing of winding cables and grinding gears. At the top floor he waited until the night light went off, then stepped into the hall. There were two apartments, one at either end. He crept to the one on the right, lit a match, read the Inspector's name off the door.

He pressed his ear against the wood and strained. He heard faint conversation inside, muffled by the walls. He could tell from the cadence they were talking French.

Thank God! Something I can understand.

He had to know what they were saying in there—all his plans for Z would depend on that. He looked around, saw some stairs near the elevator. He mounted them, came to a door, lit another match, saw an unlocked bolt. Grateful for his luck, he pulled it open, then stepped boldly out upon the roof.

Here, at least, he could see—there was light from the moon, and the city's glow around. He spotted his car parked inconspicuously across the street. The lamps that lined the Mountain Road burned sulfurous in the night.

He paused then, looked about, and felt again that he was master of Tangier. It was spread before him, this city of white geometric buildings, asleep but seething with energy, a quarter million Arabs and twenty thousand Europeans locked in an eternal brawl.

He paced the roof to its edge above Ouazzani's flat. Peering down, he saw a terrace, dimly lit by lamps inside. If only he could get down there, but there were curved, pointed iron rods protruding from the walls—protection against cat burglars like himself, he thought, and rabid dogs and rats. He'd have to climb over the spikes, then lower himself with care. There was a cornice he could cling to, and a protruding decorative ledge beneath. Yes, if he could get himself over the prongs, he might be able to climb down. But he would have to be careful—those iron points could rip apart his flesh.

He walked to the corner of the building, found the prongs more widely spaced. With his mind clear, knowing that once he descended he would be irretrievably compromised if caught, he grabbed hold of two of the hooks, tested their strength, and swung his legs between.

A moment later he was hanging for his life, his body supported only by his hands, which gripped the spokes, while he thrashed with his feet for a towhold on the ledge. He found it finally, and just in time, for his strength was quickly giving out. He paused, clinging to the side of the building, trying to control his panting and to rest.

He wasn't in shape for a caper like this. Too bad he hadn't spent his mornings jogging with the Knowles'. The mere six-flight climb to their penthouse had worn him out; now he was hanging over the side of a building eight stories above the street. A gentle wind blew across him from the Straits. It cooled his perspiration, and frightened him too, for he knew how the winds of Tangier could gather in a moment to a gale.

To regain his courage he thought back to Jackie Knowles, her mass of straw hair upon his lap, her tongue on his genitals wagging like a fox's licking salt.

He stared down. It was a five-foot drop to the terrace. Fortunately the windows were over to the side. There were potted plants down there, and laundry too. He must jump clear of them, land without a sound. He looked again, found his spot, carefully calculated the distance, pushed himself away, and dropped. He landed deftly, on the balls of his feet, dropped to a crouch and froze. A moment later he exhaled. Nobody had heard him; nobody was looking out.

I've done it!

Now he could hear them talk. The glass terrace doors were open. They were sitting in the salon just a few feet away. He didn't dare look in at them but moved stealthily behind the laundry. He realized, suddenly, that he didn't even know if they owned a dog.

He strained to listen, translate what they said. Their talk was full of pauses, and there were many words he missed.

"—don't understand. *Why?*"

"It's been so long—"

"Forever then?"

"—things he said. You can't imagine—"

"I want to read—"

"—don't have it anymore—"

"*What?*"

"Burned it."

"—"

"I knew you'd want to read—"

"—my right."

"It was between us."

"The three of us."

"—Hamid!"

A pause then. Perhaps the Inspector was standing up.

"You compromise yourself. And me."

"—so frightened, so empty, Hamid. The shop is all he has."

"—taunting me. He was going to tell me something. Then this American came in."

"If you could have seen—"

"—secrets!"

"I don't remember. Can't!"

Another silence. Lake craned his head. They were walking around, he guessed, or had turned from the window. He lost their thread, then caught it again.

"—going to talk to him again. I can make him leave—close him up—"

"What good—"

"Don't you see, Kalinka? I *have* to know!"

It all stopped then, as if they'd suddenly left the room. Their bedroom probably—if they'd gone in there he'd not hear anymore. What were they talking about? A letter, a document, something she'd destroyed. They'd been arguing about Z—no doubt of that. But he thought Ouazzani had sounded less angry than he should. Patience, gentleness—these qualities surprised him. The Inspector's voice didn't match the tone of a man who felt himself deceived.

Lake crawled closer to the glass door, but there was no more to be heard. They must have closed themselves in their bedroom. Now he'd never know what all of it had meant.

He looked up. He had to get out. But an instant later he felt despair. *How? It was impossible.* He'd never get back on the roof. There was nothing to hold on to. The ledges and cornice he'd used protruded out, and he didn't have the strength to hoist himself up. Now he was stuck. He'd gone to all this trouble, taken all these risks, learned little, understood less, and now he was going to be caught.

God, I've been a fool.

An hour later he was racing down the apartment stairs, taking the steps two at a time. He'd done a dangerous thing, taken the ultimate risk, and by some miracle, part of the chain of luck that had supported him all night, he was out of danger, free and safe. He'd waited on the terrace for an hour until he was sure the Ouazzanis were asleep. Then while his heart pumped thunderously he'd simply walked into their apartment, across their salon, opened their front door, and slipped out through the hall. It was the only way, and he'd taken it. In the lobby he stopped to gasp.

His hands were still shaking when he arrived at the Consulate, opened the garage, parked the car. In his bathroom in the residence he studied himself in the mirror, his eyes, bulging and red, the filth on his hands and suit. He stripped and stepped into the shower, ran the water hot. Then, ravenously hungry, he went to the kitchen and scrambled eggs.

Slipping into bed beside Janet, he thought of Jackie Knowles. In the morning she would call him. What would he say to her? Where would all that lead?

He knew he'd never lived before with such intensity, acquiring a mistress, spying on a spy, detecting a detective, all in the space of a few short hours. Now the possibilities were unlimited. There was nothing he couldn't do. He'd been master of the city. Tangier had whimpered at his feet.

The Raid

Often in the mornings on his way to work Hamid would drive about Tangier, moving slowly down narrow streets into obscure quarters of the town. He was not sure why he did this, since it delayed his arrival at the Sûreté, but he supposed he was searching for coherence in this complicated, shimmering city that he loved.

One morning at the beginning of the summer he parked on Esperanza Orellana in front of a carpentry shop. This spot delighted him. He liked the smell of cedar shavings that filled his car, the buzz of the saws in the background as they bit into wood. Sitting here, he thought back to the difficult night before, the row he'd had with Kalinka. He'd come home late, found her out of the house, and later, when she'd returned, she'd confessed she'd been with Zvegintzov at La Colombe.

Peter had summoned her with a long, imploring letter, she'd said, and she'd felt she'd no choice but to go to him and talk. She'd found him pathetic, friendless and alone, afraid that Hamid was out to drive him from Tangier. Peter had begged her not to say anything, to keep secret all she knew, and to persuade Hamid to stay away and leave the past alone.

How could she deny him that, she'd asked. She was filled with pity for this man she believed they'd both destroyed.

Hamid was moved, but then, when he'd asked her to produce the letter so that he too could measure the Russian's despair, she'd replied she'd burned it to spare Zvegintzov his shame. They'd argued then. Hamid had tried to make her understand. She'd said that only the future mattered, and that she didn't care about the past. Later, when they'd gone to bed, he'd lain awake for hours trying to reason his feelings out. He knew she hadn't deceived him, but there was something she shared with Zvegintzov that she still refused to reveal. What was it? What strange things had they discussed in their sing-song tongue? Why did she want to protect him? *Why?*

Tormented as he lay in bed, he'd thought for a moment that there was someone in the other room. An intruder, perhaps Peter, prowling, waiting to stab him in his sleep. He'd felt ridiculous but still he'd gotten up, and of course he'd found no one there.

It was then, the following morning, sitting in his car in front of the carpentry shop, that he began to notice certain strange goings-on at the entrance of the Hotel Américain. This dingy pension a few doors down the street specialized in impecunious tourists who could not afford a room on Avenue d'Espagne. What struck Hamid, and suddenly caught his interest, was a group of European males huddling in the doorway with Moroccan boys.

No question of what was happening—the men were slipping money to the boys, who then ran off gaily toward the beach. Payoffs, no doubt, for business transacted in the night. Hamid watched, incredulous, then drove down to the Grand Socco, where he parked in an area reserved for the police. He strode into the medina, into the lobby of the Oriental Hotel, and mounted the steps to Robin's room.

He flung open the door. "Get up!" he yelled, yanking off Robin's sheets. "On your feet, you bastard! Put on your clothes!"

He paused then. He was too angry. He needed time to regain control. "I'll wait for you in the Centrale," he said. "Get your ass down there! You've got things to explain."

A few minutes later Robin appeared in the Socco Chico, picking at the corners of his eyes. "Christ, Hamid—what have I done?"

"You've betrayed me. Sit down and talk."

Robin squinted, shook his head.

"Don't play dumb," said Hamid. "I'm in a lousy mood."

"I see that. What's wrong?"

"The Hotel Américain—that's what's wrong. You're supposed to keep me informed about places like that."

"I didn't know, I swear." He spoke too quickly. Hamid could always tell when Robin lied.

"Don't pretend," he said. "You know the place is swimming in queers."

"OK, Hamid. Stop shouting, please. You shut down one and another opens up."

"I'm talking about our arrangement, Robin. Your job is to tell me about these places. Mine is to keep them from getting out of hand."

"Oh, come on. Is that the real nature of our relationship? Wait! Don't answer!" Robin shook his head. "Look," he said, "people come to Tangier in the summer, they come down here to get laid. They want boys, boys who offer themselves, you understand—because they surely aren't seduced. All right, they need a place to find them. If you close the Américain, it'll just be someplace else."

"You still don't understand."

"What?"

"That I've been relying on you, and you've been holding back."

"Oh, for Christ's sake, Hamid. An informer has to save things up, keep the policeman's interest. It's in the nature of my work as your devoted snitch that I feed you information in little bits. That way you like me better, and I get to see you every week. Honestly, Hamid—I was going to deliver on this. Maybe even today."

"You make me sick."

"You're not angry any more?"

"Thank Allah, you bastard. Now start talking. I want it all."

"Here? In public? Just being seen with you is bad enough."

"Embarrassed? Good. I don't care—it serves you right."

Robin ordered coffee and then began to talk, rubbing every so often at his crusted eyes and unshaven cheeks. "Gottshalk owns the place. Not the building—*les fonds de commerce*. You know him—he wears dark specs and a ratty djellaba like a cape. He's an American, been here for years. He's got an 'arrangement' with the American Consulate. I thought you knew about that."

"I try *not* to remember the details about every seedy foreigner in town. What 'arrangement'? Damn it, Robin, don't spin out a tale."

"Well, Gottshalk's got this deal with the Consulate that when they have an American who's lost his passport or who's out of money and waiting for funds, they stash him temporarily in his hotel. Gottshalk lodges him, feeds him on credit, and doesn't bother to register him with the police. He gets reimbursed, of course, and a service fee besides. For this the Americans think he's great. He's very close over there to Lake and Knowles, which gives him status, because otherwise he's just a bum. Anyway, he's had hot and cold running boys for a while—"

"How long?"

"I don't know."

"Years?"

"A season or two. It's known now in London and Amsterdam. When the queens come down here they know where they can go."

"Disgusting! What's he like?"

"A bastard. Hard as nails. Charges too much and rakes it in from the boys. If they don't kick back seventy-five percent he's got a couple of goons who mess them up. But he guarantees them a place to sleep, and for a lot of boys that's good enough. It would be a pity if you closed him down, Hamid. Put a lot of kids out of work."

"Do you really care?"

"Well, I'm human."

"Yes, Robin, I suppose you are." Hamid pushed back his chair. "Not a word of this," he said. "I'm going to move on Gottshalk. I'll know who to blame if he's been warned."

As he walked back to his car, he allowed his anger to seep

away. *Robin's just an informer,* he thought. *How much can I expect?* But he knew perfectly well that Robin was more than that—that over the years he'd become a friend.

He found Aziz waiting in his office, a glass of tea in hand. Hamid looked over the reports that had piled up through the night, then announced that they were going to raid the Hotel Américain. Aziz was delighted, and seeing his pleasure Hamid explained what he had in mind. They'd mount the kind of operation he'd seen in European films—flawless, cool, sleek.

"Midnight," he said, "we'll move in. Empty the place, every room, every closet, every bed. Anyone who isn't registered we'll bring here and interrogate. Photograph them, finger-print them, warn them, and let them go. Same with the Moroccan boys—no point in holding them. What I want is a case against Gottshalk, enough to kick him out. After we close down his bordello we'll start a cleanup along the beach."

"Magnificent, Hamid. But why have we waited so long?"

"I don't know. Lethargy, I suppose. Now it pains me the way Tangier's turning into a dump. Every June the beach becomes a meat rack. We must change it back into a place to take a swim."

He spent the morning with the state prosecutor discussing pending cases, plowing through dossiers. When, finally, he returned to his office, he found a message from Farid.

The bazaar was closed when he arrived, so he parked and walked up the Boulevard looking for his brother in each of the cafes. He found him at Claridge reading a newspaper, eating lunch.

"Ah, here you are." He slid into a chair.

"I knew you'd find me, Hamid. How are you today?"

"Terrible. I've got too many cases. It's summer, and the town's gone mad."

He ordered swordfish. After the waiter left Farid put his newspaper down.

"I found the book you wanted."

"Good. Thanks."

"At the French library. They have a shelf on Indochina there. This one, about colonial Hanoi, was covered by half an inch of dust."

"Did you look at it?"

"Yes. After I cleaned it up. It's interesting, Hamid. I was quite surprised. Hanoi was something like Tangier."

"That is interesting. Tell me more."

"Well, it was an odd sort of place, like a provincial French town, but cosmopolitan too. Lots of nationalities like here—Indians, Chinese, Russians, French. And of course the natives, our equivalents—the Vietnamese, the Tonkinois."

Hamid smiled.

"A foreign quarter. Big villas. French doctors, lawyers, churches, lycées. Even a tennis club in the middle of town, and then antique shops like mine, and little shops selling native wares. Buddhist temples too—the equivalent of our mosques, at least as far as the French could see. It's very interesting. I left it at the shop. I'll give it to you after lunch." He paused. "Tell me, Hamid, why are you interested in such a book?"

"Kalinka, of course."

"I guessed that."

"I want to know everything about her. And about all the places that she's lived."

"She's telling you things now?"

Hamid nodded. "Last night, however, we hit a snag. She went to see the Russian. He told her not to tell me any more. He's afraid I'm after him, building up a case to kick him out. She knows that isn't true, but now she's hesitant to go on."

"Why's he afraid?"

"That's what I want to know. It's very curious, Farid—it seems our little Peter was once something of a spy."

His swordfish came and as he ate it he began to describe to Farid the Russian community of Hanoi. And then the childhood of Peter Zvegintzov, the only son of a middle-class Russian couple, brought up in a little room behind their shop.

"There were all these children of different nationalities," he said, "so Peter learned lots of languages early on. There was also another Russian boy approximately the same age named Stephen Zhukovsky. He and Peter became best friends.

"As I reconstruct things, they grew up together in the 1920s and 1930s just about the time the first Communists began to surface in Hanoi. There were Russians, Soviet agents, sent down to set up networks in Indochina. Possibly it was one of these who recruited Peter and Stephen at the Hanoi lycée. Anyway, Kalinka says Peter always was a Communist, not, probably, out of deep conviction but to be different, to stand out. It's easy to imagine him thinking of his recruitment as a game. Secret meetings, a cell, fun with his best friend. But then, in 1940, with the fall of France, the Indochinese administration sided with Vichy, and the Japanese arrived.

"The Vietnamese Communists, directed from China by Ho Chi Minh, decided to side with the Allies. Peter and Stephen received their orders—to link up with the Viet Minh. Now here the politics become a little murky, but I don't think it's important to follow all the twists and turns. Just think of Peter, eighteen then, already stout, wearing spectacles, full of energy, eager, and alive, embarking with his friend Stephen Zhukovsky upon a dangerous double life.

"They were drafted, both of them, into the Vichy army, where they snooped around, collected information, then passed it along to the Viet Minh. It was dangerous work, of course, but to them still something of a game. It was a while before they realized how serious it was."

Hamid finished eating, paid his and Farid's bills. Then they walked out onto the Boulevard to Farid's shop to retrieve the book. After that they turned down Rue Marco Polo, crossed the tracks that ran parallel to Avenue d'Espagne, and walked onto the beach. Hamid talked the whole way, stopping every so often to make a point. Farid listened, fascinated, head bowed, eyes always on the sand.

"Here," said Hamid, "a Vietnamese lady enters the scene, a great beauty, the contact agent for Peter and Stephen's cell. They both fall in love with her—madly in love. She is so attractive, even a seductress, and like Kalinka, I imagine, mysterious and subtle, the sort of woman who can break your heart. Her name was Pham Thi Nha, but the boys both called her Marguerite. Both of them courted her. They could speak to each other of nothing else. They were best friends and rivals too. A friendly triangle was formed.

"Stephen Zhukovsky was the one, finally, chosen to be her

lover. Peter, accepting her decision, gracefully stepped aside. Meanwhile the spying went on. The boys collected intelligence, carried messages, even helped divert a shipment of Japanese arms to guerrillas waiting in the swamps. Lots of adventures, a few close calls, bonds of fraternity between them, and all that. Peter even got hold of a photo of De Gaulle and put it with the one of Stalin he kept hidden in his boot. He still has it, Kalinka says—somewhere among his papers in the back room of La Colombe. Anyway, in 1943 Marguerite and Stephen Zhukovsky had a child. They named her Pham Thi Phoung. Peter, her godfather, suggested 'Kalinka' as her European name."

Hamid stopped. Farid glanced up.

"Go on," he said. "Go on. Go on!"

"Well, here I must rely upon research—Kalinka has no sense of politics, of course. Toward the end of the war Indochina went into turmoil. It had been run by the Vichy French, but in March of 1945 the Japanese turned suddenly against them. Perhaps because they knew they were going to lose the war, maybe because they hated people who were white—whatever the reason, they disbanded the Vichy army, and then their police started making mass arrests. It was terrible. Every Frenchman in the Langson garrison was beheaded with a ritual sword. Some of the French units made a dash for the Chinese frontier, hoping to find sanctuary with Chiang Kai-shek. Stephen and Peter managed to escape, leaving Marguerite and the baby behind. They hid out in the jungle for a while, then tried to come back. They were caught on the outskirts of Hanoi, arrested by the Japanese.

"They were tortured, both of them, hideously tortured in the summer of 1945. Peter was wounded in such a way that he would be impotent the remainder of his life. Stephen Zhukovsky was not so fortunate. He was tortured to death.

"On August 6 the Americans bombed Hiroshima. On August 16 the Japanese released all their prisoners in the colony. On August 17 Peter Zvegintzov, twenty-three years old, ruined in his manhood, wandered the rain-swept streets of Hanoi. His parents had been killed. Their shop was boarded up. Marguerite and the child had disappeared. Stephen Zhukovsky was dead. Dazed and afraid, he watched mobs of exultant Vietnamese rally before the Municipal Theater. From a staff on its main balcony the Communist party flag was finally raised.

"That's all I have so far, but you see the sort of background that's involved. It'll all come out, little by little. She'll tell it to me if Peter hasn't persuaded her to stop. He's hiding something, you see—perhaps something Kalinka doesn't know herself."

"But what, Hamid?"

He shrugged. "There've always been rumors about Peter, that he was a Communist, even some sort of Soviet spy. I heard them years ago but never found anything to back them up. But now I wonder. How did he end up here? When you mentioned that Hanoi was something like Tangier—well, I got an interesting idea."

They walked together in silence for a time, among people lying in bathing garments in the sun, children running this way and that, Europeans lounging on the terraces of the bathing clubs. They passed the Shepherd's Pie, the Packwoods' little restaurant. Hamid saw Joe Kelly sitting shirtless there, drinking, surrounded by a coterie.

"Hello, Farid!"

It was the hustler Pumpkin Pie in a tight bikini bathing suit, strutting on the sand. Hamid noticed he gave a certain sort of smile as he walked by, and that Farid responded with a signal of his own.

"You know that trash?"

Farid nodded uncomfortably, and Hamid immediately regretted what he'd said. They always avoided the subject of homosexuality, though Farid knew it was part of Hamid's job to rid the city of its reputation as a gay resort.

"Well, I must get back, Hamid. Time now to reopen my store."

They embraced, then Farid walked away. Hamid watched until he'd crossed the tracks.

He enjoyed the minutes just before midnight, sitting in his car up the street from Gottshalk's hotel. There was something almost sensuous about the wait—the prospect of action, the tension building up.

⟨ 199 ⟩

Then it all happened, precisely as he'd planned: a hushed, whirring siren; police whistles strangely soft; commands in Arabic; muffled screams; the thud of shoulders against wooden doors with feeble locks.

His men, moving with sleek precision, gracefully sprung his trap. Everyone in the hotel was caught by surprise. Soon the lobby was filled with frightened guests. Some of the Moroccan boys tried to escape across the roof, but Hamid had people posted there who snatched them as they fled. Others, wriggling under beds, were pulled out squirming by their heels. Men who were arrested nude or who'd left their passports in their rooms were politely escorted back upstairs. Aziz paired off those he'd found together, then, calling off their names, tried to match them to the registration list.

Hamid wandered about the lobby, pleased by the size of his catch and the cool, understated way the raid had been carried out. The night clerk was shaking, and Gottshalk, in his tattered djellaba, stood helpless, wrists cuffed behind his back. Hamid circled him in wonder. This disgusting man worked with the Americans; he was received by Lake and Knowles.

When Aziz had everybody sorted out, he motioned Hamid aside.

"About a dozen," he said, "caught with underage boys. And one Dutchman in bed with a girl who doesn't appear to be his wife."

Aziz blew a whistle then, and when the lobby became silent Hamid stood up on a chair. He looked around at the faces staring up at him. *I know these men,* he thought, *have seen them every summer of my life.* Rigid stances, sharp eyes, a certain anguished preying look, pursed lips, beckoning smiles—suddenly he thought of Farid. They were frightened, he could see, and flawed. For a moment he was touched. He certainly didn't hate them, but he disliked the corruption of their lust.

"Good evening," he said in French. "My name is Ouazzani. I'm chief inspector of the foreign section of the Tangier police. There have been grave violations of registration laws in this hotel, and violations of our vice laws too. Those of you who are improperly registered, or who were discovered in bed with underage Moroccan youths, will be taken now to head-quarters in our bus. There you'll be interrogated, and your consular representatives will be called if you wish. The rest of you may return to your rooms. We apologize for disturbing you and wish you a pleasant sleep. We ask, however, that you leave in the morning and seek other accommodations in town. The manager of this hotel is under arrest. Tomorrow, at noon, this building will be closed."

He repeated his announcement in English, then stepped down from the chair. Aziz released the guests entitled to return to sleep, and led the rest outside.

Hamid followed them to the Sûreté, watched them herded into a communal cell. A team of interrogators began work. Fingerprints were taken and photographs were made. It was a madhouse, the Moroccan prisoners gaping at the new-comers, the boys getting a stern lecture from Aziz.

Hamid stopped at the police canteen, drank a cup of coffee, telephoned Kalinka, told her he'd soon be home. Back up-stairs, from the corridor outside his office, he looked in at Gottshalk manacled to a chair.

"Mr. Gottshalk," he said, briskly walking in, "with you I have an airtight case. There're six or seven boys downstairs swearing out depositions right now. They say you corrupted their morals, turned them into prostitutes, and forced them to perform unnatural acts for money paid to you by foreign guests." He paced around Gottshalk, speaking calmly, paus-ing now and then to emphasize a word. "No question what's going to happen—you'll do ten years at least. What shall we do for you? Call a lawyer? Get hold of Vice-Consul Knowles? Get you pen and paper so you can write out your confession? Find you a knife so you can slit your throat?"

Gottshalk's face was twitching. His bald spot was pumping sweat.

"Inspector—could I please speak to you alone?"

"You want me to dismiss the guards?"

Gottshalk nodded.

Hamid smiled. "No bribes, my friend. Save your breath. You're finished here. The only question is whether we send you to prison or put you on a plane and ship you out."

A glimmer of hope appeared in Gottshalk's frightened eyes.

"I might expel you," said Hamid. "Permanently. Tomorrow. With all your assets frozen here. To make an example of you. To let everyone know there's no profit anymore in running a boys' hotel. Give me a complete confession, submit in writing to a confiscation of everything you own, and tomorrow you'll be put on the early plane for Madrid. Otherwise—ten years."

"You don't give me much choice."

"I give you more than you deserve."

Gottshalk looked at him in sorrow and despair.

"Quick," said Hamid, "make up your mind."

He felt quite pleased a quarter hour later as he drove home through the night streets. At last, he thought, he'd begun to act. He'd rid the town of one of its least attractive residents, and now he wondered how much longer it would take him to finally clean it out.

Kalinka was waiting up. She'd been sketching. The table where they ate was covered with drawings and pastels. He told her what he'd done, his management of the raid.

"Oh, Hamid," she said. "I had no idea you had that kind of power."

She was silent then, and he thought: *She's thinking of Peter, wondering whether I might do the same to him.*

"You wouldn't do that to Peter," she said. "I knew he was wrong when he said you would."

She was amazing, could read his mind, just as he was learning to read hers. He moved beside her, placed an arm around her shoulder, hugged her, kissed her face, her hair.

She began to talk then, after a little while, of her memories of Poland, showing him her drawings, her words pouring out. There was a school. She'd sketched it. Hamid looked at her pictures, then closed his eyes. Gray buildings. A gravel playground surrounded by a fringe of badly tended grass. Kind teachers. A long, narrow attic dormitory room. Bare lightbulbs. A row of beds. When it rained she lay awake listening to the raindrops on the roof.

Singing—he saw her in an assembly hall, her eyes fixed on foreign flags. It was a school for orphans, sons and daughters of martyred revolutionaries. Many Asian faces, Koreans and

Vietnamese. They were stirred, all of them, by the verses of the Internationale.

Gym class—he could see the children dressed in matching tunics doing calisthenics in time to a revolutionary march. Outside it is cold and gray. Snow piled on the ground. The gurgling of old steam radiators in the gym. A sour smell. Ropes to climb. A horse to vault.

Peter comes on Sundays muffled in a heavy woolen coat. He works at a factory in Warsaw. It takes him hours to reach the school. Sometimes he is gay and brings her gifts—a piece of chocolate, a ball, a doll. Other times he's sad, and she thinks he'll weep. But he doesn't. He can only stay an hour. The bus trip back, he tells her, is long and dark.

Two years pass. Hamid sees Kalinka sitting in her classes, exercising in the gym, lying with eyes open in her bed while the other girls sleep. Leaves fall. The winters are cold. She wears mittens and a little woolen cap that covers up her ears. The girls help one another, cut one another's hair. She has friends, but she can no longer remember their names. Nor her teachers. Nor what they taught.

She works with clay, makes pottery. She glazes her little bowls and is pleased by how well they look. She withdraws into herself. Her character becomes oddly formed. The traits Hamid knows so well, her dreaminess, her detachment— they take over as she sits alone for hours, sketching or staring into space. When the teachers talk of politics she falls asleep. There are pictures of Marx and Lenin in every room. Sometimes when the others sing she stands with them and mouths the words. Her teachers become concerned. They regard her as troubled and strange. They try to draw her out. They discuss her in an office while she sits alone on a hard bench outside.

One day some men come—Vietnamese. They speak gently to all the Vietnamese children, tell them a great victory has been won. Soon, they say, you will go back to your country. The children smile. Kalinka feels glad. But she doesn't really understand.

Peter tells her her mother is dead, that she died a great heroine at Dien Bien Phu. "Now," he says, "it's just the two of us alone. There are people who want to send you back to

Vietnam, but I want you to stay with me." He kisses her, whispers to her. She nods to show him she is reassured.

Peter comes to say good-by. There is snow outside. He is bundled in his black wool coat. He kisses her, tells her they'll be reunited soon, that they'll live together in a place where the air is always warm. Then he is gone and her life becomes vague, a long, uninterrupted dream. Seasons change. She receives letters. Peter writes that he is well. When she writes back she must give her letters to authorities at the school. They mail them for her. She does not know where Peter lives.

Leaves fall. Winter comes. Then summer, and autumn, and winter, and around again. One day they bring her a suitcase, tell her to pack her clothes. They give her papers, a passport. She rides an airplane to Paris. Someone meets her, puts her on another plane. When it lands Peter is waiting, ready to carry her in his arms.

That night, for the first time, she sleeps in the back room of La Colombe.

It was strange, her story, so very strange, and full, Hamid felt, of things she didn't say. Long after she fell asleep he lay awake thinking of Peter as a boy in colonial Hanoi, and Kalinka trudging through the snow between gray buildings at the Polish school. It seemed more real to him, all of that, than his raid on Gottshalk's hotel.

A week later he felt depressed. He'd been working long, hard hours in the city, resolving cases at a frightening speed. Frantic to clear up a backlog of dossiers, he'd begun to dispense justice with an iron hand. His staff was amazed. It wasn't like him to be so fierce. "Hamid is turning against the foreigners," he heard Aziz explain. "He has steeled himself against pity. He is cutting out the rot."

Was that true? He didn't know. He only wanted to reclaim Tangier. But the city was intractable. The harder he tried to reclaim it, the more deeply he felt himself engulfed. When he returned home in the evenings he listened to Kalinka, spieling out her story, snatching details here and there from the dreamy past. It was a strange existence for him, passing back and forth between two incoherent worlds. He felt a need to talk to someone decisive. He went to see Mohammed Achar.

They arranged to meet in the doctor's office behind the clinic late on a weekday night. Hamid passed through the usual squabbling water lines on his way up Rue de Chypre, through the odor of disinfectant that hung about the clinic like a fog. There was a nervous young man with Achar who was just leaving as he arrived—Driss Bennani, an architect who worked in city hall. Hamid knew him by sight, nodded to him. Bennani nodded back, then ran out.

"So, Hamid," said Achar after they embraced, "I hear you're cleaning up the beach."

"I thought you'd approve."

"I do, but still I'm surprised. My old easygoing friend, live-and-let-live Hamid, who's been so cozy with the foreigners all these years. Suddenly I hear he's getting tough. What's happened? Why the change?" The doctor poured out two glasses of herbal tea.

"I don't know," said Hamid. "The summers here make me sick."

"As well they should. But why has it taken you so long?"

Hamid shrugged. "Suddenly I detest the disorder of Tangier. I try to impose myself upon it but, of course, I fail. A funny thing, though—I'm beginning to enjoy my power. What do you think? Have I finally become corrupt?"

"Possibly. It happens to policemen. We're not living in a democracy, after all. But in your case I prefer a political explanation. I think you've become disgusted, as I've always been, by the antics of the foreigners here, and it's that disgust that's finally touched you viscerally and driven you into acting tough. I know you're not a political man, Hamid, but you take things very much to heart. You can't fail to be moved by injustice—full pools on the Mountain while our people swelter without water in Dradeb. For years I've heard people say you weren't affected by this. I always defended you. I always thought you felt it. And I always thought one day you'd make a good ally."

"Allied with whom? Is there a conspiracy going on?"

Achar smiled. "Let's not talk about conspiracies, unless we talk about the official ones being plotted in Rabat. Anyway, I wouldn't dream of trying to undermine your loyalty to the regime. But we're old friends. I'm watching your development. You're changing, Hamid, acquiring a will for order. One day you'll come to talk to me about the future, and not just the decadence of the beach."

"Actually I didn't come here to talk about that."

He described the intelligence report that an Israeli agent was coming to Tangier, his theory that he might be coming to kill a European, and Zvegintzov's tip about the Freys. "It's strange," he said. "There's a dilemma in all of this."

"I don't see one."

"Oh—of course there is. Here I have, perhaps, a perfectly fiendish pair—the Freys, Kurt and Inge Becker—people who don't deserve to stay alive. And on the other hand I have, perhaps, a killer, a man coming to murder them in Tangier. I can't sit back and allow someone to commit a crime, particularly a person who works for the secret service of an enemy state. But then who else will execute them? If the Israeli turns up, what am I to do?"

"To me, Hamid, there's no dilemma at all. Israelis and Nazis are all the same—they're foreigners. I'd say keep an eye on both of them and see who kills the other first. Then wrap up your case by killing the one who's left."

Hamid laughed. He knew Achar wasn't serious, but still his joke revealed coldness, the coldness of a surgeon who could become an executioner one day.

Achar refilled his glass. "You know," he said, "this is an exciting time to be alive in the Arab world."

"You really think so?"

"Oh, yes. There's a mood spreading, across Africa to the Persian Gulf. We Arabs, those of us who comprehend our destiny, must recognize that our revival is near at hand. Look at Europe and America, squirming before the oil cartel. It's coming for us, Hamid. A new era. You can even see it in Tangier—your friends on the Mountain reveling in decadence while down here we prepare the antibodies to extinguish their disease. Don't you feel it—the anger? We have an explosive situation here, and though I hate to say it, it's you in the police who are holding on the lid."

"This is dangerous talk, Mohammed. You shouldn't say such things to me."

"Perhaps not. But I trust you. And I hope you're interested in what I say."

"Better to change the subject. Someday, if you should happen to get yourself in trouble, it'll be good if you have a friend in the police."

"All right, Hamid—enough. How are things now at home?"

"Much better. She's stopped smoking finally. Thank you very much for that."

"You know she's been by here several times." Achar brushed his fingers across his mustache. "Actually, Hamid, she's been by quite a bit. I'm busy most of the time, though occasionally she's caught my eye. She's come here on her own it seems, approached my people and volunteered to help."

Suddenly Hamid could feel a thumping in his chest. It was the same feeling he'd had when she'd told him Zvegintzov had followed her home from the British play.

"You didn't know, then?"

Hamid banged his fist against his forehead. "Why does she do this? I'll never understand."

"Well, it's not as if—"

"What the hell have you got her doing? Scrubbing bedpans? Emptying slops?"

"Of course not, Hamid. Calm down. She's just come by a few times and helped us with our census. Driss Bennani is impressed with her, says she's been a terrific help. He's seen an interesting side to Kalinka. He says—well, I hesitate to tell you this—"

"What?"

"Well—he says she's 'a revolutionary at heart.'"

"My God!"

"That's not so bad, Hamid."

"Yes, I know. You think the same of me." He stood up. "I'm going." He walked to the door. "Good night!"

Outside the clinic he started toward his car, then stopped, turned around, and walked back up Rue de Chypre. He spent an hour strolling through the slum, following the little paths between shanties which glowed with candlelight. He listened to radios that wailed, music that overlapped and fused. He caught glimpses through split walls of people eating, quarreling, scratching their bodies. It was so squalid, Dradeb—he could hardly believe he'd been brought up in such a place. And all the time he kept thinking: *a revolutionary at heart*.

He really didn't think she'd meant to deceive him; it was vagueness, not secretiveness, that had made her neglect to tell him about her work. But then, in the back of his mind, there was a suspicion (and he despised himself for feeling it) that perhaps there was something happening between Kalinka and Achar. Or maybe even with Bennani, who'd run out so quickly when he'd walked in. Ridiculous, of course! Bennani was only a boy, and Achar was his oldest friend. But still there were things such as that time, months before, when he'd observed her sipping tea with a smuggler near the bus station, or that day he and Aziz had found her smoking with the Chinese on the laundry-strewn medina roof. How could he ever marry a woman whose past and present actions were so difficult to understand, who constantly eluded him, who was so foreign and so strange?

He paused, stood still, then violently shook his head. He had to get her into focus, had to get her clear. But then he realized that it wasn't just Kalinka. It was all the foreigners, everyone: Zvegintzov, Lake, Robin, the Freys—names gushed in, the names on all his dossiers, the names that filled the filing cabinets in his office, and constantly shuttled through his brain. For some reason he recalled a fleeting vision of Inigo sobbing, or perhaps laughing, parked one night outside Heidi's Bar. The mysteries of Tangier—there seemed no end to them. There are as many, he thought, as there are people in the town. And now Kalinka—just as I'm getting close to her a stranger glimpses something which, through all the months we've slept together, I never saw at all.

The Saint

Of all the writers in Tangier Martin Townes was the one
Robin liked the best. Yet he knew less about him than any of
the others—there was something elusive about Townes,
something ironic and concealed.

Ever since the May afternoon when they'd talked in the
Beaumonts' garden, Robin felt they shared a bond. He felt
like a specimen too. It was as if he and all the other people in
Tangier were creatures in a vivarium whom Townes observed most coolly through the blue-tinted spectacles he
always wore. Robin had been amused by Townes' suggestion
that he become a professional immoralist, a diabolic saint
and, pleased by so much attention, he'd gone to great pains
to seek Townes out. This entailed going to the Mountain, for
Townes despised the rabble of the town. He'd withdrawn
from nearly everyone, secluded himself in a glass tower on
the roof of his house where, Kranker had said, he was writing
a novel about Tangier. Robin didn't know whether this was
true, but Townes' grasp of the complexities of the European
city belied the widely held notion that he was cut off and
aloof. In fact, he seemed fully aware of all the latest gossip,

including the fact that Daniel Lake was having an affair with Jackie Knowles. He mentioned this one evening in early July when Robin stopped by for a drink.

"Interesting, isn't it?"

"But improbable," said Robin. "I wouldn't have thought Lake had the balls."

"You underrate him. He's a complicated man. Perhaps he has a desperate need for love."

"Desperate! He must be to be chasing her. She's a donkey. And her nitwit of a husband never lets her out of his sight."

"Well—what are you going to do about it? Will you mention it in your column?"

"Hmmm." Robin smiled. "These are delicate matters. Lake's got kids. I don't want to abuse my power."

"You still haven't answered my question."

"Let's just say I'd weigh the public's right to know against how exposure might harm the Lakes."

"Don't be corny, Robin. An immoralist doesn't talk like that."

"Maybe I'm not as much of an immoralist as you think. Perhaps I'm genuinely sweet and kind."

Townes laughed. "I heard about your picnic."

"It was a very nice occasion. The only bad thing about it was that nothing really bad took place."

Townes nodded. They looked at each other, laughed, and shook their heads.

"Now what I'd really like to know is who's the maniac in the church."

"I've been hoping it would turn out to be you," said Townes, "but I gather Brown has checked you out."

"God, what fools they are! Anyone you suspect?"

"Everybody. Or rather—whoever it's least likely to be. The business with the crucifixes suggests Patrick Wax. He's the sort you'd expect to find officiating at a satanic mass. But I personally think it'll turn out to be someone hitherto regarded as pious and bland. Any one of a hundred people who's felt himself abused. But getting back to your picnic, it turned out rather badly for Vincent Doyle. Kranker blabbed too much, and now everyone's laughing behind Doyle's back. Musica Codd came up to me in the market the other day.

Wanted to make sure I'd heard that Doyle carries around his silverware in his sack."

"I didn't say anything."

"Someone did. If you hadn't given the picnic, that particular bit would never have come out."

"OK. But I don't understand you, Townes. You urge me to become an immoralist, then when I do something faintly immoral, you seem to disapprove."

"I only disapprove, Robin, because you didn't follow through. You didn't mention the silverware in your column—it only got around by chance. That's your trouble, you see. You're wishy-washy. You're even a little bourgeois. To be an immoralist, and then renew yourself as a saint, you have to let all that go. You need to come up with a strong concept of yourself, then rigorously act it out."

Robin laughed. "Why are you so intent on my canonization? What on earth does it mean to you?"

"Oh, I don't know." Townes grinned. "You have so much potential. When I look at someone like you, more or less on the right track of life, I feel a compulsion to give him a little push. You're so close to what you ought to be. That's why I'm encouraging you. Cut yourself loose, Robin. Discover yourself in sin."

Robin nodded, though he still wasn't sure what Townes had in mind, or even whether he was being serious or operating on some teasing level of irony intended to provoke. "I'll try," he said. "But what about you? Are you some kind of Svengali who organizes people's lives?"

"Yes—if you like. That's not so bad. I'm a writer. I live in a world of fantasy. I think about people constantly, and also about plots. The trouble is that most of the people in Tangier are floundering in half-created dreams. If they really went to the trouble to see their fantasies through, this town would be a much more interesting place. I think you come closer than most, as does Patrick Wax, and Inigo—an extraordinary man. But let's face it—most of our friends here are pathetic. They don't even know who they're *pretending* to be. Anyway, this is too abstract. I prefer the method of your column. You name names, describe real deeds, rip off people's disguises. That to me is a virtuous occupation. I wish you'd do it more."

"Fine. Give me material. What else have you got besides this bit about Lake and Mrs. Knowles?"

"Well—let's see. I'm sure you know all about Kelly and Luscombe, how Kelly and the Drears have found a loophole in the TP bylaws, which they obtained on the sly from Derik Law, and how they're going to use it to petition for a meeting where they plan to retire Luscombe from the club. As a result Luscombe is now wandering around Tangier mumbling about a 'conspiracy' to destroy his life. It's so sad to see him perspiring, stopping people on the street to enlist their support, or sitting dazed in Heidi's Bar telling perfect strangers his bitter tale. Then there's Jean Tassigny's affair with Claude de Hoag—they carry on madly at the tennis club every day; and Françoise de Lauzon's thing with her new gardener, whom I believe she calls 'Dent de Lion,' or 'Dandelion' for short. Inspector Ouazzani too—something's bothering him. His girlfriend, perhaps. I don't know exactly, but you might be able to find out, being his snitch and all."

"Really, Townes—that's a vicious lie, started by my enemies."

Townes laughed. "Sorry," he said. "Anyway, I think I know why Kranker told that silverware story on Doyle."

"I've wondered about that. It seemed like a betrayal, since they carry on as though they're friends."

"Just a façade," said Townes. "There's a lot of bitterness there. Years ago Doyle wrote a novel, a cool, bleak thing that became an underground classic, instrumental in the creation of the myth of Doyle, the dropout exemplar. Kranker wrote a play in which he used the essence of Doyle's idea. Not the details, you understand, not even the story *exactly,* but the essence, the vision, the thing that was so particular to Doyle's point of view. But Doyle was furious, and though he's never said a word to Kranker, the thing's been eating away at him for years. Now Kranker's become hostile and begun to tell stories, like this silverware thing that makes Doyle appear an ass. You get the idea—a vicious circle of neurotic intrigue. There's no point to any of it, it's all petty and ridiculous, and yet it's typical of Tangier, true to our community and its rotting ways. *That's* what you ought to reveal in your column."

"I never heard this story before. Do you mind if I use it?"

"I doubt it would make any difference if I told you no. The point, Robin, is that if you wanted you could turn your column into a mirror. You could confront our community and all its little secrets, reflecting them back in the form of lurid gossip which in turn would become a vision of the place."

Townes excused himself, left the room. While he was gone Robin thought about what he'd said.

"You know," he said when Townes came back, "I think you're putting me on with this sainthood crap. You're really after something else. Tell me what it is."

"All right." Townes paused. "I am putting you on. I've been observing you for quite a while, Robin, and I've come to the conclusion that you're riding for a fall."

"Oh, come on—"

Townes stood up. He was often abrupt like that, sometimes even rude. "Before you go I have a present for you," he said. "A book, if you haven't forgotten how to read." He handed Robin a worn paperback edition of *The Confessions of St. Augustine.*

"Ugh! A classic! And by a saint, no less."

"Yes, Robin—by a saint indeed."

Townes walked him out to his terrace, where they paused before the view. Townes' garden framed Tangier, illuminated by the setting sun, which cast long shadows of trees upon the grass and coated the buildings below with a golden sheen. It was a powerful vision of the city, and it caught Robin by surprise.

"Funny to live up here," he said. "Tangier looks empty when you look down."

"It's a writer's view," said Townes, "too far away to see people. I can sit up in my tower"—he pointed to the glass cubicle on his roof—"and use my imagination to fill it up. From here the town is a set which I can populate as I like."

"What a wonderful place to write about Tangier."

Townes looked at him. "Yes," he said sorrowfully, "there is a novel down there. I've thought about it a lot—" He turned away and grinned.

They shook hands, then Robin walked down Townes' driveway to the street. With the tattered copy of St. Augustine stuck in the back pocket of his jeans, he wandered down from the Mountain to the medina, the smells, the crowd.

The Socco Chico, jammed with tourists, seemed especially intense that night. Hot, sweaty bodies scantily attired—they blurred before Robin's eyes. Pimples, bruises, vaccination scars—impossible to keep them straight. It's the carnival of summer, he thought, an endless moist parade, all strut and rub and furious scramble to insure oneself a delirious night.

The Socco, which he'd always loved for its overheated sense of life, turned sour for him suddenly as he sat in Cafe Centrale. How many of these bodies, he asked himself, do I really want to touch? How much of this collective genitalia do I care anymore to fondle and grasp? The same of dope and drink, the intoxicants that prefaced all encounters. How much more hashish am I prepared to smoke?

He felt strange becoming so morose, particularly in the Socco, which was his circus, his TV. The whores in their high cork shoes, the hustlers in their clinging jeans—for ten years they'd been his clowns, and their antics his release. *Perhaps,* he thought, *my trouble is I've tasted everything here too long.*

Riding for a fall—what kind of shit was that?

Townes was a voyeur who sat up on the Mountain watching people play. Still what he'd said was interesting—his point about letting go. Patrick Wax had said the same thing at the picnic, that he lacked the instinct to go in for the kill. Were they right? Was that his trouble? Would things be better for him if he began to use his column like a knife?

He was so confused by then, and so sick of the Socco, that he left his table abruptly and dragged himself through the teeming streets. People clutched at him as he passed, urged him to sit with them, tell stories, score sex or dope, but he pushed them away and in a surly mood entered the Oriental and climbed its rotting stairs.

He thought of his room, in summer, as a hotbox, a place suitable for punishment in a Japanese prisoner-of-war-camp film. Even with the windows open he feared suffocation. He stood in the middle listening to the medina sounds—Arab songs blasting from a hundred radios, the crying of a thousand babies, the screams of ten thousand cats in heat. Barking dogs, children fighting in the courtyards—all the sounds of the quarter, echoing, rebounding off the walls, seemed to roll in upon him in a great, pained, undulating wail.

He stripped off his clothes and threw them on the floor. His body too was sweaty—tomorrow he'd have to go to the beach and bathe. Then, naked, he began to pace about, giving abrupt little kicks to his shabby belongings, his broken phonograph, his piles of clippings, his teapot, his old photographs—all the junk that documented a decade. He'd throw the whole lot of it out one day, live in an empty room with nothing but a sweater and a comb. He'd order the barber to chop off his curls, then return to North America and find himself a job. Perhaps he'd work as a maintenance man on the Alaska pipeline, live with the hardhats in frigid dormitory rooms. He'd work on the tundra wastes, eat flapjacks for breakfast, moosemeat steaks at night, and then, punished by hard labor and the boring company of narrow-minded men, he would find solace in weariness and deep, undisturbed, earned sleep.

"Oh—shit," he whimpered, kicking at his discarded jeans.

"Shit again!" This time he yelped with pain. He'd stubbed his toe on something hard. It was that damn book that Townes had given him. He picked it out of his pants and flung it at his bed. Then he went to the sink, opened the faucets, stood on one foot like an ostrich, and nursed his swelling toe. When it felt a little better he limped back to the bed, and there he found Townes' note.

Dear Robin,

Because I know you're lazy, and hate to read serious things, I've devised a little game to get you started on this book. Turn to the third part of these *Confessions* and you'll see I've marked some lines. (I've also changed a word or two, just to smooth things out.) All you have to do is read what I've marked, leaving out what's in between. You'll get the point pretty fast, I think.

Yrs,
M.T.

Well, he thought, that was considerate of Townes, to go to so much trouble. He turned to Part Three and followed his instructions. What he read came out like this:

I went to Carthage, where I found myself in the midst of a hissing cauldron. I muddied the stream of friendship with the filth of lewdness and clouded its clear waters with hell's black river of lust. And yet, in spite of this rank depravity, I was vain enough to have ambitions of cutting a fine figure in the world.

I was caught up in the coils of trouble, for I was lashed with the cruel, fiery rods of jealousy, suspicion, anger, and quarrels. I enjoyed fables and fictions, which could only graze the skin, but where the fingers scratch, the skin becomes inflamed. It swells and festers with hideous pus. And the same happened to me. I exhausted myself in depravity, in the pursuit of an unholy curiosity. I sank to the bottom-most depths of skepticism and the mockery of devil worship.

I was at the top of the school of rhetoric. I was pleased with my superior status and swollen with my conceit. But I behaved far more quietly than the "wreckers," a title of ferocious devilry which the fashionable set chose for themselves. I kept company with them, and there were times when I found their friendship a pleasure, but I always had a horror of what they did when they lived up to their name. "Wreckers" was a fit name for them, for they were already adrift and total wrecks themselves. The mockery and trickery which they loved to practice on others was a secret snare of the devil, by which they were mocked and tricked themselves.

These were the companions with whom I studied the art of eloquence at that impressionable age. I fell in with a set of sensualists, men with glib tongues who ranted and raved. Yet the dishes they set before me were still loaded with dazzling fantasies, illusions with which the eye deceives the mind. I knew nothing of this at the time. I was quite unconscious of it, quite blind to it, although it stared me in the face.

For nearly nine years were yet to come during which I wallowed deep in the mire and the darkness of delusion. Often I tried to lift myself, only to plunge the deeper.

Well, he thought, *this is heady stuff.* The connections to himself, Tangier, his column, the Socco, and the Mountain crowd did not escape him; in fact, he was fascinated. And thinking these *Confessions* might yield up some secret about his destiny, he opened the book at its beginning and read on and on. Not until hours later, when he'd finished the confessional part and had come to St. Augustine's conversion, did he droop his head, extinguish the bare bulb above his bed, close his eyes, and begin to dream of boys in woolen shorts.

The next morning he was surprised to find himself elated, even though it was Thursday and his column was due at noon. He bounded out of bed, attempted a set of vigorous calisthenics, then panting and wet stood by his window and breathed deeply the rank medina air. He didn't bother to dress but walked nude to his table to give his Olivetti its weekly blowing off. He choked on the dust but stood his ground, disgusted, for there were ants climbing all over the keys of the machine. He squashed them with his forefinger, one at a time, then wiped off their remains on the wall. Finally, when everything was clean, the table crumbed and cleared of chocolate bar tinfoil bits, odds and ends of unfinished poems, and rinds of cheese, he sat down, still naked, willed himself to work, scratched at his ankles, and with flashing fingers began to type:

ABOUT TANGIER
By Robin Scott

We find Tangier, this first week of July, standing on its head. Our city is a vortex of illusions. We are seedy actors playing out delirious roles.

THE BRITISH COMMUNITY in an uproar over the latest OUT-RAGES at St. Thomas Church. Early Sunday morning, when Vicar Wick unlocked the doors, he found the great altar crucifix hacked to pieces on the floor. Deeply upset by this sacrilege, the Vicar sent out a plea for help. Jack Whyte, Tangier's "Mr. Fix It," quickly improvised another cross out of some two-by-fours lying around his shop. A new and better crucifix is now in the works, but the question remains: WHO DID THE DASTARDLY DEED? Perhaps it's a coincidence, but on Tuesday the Vicar found a black widow spider crawling across his desk. Lester Brown refused to speculate on whether there was some connection between these two events, but the wily colonel left no doubt in this reporter's mind that he thought there was. Ever since May, when an anonymous note turned up on the collection plate, and then a skewered sheep's eye the following week, Colonel Brown has made it his mission to find the perpetrator and bring him to account. Now, with the ruined crucifix and the black widow spider, the plot thickens and the hunt becomes more intense. Camilla Weltonwhist declares she will not enter the "devil's house." Dr. Radcliffe has been called to attend to Lady Pitt, who says she will not leave her bed until the culprit is caught and expelled. So—a pillar of our British society is now riddled with fury and fear. The work of a single madman, we may ask, or a symptom of our DISEASE?

DIPLOMATIC AND OTHER AFFAIRS: Much consternation now, in Tangier's diplomatic set, over the behavior of a senior representative of a major power. We're not naming any names, but if our readers care to learn more, we suggest they station themselves at odd hours by the overlook near the Rimilat Cafe. They might see an ODD COUPLE making whoopee in a BIG BLACK CAR.

Speaking of AFFAIRS, there's another one burning white hot. It's been going on in secrecy for months behind a certain prominent Mountain resident's back. A handsome young man, an older woman, and a much older husband who's often out of town. That's the triangle if you can figure it out. (Think of the tennis club if you need a hint.) Tread softly, passionate lovers, lest you inspire a *crime passionnel*.

HOW REFRESHING to take note of men loving women in Tangier! Recently Clive Whittle was heard to comment brusquely about our city's vice. As quoted to us (and we hasten to add we were not invited to the dinner where these statements were made) Her Majesty's Consul General is alleged to have said: "I don't give a fig what *they* do behind the blinds, but there'll be no mincing, no lisping, no limp wrists in *this* house!" Good luck, Clive! You may have to drop half your clientele, but in a STRANGE way, DEAR BOY, you've put your finger on the difference between "gay" and "queer." "Gay," a matter of sexual preference, is something that's neither here nor there, while "queer" has nothing to do with bed, but with a set of mannerisms "gay people" sometimes display. Well, try to understand, OLD BOY. All that lisping bitchiness which you so contemptuously despise comes from years of self-hatred engendered by just such homophobic statements as you're alleged to have made. Understand, old FRUIT?

LITERARILY SPEAKING: We have another sad tale to add to the endless misfortunes of David Klein. You'll all remember the *unfortunate accident* when David was attacked by his gardener several years ago. All's mended and well, thank God, but now another mishap has occurred. David's new "Mohammed," after washing out his best Berber rug, placed it on the garden wall to dry. A great wind came and blew it to the other side, where a gang of Dradeb urchins snatched it away. No sign of the rug yet, though the police are working on the case. Thank the Lord, David, it was just a rug, and not your ratty old toupee!

AN INTERESTING FEUD is brewing up beneath the cloak of a friendship going sour. Two of Tangier's most prominent LIT-ERATI are now talking viciously behind each other's backs. A sack of silverware, a case of "moral plagiarism"—the whole thing's too complex to lay out here. The strange thing about it, though, is that both parties still pretend they're friends. Isn't there enough hypocrisy in Tangier? What a shame it's spread to the artistic CAMP!

THEATER CLUB: "All the world's a stage, and all the men and women in it merely players. . . ." Our players' machinations continue at a heady pace. Laurence Luscombe informs us that *Emperor Jones* will be his first production in the fall. He has approached Mr. Fufu about playing the lead, but a certain AMERICAN ACTOR has sworn he'll play it in blackface himself. Meantime a copy of the TP bylaws has been surreptitiously acquired by a DISSIDENT group. There's a plot afoot to unseat the older guard by holding a meeting on a night when the voting patrons cannot attend. The undemocratic employment of democratic principles—that's the conspiracy here. Our theater club, like the church, has become a stage for vengeance, intrigue, and deceit.

CHIT-CHAT: Big party at Jimmy Sohario's Saturday night, the sixth such extravaganza in half as many weeks. Sumptuous platters overflowed; musicians beat drums till dawn.

FLASH FROM THE USA: Inigo's portrait of a certain Tangier hustler (his name will remind you of a *tart* of gourds!) has just been acquired by the Akron (Ohio) Museum for the stupendous price of sixty thousand smackeroos. Congratulations to the painter, and to his friend P.P. too. Seems some of our boys are worth a lot on canvas, a great deal more than they're worth live on sheets!

PIERRE ST. CARLTON flying in this weekend, with his usual mob of jet setters in tow. Sven Lundgren, who handles Pierre's AFFAIRS here, informs us the couturier will spend the first few days working on his tan.

HENDERSON PERRY due in August, off his Mediterranean-based yacht. Expect a big party in the usual lavish style, then a quick disappearance by our mysterious millionaire.

FAREWELL to Willard and Katie Manchester, moving to Fort Lauderdale at season's end. They'll be sorely missed in bridge-playing circles on the Mountain. Already there's talk of a "drink the dregs" party to see them off.

FINALLY A WORD OF REGRET about the closing of the Hotel Américain, unofficial landmark of Tangier's, uh, "gay set." Its proprietor, Hans Gottshalk, has been expelled on a morals charge, and, we're told, he will never return. Some of us who've been here a while were reminiscing the other night about the hotel's filthy corridors, its stinking toilets, its sagging mattresses, and its seedy owner, who so often tried to rob us blind. Tangier will be the richer for his loss, and yet . . . and yet . . . AN ERA ENDS.

Robin didn't need to read his column over to know how mean it was. But having written it, he had no intention of changing a single word. He would hand it in exactly as he had written it, with the vague hope that by the authenticity of his malice he would find a way to propel himself out of the mire and delusion of Tangier.

The Lovers

Late one July afternoon when Tangier was just beginning to cool down, Jean Tassigny was driving to the Mountain from the Emsallah Tennis Club when he noticed Tessa and David Hawkins' Arabian geldings tied up in front of La Colombe. Vanessa Bolton's little Porsche was parked there too, and Hervé Beaumont's Fiat coupe. Jean stopped, pulled on his tennis sweater, and walked inside to buy a *Dépêche de Tanger*.

The little shop was jammed. Peter Zvegintzov was darting about, frantically trying to serve his customers. The Manchesters were browsing through horticultural magazines, and Skiddy de Bayonne was sniffing imported teas. Jean picked up his paper, then embraced Vanessa Bolton. David Hawkins, crop stuck into his boot, rushed over to give him a double kiss. Jean waved to David's sister, Tessa, who was deep in conversation with Hervé Beaumont. Jean knew Tessa was sleeping with Hervé's sister Florence, but whether with her own brother too he wasn't sure. Still his suspicions made him feel sophisticated, a part of *tout Tanger*. Though he'd been living in the city less than a year, he'd already acquired a sense of its complexities and overlapping social spheres.

Half an hour later, at home, reading on his bed, Jean felt his heart suddenly begin to pound. He read the offending lines again. There was no mistake. Robin Scott had found out about his affair with Claude and had printed it in his wretched column.

His abdomen grew weak. He felt as if he'd just been kicked. He had to tell Claude, tell her at once, but she was downstairs in the salon with her father sipping an apéritif. Had General Bresson seen it? Probably not. He was contemptuous of gossip and didn't read English very well. But Joop de Hoag could read English perfectly, and was due back in Tangier in two more days. Scott had mentioned the possibility of a *crime passionnel*. Was Monsieur de Hoag really capable of that?

Jean remained upstairs, waiting for the General to leave. But when it became apparent he was staying on for dinner, Jean dressed and descended to the salon. There he endured an hour of tedious small talk, gazing desperately at Claude all the while. But the more boldly he tried to attract her attention, the more coolly she pretended she didn't understand; finally, seeing she was annoyed, he submitted to an interminable wait.

At dinner the General reminisced about Algeria. "Morocco," he said, "was pleasant during the Protectorate, but in Algeria life was truly sweet. It was France, with all the virtues of the Republic and the additional luxury of slaves."

The man was insufferable, but Jean nodded all the same. No point in antagonizing him—Jean only wished he'd leave. Hours later Jean escorted him to his car, and after he'd driven off, he looked down upon Tangier. At night, from the Mountain, it was a distant field of flickering lamps, a thousand beacons beckoning lovers to romantic passageways and glowing minarets.

Jean sighed, walked back to the villa. Claude had already retired to her room. He helped himself to a cognac, waiting for the servants to finish clearing up. When they were done, he gulped the last of his drink and hurried up the stairs.

"Fool!" She nearly spat at him. "Do you want my father to find out?" Then, before he could answer, she smiled, threw her arms around him, and begged him to undress.

He pulled out Robin's column, passed it to her with a trembling hand.

"What's this? 'Burning white hot—an older woman—passionate lovers—*crime passionnel*.' " She threw it on the floor. "Trash!"

Jean flung himself on the bed, and after a while, after she'd paced the room, she sat beside him, lifted his head onto her lap, and ran her fingers through his hair.

"I could kill Robin for this! But don't worry—Joop won't see it. He doesn't read the *Dépêche*. He'll be busy when he gets back."

"What if someone tells him?"

"No one will."

"Your father? Or one of the British? They love to write anonymous notes."

"In that case I'll deny it. I'll say it isn't true. I've tipped a fortune to the servants. He'll have to accept my word."

"What if he doesn't? He'll watch us. He'll be suspicious. Robin found out. Too many people know."

"Never mind," she said. "We'll be careful. Perhaps, at times, we have been indiscreet."

He looked up at her, thinking of all the times she'd flaunted their affection. She loved danger, courted it, used it to enhance her pleasure and provoke his fear.

"What would he do?" he asked.

"Joop? Oh—he'd kill us, I suppose. Or perhaps he'd just kill you." She laughed, a deep, throaty laugh. Then she pulled his ears.

He spent the night in her bed, but at dawn, before the servants were awake, he got up quietly and stole back to his room. He disliked leaving her, often dreamed of lazy early morning bouts of love, breakfast on her terrace facing the sea, the two of them, naked to the morning sun, sipping coffee as they caressed. But that was impossible. Their whole situation was impossible, though Claude seemed to thrive on its risk.

A year earlier, when Jean Tassigny was interviewed in Paris by Joop de Hoag, he wasn't at all certain exactly what he was being hired to do. The Dutchman was vague about the details, and Jean was too excited to inquire. The idea of living in Tangier was more important to him than the job, and besides Monsieur de Hoag had given him assurances that his training would be invaluable to a career in high finance.

A few weeks after the interview Jean received a formal letter. He'd receive fifteen hundred francs a month, and food and lodgings at the de Hoag house. He'd be treated, in Monsieur de Hoag's words, "as a member of my family," for which, in return, he'd act as Joop de Hoag's *homme de confiance*.

He arrived in Tangier on a windless autumn day when the light sparkled off white buildings, etching the town against sky and sea. He was dazzled by this effect, and also by the de Hoag house—a great, square, earth-colored mansion that looked as permanent and stately as a bank. Its gleaming double doors of brass swung slowly open like the entrance to a vault, and on the other side, from a terrace cut into rock, he looked upon the fabled city that guarded the Mediterranean Sea. It spread like gleaming mercury back from the bay, surrounded by forests of wild pine and the mountains of the Rif. But there was more than the wondrous clarity of light and the views that ravished him that day. There was a woman, the most beautiful he'd ever seen—Monsieur de Hoag's young wife, Claude.

Claude. Mysterious as the moonlit Casbah, he thought, guarded as the medina walls. He made up names for her— "Tangier Nightbird," "Aphrodite of the Mountain"—wrote them out on slips of paper, then burned the slips and scattered the ashes upon the sea. Why wasn't he a poet? Why couldn't he discover her in a name? It would take a Rimbaud to do that, he thought, but he became obsessed, and though untalented he tried.

Each morning he and Monsieur de Hoag left early for their office, a shabby building near the port. Here he pored over ledgers, studied reports of Brazilian diamond mines, enciphered de Hoag's orders to buy and sell, and telexed them abroad. He learned leverage and arbitrage, the mechanisms of Liechtenstein corporations and numbered Swiss accounts. De Hoag showed him how to move silver bullion through three markets in a week, take a position in Dutch gilders while the Deutschemark fluctuated down, ride the Italian lira, liquidate cocoa futures at the proper time, then move the profits back into gold, the only commodity a man could trust.

There was an exhausting excitement about these forays in and out of gold, deep, intense pondering up to the moment of the move, terrifying tension during the wild speculative phase, and then relief, vast relief, when once again the money was safe. Five sets of midday tennis did not leave Jean so fatigued.

De Hoag taught much, but there were things he would not reveal: the identities of his clients and his informants in Johannesburg and Geneva—matters too confidential, it seemed, even for an *homme de confiance*. Still Jean was patient, certain he'd learn them in time. And, meanwhile, he thought of Claude.

It was an ecstatic torment to face her over dinner, her dark gleaming lips, her wild turquoise eyes. They'd sit, the three of them, when the de Hoags were not invited out, at the end of a long refectory table laden with china, candelabra, flowers. He and Monsieur de Hoag wore smoking jackets; Claude, in the middle, wore a strapless gown and a diamond necklace that glittered upon her neck. They ate while silent liveried Moroccans served, and talked of Tangier, its society, its vagaries and strife. Often, too, Claude's father would come, and then Jean would be seated at the far end. The retired general and Monsieur de Hoag would speak of world events while he and Claude exchanged smiles through the candle flames.

He wondered what she thought of him then, if she was really conscious that he was there. She often seemed aloof, though there were times when she was kind: she held a reception to introduce him to the young people and gave him permission to use her car.

In those first months, while he explored Tangier, found his way into its low-life bars, discovered the special quality of its intoxicants, the warming, ballooning power of its kif, he was content to regard Claude de Hoag as an untouchable object beyond his reach. But as time passed and he grew weary of the formal rituals of the Mountain, he fell into the habit of retiring to his bedroom after work, facing a window from an armchair, and watching as the sun set behind the house and the city faded slowly from his sight. Then, when it was dark and like magic Tangier took on another shape—redrawn, it seemed, by lines of electric lamps—he'd fall into reveries in which he imagined himself and Claude moving separately through a night maze of streets toward a fog-shrouded square where they embraced. At these moments, when he dreamed of wrapping her in his arms, his fantasies became as real to him as anything in his life. He'd imagine the warmth of her through her clothes, and his body would throb with desire.

It was so difficult then to face her, speak to her of inane little things, use the "vous" form, smile in the mornings, refer to her, always, as "Madame."

Once, when he saw her walking her dogs alone along the beach below the cliffs, he sensed that she was lonely and that he might have her if he wished. He even dreamed of how he might declare himself, practiced the gesture by which he would take her hand, kiss it, then return it to her cheek, all the while staring at her with a mixture of longing and tragic obsessiveness in his eyes. There were no words in this fantasy, only glances, gestures that spoke eloquently of his desire, a silent, tranquil ballet by which he asked for her and she accepted him, promising with a smile that in time their silent contract would be sealed.

He imagined this scene taking place in her garden against a backdrop of a flawless sky, with the coast of Spain set hazily behind and the African sun beating upon eucalyptus which dappled the light before it grazed her face. She would be dressed in a flimsy cotton caftan dyed blue by Toureq artisans in the south. A strand of graduated pearls would glow soft against her throat. He was surprised by the compression of this vision, but was wise enough to understand that he obtained more pleasure from the formal contemplation of his passion than from coarse fantasies of its display.

He began then to read romantic novels, to quench an endless thirst for love. He felt like a shopgirl at first, pathetic, deprived, but when he discovered Stendhal's *Lucien Leuwen* he quickly lost his shame. He read the book slowly, carefully, rereading certain passages many times. He wanted to make the pleasure last, inhale deeply of each lovesick fume. He reexperienced his growing love for Claude as Lucien's love crystallized for Madame de Chasteller, and although he knew he was being foolish, he persisted, seeking escape from the torment of living beside a woman he adored and yet could not possess.

He needed an escape too from Monsieur de Hoag, who was often hard with him and difficult to please. Whenever Jean offered a suggestion at the office, de Hoag turned on him with a sarcastic smile. "Perhaps, Jean," he'd ask, "you have capital of your own to risk? What? No? Well in that case, my boy, may I suggest you conclude your apprenticeship before proposing absurd ventures doomed to fail."

By November their relationship had begun to change. Jean had the feeling that de Hoag had been insincere with him, that he was being exploited, used as a clerk, that de Hoag had no intention of handing him responsibilities or ever allowing him to make decisions on his own. Perhaps, he thought, it's because I'm young; perhaps he dislikes me because he's jealous of my strength and looks. Joop de Hoag was an ugly man, small, fat, bald, almost repulsive when he smiled. His eyes were small, squirrelish, unyielding, and his mouth was tight with greed.

Why had Claude married him? How could she bear to share his bed? De Hoag had bought her—Jean was sure of that. General Bresson had sold her to him when she was barely out of school. Now the General was rich, and the Dutchman owned a stunning wife.

There was another thing that bothered him: de Hoag's alliance with Omar Salah. Jean knew the chief of customs from the tennis club, where they'd played together several times. The man's conduct was appalling: he cheated on line calls, served before his opponent was prepared, and cursed in Arabic as he rushed the net. De Hoag was involved with him in shady deals, secret, illegal bullion accounts for Salah's rich Moroccan friends. Jean had no proof of this (the details were locked in Monsieur de Hoag's private safe) but he found the idea odious and used it to justify the adulteries in his dreams.

After Christmas the rains began, great torrential showers. Claude left Tangier to spend the winter with friends in

Kenya, and a few weeks later Monsieur de Hoag set off for São Paulo to inspect his holdings there. Jean, alone with the servants in the old villa, wandered from room to room at night. Water slashed upon the roof, mud slid down the Mountain. Tangier was wet and dark, its cafes were dreary, full of Moroccans shrouded in hoods that gave off an odor of mildewed wool.

Somehow he got through the winter, consoled by the Hawkins', the Beaumonts, Inigo, Vanessa Bolton, Robin Scott. And then, in spring, Tangier became his mistress—he fell in love with the city once again.

He lavished love upon it as before he'd lavished love on Claude. Its arches, its gardens, its whiteness enchanted him, filled him with tenderness, compelled him to explore. Flowers were bursting out, blossoms on the bougainvillaea, lace on the jacaranda trees. He walked the Boulevard, strode through the Socco, discovered the markets, the souks, found places where men beat copper, worked leather, fashioned clay, spun wool. He spent hours in the medina, listening for music that erupted in sudden bursts from shadowed doors. He visited the spice shops, priced ambergris, tasted olives, almonds, dates, then prowled the junk stores looking for Berber jewelry, pausing by fountains to watch women washing clothes. He breathed the rankness of the medina, the dust of the Casbah walls. The beaches, white, untouched, glowed like platinum in the sun. On golden Sundays he sat on Avenue d'Espagne watching the waves thunder against the jetties in the bay. This was a city, he thought, made for lovers, a city built for passion, for long kisses and secret trysts. Its faint putrescence, its architectural decay provided shelter for his lust.

And then Claude came back from Kenya, tanned, aglow. The house was alive again. She worked her garden, cut flowers, placed them everywhere in bowls. She seemed to smile at him more often, and even Monsieur de Hoag was less hard with him than before.

He'd been foolish, he thought, to have dreamed of loving her. Tangier was a city so palpable with romance that it had forced him to invent a lover lest the brilliant setting go to waste.

He decided to concentrate on tennis, in the hope that the discipline of vigorous exercise would clear her from his mind. He began to get up early, run down the Mountain to improve his wind. He played an hour before breakfast with a trainer, and after work returned and played again till dusk. He picked up matches with Spanish businessmen and young, aggressive Moroccans. His game improved. He won a tournament. His body tanned. He became lean and hard.

One afternoon when he returned from the courts Claude stopped him in the hall. She wanted to take up tennis, she said, and asked him if he'd help. He told her that of course he would, and so, with Monsieur de Hoag's approval, they went together to the little tennis shop on Rue Goya and he watched as she was outfitted with a racket, shoes, and clothes.

She was awkward at first, broke her swing at the wrist, but he coached her until she could play a decent game. He ran her about the court, fed her backhands, slices, forehands, serves, and when he noticed an error in her form he crossed to her side of the net, stood behind her, placed his hand beside hers on the racket, and slowly moved her through the strokes.

It was then that his adoration was revived. Her body became demystified. He became accustomed to touching her, seeing her bare arms and legs, looking at her face beaded with perspiration, thinking of her as a woman, warm, alive. His dreams of the autumn, formal ballets played out against sun-dappled seascapes, gave way quite suddenly to moist fantasies of flesh, thrashing limbs, grasping hands, sucking tongues and mouths.

He felt then that they shared a physical attraction, all the more powerful because it was unspoken and taboo. He'd catch her watching him, and sometimes, when he stood behind her pressed against her back, he'd feel her spine tremble where they touched as if her body, heated by exercise, was crying out. He knew then that he only had to wait, that sometime soon, at the proper moment, when they were alone or in public unobserved, he had only to let his hand linger a moment too long and she would not be able to resist.

But when? When might he do it? When might he seize

her, kiss her, caress her, cause her to moan and heave? How would they become lovers? When?

It would not be easy, for Tangier was small. The people of the town liked nothing better than to spy upon their neighbors and unravel their affairs. So the tennis court became a stage where they enacted an erotic dance. They used the public game to disguise their private play. Each rally held a hidden meaning, each exchange of shots was a coupling in code. A soft service became a caress. A smash was an aggressive thrust. Sometimes he'd toy with her, feed her soft seductive lobs, and then, when she was near the net, he'd send a passing shot hurtling by her side. They'd smile at each other as if to acknowledge the meaning of the play. They were tennis lovers. Their courtship was the game. With swishing rackets they flirted hour after hour, vigorously twitching each other's lust.

Afterward, on the club terrace, drinking beer in sweat-soaked clothes, Jean would recognize the glint of desire in her eyes, but he said nothing, determined she should make the first advance.

She did, finally, on a hot May afternoon. Monsieur de Hoag was in Geneva on a business trip. Jean had left the office early to join Claude on the courts at noon. They played hard, the heat was terrific, and afterward Claude suggested they take a drive.

It was a cloudless, windy day of violent waves on the Atlantic shore. She chose a deserted little bay between Cap Spartel and Robinson Plage. They parked on the cliffs, climbed down to the beach, and without a word started to undress. Finally, standing bare, they turned to one another and stared. There was a pause as they ached and tensed, the sort of pause, it seemed to Jean, that must always occur before a passionate event. Then she came to him, circled his waist, pressed her cheek against his shoulder. He felt her shudder as he wrapped her in his arms.

They made love in a cranny in the cliffs, searing, thrusting, violent. Then, pulled apart, they lay on their backs in the sand, chests heaving, listening to the surf. Jean wanted to speak, but all his thoughts were chaotic. He was conscious only that their act had been momentous, and that by it everything in his life was now, irrevocably, changed.

They made love again. This time she rode him. He gazed up at her, her face held high, her turquoise eyes upon the sea reflecting back the sun. She rode and rode, never looking down. Waves smashed against the sand. He felt that they were joined.

Afterward they swam, then licked the salt off each other's cheeks.

At the house that night she led him to her suite. The weeks of tennis had built up such a backlog of desire that it took them until dawn to use it up. They were savage with each other, devouring, excessive. He ravished her, again and again, and she provoked him further with demands. Finally, when they were finished, Jean felt they'd pushed to the limits of their polarity. He was proud of his manhood, and falling off to sleep he was conscious that his sense of it had been enlarged.

When Monsieur de Hoag came back and they could no longer be alone, they'd brush against each other in the villa halls. Their hands would touch fleetingly as they'd seat themselves for dinner. Over breakfast in the mornings they could hardly bear the stress.

After a few days Claude could stand it no longer. She suddenly stopped playing tennis in the middle of a match. They got into her car and drove madly down the coast. In Asilah, in a Portuguese hotel, they made love on a stained old mattress while dry thunder rumbled in the sky.

Tangier embraced them. Something tragic about the city, Jean thought, provided resonance for their affair. He thought of himself as a man living in a decaying temple; he prayed at an altar of erotic love while a storm raged outside.

Through May and June Monsieur de Hoag was constantly away, on a series of brief business trips to Zurich, Monaco, and Rome. On one of these occasions Jean and Claude were invited together to Barclay's house, a strange, irrelevant dinner, Jean thought, where Claude's father had acted like a fool. Apropos of nothing the General turned to the Governor and began complaining about his phone. Jean, embarrassed, looking around, confronted Omar Salah glaring at him with hate.

Afterward he told Claude, then asked if she thought Salah suspected their affair.

"It wasn't Salah who was watching you," she said with a scornful laugh. "It was Barclay. He couldn't tear his eyes away."

"But why?"

"He's an English pederast. Are you blind, Jean? Haven't you noticed him on the terrace of the tennis club devouring you as if you were his feast?" And then, fondling his testicles: "How Peter Barclay would love to get his hands on these!"

Joop de Hoag, she told him, only had one ball. The other, undescended, had atrophied inside. "He disgusts me," she said with a grimace. "Physically he disgusts me. I despise his body and loathe his wealth."

She kissed him a while, then suddenly turned over on her back. "I lied to you, Jean," she said. "Last year I slept with Salah. We spent a weekend together in Marrakech. Perhaps he suspects us. I don't know."

He could hardly believe it, but when he questioned her she refused to tell him any more.

"Tangier is complicated," she said. "Things here are not so simple as they seem."

Yes, there was something torturous about Tangier, a sense he had of tension and labyrinthine density all around. Was the romantic charm of this old city merely its façade? Was it an abyss into which he'd flung himself for love?

He lay awake that night listening to the distant cries of the muezzin, thinking about women and deceit. He was twenty-three; Claude was thirty-five. Together their bodies sang, but there was disconnection between their minds. He'd perceived this in her before, sometimes when they were making love: a lack of focus, a concentration upon herself, her eyes, always averted, fixed on some distant point. Is it possible, he asked himself, that she and Salah are still involved? Why would he stare at me like that? Could she have told him? Is she mad?

Sometimes he thought that she was. She seemed to want to dare the world to discover them, to take chances no sane person in her position would want to take. She insisted they rent horses and gallop publicly down the Spartel beach. On a tennis ball with a pen she wrote that she loved him, then demanded he smash aces until her words were worn away.

One morning they played very early at the club, even before Monsieur de Hoag was awake. After a hard set she came with him into the men's changing room. Claiming she was excited by the danger and the smell, she insisted he make love to her on the wooden bench between the lockers. He complied because it was still early and no one else was about, but in the middle of the act he opened his eyes and saw the crippled boy who raked the courts watching them from the door. He didn't tell Claude but later he was scared. He knew that now that one Arab had learned their secret, all Tangier had learned it too.

There was something corrupting about the city, he thought, something infectious about its rot. His golden love for Claude had tarnished to a mellow rust. He was beginning to enjoy her whirlpool, her sense of treachery, her bizarre desires.

Together they went to see Inigo, to confide in him, confess their affair. The painter, flattered to be chosen as their confidant, invited them to make a tour of his house. He was charming, almost childlike, as he led them through room after room, each connected to the next by a Moorish arch, each containing a finished painting hanging from the wall by chains. In his studio he showed them an uncompleted portrait of Patrick Wax. The old man was seated before a display of crucifixes; a Pekingese, sprouting a pink erection, gazed out from beneath Wax's chair.

When they had seen everything, and had finished gasping over the perfection of his technique, Inigo led them to a little room beside his pool. "This is a steambath," he said, opening a valve. "I built it to remind myself of the many amusing people I've met in the bathhouses of New York."

Claude was delighted, clapped her hands. "Please, Inigo," she said, "let Jean make love to me here. You can watch us if you like."

For a moment Jean was stunned, then excited by her idea. *How far I've come,* he thought, *since I dreamed of her in the fall.*

Inigo released more steam, smiled, and left to fetch his crayons. They were already undressed, locked on the floor of wooden slats, when he returned and began to sketch.

Afterward they knelt beside him, naked, their bodies slick.

Peering at his drawing, they discovered themselves as vague, amorphous figures lost in mist. It was a tour de force of draftsmanship. Inigo ripped it from his sketchbook and presented it to Claude as a gift. He placed his arms around their bare shoulders, hugged them tight, then lit and passed a kif cigarette.

"I have a new project for a painting," he said. "Six cocks. Just six. The midsections of their owners too, of course— navels, thighs, hairs. The cocks not hard, not erect, just hanging loose. The title: *Six Cocks at Midday*."

He looked at Jean, and then back to Claude. "With your permission, Madame, I should like to include his in the work."

Jean squirmed with embarrassment, but Claude giggled with glee.

"I'm perfectly serious," said the painter, reaching down and gently taking hold of Jean's organ with his hand. "Good proportions. Good heft. Perhaps I will locate it third from the left, a little closer to the foreground plane, standing out a bit from the other five. You understand the reference, of course: *Six Persimmons* by the Zen painter Mu Ch'i."

Such erudition! People didn't speak like that in Paris. Jean Tassigny was happy he'd come to live in Tangier. In this white, glittering city one could discover who one was. One could dive through a gleaming surface of idealizations and illusions, and swim about in murky depths.

Now there was danger.

Two days after they read about themselves in Robin's column, Jean and Claude drove out to the airport to meet Monsieur de Hoag. He was flying in from Lisbon on a morning flight. The field was only fifteen minutes from the house, but they left an hour early to drive along the sea.

Claude parked above the "Grottoes of Hercules," caves in the cliffs that marked the entrance to the Straits. They walked down toward the ruin of an ancient Roman sardine factory, eroded by two thousand years of winds and drifting sands. The beach was deserted. They stripped, plunged into the sea, then returned to the sand and made love.

It was a defiant act, well calculated by Claude, for she

knew this spot was on the line of approach to the main runway of the Tangier airport. When they were finished, they lay naked to the sun and watched the plane sail in. It was not five hundred feet above them and seemed to float as it crossed the sky. Probably no one in the plane could see them, and certainly no one could have made them out. But still, it seemed to Jean, it was a strange and desperate thing to do.

After the plane passed and began to bank they rushed to the car, dressing as they ran. Jean drove quickly to the terminal. They arrived in time to mount the observation deck and watch the passengers cross the tarmac to the lounge.

A few minutes later Jean stood back while Claude ran to her husband, embraced him, welcomed him home to Tangier. He stepped forward then to formally shake his employer's hand. Joop de Hoag handed him the baggage checks. Jean felt pity for him, and terror.

The Spy

Early one morning in the middle of July Hamid Ouazzani was driving along Vasco de Gama when he spied the Foster Knowles' jogging group moving like an apparition through the mist. He stopped to watch. They were running on a trail parallel to the Jew's River. He could make out Foster in the lead, taking awkward, gangling strides, followed by a bobbing line of men and women of assorted heights. Hamid recognized some of them: Clive Whittle, Madame Fufu, Jack Whyte, and, at the end, the ferocious Jackie Knowles yelling harsh encouragements to speed up the pace. He fixed on her swinging ponytail, watched it grow smaller as she was swallowed by the mist. He thought of Europeans locked in their *danse macabre* and sighed over the fate of Daniel Lake.

He knew from his surveillance that the Consul General was involved with Mrs. Knowles, a ridiculous affair, it seemed to him, considering the abandonment with which Lake was carrying it on. His indiscretions were now the talk of Tangier. He'd been observed kissing her in the balcony of the Mauritania Cinema, and groping with her in the official American car. Hamid didn't want to judge Lake. His posture as a policeman was to understand the foreign mind. But the Consul's behavior was inexplicable. Whenever Hamid thought of him he sighed with sympathy for a human being in distress.

Sympathy. For years he'd lavished it on foreigners. Now he resented them for taking up his time. His capacity, which had once seemed infinite, to hear confessions and then absolve, was diminishing little by little as each July day passed. The summer was at its height, his office was flooded with cases, but his attention was focused on Kalinka, his search to understand her, uncover her dreamy past.

Every night now they talked, though both of them were tired, she from her work at Achar's clinic, he from his hours at the Sûreté. She was assisting Driss Bennani with a "census" of the slumdwellers—she called it a "census" though Hamid felt it was more than that. But when he hinted to her that he disapproved, she waved his objections away. "Are you jealous?" she asked playfully. "Do you want me to stay home like a Moroccan squaw?" He shook his head and did not persist. Her tongue had become sharper since she'd started to work, and she didn't forget things anymore.

Most of her memories were based on conversations she'd overheard, or things her mother had told her, but still there was a sharpness to these scenes as if she'd observed them all herself. There were inconsistencies, of course, pieces that didn't fit, but when Hamid listened to her and closed his eyes her memories came alive.

He had a vision of Peter Zvegintzov: he is in hiding when the Viet Minh come to power, crouching by day in the boarded-up back room of his parents' shop, going out at night, foraging for bread. But then, a week or so later, after order is restored, Peter embarks upon an obsessive search for Marguerite and Stephen Zhukovsky's child. He walks the back streets of Hanoi, the rutted dirt streets where the Vietnamese live, passes abandoned trucks and tanks, and Catholic families packing up to leave. He asks questions, walks and walks, but can find no trace of them at all.

At last, one evening, beginning to think that they are dead, he returns to his shop, where he finds a waiting boy. The boy leads him to a roofless shanty in the refugee district on the southern edge of town where he finds Marguerite and Kalinka shivering in the rain.

A year later—the end of 1946—the French are back in control. The Viet Minh have been doublecrossed by De Gaulle and Chiang Kai-shek. The French have slaughtered twenty thousand Vietnamese in Haiphong. Ho Chi Minh, retreating to the jungles, has begun the Indochina war.

Peter sits in the back room staring at the wall. Kalinka, an infant, plays with groceries on the floor. Marguerite sweeps out the shop with a bamboo broom. It scratches against the wood—Kalinka recalls the noise.

Peter is shattered. A man destroyed, he screams in the night, then moans and weeps. His torture by the Japanese has left him with fear and scars. But Marguerite nurses him and somehow finds them food. "Survive, Peter!" she tells him. "A man can recover from wounds. Take sustenance in ideals, fraternity, revolution, the struggle to forge a society that is just."

Early in 1947 Peter reopens his parents' shop, a glorified grocery store, a prototype for La Colombe. He is busy for weeks replenishing his stock, building new and higher shelves. He has strung the curtain that divides the back room, separating Marguerite and Kalinka's bed from his. He decorates the outside of the store with flashing Christmas lights, then announces the reopening in the French-language press. Customers come in. He offers them special service. They ask about Marguerite. "My concubine," says Peter, "and Kalinka, my child."

Thus begins the network of lies that is to become a screen around their lives. The shop is a front, a center for espionage carried out from the back room by Marguerite. Hamid has a clear vision of her—a fascinating woman he wishes he could have known. She is strong, made of iron, burning with revolutionary zeal, but also kind and capable of great tenderness, a woman who always smiles.

Peter runs the shop; Marguerite runs the agents. They come and go, bringing instructions, carrying back her information to the jungles and the war. One day at dawn a man in black pajamas appears. He is a courier come to deliver her commission. She has attained the rank of major. She is among the most effective cadre in Hanoi.

Peter bounces Kalinka on his knee, up and down, up and down. Through the window she can see her mother bicycling up the street. Marguerite has gone on a mission. Peter doesn't know when she'll return. That night he reads Kalinka a fairy tale, then kisses her and turns off the light. She lies on the big bed, the bed she shares with her mother. She can hear Peter undressing on the other side of the curtain. He is humming to himself. She feels safe.

Years pass. Kalinka grows up. Business at the shop expands. The front of the store is crowded with officers' wives leaving their letters to be weighed and mailed and talking among themselves. Peter, a busybody, a gossip, shrewdly draws them out. He giggles at inanities. People take him for a fool. Always he is darting back and forth, disappearing into the back room. He is relaying information to Marguerite on troop movements, transfers, local politics, morale.

When the shop is closed for lunch Marguerite sets a teapot on the fire. Peter steams the letters open. He has discovered the secrets of flaps and seals.

All goes well until 1952, when suddenly there is consternation in the shop. Kalinka, nine years old, comes home one day from school. She greets Peter and her mother, sets her satchel down, but neither one of them looks up. For days after that she can feel their tension—French counterintelligence has discovered Peter's Soviet connections before the war. They suspect him of being a Russian field officer coordinating deliveries of arms to the Viet Minh. He is being watched. Strangers come in. They make small purchases and drill Peter with their eyes. There is a car parked across the street. Two men sit in it reading newspapers. The deliverymen who carry Marguerite's reports are warned to stay away.

Conferences. Meetings. Hushed conversations. Kalinka hears them plotting through the night. It is Marguerite, after all, who poses the real danger to the French, but it is Peter, finally, who is arrested—the French have taken her for an ignorant Tonkinoise.

Peter's interrogation—no beatings this time, nothing like his treatment by the Japanese. Bright lights in his eyes, hours without sleep. Finally he confesses to great and monstrous crimes, all rehearsed so many nights with Marguerite. The French, bewildered by the scope of his confession, take him for a major spy. He is too important to be imprisoned. They decide to expel him to Russia, a homeland he's never seen.

Much emotion that final hour when Marguerite and Kalinka visit him in jail. No possibility of Marguerite leaving too—she must stay behind to continue with the fight. But Kalinka is another matter. They discuss her future while she holds her mother's hand. If anything were to happen to Marguerite, Kalinka would be orphaned and alone. Finally it is decided—she will leave with Peter. Someday, sometime, when the war is over, they will all be reunited in Hanoi. A last exchange of hugs. Kalinka and Peter board the boat. Her last memory of her mother is the sight of her standing beside her bicycle waving to them from the pier.

Thus Kalinka's story was completed up to the time of her arrival in Tangier, a jigsaw puzzle of a life in which Hamid had searched for matching edges, gradually filled in holes and gaps. Still, for him, the biggest gap was not yet filled: *Why had Peter settled in Tangier, and why had he insisted that Kalinka pretend to be his wife?*

He wondered why this was so important, why, having learned so much, he couldn't leave these matters alone. *Am I*, he asked himself, *behaving like a lover or a detective?* Both, he decided finally—*I can't help myself; I have to know.* Was it because Kalinka was getting away from him, growing, changing, beginning to contradict the personality he thought he had understood as, so laboriously, he'd unraveled her early life? He couldn't say. He knew only that solving the relationship between her and Peter had become an obsession, the problem to which his great troubling questions about all the foreigners had finally been reduced.

At 2:00 A.M. one morning the telephone rang, jarring Hamid from sleep. Eyes still closed, he grasped about for the receiver, then accidentally knocked it to the floor.

Kalinka turned on the lights. "I can hear someone talking," she said.

Hamid strained his ears and heard it too, an urgent garble of Arabic, distant and indistinct. "Yes?" he said, retrieving the receiver. "Yes? Yes?"

"Aziz, Inspector. I'm at the Sûreté."

"You want me to come down there too, I suppose." He sat up, adjusted his pillows. Kalinka covered up her ears and yawned.

"We need you, Hamid. We've got a fiasco down here. I wouldn't call at this hour if I weren't facing special difficulties—"

"All right, Aziz. I'll see you in a little while."

He hung up and began to dress. "There's a certain ironic tone," he explained to Kalinka, "that finds its way, occasionally, into Aziz's voice. Then I know I'm in for it. Absurd passions. A glimpse at the rot of the West." He slipped into his moccasins. "It's the best part of my job."

There was not a car on Hassan II as he drove quickly through the night, only a few souls still lingering at the cafes off Place de France. Aziz was waiting on the steps of the Sûreté, pacing back and forth, puffing nervously on a cigarette.

"This one's something, Hamid—prominent persons, overtones of sex. I have the principals separated now. A few minutes ago, when we put them all together, they started to fight like medina cats."

Poor Aziz, he thought, *so loyal, so intelligent, but when it comes to the foreigners he still gets flustered and confused.*

"Don't worry." Hamid slapped him on the back. "We'll straighten this out soon enough. We'll go to my office. I want to hear everything in sequence. We must conduct our business in an orderly way."

He stopped off at a lavatory to splash cold water on his face. He wanted, always, to appear clear-headed and set a calm example for his staff.

When, finally, they were seated in the office, Aziz began to talk. Hamid was pleased by the cogency of his delivery and by gestures he recognized as his own.

"About an hour ago our operator received a call. The night clerk at the Hotel Continental reported a disturbance in one of his rooms. Since the Continental is in the Dar Baroud sector of the medina, the operator referred the complaint to the First Arrondisement. A pair of officers responded, arrests were made, and since foreigners were involved all the parties were brought down here. This is what we have: Mohammed Seraj, better known as Pumpkin Pie; an old whore who goes under the name of Sylvia; two young prostitutes, a boy and a girl, each about sixteen years old; Mr. and Mrs. Codd."

"Ashton and Musica Codd?"

Aziz gave a triumphant grin. "The Codds claim the role of complainants, but there's a difference of opinion on that. For one thing, they were arrested nude. And our investigating officers say Codd tried to thrash them with his walking stick. Pumpkin Pie claims they hired him to convince the teenagers to perform unnatural sexual acts. He says the whole fracas began when he refused and they turned on him in rage. The old whore claims she just happened to be in the next room and came out only when she heard the noise. The teenagers say she's their mother, and that she's in the business of renting them out."

"What do the Codds say to that?"

"They're claiming they were framed. They were 'interviewing' the kids, they say, when the whore arrived suddenly with Pumpkin Pie. These two tried to blackmail them, and when they refused to pay out they were brutally stripped and robbed. Codd says he assumed our men were other members of the gang. He merely tried to defend himself with the only implement he had at hand."

"Whew! All right, Aziz. Arrange six chairs in a crescent around my desk. Bring everybody in. I'm going down to the canteen. I need a cup of coffee before I deal with this."

He knew he was in for it on his way back upstairs, even before he reached his floor. The clamor of their shrieks echoed in the corridor. He could hear Aziz shouting at them in Arabic and French, warning them that when the Inspector arrived they'd better be still and behave.

"Shut up," he yelled, walking back into his office. "This is a department of criminal investigation, not a zoo."

He looked at them, fixed each one of them in turn. Pumpkin Pie, in a soiled undershirt, held himself with the arrogance of a hustler who felt himself desired. The old whore was pathetic—fat and wasted, her face contorted in a toothless grin. The two children were beautiful, but Hamid knew they were capable of infinite lies. And the Codds—

Hamid recognized the grimace of shame. Their clothing was disheveled, their faces stained with mercurochrome dots. The famous old Irish playwright and his wife sat as proudly as they could, determined, he could see, to brave things out.

"A sorry-looking group," he said to Aziz in French. "Is anybody injured? Is everyone all right?"

"Superficial cuts, Inspector. Our officers were beaten worst of all."

"The old bugger hit me with his walking stick," said Pumpkin Pie. "I'm going to sue him for damages as soon as I'm released."

"What makes you think you're going to be released?" Hamid asked.

"They're perverts, Inspector. Can't you see?"

"He says the two of you are perverts," Hamid said in English to the Codds.

"He did, did he? Well—he's a blackmailer." Codd brandished his fist. "He tried to frame us. He ought to be locked away."

"Publicly thrashed, I'd say," said Mrs. Codd.

"Piss on you, bitch," said Pie in Arabic. "Your cunt stinks like a rotten fish."

"Shut up!" screamed Aziz.

"What did he say?" asked Codd.

"I'm afraid, Mr. Codd, he was insulting your wife."

"This is absurd, Inspector. I demand that we be released. Surely you're not going to take the word of scum like this against people like my wife and me. We're tired. We're willing to drop our charges. All we ask is that you release us so we may return to our home and go to sleep."

"That's all very well, Mr. Codd," said Hamid. "But your charges aren't the only ones we're dealing with tonight."

"It was all a misunderstanding. I'm sorry about the officers. I'll gladly pay them damages. It was a trivial misunderstanding—nothing more."

Hamid shook his head. "Not so trivial as all that. Solicitation of minors, attacking a policeman, engaging in a brawl, false registration at a hotel. These are serious crimes that could lead to your expulsion. What a tragedy for you to end your residency here that way."

Hamid sat back then and watched them squirm. Musica Codd held back a sob. Ashton sat stiff and pale.

"Before we begin our investigation, I can call in Clive Whittle if you wish."

"That won't be necessary." Codd vigorously shook his head. "I'm quite certain we can straighten this out for ourselves."

"Very well," said Hamid, "but I insist on hearing the truth. This absurd story about your 'interviewing' these children is not something I'm prepared to believe."

"But—"

"Let me finish. It's a foolish, impractical lie. If you're going to stick to that, you'll only force me to pursue this case. Then this matter, in all its obscene detail, will become the delight of our local press."

Musica choked. Ashton bowed his head.

"It's a well-known fact, Mr. Codd, that both you and your wife have, for some time, been trying to arrange yourselves a *partouze*. It seems as though you've finally succeeded, though perhaps not with the result you had in mind. Do you deny any of this? What were you doing with these children? Do you really expect me to believe you were set up for blackmail by ignorant thugs like these?"

He turned away before Codd had a chance to answer, switched to Arabic, and addressed himself to the whore. "What have you got to say, you bag of bones?" he asked.

Sylvia set her mouth to show she wasn't going to talk.

"You set this whole thing up with Mohammed here. He made a deal with you, didn't he? How much money do you get for selling the bodies of your kids?"

"That's a lie, Inspector!" Pumpkin Pie screamed out.

"Shut up! I haven't gotten to you yet!"

"They're perverts! This is my country! We're brothers in Islam! You cannot side with them!"

"If he says another word, Aziz, take him back downstairs."

Aziz nodded, delighted by the whole affair. Hamid rubbed his eyes. Already he was bored.

"All right," he said, "we have testimony that contradicts. Clearly you children are the key. Now listen, and tell me if I'm right. Your mother told you to go with Mohammed and meet this English couple in the room. She told you to do whatever the English wanted. Isn't that correct?"

Both children nodded eagerly.

"So," he said sympathetically, "tell me what went wrong."

"We didn't want to do it," said the boy.

"Yes. I understand. But why the fight?"

"Him!" The girl pointed at Pie. "He told us we had to or he'd beat us up."

"Go on."

"Well," said the boy, "we were scared so we went along. But when we saw the infidels we didn't want to anymore."

"They were too old," said the girl.

"Their flesh was gray and fat."

"We refused. And then the infidels got mad."

"They started to scream at us."

"Our mother and Mohammed came in to find out what was wrong."

"And then what happened?"

"Then the infidels and Mohammed began to quarrel. Mohammed told the infidels they'd have to pay extra because they were so ugly and old. The infidels refused to pay, and then they started to fight. A little later the police arrived."

It all sounded perfectly reasonable to Hamid, including the part about asking for extra money from the Codds. The case was simple. It more or less solved itself. All of them were guilty. He wondered what to do. He felt a strong disgust and was gnawed at by the notion that no matter how he handled this affair it would end up being a waste of time. He turned to the Codds, translated what the children had said.

"Well," he asked, "have you anything to add?"

"We've been stupid, Inspector," said Codd, "terribly stupid. And of course we're deeply ashamed." The Codds looked at each other, then averted their eyes. "I don't know what more to say."

Contrition—Hamid had heard it all before. Suddenly he was tired of Europeans, their nasty escapades, their evasive, pleading eyes.

"I don't know either, Mr. Codd," he said. "All my life I've tried to understand people like you. You come down here, set yourselves up on the Mountain, and then, not content with your luxurious lives, you insist on disgracing yourselves in the gutters of Tangier. Why? Can you explain it? Is it something about our town? Or is it nothing more than the natural weaknesses of your all-too-imperfect flesh?"

He waited for them to answer, and when they did not he shook his head. "I don't know what to do with you. There's a side of me that wants to be harsh. But I find I have no desire to listen to your confessions or lock you up and watch you writhe. In fact, I think that would be meaningless. You've made fools of yourselves. You've been absurd. You are what you are, and you've done what you've done. You don't even offer me an excuse."

He looked at them again, taking no particular pleasure in their embarrassment or in his power, as an Inspector, to settle their case as he liked. They were so pathetic, such grotesque antiques, that he felt sick looking at them, sick of their lechery and wounded pride.

"All right," he said suddenly, "leave. Go home. Next time there'll be no mercy. Now get out of here quick, before I change my mind."

Ashton Codd started to say something, but Hamid waved his hand. He was not interested in gratitude. He felt tired and filled with scorn.

"So," said Aziz when they were gone, "do we release the others too?"

"Yes. Throw them out, all of them. Let's go home and get some sleep."

When they were all released he gave Aziz a lift. Finally, at home, standing on his terrace, he stared out at the Mountain and listened to the wind.

The only pleasure he found those hot July days occurred during his noontime marches down the beach. He liked swaggering on the sand, pointing at people and ordering them removed. He felt then that he was doing something, perhaps purifying Tangier, but he learned from Aziz that these actions were not universally admired in other bureaus of the police. One day the Prefect himself suggested Hamid could overplay his hand.

"Look, Hamid," he said, "what are you trying to prove?

Your cleanups don't accomplish anything. You just chase the scum someplace else."

"Perhaps," said Hamid, "but at least the beach is clean. There's less crime now around the hotels."

"My advice is to stick to foreigners and not worry so much about vice. Inspectors sometimes go too far and then they find themselves transferred. Ever been to Ksar es Souk? In the Sahara the sun shrivels up your tongue."

It was a threat without substance, and it failed to fill him with any fear. Still he wondered if he was doing good, if his cleanup was anything more than a charade.

The day he spotted the joggers on Vasco de Gama turned out to be the hottest of July. As he drove about Tangier, feeling the heat rise hour by hour, he had an inkling of what August would be like, and bit his lip in dread. It would be Ramadan, coinciding with the hottest month as it did once in twenty-five years. Sunrise to sunset without food or a drop to drink—in August that would be more than fasting; that would be agony without respite.

He spent the day visiting his men, trying to sort out crimes of substance from a backlog of unresolved complaints. He was tired of sex crimes and smugglers of hashish, tempests on the Mountain, vagrant hippies, trivial disputes. Something was happening in Tangier, but he didn't know what it was. He could feel the tension all around but couldn't put his finger on its cause.

He passed people as he drove: Robin Scott giggling in a cafe, Laurence Luscombe walking wearily on the Boulevard, stooping in the heat. The old actor's face was pale as chalk. His wisps of whitened hair blew crazily in the blowtorch wind.

He noticed the Freys' limousine parked before a bank. Though he knew they were the notorious Beckers, he also knew there was nothing he could do. Since they were rich, they could keep an extradition order from ever getting to the courts. His only hope, he felt, was to keep up a patient watch. If an Israeli agent ever did turn up, he might manage to catch them all in a tour de force.

Heading back to the Sûreté, he saw Vicar Wick leaving

Madame Porte's *salon de thé*. The man's gait was nervous, his face haggard, tense. There was something about him that struck Hamid—as if he were enduring an enormous strain.

Finally at seven, exhausted by another incoherent day, he picked up the book Farid had found for him, left his office, and walked downtown. He fought his way through the throngs that crowded Boulevard Pasteur at dusk, passed a band marching back and forth, blowing trumpets and beating drums.

When he walked into his brother's store, Farid's assistant was showing a necklace. His customer, a French lady accompanied by a boxer dog, was debating the merits of the piece and the astronomical asking price. Hamid interrupted, asked the assistant for Farid. The bartering continued. The assistant pointed to the stairs. Hamid mounted them quietly—only later he asked himself why. He hadn't intended to surprise his brother, but he didn't want to disturb the negotiations in the shop. He had just stepped into the dim upstairs room, the room where Farid stored and showed his rugs, was looking around, wondering where his brother was, when he heard a groan quickly followed by a gasp. He moved slowly, quietly, toward a mound of rugs piled near the wall. He heard the sound again and, following his policeman's instincts, moved closer so he could look behind.

He guessed they'd heard his footsteps—the next moment their startled eyes looked into his: Farid and Hervé Beaumont, the olive-skinned body of his brother, the pale one of the European boy, entwined, naked on the floor.

The bargaining downstairs had become shrill—he could hear the high-pitched cries of the Frenchwoman demanding a concession in the price. Hervé began to giggle, then to rock his body back and forth, but Farid remained still, his face impassive, a look Hamid remembered from their boyhood, as if he expected to be hit.

A long moment passed between them as they searched each other's eyes. Later Hamid had the impression that they'd tried to peer into each other's brains. But then the mood was broken by a bark—the Frenchwoman's boxer downstairs.

"I just came by to return the book," he said. He laid it on top of the rugs, turned, and walked away.

Downstairs Farid's assistant was standing in the doorway talking to another assistant shopkeeper from across the street. "What a bitch," he was saying as Hamid brushed by. "When I met her price she laughed at me, yanked at her dog, and left."

"Yes," said the other, "they're all like that this year. Pigs' vaginas, tourist trash—"

A few days after he surprised his brother, Hamid decided to abandon his cleanup of the beach. He also decided that the time had come to confront Zvegintzov without letting him wriggle away.

He pulled up in front of La Colombe at ten o'clock, long after the shop had closed. This time there'd be no interruptions, customers intruding, or telephone ringing in the back. Pausing in his car, he studied the iron grill pulled down over the store's façade. He remembered sitting out here one afternoon in May wanting to warn Peter about following Kalinka, then hesitating and finally driving off. This time it was different. He knew the questions he must ask. He also knew that Peter was afraid of him, though he had no desire to exploit that fear.

When, finally, he walked across the street, he heard drumming and music clashing within Dradeb. There were many weddings in the slum that summer night. If he and Kalinka decided to be married, would they celebrate the traditional way?

He looked in through the grill. The lights were off, and there was no sign of movement in the shop. No bell either, so he shook the grill, then noticed a ribbon of light beneath an inner door. *He's in the back room,* he thought, *that back room where Kalinka spent so many years.* He walked around the side of the building to a window where a shade was drawn.

He rapped on the glass. Nothing. He rapped harder. Still no sign. He was about to call out Peter's name when suddenly the shade snapped up.

"Peter—"

"Who's there?" His face was only inches away, but the reflections on the glass must have confused his sight.

"It's me, Hamid."

"What do you want?"

"Open up."

"It's late."

"I want to talk to you. Open up."

Peter glared out, blinking his eyes. Then he yanked down the shade.

Hamid walked to the front of the shop. A minute later a flourescent light sputtered on. Peter opened the inside door and spoke to him through the grill.

"I'm closed, Hamid. Come around in the morning."

"No, Peter. *Now*. We must talk together *now*."

Peter hesitated, then he knelt to unclasp the padlocks which attached the grill. He fumbled but finally managed to undo them. He raised the grill just high enough so Hamid could enter if he stooped.

"You frightened me half to death, Hamid. You should know better than to frighten a man at night."

"I'm sorry, Peter, but the night is best. We're always interrupted during business hours."

"Well—you're inside now. You might as well sit down."

He pulled out a stool, set it in the center of the room, then sat down himself on the yellow hassock where Kalinka used to perch.

"So, Hamid—you've come to expel me. I've been expecting this. I've even packed a bag."

"I'm not here for that."

"Oh? Really? Then how much longer is the suspense to last?"

"Look, Peter, you must get this through your head. I've no intention of expelling you."

Peter was silent.

"You don't believe me."

"Why should I believe you? You've been after me for months."

"You have it wrong. I've only come to talk."

"You want the facts, don't you—the *incriminating* facts?"

"Incriminating to whom?"

"To me, of course. I'm not stupid, Hamid, though you may think I've been at times. Your dossiers—I know all about them. And that all these months you've been building up your case."

Hamid squinted at him. The light in the shop was dim. Peter seemed so loathsome, such a loathsome little man.

"Really, Peter, you have things wrong," he said. "Kalinka and I have been trying to reconstruct the past, and since you're a part of it, you're involved as well."

"Am I supposed to believe that's why you're here?"

"Why not? I could have kicked you out anytime."

"Yes. That's true."

"Why are you so frightened then?"

"Because you have *power,* Hamid. I know all about that, you see. I've been kicked out of a country before." He paused. "Now there's no place for me to go. There's barely a country left that will take me in. You've already got Kalinka, Hamid. If you expel me I'll lose everything. I'll even lose my shop."

A silence. Hamid wondered how he could break through so many layers of fear.

"Peter, I give you my word. I have no wish to see you lose your shop. Tell me what I need to know and I'll never trouble you again."

"And if I incriminate myself?"

"You won't. Not with me. Everything you say will be in confidence. I'm sincere, Peter. You must take me at my word."

Peter stared at him a long while—Hamid imagined him weighing out his trust with the same caution he used when he weighed a letter on his postal scale.

"All right," he said finally, "ask your questions. I don't promise that I'll answer them, but we'll see—"

"I know most of it already, I think—your membership in the party, your friendship with Zhukovsky, Kalinka's mother, Zhukovsky's death, your expulsion from Hanoi."

"And Poland?"

"Yes. That too. Kalinka's years in school. You were working in a factory there, she said."

"A shoe factory near Warsaw. It wasn't much of a job."

"But then you left and came down here. That's my question, Peter. *Why Tangier?*"

"Ah—" Peter shook his head. "That was a difficult time for me. I was really up against it—up against the wall."

"Tell me about it."

Peter shook his head again, paused as if to clear his memory. Then he coughed and exhaled.

"It was 1954, just after the settlement, the Geneva Conference that ended the Indochina war. I was summoned to the Vietnamese legation in Warsaw. A man there, an old partisan, told me that Major Pham Thi Nha had been killed at the battle of Dien Bien Phu. She'd volunteered to join the siege and, on the twentieth day or so, had somehow gotten killed. I never found out how—a bomb from an airplane, a shell from the French fort. It didn't matter anyway. All that mattered was that she was dead. I was still reeling from that when this man told me his government wanted Kalinka back. At first I tried to argue with him. Kalinka belonged with me. I'd promised her mother. I'd put her in school. I was prepared to bring her up. But there was no arguing. A directive had been issued. Kalinka was an orphan, the daughter of a heroine of the resistance. She qualified for special treatment now. Her place was in Vietnam. Well, in that case, I said, I would go back there with her too. The man smiled at me and shook his head. 'We've won the war,' he said. 'We don't need foreign agents anymore.'

"I knew then they'd never let me back. Marguerite was dead, and they wanted Kalinka too. I was desperate. You can imagine how desperate I was. The thought of losing her—I couldn't accept it. And I knew I had to do something fast if I was to keep her from being taken away.

"I stayed up all that night, thinking, thinking, and the only thought that came to mind was the Bureau, the KGB. They'd sent me to Poland in the first place, found the school, helped me get my job, and they'd told me that if I ever needed help I could always count on them. I was an old agent, you see. They take care of us in a way. I didn't want to go to them. I wasn't even a Communist anymore. I didn't give a damn about any of it, but I was desperate and the Bureau seemed the only place to turn.

"Their offices were in an annex to the Russian Embassy, an old palace cut up into a thousand tiny stalls. There were three of them who interviewed me. I told them my story and begged them to help. There was no problem, they said. All I had to do was reinstate myself. Then all my troubles would be solved, and Kalinka would be safe.

"It wasn't long before I realized what that meant. They offered me a deal. I had certain skills, remember, knew lots of languages and had had experience in intelligence work. All I had to do was agree to work for them again and they'd see to it that Kalinka stayed at school.

"Of course, I'd presented them with the sort of situation they like the best—someone very close to hold over your head, so you do everything they ask. Now understand me, Hamid—*I didn't want to be a spy again.* But I was desperate, and that was the only way I knew to keep Kalinka out of Vietnam. So I agreed, and a few months later I was sent down here."

"*Why?* There's nothing here."

"That's true now, though in those days it wasn't clear. I came down in 1955. North Africa was on the verge of change. The Algerian rebellion was starting up. Moroccan independence was nearly won. Tangier was an international city. It had been filled with spies since the Second World War. No one knew what was going to happen. It seemed a good place for a deep-cover agent to set himself up and burrow in. So I came down. I had a Polish passport—nothing special about that. I worked as a clerk in a bank, establishing my residency. Then I got a job as comptroller for a small import-export house. Well, suddenly the situation changed. The French and Spanish pulled out, Mohammed V became the Sultan, and Tangier became part of Morocco once again. With the end of Tangier as an international city there was hardly anything for me to do."

"Then why didn't they pull you out? Send you someplace else?"

He shook his head. "I don't know. Perhaps they thought I was perfect for this place."

Hamid, watching him, knew precisely what he meant. There was something second-rate about Peter, something obviously mediocre that helped him blend with the other working foreigners, the Spanish shoemakers and Italian barbers, the Dutch clerks and French auto shop repairmen in the town. Who would ever suspect that he was anything but what he seemed, a second-rate European with a vague and mediocre past?

"I had nothing to do all that time. Really nothing that could incriminate me now. I want you to understand that, Hamid. I never did anything against your country. I was just here to keep an eye on things."

"What things?"

"Oh, the ships, you know, coming and going through the Straits. I had some boys who watched them for me, and I wrote down what they saw. I never knew what passed through at night, of course, or when it was foggy and they couldn't see."

"But that's ludicrous—to cover the Straits like that."

"Yes, yes—I know. But I subscribed to the shipping newspapers and got lots of information out of them. I mailed my reports to a postal box in Rome. Just lists of ships and the approximate times they passed. Anyone could have done it. Sometimes I just made it up."

"They never checked?"

He shook his head. "I guess it didn't matter so long as it sounded right. Anyway, I was busy. I was setting up this shop. You see—I'd saved a little, looked around, and decided a shop was needed here. I'd always wanted another shop, like the one my parents had. I'd inherited their place, spent wonderful years there with Marguerite. So I set up La Colombe, modeled exactly on the Hanoi store. And I was successful almost from the start."

Peter took great delight explaining how he'd expanded his business through the years, from merely selling merchandise to offering his customers *grand service*. Soon he became a clearinghouse for servants, a man who could be depended upon to find a good night watchman or fix a telephone. And all that time he'd worried about Kalinka—her letters were so infrequent, lonely, and strangely sad. He wanted her back, but knew he must be patient. He kept up his reporting on the ships until, one day, a man appeared.

He was an important man—Peter was sure of that. A man named Prozov, a man accustomed to command. He spoke in Russian and knew all about Peter's past: Indochina, his expulsion by the French, his hopes of being reunited with Kalinka too. He was prepared to arrange that, he said, if Peter would provide a little service first. A little job. A little mission. Nothing especially dangerous, though there was always a certain risk. And if Peter refused—well, Kalinka might have to stay in Poland for many years.

He took Peter's car, drove off, disappeared with it for several days. When he returned he told Peter to drive it to Algiers. Peter was scared then, really scared. There was something, he knew, hidden in his car. He didn't know what it was, and he didn't want to know. The French had a dossier on him—in Indochina they'd marked him as a Soviet spy. Now there were rumors they were using torture in Algeria. Remembering his experiences with the Japanese, he trembled at the thought of being interrogated once again.

But still he did it. It was his only chance to get Kalinka back. And his mind was sharp—he was canny when he had to be. It occurred to him, driving across northern Morocco toward the Algerian frontier, his hands shaking as he gripped the wheel, frightened to death with no idea of what might be welded to the bottom of his car, that if he did get across, did fulfill the mission, he had no guarantee the KGB would keep their word. They could doublecross him, refuse to keep the bargain—so long as they had Kalinka they could use him again and again. So driving along, checking to see he wasn't followed, glancing every few seconds at the rear-view mirror, he realized that the only way he'd ever get her back would be to end his usefulness to the Bureau by making them think the French knew who he was. If he could do that they'd have no further use for him, and therefore no reason to hold Kalinka anymore.

It was a fascinating notion, and he toyed with it the entire way, wondering how he could manage it, if in fact it was worth the risk. He was proud of the way he behaved at the frontier, like any ordinary European heading toward Algiers to have some fun. He stopped in Oran, bought the newspapers, and then got an idea of what might be in his car. The French were conducting a series of nuclear tests in the Sahara. Perhaps he was carrying equipment to monitor the blasts.

He thought about betrayal, could think of nothing else, as he entered Algiers through a driving, torrential rain. Then he got lost in a maze of traffic circles and one-way streets; finally found his meeting place by the Jardin Exotique. He waited there, shivering in his car, until his contact came. It was an Algerian this time, someone he'd never seen, who directed him up a hill to a region of villas with walled-in grounds. The Algerian pointed to a house, got out, swung open a set of gates. Peter drove straight through into a garage, took out his suitcase, and was driven back downtown in another car.

They'd booked him into a businessmen's hotel. He spent a night of torment there on a sagging mattress, slapping mosquitoes off his chest. All he had to do, he thought, was call the French police. If he turned informant, offered himself as a double agent, they'd make it look as though they'd been watching him for years. The Russians would see he had no further use, and then would let Kalinka go. It was a gamble, of course, the gamble of a lifetime, but one he was willing to take. He was about to call the French, had actually picked up the phone, when suddenly he remembered something which gave him second thoughts. Why had they let him see the garage where presumably they'd take apart his car? They didn't work like that, kept things compartmentalized— unless, of course, it was all a trap. Yes—then he was sure of it and knew he couldn't take the chance. If he called the French, told them about his car, and they went to the villa and found no trace, the Russians would know he was a double agent and he'd be dead within the hour. So he did nothing, sat in his hotel room, stared out mournfully at the rain. And on the morning of the third day Prozov finally called.

"We're pleased with what you did," he said. "Your work is finished now. You'll find your car parked in front of the hotel, and you can expect delivery of the Polish goods."

That was it—a miracle. They actually kept their word. He never heard from them again. Kalinka arrived two months later with a Polish passport bearing his own last name. He fixed up the back room of the shop so it would remind her of Hanoi.

"So you see, Hamid, you really have no good reason to throw me out. I never spied against Morocco—I never had the chance. Everything was for Kalinka, to get her here and keep her safe. I pretended we were married, and no one suspected we were not. She was only sixteen then, but her face was timeless like Marguerite's. Even the Vietnamese wouldn't take her away when they found out we were man and wife."

Had Peter really thought the Vietnamese would care enough to send someone to Tangier to snatch her back? It was ridiculous, absurd, yet Peter had rigorously carried this fiction out, even, years later, coming to Hamid's flat to demand an explanation, because, as he'd put it at the time, "I'm the husband. I have certain rights."

Kalinka, Hamid thought, must have been extremely troubled to have submitted to such a situation for so long. But she was indifferent, as she still was to so many things, and if it had pleased Peter to introduce her as his wife, then she'd played out that role without complaint. Peter had fed her, protected her, made her the focus of his life. And all that time they'd slept in separate beds in the back room of his shop.

"I admire you, Peter," he said. "That was brilliant the way you calculated things. Not calling the French; seeing through the Russian trap. Yes, I admire you for that."

Peter beamed.

"You know," Hamid said, "I've known you for many years, but I've never been in your back room."

Peter laughed. "Nothing there," he said. "No secrets, Hamid. Just my papers and accounts. But come in, if you like."

They stood up, and Hamid followed Peter to the door. It was a shabby room, and Peter looked shabby standing in the middle of it, talking, gesturing, scratching at his head.

"Here's the curtain, pulled back now, but in the old days we used it to separate the room at night. This was her bed, bigger than mine, you see—Marguerite and Kalinka shared a big bed like that. I've set things up pretty much the same in here. Their bed was always on the right, and mine was near the window, just as now—"

He mumbled on, lost in his memories, while Hamid stared at him and gaped. Suddenly he understood: it was nostalgia for the life Peter had led with Marguerite that had caused him to force Kalinka to take her mother's place. So pitiful, this fantasy, and so cruel the way he'd made her play it out. Just the thought of Kalinka sleeping here and wandering around Tangier so many years playing his preposterous game—Hamid shook his head in grief. The hashish probably saved her, he thought. Only in its fog could she escape Peter's twisted, terrifying love.

"Oh, I know you love her, Hamid. You're strong, you treat her well. But still I need her too, if only to talk with her in the old language we used to use. All this time, you see, I've been afraid you'd find out I was a spy. Then you'd throw me out, and I wouldn't see her anymore."

A spy—he was afraid I'd find out that! It was so pathetic, his fear, all his illusions about himself. He'd been nothing, an inaccurate spotter of ships, a clerk, and once a messenger to Algiers.

"Don't worry, Peter. Nothing will happen to you now. And of course you may speak with Kalinka sometimes. I won't feel compromised."

Peter beamed again.

"One more question, though, before I leave. I know the Japanese killed Kalinka's father. I've wondered why they didn't kill you too."

"Ah—well, you see, Hamid, Stephen was a real Communist. He held his tongue. But I—I talked a lot."

As Peter hung his head then, out of shame, Hamid felt all his anger melt away. He knew now for sure that Peter was harmless, a broken man, a burned-out case.

They shook hands, and then Hamid left, pausing a moment outside the shop. He thought of Peter inside, so deluded, so obsequious, somehow managing to function in Tangier. He's found his niche, he thought, and he'll survive, so long as Kalinka remains nearby. He'll operate this shop, this little museum, listen to gossip, perhaps steam open a letter or two a week, endure insults from his customers, flick his feather duster to hide his scars, and go to bed each night haunted by memories and ghosts.

Thinking about that, driving through Dradeb, through the wedding throngs which jammed the narrow street, Hamid felt a wave of sympathy break from the reservoir he'd thought was dry. It washed over Peter, so battered, so wounded, by the forces that had shaped his life.

At last, he thought, *I understand.*

He wept then in his car, driving through the slum, wept with pity for Peter Zvegintzov, the fussy little shopkeeper, and for Kalinka wandering the city trying to escape her nightmare in hashish and dreams. He wept too for the pain of Stephen Zhukovsky, screaming in a Hanoi jail, and for Marguerite Pham Thi Nha, loading artillery at Dien Bien Phu, smiling beneath the brim of her conical straw hat.

Emerging from Dradeb, honking his way through the last of the revelers that summer night, he still had tears in his eyes. He was in a rush to get home, hold Kalinka, ask her to marry him. He wanted to shield her from the savage storms of life.

III.

RAMADAN. *It settled upon our town with the August haze and a dry, hot Saharan wind. At dawn a cannon roared out from the port to tell the faithful to begin the daily fast. At dusk it roared again, arousing a clamor from all the mosques. Then the spicy smell of harira soup perfumed the air, and we were bewitched by the sounds of Arab flutes.*

But then, as the fast progressed, anger engulfed Tangier: dogs became vicious, babies shrieked, quarrels broke out in all the quarters—the wells were running dry.

The holy month divided Tangier into two cities: a city of foreigners exalting in our season, and an Arab city of brooding multitudes who regarded us with an unflinching gaze. Their Tangier became the backdrop before which we pranced and played, living sweetly in the interstices of their rage. . . .

A Visit
to the Mountain

Early one broiling August afternoon Laurence Luscombe left Dradeb. The sun nearly blinded him as he stepped outside his house, then paused by the overflowing septic that oozed beside his door. All the houses on his alley fed into it, and the stench was terrible, human wastes marinating in the heat. The fumes, strong as sulfur, burned his nostrils. He staggered for a moment and held his breath.

It was all so foul, a reminder of his decline, but on twelve hundred pounds a year there was nowhere else for him to live. As it was, he hardly got by in Tangier, eating fruit and small quantities of the cheapest fish, walking everywhere, no matter how fierce the heat, even depriving himself of coffee and beer. He'd kept his pride, he thought; so far no one had tried to steal that. He still showered fastidiously at Derik Law's, though it was an agony to walk there every day.

And yet—he was shabby. He knew it, could feel very clearly that he was. Sometimes, when he approached people, they smiled and turned away. When he spoke to them about his troubles they winced and hurried off. Why? What was it about him that inspired such distaste? Perhaps, he thought, he smelled of failure, or showed too clearly the ravages of age.

He was pale and gaunt, with brown spots on his face. His hair was nothing but a few dry white wisps, and his clothes, unironed, hung loose upon his frame. A memento mori—perhaps that was now his role, staggering about, stalking Tangier, reminding people of death.

He set off down the main street of Dradeb, empty except for some ragged children playing cheerlessly in the dust. Men and women were sleeping through the midday heat, weakened by thirst and hunger—their abominable, pointless fast. Luscombe hated Ramadan, had hated it since he'd come to Tangier. Mail was misdelivered. The Arabs were all on edge. At dusk the city abounded in accidents caused by distracted drivers hurrying home for soup.

He crossed the Jew's River, paused on the narrow bridge, then looked up at the Mountain, so high, so far away, so steep. Today he would climb it, despite the raging sun. He spent a few moments working up his will, then set off on the trek.

"It's a conspiracy—don't you see? Everyone says it is now."

Luscombe looked straight at Peter Barclay, beside Camilla Weltonwhist on the couch. His iron-gray hair caught the sun, his cane lay across his lap. Her diamond collar gleamed against her throat. Her torso looked like a vase.

Clearly they were irritated with him, but still they were trying to be polite. He'd done the unpardonable, intruded unannounced. He'd interrupted their backgammon game. He should have phoned them first.

"But I don't understand," said Camilla, blinking at him confused. "Why did they pick that particular date? I must say, it's *quite* inconvenient. Why do you suppose they didn't think about that?"

"But they *did* think about it," Luscombe said. Barclay, he noticed, was fidgeting with the dice. "That's what I've been trying to say to you. They *intended* that it be inconvenient. That's the conspiracy, you see."

"Oh." She settled back, still not grasping his point. His situation, he felt, wasn't all that complicated, but she didn't seem to want to understand.

"Now let me get this straight, Larry." Barclay leaned forward, displaying his shiny teeth. "You say your actors have petitioned for a meeting with the intention of taking over the club, and that according to the bylaws of the Tangier Players you must meet with them at the time they've set."

"That's it. Exactly. Now you see why—"

"Damn peculiar bylaws, if you ask me."

"Peculiar indeed." Camilla nodded her head.

They both looked at him sharply, as if he were responsible for his predicament and had no business complaining about it to them. Barclay smiled, but Camilla glared. He'd seen her glare like that at the market, shopping for luncheon parties, ordering lamb chops by the dozen, hiring boys to carry her groceries to her Rolls.

"I only intended that the club be democratic. I wrote the bylaws to insure majority rule. That was years ago. I never imagined they'd be used against me. It never entered my head."

"Should have, Larry. You should have thought of it." Barclay edged forward, determined to win the point. "I must say, it's rather shrewd of Kelly." He grinned. "I hadn't realized he was so crafty. Must give him credit for that."

The two of them, Barclay and Weltonwhist, nodded vigorously and exchanged a knowing glance. They seemed more impressed with Kelly's craftiness than with his own quite desperate plight.

"Oh, yes, he's shrewd," Luscombe said. "Kelly's crafty like a fox. But he mustn't be allowed to get away with it. That's what I've come to say. We must all fight him together. Teach him a lesson. Collapse the conspiracy right on his head."

A silence. Camilla looked over at Barclay, who was staring off into space. Evidently he was weighing the consequences, considering what the two of them should do.

This time I need you, Luscombe thought. *This time you mustn't let me down.* He'd climbed the Mountain expressly to win over Barclay's support. With Barclay the Mountain would rally to his side; without him he'd surely lose TP.

"You see," he said, quite frantic, hoping to arouse their sense of fair play, "everyone in town's known about these parties for weeks, so Kelly asked for a meeting on just the particular night when he was certain you patrons wouldn't come. He's counting on your being frivolous—that's the core of his plan. Without you he'll have the votes to take over the club. He'll get the treasury—that's two hundred pounds! The lights. The flats. Even the contract with the Spanish Polytechnical school."

He stopped, astonished by his tone, so desperate now, so excited, much too loud and excited for Mrs. Weltonwhist's salon. "Might I have a glass of water?" he asked, realizing he'd been sitting in her house for a quarter of an hour without her offering him anything to drink.

"Oh, yes, of course." She rang for her butler. Barclay squinted at him, annoyed.

"Well, Camilla dear," he said, turning to her with a savage little smile. "I'm afraid there isn't anything we can do for Larry here. Really, it's an awful shame."

"But surely, Peter, we might manage—"

"No, darling. No possible way." He turned to Luscombe. "We're both invited to Henderson Perry's that night, and we must be there promptly at eight. That's the protocol. Ordinarily it wouldn't matter, but Henderson's invited a batch of Moroccan royals, so of course, you see, we can't be late."

"That's all right, Peter. The TP meeting's set for seven. All you have to do is turn up and vote, then go on to Perry's with time to spare."

He was relieved then, even amused; Kelly was clever, but he'd miscalculated about the time. He was just beginning to relax, certain now that things were going to work out, when Barclay frowned and shook his head.

"I'm sorry, Larry, but it's not so simple. These club meetings have a way of running on. Both of us need time to rest and dress, and Camilla's promised to do Henderson's bouquets."

"But you at least—"

"No. Sorry, Larry. It's not convenient. I'm just not going to have the time."

"But *please,* you *must*—"

"It's not that we don't *want* to come, you see, but we're previously committed and now it's too late for us to wriggle free."

"One can't be rude, you know," Camilla said. "I know this is important to you, but surely you're not asking that."

Luscombe slumped back, stunned by their refusal. They'd kicked the breath right out of him. Now he felt too weary to complain. "Convenient," "rude"—those were the things that were important to them. Everything had to be arranged for *their* convenience. They needed a guarantee they'd be *amused*. He looked at them sitting there, pitying him with smiles. What did they care, after all, that the actors had turned against him? What did it matter to them that Kelly would turn TP to trash? They didn't care—not the slightest bit. He realized how stupid he'd been to think they ever would.

"There *are* other voting patrons," Camilla said. "Surely you haven't been depending on us." It was more of a reproach than a helpful suggestion. He'd shown poor form, in her eyes, by placing the onus on them.

"I've tried Vanessa Bolton," he said, "but she's going to Perry's too. The Codds are invited to Countess de Lauzon's, and on to the Manchesters' as well."

"Ugh!" said Barclay, curling his lip. "The Manchesters—they're having some kind of leftover thing. But there it is, you see—Françoise is having a party too."

"What about Percy Bainbridge?" Camilla asked. "He's a patron. At least I think he is."

"I've been to see him, but he won't make a commitment. He's been waiting for you to take the lead."

"Waiting to be invited to Henderson's, you mean." Barclay laughed. "Poor Percy—he'll wait forever for that."

Camilla snickered, and then the two of them exchanged another glance. They were fascinated by gossip, who was invited, who was not.

"Oh, dear me," she said. "Isn't there anybody else?"

"There're the Whittles, but I haven't approached them yet."

"Don't!" commanded Barclay. "That wouldn't do at all. You must be sensitive, Larry. You must think before you impose. Everyone wants to help, of course, but if you're pushy, well, then—" He shrugged.

So that was it: he'd been too *pushy,* and he'd *imposed* on them much too long. He stood up abruptly. They'd given the signal. Now it was time for him to go.

"There's the Vicar, isn't there?"

"Yes, Camilla! And he *just might be willing* to come."
Barclay looked up, clicked his teeth. "Tell you what—I'll have
a word with him. Vicar always takes my advice."

"There," said Camilla with a sigh. "There—you'll have
Vicar Wick. You can't say we didn't help you, Larry. I knew
Peter would come up with something in the end."

It was hopeless. They didn't understand. Or perhaps they
understood too well. Even if the Vicar came he'd have only
three votes. They were both gazing at him now, impatient
that he leave.

Suddenly he felt unsteady, afraid he was going to faint.
Perhaps he'd stood up too quickly. Camilla took hold of his
arm.

"Now, now, Larry," she said, guiding him across the room.

"Sorry, Larry," said Barclay, not bothering to rise.
"Courage, old boy. Good luck!"

Camilla led him to the door, then most smoothly showed
him out. "When the summer's over and things have quieted
down," she said, "you must be sure and come around again.
Some afternoon, perhaps, when everything's less frantic.
We'll sit out in the garden and take some tea."

There was a moment of confusion. He was still clutching
her glass. He thrust it into her hand, saw a weak, distant
smile, then a nod of dismissal as she shut the door.

He stood alone outside, dazed by the whole exchange. She
hadn't even invited him for lunch; all he rated was a cup of
tea. It didn't matter really—at this point nothing did. The
petty slights, the little glances and winks—what difference
now if he was going to lose the club? He'd climbed the
Mountain on the strength of a futile hope, and now everything was finished, all was lost. The Tangier Players, his creation, had slipped from his infirm grasp, on account, it
seemed, of Peter Barclay's whim and a commitment by Mrs.
Weltonwhist to prepare Henderson Perry's bouquets.

He walked away quivering, shoulders hunched, eyes
smarting from the harshness of the light. He stopped every
so often to wipe his brow, pant and gasp for breath. They'd
resumed their backgammon game by now, or perhaps they
were still dissecting him. He'd known such people all his life,
knew the way they rolled their eyes, the tone they used to
express disdain.

He walked as rapidly as he could in no particular direction, anxious to get as far as possible from the house. Time passed. He wandered aimlessly farther up the Mountain, past villas, then into meadows, up always toward the Mountain's crest. He followed narrow, rocky paths, passed ancient wells and children tending goats. There was an old mosque up there, a quiet place he'd stumbled upon years before. He climbed higher, searching, but couldn't find it. He lost track of where he was.

After a while he stopped, exhausted, feeling pain in all his joints. There was a band of burning across his chest. The walk had worn him out. He looked around, spied an outcropping of rock, went to it, sat down to rest. Life was so unfair. For ten years he'd struggled. And then—one humiliation after another had piled on since May, until now, in August, his world had turned to ash.

He gazed down upon Tangier. The city glowed miles below. It baked away beneath the brutal sun, a secret city, closed upon itself. How lonely it looks, he thought, that decaying town of ancient streets. For a decade his life there had been sweet. Now everything was over, and the city was growing mean.

Yes, it was more than TP that was over for him now. It was Tangier that was finished too. A way of life. A sweet embrace. That season had come now to its end. The Moroccans had turned against the Europeans. They didn't want to live with foreigners anymore. The era of the Mountain would soon be over, and those who'd just scorned him would soon be scorned themselves.

His eyes glazed as he began to think about himself, look back upon his life, take the measure of his worth. He'd spent years, he realized, in cheap theatrical hotels, hovels not much better than his shanty in Dradeb. He'd spent a lifetime trying to preserve his dignity in the face of all the humiliations an actor must endure. What had it meant—his life upon the stage? Not much, he thought—barely anything at all. He'd played uncles and butlers and inspectors from Scotland Yard, small, neat, lonely little men with a moment or two of grandeur, a line or two of wit. Theater, he'd told himself, was nothing if it was not an art, but he'd always known this wasn't so, that it was a shabby life, a glittering sham.

He had a revelation then of what he truly was: a discarded old actor, irrelevant, gone to grief, gazing down upon a foreign city that had never recognized his talent and had always been hostile to his dream. He was an extraneous, foolish old man, clutching tight to a ridiculous creation while others, equally foolish, pried hard to unloose his grasp. He lowered his head, covered his face, prepared to sob with pity for himself. But all he could conjure to express despair was a bone-dry bitter laugh.

And yet—he loved Tangier. Uncovering his eyes, looking down again, he was moved by its beauty, its whiteness through the August haze. Then he was overwhelmed by a sense of his own mortality: soon death would overtake him, though Tangier would survive.

Death. He'd thought about that a lot of late, pausing at midday sometimes on the sweltering streets, staring off into space, or lying naked on his sagging bed at night praying for a cooling breeze. But still he was glad he'd climbed so high, had taken in this stunning view. He knew with utter certainty now that he would not live to see another summer in Tangier.

The Code
Machine

Sitting in his office one Sunday afternoon in August, waiting for Peter Zvegintzov, Lake felt that he was finally putting things in order, and that the climax of everything was near. For weeks he'd thought of his life as a film in which two opposing stories were intercut: his descent into a pit of sensuality with Jackie, and the execution of his plan for Z.

He'd tried to simplify, had taken certain steps. He'd sent his wife and sons back to Minnesota for the month, on the pretext that his mother needed company and that the boys would profit from a change of scene. Then he'd distracted Foster, inventing all sorts of time-consuming tasks. He'd sent him into the city to study social currents, and several weeks ago on an inspection tour of northern Morocco which, he hoped, would last at least a month.

Lake sat back in his swivel chair, smiled, and closed his eyes. Now finally rid of his wife and his lover's husband, he could concentrate on the great adventure of his life. In less than an hour the Russian would be closing up his shop. Lake had invited him to the empty air-conditioned Consulate to mount the final stage of his assault.

The telephone rang, harsh, abrupt. Lake was startled. He sat up straight. Who the hell was it, he wondered, reaching for the phone. Not some stranded tourist, he hoped, or Zvegintzov begging off.

"Hello."

"It's me."

It was Jackie, her voice mellow and breathy. She called him all the time now, day and night.

"Is that you?" she asked.

"Of course it's me," he said. "Who else would be here on a Sunday? Who'd you think it was?"

"Just wondered how the work's going," she said. "I'm lying here in bed now, absolutely stark. Gosh, I'm horny, Dan. My legs are thrashing. I'm just dying for you to come."

"Well," he said, pleased by the image of her spread out, tempestuous with desire, "you're going to have to wait quite a while, Jackie dear. I've still got a hell of a lot of paperwork to do."

"OK, Dan. That's OK. Just wanted you to know I'm waiting for you here." She made a squeaky little kissing noise just before hanging up.

Horny! Christ! When was she not?

She was a man-eater, insatiable. There were marks all over him that testified to her passion. When she was excited she clawed him like a tigress. Though she proclaimed herself a vegetarian, she devoured his flesh like meat. They'd screwed, he guessed, over every chair and table in the office, on top of his big State Department desk, even against the dictionary stand. Her gymnast's body was capable of incredible contortions. Sex to her was joyous exercise.

It was marvelous to be involved with such a creature, not much good for anything, he thought, except to screw. He'd been contemptuous of her at first, had found her utterly moronic, but after a while, when she'd reduced him to the state of a happy animal, he began to find great virtue in her guiltless pursuit of sex. He let her lead him then, turned his body over to her to use. And use it she did, pleasuring and exhausting him, restoring his vigor, curing his insomnia, sweeping away the worries that had been cluttering up his mind.

She even had him doing calisthenics now. ("Got to work off all the flab, Dan! Got to get yourself back in shape!") She taught him how to jog in place and stand on his head against the wall. He did a dozen pushups every morning and skipped rope nude at night.

At first her addiction to athletics put him off. They'd be screwing away, lost in a rhythmic daze, and then he'd begin to hear her counting off the strokes. "One, two, three, four!" Christ! It was like being in boot camp or training at a YMCA gym. But eventually he got used to it, and her athletic imagery too. The more he thought about it, the more impressed he was by her imaginative powers. Going to bed was "going to the mats." Afterward they'd "hit the showers," then have a "skull session" to figure out "new plays." When she wasn't ready, and needed more oral stimulation, she'd suggest he "take another lap."

She was full of tricks too, such as fondling his organ through the rough mesh of her pantyhose, or taking the rubberband off her ponytail and letting her long hair fall upon his genitals like a gentle, tickling rain. She'd shake her head slowly then, side to side, using her hair to arouse.

Sometimes she called him up at the office to ask if he was "horny" or to make an obscene suggestion in her cheerful, breathy voice. She was a maniac for oral sex, and would suggest it to him at the oddest times. "I want to give you head, Dan," she whispered once at a reception for the officers of a Sixth Fleet submarine. Christ—she was unbelievable. He couldn't think of anything but her golden pubic fleece. Once she came into La Colombe when he was down on his hands and knees helping Zvegintzov fix his ice cream freezer. At the sight of her calves (she was wearing shorts) he trembled so much he dropped his screwdriver on the floor.

From the beginning he'd been worried about Foster, and what he'd do if he found out. But Foster was obtuse. Or, as Jackie put it: "He doesn't know his ass." She said awful things about him, revealed intimate details that made Lake wince, such as how, after jogging, he "couldn't get it up," or describing how she'd caught him once "whacking off in the john." Their marriage sounded as rotten as his and Janet's, the difference being that they'd tried to spice it up. She told how the Codds had approached them about the possibilities of "doing a quartet," and then how negotiations had broken down when she and Foster had viewed them in bathing garb beside Percy Bainbridge's pool.

Still he was wary, and one time badly scared. Shortly after the beginning of the affair Foster burst into his office clutching a copy of the *Dépêche de Tanger*. He plunked the paper down in the middle of the desk, then stabbed at Robin Scott's gossip column with his thumb. "Get a load of this," he said, pointing to a passage underlined.

Lake read it slowly, then looked up, expecting Foster to punch him in the teeth.

But Foster was laughing. "Get it?" he asked. "Uganda! A major power! Jesus—what a joke!"

"Uganda?" Lake searched his face. He couldn't follow Foster's drift.

"It's Fufu, Dan. Hell—I thought you knew. He's got mistresses all over town."

Lake was incredulous. Was Foster really such a fool? There it was in black and white, a clear reference to Jackie and himself. "A senior representative of a major power," Scott had written, "making whoopee in a big black car." Could anything be more incriminating than that? He wondered if Foster was playing dumb. But that night Jackie reassured him. "He doesn't know shit from shinola," she said, handing him a kif cigarette.

She'd been trying for a month to turn him on to pot, but he'd been resisting as best he could. "It's groovy," she told him, "prolongs orgasms, stuff like that." She showed him how to inhale the smoke, then hold it in his lungs.

He didn't like it. It made him dizzy. He much preferred to drink. "Come on, Dan—don't be a stiff. You've got to smoke the local grass to understand a place." He told her he didn't give a damn about understanding Tangier, but when she convinced him finally to share a joint, he felt like a buoy floating loose at sea.

In the early days he'd picked her up on street corners, then driven her out to the lovers' lane at Rimilat. But after they read about themselves in Robin's column, they began meeting in his office late at night. They'd screw like crazy there, while Janet slept in the adjoining residence, and Foster, dozing in his flat, assumed Jackie was out for an evening jog. After a while, however, these quick, impassioned meetings were insufficient to their needs. They longed for more subtle, extended sessions, free of fear that their spouses might intrude.

It had been easy persuading Janet to take the boys to Minnesota. Getting rid of Foster had been something else. Lake devised the political reporting project to get him out of the building. Then he met with Jackie in the empty residence and made love to her for hours at a time. Foster, however, was energetic, and began to turn up at odd moments with hysterical reports. He claimed conditions in Tangier were not so placid as they seemed. He said the city was ready to erupt.

"Nonsense," Lake told him, evading Foster's eyes, his own hand in his pocket nursing his sore cock beneath the desk. "Where do you get this stuff, for Christ's sake? The town's prosperous. The lousy tourist season's at its height."

"Well—I've been sniffing around, Dan, just like you said. I've been getting the Moroccan point of view."

"And?"

"And they're pissed, Dan. There's too much corruption. And the government's started up a draft. Seems the King's Saharan initiatives chewed up his army. He needs new recruits, so they're drafting them like crazy—one man from each family, they say, to fight dissident tribesmen in the south. There's a lot of tension now. The people don't like it, especially in Dradeb. A lot of anger in the city now. The lid's about to blow."

"Jesus, Foster, how many times have I got to tell you? In the foreign service we don't use words like 'pissed.' "

"Sorry."

"You've got to be specific. Impressions aren't enough."

"I've got specifics. Like this business about the soup."

"What business? What soup?" Lake shook his head, annoyed.

"This Ramadan thing," Foster explained. "It's really got Dradeb riled. See—there's this tradition. On the first night of Ramadan the King gives soup to the poor. Harira soup, to break the fast—it's supposed to be rich, full of vegetables and meat. Anyway, this year the King paid for it, but as the money trickled down all the middlemen took their cut. By the time the soup got to Dradeb it was nothing but this thin brown goo."

"So, what did they expect? Everyone knows there's graft."

Foster shook his head. "They're agitators down there, Dan. Like this surgeon guy, Achar. He went around with the soup truck making speeches. Ladled the stuff onto the ground. Said it symbolized the country's rot."

"Yeah? What else did he say?"

"A lot of stuff against the regime. Very antiforeigner too. Like it was all a plot or something, and the people didn't have to take it anymore."

"Hmmm," said Lake, taking all this in. "Maybe you're on to something after all. Write it up and we'll report it to Rabat. Put it in decent English if you can."

It was Jackie, finally, who came up with the idea of sending Foster out of town.

"Just get rid of him," she said. "Get the jerk out of our hair."

The idea of traveling alone across northern Morocco, making contacts and reporting on the political scene, should have intrigued Foster, if only because of the adventure involved. But for all his jogging he turned out to be soft. He balked at the idea, claimed he was needed in Tangier, to handle visas and visit arrested Americans in jail.

"He's really a schnook," Jackie said after Lake had ordered him to go. "I'd like to divorce him, but then I wouldn't know what to do. Join the Women's Army Corps, I suppose, or maybe take a masters in phys. ed." Lake felt touched by her limited ambitions. Something about the contrast between her naiveté and her expertise in bed struck him as entrancing and profound.

With Foster finally out of the way, he was free to zero in on Z.

At the beginning he had no idea why he was cultivating the man. He'd been fascinated, of course, by his file— Zvegintzov's past as a Soviet agent and the warning that "personal contact by consular officials" was specifically "not advised." There'd been something contrary, he realized, about his pursuit of Z, something deliberately disobedient that drove him on. Assigning Foster to watch the shop, then going there nearly every day, inviting the Russian to dinner at the Consulate, spying on him through his window late at night—it was as if all of that was a way to thumb his nose at the Department, which had exiled him so unfairly to Tangier.

Yes, he'd been fascinated by the idea of becoming friends with a Russian agent, ignoring instructions, doing what he pleased. It was a way to assert his independence, but still, he felt, there was something more. A link—that was it; the link he felt with Z. Two men used up, two old cold warriors stationed in the backwater of Tangier. There was much in common, he thought, though they were employed by opposing powers. Two men mired in boredom, thrown on the ash heap by superiors indifferent to their fates.

The trouble was that despite a veneer of intimacy, the Russian never really opened up. His fleshy face remained noncommital. He sidestepped Lake's overtures and kept himself aloof.

But then one day it came to Lake—the real reason behind it all, an explanation of what he was doing, a justification for his pursuit. He'd seen it in a moment, a revelation that struck him like a bullet and exploded a whole new level of ideas. It was very simple really, a mission he'd been destined to fulfill. The reason he'd been pursuing Z was to cause the Russian to *defect*.

Once he realized that, everything started making sense. He became flooded with fantasies of such intensity that even his interest in Jackie began to wane. He knew it would not be easy to cause defection. Russian agents were known for their fanaticism, their hardness to reason and the soft life styles of the West. But still he imagined himself engaging Z in a debate. They would wrestle together over the salvation of his soul.

Z would waver at first, then pull back. The struggle would teeter this way, totter that. But Lake would prepare himself well, laying the groundwork for a solid friendship while dropping increasingly unsettling hints and boning up on crucial Marxist texts. In the end he would send Z off to Washington, where for months the Russian would spill his guts.

He'd have much to tell of the intrigues in Indochina, and vital information on the North African spy nets. With luck he might even be converted to a double agent, then used to feed back false information to the Soviets. Or he might opt for a new identity in some Midwestern state, where he could begin his life again, perhaps open up another shop.

Lake knew it was a grandiose idea, and also treacherous with risk. He'd be putting his entire career on the line—if he failed he'd be fired for sure. But still, it seemed to him, he had very little choice. Better to end in glory or defeat than to die slowly of boredom and despair.

The day after he got the idea he began to intensify his assault, extending his visits to the shop, stopping in at odd hours when no one else was there, buying paperback espionage novels on Peter's recommendation, reading them and then returning to discuss the intricacies of their plots.

"Now, Peter," he'd ask, "if you'd been the spy here, would you have done the thing this way?" The two of them would then talk it out, their conversation laced with friendly tension and double entendres. Z would dance about behind his counter, hopping from foot to foot. His eyes would dart back and forth behind his spectacles. He'd cough and sputter and try to change the topic to something else.

"Now, Peter," Lake had said another time, apropos of nothing at all, "*if* I were a spy and wanted to set up a network in Tangier, first thing *I'd* do would be to get hold of a little shop like this. Place is a natural, a crossroads, great situation for a drop. I could keep an eye on everything, position myself in the center of the web. Like a spider, Peter, spinning wider concentric circles all the time."

Z had stiffened at that, but then Lake had smiled, and the Russian had relaxed. Lake wanted him to wonder whether he was merely being teased or whether he was being snared in a complicated plot.

One day he came in and spoke blandly about the weather. Then, as soon as Peter let down his guard, he threw him a tricky curve. "When I read about these deep-cover agents," he'd said, "I feel sorry for them, their loneliness, their difficult, dangerous lives. How tempting it must be for them to turn themselves in, to 'come in from the cold' as the expression goes—"

Peter, Lake thought, had betrayed himself, grasping one hand in the other, blinking involuntarily, turning to straighten merchandise on the shelves. Lake felt he'd touched him and resolved to keep the pressure up. When, finally, he offered the alternative of defection, Z would be grateful and relieved.

The trouble was he didn't get much feedback, nothing but these occasional signs of strain. The Russian would stare at him attentively, or glance up with a grin, but he never countered with a quip of his own and sidestepped when Lake became direct. It was impossible to know what the man was really thinking. Lake felt he was working blind. The more unsubtle he became, the more Z backed away. Often when he left the shop, he felt the pieces weren't falling into place.

It was getting to be time, he knew, to make his move, time to stop pussyfooting around. The previous Friday, when he'd dropped in at La Colombe, he'd asked Peter to meet him at the Consulate Sunday afternoon. "Come on over after you close," he'd said, "after the church crowd's passed on through. I'll show you around the building. Then we'll have ourselves a little talk."

Now it was Sunday, nearly four o'clock. Peter, he guessed, would just be closing up La Colombe. He took the elevator down to the Consulate's lobby floor. He wanted to be there waiting when he arrived.

The glass that faced the street was one-way, mirrored, put in at great expense. The object was to cause confusion in case there was a terrorist attack. Lake paced the lobby, pausing every so often to straighten a stack of "customs hints" brochures. On the wall by his order was posted an enormous sign listing the Americans languishing in Malabata prison on account of drug arrests.

Lake loved this building, so antiseptic, so clean, an air-conditioned American oasis, his fortress against Tangier. Here the corridors were straight, the elevators were silent, the city was hermetically sealed off. Everything was new, made of glass and steel, so unlike the teeming streets outside.

A few minutes later he saw Z pull up, then watched, unseen, as the Russian locked his car. Peter mounted the Consulate steps, struggled with the locked front door. He paused, pulled out a handkerchief, and applied it to his dripping face.

Christ—if he's afraid to ring the bell, then I've really got him by the balls.

Peter did ring finally, and Lake waited a full minute before he opened up. He just stood there, ten feet away, face to face with Z, feeling powerful because he was invisible, carefully inspecting the Russian's face. Z was stubborn, all right, crafty, but he looked vulnerable outside his shop. Lake enjoyed the idea of watching coolly from the lobby while the Russian perspired in the sun.

"Peter." He opened the door. Z edged his way inside. "No one here," said Lake, "just the two of us. Come in—I'll show you around."

He led Z through the building, down corridors, into offices, even into the garage. Finally he brought him upstairs to the Consul General's suite, then seated himself behind his desk, before his ensign and the American flag.

"You're the first Russian to get the grand tour, Peter. VIP treatment—nothing less."

"Thanks, Dan." Peter peered around. "You Americans know how to live."

"Yes," said Lake. "No little grubby cubbyholes for us. And the whole building's regularly debugged. We don't want anyone listening in, you know, listening in to all our secrets from some back room behind some shop."

He grinned. Zvegintzov tightened up.

"Come on, Peter. I'm only kidding around. Let's face it, it's terrific the two of us are friends. Here we are, citizens of opposing powers, yet we really like each other, so to hell with the struggle out there." He motioned with his arm toward the Straits of Gibraltar, indicating Europe and the world beyond. He was pleased by this extravagance of gesture, and the perplexed expression on Peter's face.

"There *is* something between us, isn't there, Peter?" he asked, narrowing his eyes. "This little wedge of suspicion, this little game we've been playing since we've met."

Z smiled weakly, then he shrugged. Lake sat up straight. Suddenly he slapped the desk.

"Oh, hell, Peter—drop your guard for once. Let's forget all this cat-and-mouse stuff. Christ—don't you see? We're buddies now. We're pals."

Z nodded cautiously and stared down at the rug.

Work the old seesaw. Keep him on edge, Lake thought. *Change the mood. Don't let him settle down.*

"You know, Peter," he said, trying to work some sympathy into his voice, "when you think about it there's a limit to the things a man can be expected to endure. There's only so long a man can go on living with deceit. Know what I mean? Ever think of crossing over? What a terrific feeling that would be?"

Peter stared at him quizzically. Lake toughened up his eyes.

"*Defection,* Peter. That's what I'm talking about. *Defection.* Giving yourself a second chance."

Z was staring very curiously now. Lake congratulated himself—he had the Russian hooked.

"Of course, the question in such a case would be—well, there'd be many questions in a man's mind. Such as how he'd be received by the other side, and how well he'd be protected from the people he'd worked for before. How much would he be expected to betray? How many of the old beans would he be expected to spill? And then there'd be the question of confidence, the person he'd defect to, the guy into whose hands he'd, quite literally, be placing his life."

He looked at Z again, highly attentive now. Is there a Russian agent anywhere, he wondered, whose mouth isn't full of rotten teeth?

"And motivations! Let's not forget about them! A man who'd defect—he'd have to have a motive for doing that. It might be a matter of high moral principle. Maybe it would have to do with his political beliefs. Or it could just be that he wanted to change the nature of his life. An escape maybe from something in the past. A complicated personal situation, say, involving his wife, or someone else. Comfort. Money. Change. It could be a combination of any of these things. Or all of them. Or even something else. You see, Peter, the possibilities are infinite, but the end is pretty much the same. I wonder how many men wouldn't jump at a chance to start everything over, with a clean slate, without the stigma of a past—"

He felt himself becoming increasingly excited, more and

more manic as he talked on. He was pleased by his eloquence and stunned by his daring. His voice, he noted, was steady as a rock. For a moment it occurred to him to pause, give Peter a chance to reply. But having achieved a certain momentum he had no choice, he felt, but to gush on.

"Now speaking theoretically, Peter—and, of course, theoretical is what this conversation is—let's assume for a moment that there were two men who were quite good friends, and let's assume further, simply for the sake of this discussion, that one of these men wanted to defect to the other's side. Now the first one, the spy, say, the guy who wanted to make the change, he'd have certain apprehensions, as we can both well imagine, about the credibility of any offer from his friend. I mean—that would be perfectly natural. Spies are human beings, after all. He'd have made his decision, you see, completely on his own, but still, being human, he'd be stupid not to have some doubts. The change would be voluntary, a product of his will. But he'd have to be certain he could really trust the other guy. He'd have to have great confidence and not think he was being used. Confidence. Mutual confidence. That's basic to what I'm trying to convey."

He sat back then and smiled. "You understand me, don't you? Yes—I think you do."

"Well," said Peter after a while, "I think I understand you. More or less."

"Good. Good. That's very important. It's vitally important that we understand each other today. Frankly, I wasn't sure we'd reach an understanding so very fast. Sometimes I've felt, well, there's been this—a certain strain."

Zvegintzov cleared his throat. "You haven't always been so candid with me."

"But you find me candid today?"

"Oh, yes. Today I do."

"And?"

"Well—"

"Yes?"

Zvegintzov shrugged. "Let's just say—I think I understand."

"Good!" Lake jumped to his feet. He had Peter now, balls to the wall, but still there was something missing, a commitment, an act of faith. *Confidence*—that was it. If he wanted Z to have confidence, he would have to show that he had confidence in him.

A sign. He needed a sign. Something that would cinch it, sew the defection up. Suffused by a sense of well-being, convinced that success was within his grasp, he began to search for a solution, while his heart beat thunderously inside his chest.

Of course! He had it now.

"Come, Peter," he commanded softly, startled by the brilliance of his idea. "Come. I want to show you something. A special section of the Consulate. A section no foreigner's ever seen."

He moved decisively toward the rear door of his suite, into the secure area, the little corridor through which only he and Foster were allowed to pass. He paused at the vault, knelt to turn the knobs. When finally he heard the click, he stood up, motioned Peter back, then swung open the steel door.

He was breaking security, he knew, breaking every rule in the book. But if his plan worked, none of that would matter. It was impossible to live without taking risks.

"Look, Peter. Look!" The two of them peered inside. Lake gestured toward the bank of green steel filing cabinets that lined the inner wall. "Our files, all our secrets, everything we've done in Tangier since 1935. It's all here—even our extensive dossier on you. See that computer thing over there? That's the gadget we use to crack messages and put them into code."

They stared, both of them, at the gleaming cryptographic device.

"What do you think? Come on, Peter! Tell me what you feel?"

"I—I'm flabbergasted," Peter said.

"Of course. Of course you are! A man like you, a man with a well-trained eye. Just to have a look at a machine like that—Christ! Your people would give a fortune to be here now. You can't put a price on a moment like this, but here I am showing it to you. I *trust* you, Peter—I want you to understand. Now I ask you to put your trust in me."

A pause then as they stood side by side staring at the code machine. Lake could hear Z exhaling in heavy gasps. Suddenly he felt weak, overwhelmed by what he'd done.

The Labyrinth

Throughout the summer, but particularly in August, certain undesirable elements began to appear in Tangier. Hamid noticed them—pickpockets of uncanny skill and verve, and gangs of dark-browed adolescent thugs. The latter seemed to specialize in harassment, insults and jostles on the Boulevard and, sometimes, outright attacks on foreign residents of the town.

Among the first of their victims was the accident-prone writer David Klein, discovered nude and beaten bloody on a lonely stretch of beach beneath the Amar woods. He'd been sunning himself, he told Hamid, immersed in a biography of Oscar Wilde, when he was suddenly surrounded by a gang of grinning toughs. They closed in, then took turns kicking him, aroused by his squeals and pleas. Shortly after Dr. Radcliffe patched him up, Klein left Tangier for good.

Next was Philippa Whittle, wife of Clive Whittle, the British Consul General, an imperious lady much admired for her charitable good works. She was walking in broad daylight on Avenue Christophe Colombe, when a gang swarmed upon her, punched her to the ground, stole her purse, and robbed her shoes. Whittle made stern representations to the Prefect, and then, when Hamid failed to find his wife's attackers, he filed a diplomatic protest in Rabat. But as hard as Hamid tried, he could find no witnesses to the event. Either the woman was an hysteric or people in the neighborhood were covering up out of sympathy for the attacking gang.

It was Sven Lundgren, the little dentist, who suffered the worst abuse. He was standing one evening by the rail tracks, recruiting for Pierre St. Carlton, when suddenly he was jumped by a youth who lashed his face with a steel chain. For a while it looked as though Sven might lose an eye, but St. Carlton flew him up to Paris, where a doctor saved his sight.

There was no pattern to these assaults. They seemed to occur without provocation or plan, savage outbursts from unidentified persons who had somehow infiltrated Tangier. The European community was, naturally, upset but, according to Robin Scott's column, equally determined that no herd of youths was going to ruin its summer fun. At night, safe in their villas, lulled by the gentle bleating of Arab flutes, the Europeans told each other that after Ramadan the city would resume its former calm.

Hamid was not so sure. These assaults on foreigners distressed him greatly, and he felt there was more to them than the stresses of the fast. Something was changing in the city—there was tension and anger now. For some time he'd sensed this change; now he tried to understand its cause.

The draft was one thing—it was so stupid, he felt, to draft people during the holy month, but the provincial administrators didn't seem to care. The recruiters, minor despots, were pitiless in their pursuit, rounding up young men, shipping them off to army camps, oblivious to the anger they aroused.

As the draft began to gain momentum and the water crisis worsened, Hamid observed flocks of petitioners mobbed outside city hall. One time, when he was driving by, he saw some women fling themselves before a limousine. When the chauffeur stopped and the women pressed themselves against the car, Hamid had a glimpse of the tense and frightened Governor of Tangier nodding gravely at grievances being shouted at him through the glass. A few seconds later, after the limousine had pulled away, he overheard the women muttering among themselves. *"Walu,"* they said, "we'll get nothing out of him."

It had been years since he'd heard such bitter words—not since his boyhood, the time of struggle against the Spanish and the French. And he heard other things too that gave him pause, mumblings from policemen, reported to him by Aziz, about Mohammed Achar and his protegé Driss Bennani, things they were alleged to be saying to the people of Dradeb. There was no proof as yet, no evidence against them, but Aziz told him that certain officers were trying hard to build a case. Achar and Bennani were careful, avoided direct attacks upon the King, but according to Aziz they left little doubt that they were complaining of his regime.

Aziz hesitated after he told him this, as if he wanted to add something more.

Hamid met his eyes. "I understand," he said. "I'll speak to her tonight."

He tried. He put it to Kalinka as calmly as he could. "I'd appreciate it," he said, "if you'd stay away from the clinic for a while. I know you like your work there, but there's some trouble now. Achar and Bennani are stirring things up, and it would be better for me if you stayed away."

She surprised him then—she argued back. "It's my work," she said. "I can't do it if I stay away."

"Of course, Kalinka—I know that. But please don't go down there anymore."

"Why? Tell me why, Hamid."

"Well—" How could he explain? "I have some enemies in the police, and these men are watching Achar. By connecting Achar with you they could make it look as though I'm involved."

"But you're not, Hamid—"

"Of course I'm not. But you live with me, and you're working there." He looked at her.

She frowned. "I'm sorry," she said. "This is what I want to do."

Suddenly he was furious. Didn't she care about his career? He stood up, started to leave the room.

"I just can't give it up," she cried. He stopped, turned to

look at her. Her hands were set upon her cheeks. "There's such excitement down there, people doing things, trying to set things right. There's so much more to Tangier than I ever thought, Hamid. So much more than the people who go to Peter's store."

"Are you saying I waste my time?"

"No, not that—"

"You're beginning to sound like Achar."

"Well, he has been an influence, I admit—"

"Oh, yes. An influence. And you've certainly caught his mood. You have, Kalinka. Yes, you have. I know him. He's persuasive. And very attractive too."

She stared at him. "What are you trying to say?"

"That I'm sick of hearing about how noble he is. 'Achar says this.' 'Bennani's doing that.' You're more interested in them than in your life with me."

"That's not true!"

"I hope not."

"Well, it isn't."

"Good. That's good. Now listen, Kalinka, I can't control you. You're a grown-up woman, and you're not my wife. But if we're going to be married, then that's something else. You can't go around and compromise my position. Perhaps you'd better think about that."

"I have thought about it."

"And?"

"Well, I'm not so sure we should be married, Hamid. At least not yet—not for a while."

He looked at her, saw that she was serious, nodded, and left the room. Standing out on the terrace, looking across the city, he had the sense that everything between them was suddenly different. What was happening to her? Why had she become so willful? And he—why was he so difficult, making an issue out of her work just because of a hint from Aziz? He wasn't really jealous of Achar, though there was always the possibility, he realized, that if he tried to dominate Kalinka too much he could drive her straight into the doctor's arms. No, it wasn't that—his real fear was of disorder, the disorder he believed she was helping to sow in Dradeb, and the disorder that now seemed to have entered their home.

He'd wanted to marry her, had only held back until he could clear up some questions about her past. But now that that was solved, her relationship with Peter finally understood, she informed him that she wasn't yet ready herself and that as far as she was concerned their wedding could wait. That was something he hadn't anticipated. She had caught him in his pride.

They were quiet at dinner, excessively polite, then afterward moved about the apartment trying to stay out of each other's way. Finally, just before they went to bed, she broke the tension, for which he was grateful and relieved. She offered him a compromise which he immediately accepted. She'd be willing to stay out of the clinic, she said, but wanted to continue working on the census in the slum.

Census. It sounded more like a petition of grievances to him, something Bennani had organized, a door-to-door survey of what people thought, what they wanted in Dradeb, their sorrows, their complaints.

She cared about it, he could see, and that touched him, to his surprise. He remembered, months before, fearing she might change if she could give up her hashish. He'd wondered then if she'd become a different person and, if she did, whether he'd still love her as much. Well, he thought, she has become different, a quite extraordinary person, and there is no question about how I feel—I love her now even more than before.

Sometimes it was just little things that moved him, such as her insistence on participating in the fast. She didn't have to, wasn't a Moslem, but she couldn't bear the idea of everyone suffering except herself. It was hard not to admire her for that, her compassion, her empathy with anyone deprived.

As always, he'd found, the first few days of Ramadan weren't so bad, but having her as his companion in the misery made them even easier to endure. He was proud of her discipline, her ability to suffer all day without food or drink, until the moment when the cannon sounded and the mosques announced the night's release. Then he and Kalinka drank their full of soup and stuffed themselves with honey-cakes. Afterward he swept her in his arms and carried her to their bed.

Here they fondled each other for hours to the music of the city's flutes, soaring out of the pain of self-denial into realms of ecstasy and desire. Tangier seemed different then, so different from the dour city of the fast. They listened to their neighbors celebrating and agreed the nights were charmed.

Yes, she was a different person now, had actually grown, it seemed. Ever since he'd raised the veil from her past she'd become strong, incisive, and direct. Before, he'd seen no way to connect her to the world which he policed. She'd always been separate from the city, his private mystery, but now he felt there was a relationship between his public life and his life with her.

It wasn't just her work, this grievance census she was taking in Dradeb. It was something more, another kind of link. She mentioned it to him that night they fought and made up, an idea she had about the meaning of her mother's life.

"I think," she said after they'd made love and were in bed listening to the flutes, "that all those years that Peter was pretending, trying to duplicate his comradeship with mama— oh, you know, Hamid, starting a store here, arranging the beds the same, even making me pretend to be his wife—that all that time he was smothering me with rituals and lies. I couldn't breathe then, find myself, find out who I was. But now I'm free, thanks to you. I've stopped smoking. I've read books on Vietnam. Now, finally, I understand what mother did. And, listen Hamid, there's a connection too between Hanoi and Tangier, between what happened there and what I feel here."

He sat up abruptly when she said that. He was astounded, unsettled, even shocked. "No, no," he said, "it's not the same. Oh, in superficial ways, yes. But we're not a colony anymore."

"But it *is* the same, Hamid, at least to me. Mama wanted much more than to put out the French. She wanted to change the country. Change the way people lived."

"Where do you get these ideas, Kalinka? From Achar, of course—"

She slapped him playfully. "I have my own ideas. Where do I get them? From using my eyes, like you." She raised her body and grasped his face between her hands. "You should know, Hamid. You, of all people, should know. You were born down there. No water. The degradation. Surely you remember what Dradeb is like. What difference does it make to the people down there if they're ruled by the French or a Moroccan king?" She paused, shook her head. "It doesn't make any difference. None at all. All they care about is that someone care for them and that no one trample them—that they aren't hurt by life."

He turned away. She was right, he knew it, could remember his feelings as he'd gazed up at the Mountain as a boy. But he'd put them aside, replacing his hurt at the indifference of the Europeans by a fascination with their styles of life. He wanted to tell her about that, and about all the hurt he'd once felt, but he was afraid that if he started he would talk too much, say things that would not become him, appear less of a man, and by that risk losing her respect.

"Tell me, Kalinka," he asked, "what did you do? In the old days, I mean—all those years, those twenty years or so you wandered around Tangier? What did you feel then? What did you think?"

She smiled. "Lost in smoke," she said. "I walked the streets, went about my errands, looked at the sea, picked flowers, sat around the shop. I didn't feel anything then. I didn't understand. Thank you, Hamid, for rescuing me."

It was a miracle, they both decided, that they'd found each other in Tangier. He felt grateful to Peter Zvegintzov for having brought her to the town.

Now, when he saw the Russian on the street or bustling about behind his counter through the window of his shop, Hamid felt no anger against him, no need to hound him or confront him anymore. All the old tension was gone, replaced now by pity. He'd made a resolve never to bother Peter again, not even to use him as an informant despite his access to the European world. And he'd told Aziz to forget about him too.

After that night when he and Peter had talked he had felt a softening, an erosion of the toughness that had seized him in July. After that night he felt more strongly than ever the loneliness of the foreigners, the awful, isolated loneliness in which they seemed to live. Zvegintzov, Luscombe, Inigo, the Freys; even the philanderers, Lake, Baldeschi, Fufu; the ac-

tive homosexuals, men like Robin Scott and Patrick Wax—
they evoked his pity, for he felt they lived in cages, separated
from life, cut off from it by lack of love. And he felt an almost
tragic stillness on the Mountain that fit in with this feeling
too. He was stirred by sadness when he drove up there. The
Mountain was so distant, so passionless, as opposed to
Tangier, a cauldron of tension and rage, an Arab city, his
town, his home. He couldn't explain this difference, and unable to reconcile the Mountain and the city he took refuge in
his love for Kalinka, the warmth of her beside him in the
night.

Yet every so often a feud would erupt among the foreigners, and then this new, sad sympathy he felt would shift
quickly to contempt. Such a change occurred on the eighth
day of the fast. Suddenly his office was filled with shrieking
people. Angry name calling and recriminations filled the air.

Within the space of twenty-four hours Colonel Brown's
Dalmatian attacked the Ashton Codds' teenage maid, Peter
Barclay's schnauzer tore open the leg of Skiddy de Bayonne's
gardener, Vanessa Bolton's Alsatian bitch set upon the Hawkins' groom, and Katie Manchester's cocker spaniel bit the
buttocks of Camilla Weltonwhist's chauffeur.

There was a common element in these events, Europeans'
pets attacking Moroccan flesh. But it was not a simple case of
Europeans against Moroccans—the feud developed another
way. It became a matter of employers of bitten servants
versus the owners of attacking beasts. The Codds, for instance, were adamant in their demand that Colonel Brown's
Dalmatian be put to death.

Hamid tried, as best he could, to sort the matter out. He
called the province veterinarian, who agreed to take the dogs
away for observation at a kennel near the crumbling *corrida
de toros* on the eastern edge of town. Here they were visited
daily by incensed owners bearing platters of ground-up meat,
while each morning the injured servants were accompanied
by their masters to the antirabies injection line at the Insti-
tute Pasteur.

The rabies scare blew over in a week. The saliva tests
proved negative, and the animals were returned to loving
homes. But though the alarm proved false, the bitterness did

not subside. People swore they'd get even no matter how long it took.

There was no logic, he knew, to these European feuds, yet the city seemed riddled with them—hatreds and vendettas that possessed the foreigners, a form of sustenance by which they renewed themselves and by which, he sometimes felt, they'd be devoured.

When he described the dog-and-servant feud to Kalinka, she shook her head and laughed.

"I know you think it's funny," he said, "but it took three days to straighten out."

"Oh, Hamid, I'm sorry," she said. "It's just so ridiculous—that you have to spend your time on such silly things."

"Yes, it is ridiculous. I know. All my work. All of it."

"Oh, Hamid—" She edged closer to him, took hold of his hand. "Poor Hamid, so much trouble you have, so many troubling affairs."

"What can I do? I'm supposed to police these people."

"Can you transfer to another section, get away from them for a while?"

He shrugged. It had taken him years to get where he was. He'd always wanted to be chief of the foreign section. Now he had the job, and all the misery of it too.

"Listen," she said, "please don't be angry with me, Hamid. You've helped me so much, freeing me from hashish, talking with me, helping me so I could face the world and discover who I am. Well, maybe now I can help you a little too. Because you're a prisoner, Hamid—a prisoner of the Mountain. There're so many more important things than the things that happen there. Injustice, cruelty—I see it so clearly now, and you must free yourself so you can deal with them."

Injustice, cruelty. She was speaking of Dradeb, of course, and in the same words used so often by Achar. Had the surgeon put her up to this? Were he and Bennani using her to get him to help them in Dradeb? He dismissed the notion as absurd, but it set him to thinking about his life.

He had thought that if he could understand Zvegintzov and Kalinka, get to the bottom of their past, then the mystery of all the foreigners would be revealed, and the motives for all their curious actions would become clear to him at last. It hadn't happened. He was still confused, and now Kalinka was implying that he had a narrow vision of the world. *A prisoner of the Mountain*—was she right about that? He wondered. Could she by some intuitive route have come in a few weeks to a comprehensive grasp of the city while he'd become lost in a sideshow, the foreign colony, so many years? This notion—that for years he'd been missing Tangier's essential point—was too terrible to face.

It's the fast, he thought, that's clouding up my mind. He'd begun to get headaches from lack of food and interrupted sleep, could hardly bear any longer the deprivation of water in the day. Even his meetings with Robin at the Haffa Cafe seemed boring and irrelevant now. While his favorite informer spieled out gossip, he stared in agony across the Straits.

"—Percy Bainbridge, you know, Hamid, the failed inventor, the sycophant—well, he just won a fortune at the Casino Municipal. Amazing! And, oh dear! I nearly forgot—Inigo's broken off with Pumpkin Pie. Yes, it's finally happened. He's gotten rid of that crazy lad. Now he's secluded himself to work on an enormous canvas, a double portrait, erotic to be sure, of Tessa and David Hawkins, our incestuously involved brother-and-sister horsebackriding act—"

Who were these people? Did he know them? How many years had he wasted caring about their pointless lives?

"—Anyway, let me tell you, I've great plans for little Pie. Now that he's 'wild chicken,' out of Inigo's sphere, I'm going to put him together with Hervé Beaumont, who keeps telling me he wants to become a full-time queen. Pie's a little dangerous, but Hervé can handle that. There's no better hustler around, I think, to teach a boy all the tricks—"

Hamid turned away. Robin's mention of Hervé Beaumont brought back sad thoughts of Farid. He'd seen his brother many times since his intrusion in the rug room, but neither of them had spoken of the incident, as if it hadn't happened and Hamid hadn't seen what he had seen. It didn't matter anyway, he supposed. They were brothers and loved each other as brothers should. Farid was entitled to live his life as he liked. And yet it seemed to Hamid that in that moment in the rug room he had stood between opposing worlds which he could not put together in his mind.

Could Kalinka help him reconcile the foreigners' Tangier

which he policed with the Arab city in which he lived? Could she give him a vision of Tangier in which all its facets would finally be clearly joined? She'd said he'd liberated her from hashish, and now she would free him from the Mountain. Was that possible? Was she right? Could she really have become so strong?

He had a dream. He was lost in a medina—not the medina of Tangier, for he knew his way through that, but a new and strange medina, a maze of alleyways and buildings, narrow streets that turned at odd angles, filled with people crying out in European tongues. Yes, that was what was strange—there were no Arabs in these streets. It was a medina for Europeans, which was impossible of course, a European labyrinth in which he was caught and trapped and lost. But then Kalinka appeared, slim and straight in a Vietnamese dress. She beckoned to him. He followed her. She became his guide, led him through the labyrinth, and showed him how he might escape.

A Night
of Five Parties

Two-thirds of the way through Ramadan the foreign community of Tangier became possessed. The social madness, the effort to transform a disastrous summer into a glittering fête, reached a peak when five parties of varying elegance and size were scheduled for a single August night.

Everyone's appetite had been whetted, prior to that sweltering evening, by the presence in Tangier harbor of Henderson Perry's enormous yacht. That magnificent boat, *The Houston Gusher,* anchored in plain sight seemed to advertise the festivities to come.

Those fortunate enough to be invited to Perry's "Castlemaine" would have a chance to devour his Beluga caviar and God only knew how many bottles of his fine champagne. The American Ambassador and half the Moroccan royal family were coming up from Rabat. There was even a rumor (incorrect, as it turned out) that the Shah of Iran would secretly fly in.

In the event that one were not invited to Perry's, the situation was still not bleak. Countess de Lauzon was throwing a rival affair—"an evening of fantasy," she said—at which her guests, the sons of Sodom and the daughters of Gomorrah, were encouraged to appear in outrageous dress.

Then there were the Manchesters, who'd invited their friends to "drink the dregs" on the eve of their departure for Fort Lauderdale. Willard and Katie weren't aware of the other parties when they sent their invitations out, and later, on account of pride, they couldn't change the date. It didn't matter anyway, according to Robin Scott, since their circle barely touched the higher orbits. Peter Zvegintzov, Dan Lake, the Foster Knowles', and the Clive Whittles had accepted, the Fufus were probables, and the Ashton Codds had promised to "try."

The gathering of Tangier Players club members at Jill and David Packwood's Shepherd's Pie was the lowest of the parties in social terms, but held the promise of high drama nonetheless. The Packwoods' little restaurant on the beach would be closed to tourists for the night. Once a nasty bit of TP business was concluded, there would be a beer-and-sausages party to celebrate the end of Laurence Luscombe's reign.

Finally there was a soirée at Jimmy Sohario's, "a party to unwind from parties," as it was billed. Everyone was invited: duchesses, diplomats, hustlers off the streets. The idea was to slip away from the Manchesters', the Packwoods', Henderson Perry's, or Françoise de Lauzon's just after midnight when things were cooling down, then hurry over to Jimmy's "Excalibur," where the revelries would last till dawn.

Tangier was ready, poised for all of this, when the unexpected news of Vicar Wick's suicide broke like a summer storm. A cloud of confusion hung above the Mountain. Lightning bolts of sorrow pierced British breasts.

But then, as the contents of the Vicar's diaries became known, the shock and grief began to lift. The sorrowful image of him dangling from a rafter in the nave of St. Thomas in a noose of his own contriving gave way to a sense, generally shared, that the old boy had got what he deserved.

Word of his scandalous diaries traveled fast. His expressions of hatred, his detestation of his loyal flock, were greeted with stunned outrage. He held them all responsible, it seemed, for the evils that had descended upon the church: the anonymous notes, the pierced sheep's eye, even the hacking of the altar crucifix. People were prepared to forgive the curse of madness, to say "There but for the grace of God go I," but the Vicar's accusations against them, his hatred so monstrously misplaced, eroded any sympathy they might have felt.

Lester Brown certainly felt that way. "My God," he said, wiping the sweat from his gleaming pate, "how that awful man led me on. He had me spying on people, making lists of suspects whom he knew were innocent all the time. Kept talking about the future of St. Thomas, the hypocrite, as if he ever really gave a good goddamn."

Lester might have had good cause to feel betrayed, but there were others who, though less intimately involved, expressed great fury too. How can this be? they asked, bitter and confused. How could this man whom we honored, made curator of our faith, have stabbed us so cruelly in the back? Other, less pretty phrases were bandied about the Mountain. "A kick in the ass," said Percy Bainbridge. "A knee to the balls," said Patrick Wax. The furor, which raged like a tornado, brought many Englishmen to tears, not in memory of their late vicar, to be sure, but for what his actions told them about themselves.

The Mountain recovered after a while, making a conscious effort to dismiss the matter from its collective mind. "We're not accountable," Peter Barclay told his friends, "not accountable in any way. Besides, we must try to occupy ourselves. The parties, for instance—it'll do us good to let off steam. In the autumn there'll be plenty of time to find someone new to lead the church."

So the storm passed, nearly as quickly as it had come. Spiritually regrouped, the Europeans marched on with their lives. There was much to think about those torrid August days; Tangier was restless, and a night of five parties loomed.

Hamid longed for an air conditioner, anything to relieve the heat. The churning fan that hung from the ceiling of his office made a sirocco of the stifling air. There was a water cooler out in the corridor and a machine that dispensed paper cups. He brushed by it many times each day. He hated it. It mocked his thirst.

Such a clutter on his desk, such a jumble of cases he could never solve. He hurt from Ramadan, suffered from the fast. One was not supposed even to swallow one's own saliva, or insult Allah by smoking a cigarette. It was mad, he knew, to abide by these rigid rules, especially since he did not think of himself as a particularly religious man. The President of Tunisia had told his people that the Koranic laws no longer applied, but Morocco was different, a fanatic theocratic state. The pressure to conform was enormous. Only combat battalions were exempt.

Truly, he thought, it had been an awful summer, miserably hot, filled with crimes. Then there'd been the suicide, less astounding as an isolated act than for the hatred and bitterness it aroused. The original note addressed to Barclay, which had triggered the Vicar's loss of faith, had never harmed its intended target, and its author, whoever he was, was still unpunished and unknown. But the Vicar, who'd taken on the burden of that author's guilt, was now despised in death.

Ah, he thought, *the infinite complexities of the foreigners, the inscrutable workings of their minds.* But really the whole business bored him now—the Mountain seemed alien in the face of the agonies of the fast.

Still there were things to do, distractions from his thirst. He'd just received orders to put aside his outstanding cases. Members of the royal family were due in Tangier at eight o'clock, and their security had to be arranged. Aziz had made up a special duty roster and was out now fetching a map of the Mountain Road. Soon the two of them would sit down, mark it up, decide where to post the men. The problem, as always, would be to protect the corridor through Dradeb.

Laurence Luscombe made his way down Rue Marco Polo, tilting back his body as he walked. The narrow little street was steep and treacherous; he was careful not to trip. The bright lights of Avenue d'Espagne lay ahead. It wasn't night yet, but it was Ramadan and someone had forgotten to turn them off.

He whistled "Mad Dogs and Englishmen" to keep his courage up. Across the tracks, lining the beach, were the little bathing clubs, the bars and restaurants, and the Shepherd's Pie. It was a few minutes past seven. The others, he knew, were already there. They were prompt at least—that was one thing he could say. God knew he'd trained them long enough, taught them how important it was to be on stage on time.

It was a deliberate choice on his part to show up five minutes late. He'd planned things, practiced his speech before his mirror, refined every gesture, timed each gulp and pause. He was going to give a performance tonight, perhaps the greatest of his career. He was confident, well rehearsed, but a little nervous too. There was, as always, the dread of rejection, the thought that the audience might hiss or boo.

Ah—there was Derik Law's little Humber by the curb, the Calloways' cream-colored Buick, Joe Kelly's Renault 16. Yes, they were there all right, probably wondering where he was. The Drears, and Jack Whyte, Jill and David Packwood, of course. Well—let them wait a minute longer. Let them just simmer in there. Let them stew.

He started to cross Avenue d'Espagne but leaped back to avoid a bus. Lord, it was terrible the way these famished Moroccans drove. They aimed right at you, as if they wanted to run you down. Well, maybe they did, he thought.

He walked a few more paces down the sidewalk, then attempted to cross again. This time he made it, over to the railroad side. He crossed the tracks, stepped onto the beach, trudged his way across the sand to the door of the Shepherd's Pie.

What a dump it was, the Packwoods' place. "English Spoken Here" a big sign said. There was another one below: "Private Party. Closed Tonight." He recognized David Packwood's sloppy lettering, the same dribbling style he used on TP sets. It *was* a dump. Imagine calling a restaurant the Shepherd's Pie. So coarse. So non-U. It could be worse, he thought. They could have called it the Fish and Chips.

What could one expect anyway? The Packwoods were trash, like the Drears and the Calloways. They had their little summer business, their little bar and restaurant on the beach. Four thousand, five thousand quid—they claimed they cleared that much catering to Cockney British tourists, the aftershave perfumed set, the Piccadilly queers. Well, they made a living at it, enough to see them through the winter months, though Jill always looked a fright when the summer was over—David kept her cooped up in that closet of a kitchen turning out those disgusting greasy pies.

He checked his watch. Too late to turn back now. He made his way to the door, paused a moment, screwed up his courage, pushed it open, and stepped inside.

There they were, the lot of them, looking at him just the way he knew they would. Guilt! Shame! It was written all over them. The shame of it, to call a meeting when they knew perfectly well his supporters couldn't come. Well, let them stare, damn them. It didn't make any difference now. He took them in, one by one, met each set of eyes straight on. They lowered theirs, of course—except for Kelly. That scarred-up little bastard *had* no shame.

To hell with them! To hell with Kelly too! They'd beaten him; the game was over now. Derik would have stood by him if he'd decided to fight it out. Barclay had said the Vicar would too, but then the Vicar had killed himself.

"Evening," he said in a gentle, fatherly voice which had nothing to do with the way he felt. "Sorry to be late. Don't want to delay the routine. Sunset years, you know. Can hardly keep up with you youngsters anymore."

He smiled then, as broad and charming as he could. They were staring at him quite curiously now. They'd been expecting something else. He knew what that was: a broken man, whining, pathetic, enraged. They'd come for blood, to see the old bull slain. Torment him, kill him, haul him away. Well, he'd not give them the pleasure of seeing that; he'd give them a lesson in class.

"Listen," he said, stepping to the center of the room, using the space between the tables as if it were a stage, "there're a few words I want to say before we get on with business." They were all ears then, craned forward in their seats. He smiled at them kindly and looked around again. His timing had been good—he'd thrown them off their guard.

"I was seventy-five this year, you know." A little grin then, just as he'd rehearsed. "There comes a time when a man has to face the fact that he's, well, past his prime. Then it's time

⟨ 300 ⟩

to step aside, for someone younger, with a steadier hand. I've been giving that a lot of thought of late, and I've decided it's time now to retire."

He heard a murmur, looked around, saw that Jessica Drear had raised her brows.

"I know this comes unexpectedly. We're meeting here to decide about next year's plays. But I thought I owed it to you to say this first, so that the new man, whoever he may be, will have a chance to put his stamp on the season that lies ahead. Now I don't want to be sentimental, lay on the syrup and all that. I just want to say how much I love you and how much working with you these last years has meant. Jill and David. Rick and Anne. Derik. Jack. Jessica and Jessamyn. Joe. We've failed at times—all of us have made mistakes. But, by Jove, we've tried, tried hard to put on good plays. They can't take that away from us. No one can. So—I just want to thank you for your loyalty to me, and for just being the great people that you are."

He paused, choked with rehearsed emotion, looked around, sensed his speech was having its effect. That line about loyalty—that had hit them where they hurt. He could feel them softening, knew he had them won—an actor's power, and he savored it a while before he continued on.

"Finally, a personal note. It isn't easy for an old actor to leave the stage, make his final bow. For almost sixty years I've trooped the boards—that seems now a long, long time. They say old soldiers never die, that they just fade away. Old actors—well, I don't know what they say about them. But this old actor will always be there in the hall to clap for all of you."

Another pause, this time a long one. He knew his final words must sound most deeply felt.

"We've had our quarrels. We've shouted and screamed. We've laughed a lot, and wept a little too. But that's the theater. That's what it's about. A clash of intellects. Temperaments aflame. Before I open our meeting to business—and the business tonight will be to select a new leader for our club—let me just quote a few lines from the *Tempest,* old Prospero's farewell. It says what's in my heart:

⟨ 301 ⟩

> *But this rough magic*
> *I here abjure; and when I have required*
> *Some heavenly music, which even now I do,*
> *To work mine end upon their senses that*
> *This airy charm is for, I'll break my staff,*
> *Bury it certain fathoms in the earth,*
> *And deeper than did ever plummet sound*
> *I'll drown my book.*

He sat down then, to their utterly stupefied silence. All of them were pulsing with sentiment—except for Kelly, who glared at him and scowled. Luscombe couldn't blame him; his evening had been stolen by design. But Jill Packwood was weeping, and she was hard as nails. Jack Whyte's eyes were glistening. Jessica Drear held her face in sweating palms.

Derik Law stood up then, just as the two of them had planned. He began the song, and of course the others followed, eyes upon him, big and red, weeping and smiling and nodding all at the same time:

> *For he's a jolly good fellow!*
> *For he's a jolly good fellow!*
> *For he's a jolly good fellow!*
> *That nobody can deny!*

Lake had been circulating at the Manchesters' for an hour, waiting for Z to show up.

"Oh, he'll come. He promised," said Willard, snapping the shutter of his Instamatic, filling the room with a blinding flash.

"He'll be here eventually, Dan," Katie said. "Now go try some of my tuna spread."

Her tuna spread! It was sickening, tasted as though it were made of fur. The whole damn party was an outrage. Lake couldn't believe he was really there. He'd come only because Z was supposed to come, and he had to confront the Russian face to face. Otherwise he would have stayed home. It was a humiliation to be at the Manchesters' while the Ambassador was up at Henderson Perry's, mixing with the royals and *tout Tanger*.

The Manchesters! Christ! They'd invited him to "drink the

dregs"! They'd served up the dregs, all right—Spanish "scotch," Argentine "vodka," all those undrinkable blended whiskeys they'd gotten for Christmas through the years. The potato chips were soggy. The canapes were a disgrace. The hall was filled with packing cases. The servants were sullen, worried about their tips.

"Great to meet you," he heard Willard say to a bunch of newcomers to Tangier. "Come visit us in Florida. We're moving there, you know." This was supposed to be a going-away party for the Manchesters' closest friends, but those friends were out on the terrace, talking among themselves, while the Manchesters stood alone in the living room saying tearful farewells to people they didn't know, snapping their pictures, even inviting them to visit them in the States.

It was insane. Madness. And still Z hadn't come. Lake was worried about that, that ever since he'd shown him the code machine the Russian had avoided seeing him alone. When he came into the shop Peter behaved as if nothing had happened, as if they'd never had that conversation in his office the Sunday past. Lake couldn't figure it out. He thought everything had been arranged. Z had as much as said he'd be willing to defect. What the hell had happened? Tonight he was going to find out.

The Manchesters were such boobs. How could he ever have thought of them as friends? They'd brought out every bit of junk they didn't want as offerings to their guests. There was a pile of stuff on the dining room table which Katie kept loading into people's arms. Wrinkled old maps of Morocco from the glove compartment of their car. A swollen can without a label (botulism for sure, he thought). A bottle of home-pickled watermelon rinds. Coat hangers and bent curtain rods. A fondue pot with an enormous crack. They must be nuts, he thought, trying to flog off stuff like that. Why didn't they just heave it in the trash? As it was they'd tried to sell everything they didn't want: potted plants, an ironing board, some innertubes, a rusted lawn mower. But this other stuff—they had to be kidding, though there was Katie trying to stick Rick Calloway with a dozen lifeless tennis balls.

He stared around the room for a while, then tried to attract the attention of Jackie Knowles. But she and Foster were snuggling in the dining room like a couple of dodo birds in heat. Ever since Foster had come back from the north, all the gas seemed to have gone out of their affair. Why? He still wasn't sure, except that Foster had returned weathered and tanned, sporting a little Vandyke beard. It made him look all the more ridiculous, what with his blond hair curling down his neck. But that little beard seemed to be working wonders on Jackie. She called it "neat," said it felt good when Foster gave her head.

That was enough for Lake. He wasn't about to share Jackie with her husband or be satisfied with "sloppy seconds." If the Knowles' had solved their sexual problems, that was fine with him. He and Jackie had had their fling. He told her to cool it for a while.

Suddenly he turned around—there was something buzzing in his ear. It was Anne Calloway talking away. Evidently she'd been speaking to him for quite a time.

"—There we were," she said, "sitting there at the Shepherd's Pie, all set to give Larry the old heave-ho from the club. You won't believe what happened an hour or so ago. God almighty, what a scene!"

"What *did* happen, Anne?" he asked, watching the door in case Zvegintzov came in.

"Like I said, Dan, we were waiting there when Larry showed up and flat resigned. Gave a brilliant farewell speech too. Broke us up, I'll tell you. Absolutely broke our hearts. Anyway, next thing you know we've all forgotten we called the meeting to bounce him out. Reelected him president of TP for life. Then created a new job, managing director, so Kelly wouldn't feel put down. You should have seen Kelly's face! He was furious. Stormed right out. But what could we do? Couldn't throw out Larry after all he'd said. They're still down there, the rest of them, eating sausage and guzzling beer—"

Anne Calloway was still chattering, though he'd nearly turned his back. He could see Fufu out on the terrace, spittle shooting from his mouth, holding forth on his favorite scenario, the one that ended with South Africa in a sheet of flames.

"Things are smelling bad here, Dan." It was Willard who'd sidled up. "We've loved Tangier, really have. We've had some terrific years. But now we're glad to be getting out. Whole country's rotten to the core."

Jesus Christ!

Lake couldn't believe his eyes. Old Ashton Codd was swiping the hors d'oeuvres, stuffing a great batch of those foul tuna canapes into his pockets, then looking around to be sure he wasn't seen. Lake turned away, sick to his stomach. It was horrible, just imagining all that furry tunafish sticking to the insides of Ashton's pants. *What a nuthouse!* Baldeschi was feeling up the new secretary at the British Consulate. Philippa Whittle, making her first appearance since she'd been attacked, glared around with the crisp and wary look of a woman who'd suffered an awful fright.

Z! Where was the little bastard anyway? Pinning him down was like trying to nail a glob of jello to the floor. Ah— there he was, the Commie punk. He'd finally shown up, was standing by the door. Now was the time to move in, trap him against the wall.

"Who you supposed to be, lad?" asked Patrick Wax, crossing the crowded salon at Françoise de Lauzon's. He looked sharply at Robin, up and down.

"Robin Hood, of course," Robin replied. "Who the hell did you think?"

"Yes," said Wax, stepping back a pace, squinting at Robin again. "I see that now. You're all dressed in green. I presume that silly little stick is supposed to be your bow. Well, Robin, very nice indeed. Just think of the rest of us as your *very merry* men." He laughed, then smacked Robin on the back. "Good try, lad. We're all aware of your impecunious state. Françoise will forgive you. At least I *think* she will."

Wax crossed the room to embrace someone else. He'd come as "Jack *and* the Beanstalk," dressed as a swishy yokel, carrying a huge green phallus in his hand.

Robin didn't know if Françoise would forgive him, and he didn't give a good goddamn. He'd done the best he could with his costume, taking a metaphorical approach. He'd improvised a hood out of an old scarf he'd found beneath his bed, then scratched up a bent piece of driftwood from the beach and strung it with a bit of string.

He loathed costume parties, refused to take them seriously. It was particularly awful, he felt, to be at Françoise's "fantasy evening" tonight. Nothing was worse than to be at the second best. Far better, he thought, to be at the bottom, at the Manchesters' thing, or with the TP scum at the Shepherd's Pie. He knew that Henderson Perry's party would almost certainly be a bore, but to be seen tonight at Françoise de Lauzon's was to have it proclaimed that one hadn't made the grade.

Still there were a lot of people there, seventy or eighty at least. The room was a sea of costumes, and there were people skinny-dipping in the pool. Robin pulled out a wad of paper and began to jot down notes. He'd get back at Perry when he wrote his column—he'd stretch the truth, make Françoise's party sound like better fun.

Florence Beaumont, he noted, made a nice Cinderella; Inigo was her Prince Charming in tow. Percy Bainbridge played an aging Mary Poppins. (Barclay had helped him with the nanny's outfit, Percy'd claimed.) Darryl Kranker was a lisping Sinbad the Sailor, and Hervé Beaumont looked cute as the Lone Ranger, with a couple of silver-painted water pistols and an effeminate horn-rimmed mask.

Some people were so elaborately made up that Robin had difficulty discovering who they were. Heidi Steigmüller, the proprietress of Heidi's Bar, wore a rubber mask modeled on the features of Charles De Gaulle. Countess de Lauzon, the quintessential faghag, was Count Dracula, her appearance rivaling Bela Lugosi, while Inge Frey had come as Little Red Riding Hood and Kurt Frey as the Big Bad Wolf. There was, Robin realized, an air of savagery in the room, and all sorts of wicked things going on around the pool. Everyone knew the better party was up at "Castlemaine," but they were all trying to ignore that fact.

Patrick Wax, he thought, put it best when, at one point during the evening, he came up and shook his head. "For a bash like this," he said to Robin, "it's even too much trouble to bathe."

Monsieur de Hoag was driving. Claude, very quiet, sat in the back of the Mercedes with General Bresson. Jean Tassigny, beside Monsieur de Hoag, peered ahead into the night. He watched the Mountain Road narrow and steepen as they climbed through darkness toward the crest.

They were stopped at one point by security police, who swept the car with flashlights, then politely waved them on. Jean turned to look at Claude as the beam passed across her face. She sat still, like a sculpture, staring straight ahead, as cold and pale as marble, he thought, except for her turquoise eyes and the diamond necklace that glowed against her throat.

A little later he looked back again, saw the lights of Tangier glittering far below. Then they were stopped at great iron gates. They gave their names and were waved through to the grounds. They followed a road that ran parallel to the cliffs, past terraces, gardens, pools cut into rock. Finally the road curved and "Castlemaine" came into sight. Jean gasped as they approached it, a huge Moorish palace lit from within by thousands of flickering candles, its great tower looming in the night.

In the front hall they were searched by royal bodyguards, patted lightly through their clothes. Jean thought this frisking was performed with skill, but General Bresson was indignant all the same. "I don't know why they're afraid of *us*," he muttered. "*We* don't want to kill them. *We*'re not Moroccan, after all."

They were escorted into a huge reception room where scores of people milled about. Jean recognized the American Ambassador right away; the man had once run for vice-president of the United States.

The Hawkins' were there—the last time Jean had seen them they'd been posing nude for the erotic double portrait by Inigo. Pierre St. Carlton, in a gray velvet suit, chatted with Vanessa Bolton against a wall. Jean was introduced to a number of Brazilians, a grandee of Spain, some confident businessmen from Iran. There was a famous Greek actress who wore fabulous jewels, and an Italian leading man invited up from Marrakech, where an historical film was being shot. Omar Salah came up to them, kissed Claude's hand. Then he put his arm across the shoulders of Monsieur de Hoag and guided him away.

They were waiting, Jean understood, for members of the Moroccan royal family, off somewhere with Henderson Perry in another part of the house. Jean brushed close to Claude, tried clandestinely to take her hand. She showed her annoyance by turning away: she was like that sometimes, ready one minute to risk exposure, furious the next because he'd dared to look at her and smile. He shrugged and started toward the Hawkins', passing near Peter Barclay and Camilla Weltonwhist on his way.

"The trouble with Henderson," he overheard Barclay explain, "is that he has no taste at all. Look at these third-rate paintings. He lives like a very rich dentist, don't you think?"

Jean nodded to himself. The interior of "Castlemaine" was disappointing, especially after the fabulous entrance through the grounds. The walls were covered with dark pictures in heavy frames. There were a few Moroccan antiques, candelabra from Farid Ouazzani's shop, but most of the furniture was contemporary and expensive, the sort one might find in the waiting room of a society physician on Boulevard Malesherbes.

Jean tried to talk to the Hawkins', who were uncommunicative and wrapped up in themselves. When he looked back at Claude, he saw her speaking with Salah. The chief of customs was making forceful gestures with his hands. Claude, he was happy to see, was staring back at him unimpressed.

Vanessa Bolton caught his eye, motioned him to her side. "We must stick together," she said, kissing both his cheeks. "We're the only young people except the Hawkins', who of course are stoned."

She brought him into her conversation with St. Carlton. The couturier was holding forth on the phenomenon of American millionaires. "Perry's from Texas," he said, "the only place in the world besides Tangier where people still think titles count. The man's phenomenal. Absolutely ruthless and filthy rich. You've seen the yacht, of course."

"Speaking of toys," said Vanessa.

"Yes, my dear." St. Carlton raised his eyebrows. "All the talk is true. Perry adores them. There's a room here someplace filled with electric trains. And perpetual motion machines—my God! There're all sorts of them around the halls."

"We must look around later, Jean," Vanessa said. "There're such lovely gadgets—"

"Yes," said St. Carlton. "And then there's his cryonics stuff."

"Cryonics?"

"Oh, yes, my dears. He's got equipment that accompanies him everywhere—cylinders of liquid oxygen, a preservation box. If he contracts cancer or falls ill of an incurable disease, his people have been instructed to freeze him in a flash. The idea, you see, is that eventually medical science will find a cure. Then he can be defrosted and treated, even a hundred years from now. Mad? Maybe. The poor man wants to live forever. But who doesn't? Just tell me that."

St. Carlton paused, gazed across the room. "Look at that viper," he said, pointing toward Barclay. Then suddenly he brought his hand up to his mouth. "Oh, dear—here they come, I think. We must all remember to curtsy and bow. I always get goose pimples around royalty. Then, damn it, I forget—"

Henderson Perry, a neat little man, led the six Moroccan royals into the room. There was something impersonal about his style, more of the tycoon giving foreign dignitaries a tour of a factory than of a man hosting a party in his house.

There was a hush as they appeared. All the guests fell back. Perry led the royals to the center of the room, then introduced them one by one.

There were three princesses, sisters of the King; two princes, brothers; and the adolescent Prince Heritier, which explained the elaborate security around the house. Jean found them a curiously unimpressive group, rather short, darker than most Moroccans he knew, slightly awkward, he thought, with quite ordinary Moroccan features, the sort he'd expect to see in the Socco on a market day.

He watched as they moved about, greeting Perry's dazzled guests. When they reached the de Hoags he was moved by the sight of Claude bowing with elegance, never lowering her turquoise eyes.

Now that's a real princess, he thought, suffused suddenly

by waves of love. He wanted to go to her, take her hand, lead her away from this stuffy party out to Cap Spartel, where they could lie together on the sand and make love to the rhythm of the surf.

At dinner Perry, Barclay, the royals, the movie stars, and the Ambassador were seated at a big table on the terrace protected from the wind by a screen of glass. Jean sat with Vanessa Bolton, Pierre St. Carlton, and one of the Iranian wives. St. Carlton did most of the talking, gossiping away and complaining of the "sparseness" of Camilla Weltonwhist's bouquets.

Jean barely touched his food. He was too preoccupied with Claude. She was sitting with Salah, Lady Pitt, and Skiddy de Bayonne. He stole furtive glances at her all through dinner, but she never once returned his gaze.

After the meal the guests were led away for coffee to a huge room where musicians beat on drums. Soon bellydancers appeared and began to roll their stomachs. There was nothing erotic about them, Jean thought, and he slid, after a while, into a state of soft malaise. He'd drunk too much champagne and now dreamed of Claude, all the things they'd done, the wonder of her eyes, the mystery of her smile.

He was in the midst of this when Vanessa Bolton grabbed his hand. "Now's our chance," she whispered. "Perry's about to take the royals on a tour."

Jean nodded, stood up. Together they edged their way outside. Perry was already in the hall explaining the principles of perpetual motion. Jean, glancing back just as they were leaving, saw Monsieur de Hoag, but not a trace of Claude.

The tour was delightful. Perry liked showing off, and the Moroccans, all connoisseurs of Western gadgetry, were most responsive to the charms of his machines. They looked in at his kitchen and his communications center in the tower, full of transmitters and a telex by which he kept track of his business interests around the world.

Perry guided them into his room of electric trains, then sat down at a console and started them by remote control. Soon the Crown Prince was busy lowering barriers, flashing signals, while Perry explained that the network was "fail safe"— if a collision were imminent, the power automatically cut off.

A good thing, Jean thought, since the Prince seemed reckless. He pitied Morocco when this young man became the King.

The tour continued. They mounted stairs, wound through corridors, looked out at different views. When they came at last to Perry's personal suite, Vanessa excused herself, but a few minutes later she sneaked up behind Jean and whispered in his ear. "Pretend you have to pee," she said. "Then use the bathroom on the right."

Jean, obedient, did as he was told, and for his trouble was vastly entertained. There was a sunken tub in the middle of the bathroom floor with little piers built along its sides, and a great fleet of miniature boats floating there, neatly tied. There were tiny warships, toy yachts, meticulous reproductions of famous craft—a whole flotilla, perfect in every detail, all with wind-up motors to make them sail.

He laughed then, finally touched by Henderson Perry, his magic world, his secret vice. This legendary tycoon, reputed to be so ruthless, liked to play in his tub with tiny boats, like any toy-struck American boy.

When he left he found the others by a window. Perry was demonstrating a telescope. It was an infrared model, based on devices developed during the Vietnam war. One could see people in the dark with it, Perry explained: the human body gave off waves of heat.

Perry offered the scope to the Crown Prince, who stepped up to it and scanned the grounds. Jean and the others were standing behind him waiting their turns to look, when suddenly the Prince let out with a giggle and pulled at the gown of his youngest aunt.

She took hold of the instrument, gazed through it, then she too began to laugh. Soon all the royals were pushing and shoving. There was much chattering in Arabic and wild gesturing with hands.

Henderson Perry, a little confused, watched them with a smile. "I don't know what they see out there that's so damn funny," he said. "Whatever it is, it must be pretty good."

After a while, when the royals had tired of their game, Jean, who was nearest, stepped up to the telescope to look through it for himself. Being careful not to move the instrument, he brought his eye down slowly to the lens. He was bewildered at first—the infrared effect made things look strange. But a moment later he felt a rush of pain. It was Claude, he was sure, not inches from his eye, somewhere out there in the gardens of "Castlemaine," naked, he could see, and with a man. Jean stared, felt sick, then turned away. She was making love with the customs' chief, Omar Salah.

Lake knew he'd had it. Everything had backfired. He felt crazy, about to run amuck.

He was driving down the Mountain at a furious speed, like a kamikaze pilot daring death. His tires squealed as he took the curves. The American flag on his fender snapped crazily in the wind. His lights caught someone standing in the road, a policeman maybe—he wasn't sure. He stabbed about with his toe, searching for the high-beam switch. By mistake he activated the windshield wipers. He nearly hit the cop, swerved away just in time.

Better slow down, he thought, trying to turn the wipers off. At the bottom of the hill, just before the Jew's River bridge, he brought the car to a screeching halt, then lay his head against the wheel.

That noise!

The awful sound stopped as he jolted back. He'd been pressing his forehead against the horn.

If I just don't lose my head, then maybe things will be all right. But he knew they wouldn't, that there wasn't any way he could obliterate the past, not just the last fifteen minutes, but the whole time he'd been in Tangier, his whole damn sorrowful life. He leaned forward, peered out at the street. No one there; Dradeb was quiet. He turned, fastening his eyes on La Colombe.

That bastard! That stinking Russian bastard! That goddamn son of a bitch!

Feeling himself beginning to go mad again, he fought to regain control. He had to keep cool, not allow himself to crack. He had to figure out what to do.

Z had been blunt when he'd made his proposition a quarter of an hour before, out on the terrace at the Manchesters, with thirty people milling around, and that asshole Willard standing there, snapping pictures for his memory book.

Proposition! Ha! Blackmail was a better word. Zvegintzov said that if he heard another word about defection he'd tell the American Embassy about everything Lake had done. "Everything"—that was the word he'd used, drawing out the syllables in his obnoxious Slavic whine.

"Such as what?" Lake had asked, feeling an awful burning in his chest.

"Such as how you broke security," Z'd replied. "Such as how you invited me into the communications room at the Consulate, then offered to defect to me with an American code machine in hand."

"Don't be stupid, Peter. No one's going to believe that."

"They will," he said, "when they see my evidence, the photographs I took inside the vault."

Photographs! What photographs? His palms were sweating then. Zvegintzov pulled the little Minox out of his pocket, waved it around, nearly stuck it in his nose.

Christ! It could be true. Z could have done it without his noticing anything, without his even hearing the shutter click. He'd been so wrapped up in himself then, so flushed with feelings of power and success. Now the bastard was threatening him. Blackmail—it was nothing less.

"What do you want from me, Peter?" he'd asked. "How much money do you want?"

"I don't want money," Peter replied, "I just want you to leave me alone. Stop harassing me, Lake, and tell your people to lay off too. Or I'll give my pictures to the Russians and ruin your career."

That was it, the blow that had done him in. He went blind with fury, could have strangled the bastard then and there. But he hadn't—had been too scared. Instead he'd run out of the house, knocking a fondue pot out of Katie's arms. He'd heard it crash to smithereens just as he'd slammed the door, heard someone calling after him ("Dan, Dan"—it sounded like Jackie) as he'd started the car and begun the wild drive down toward Tangier.

Well, now he'd had it. He'd done so many stupid things, playing the spy, underrating Zvegintzov, vastly overrating himself, compromising his country besides. Impossible to let Z hold those photographs over his head, which left him, he realized, with little choice. The Ambassador was in town.

Lake knew what he had to do. He'd have to drive up to Henderson Perry's, call the Ambassador out, confess everything, and resign, right there, tonight.

A little after midnight Robin was driving up the Mountain in Hervé Beaumont's car when he noticed a light in the glass studio on the top of Martin Townes' house.

"Slow a little, Hervé," he said, squinting at the tower and smiling to himself. Everyone else in Tangier was at a party, he and Hervé were on their way to Jimmy Sohario's, but there sat Townes, scribbling away, working into the night.

He was glad when they finally reached "Excalibur," such a change from the atmosphere at Françoise de Lauzon's. Jimmy, a diminutive and affable Indonesian, was always an excellent host. His food was the best on the Mountain, and his villa one of the most fabulous in Tangier. Robin thought of its interior as a bestiary since so many parts of animals were displayed. The chairs were made of entwined antlers, the wastebaskets were hollowed-out elephants' feet, the floors were covered with zebra skin rugs, and the walls were adorned with polished giant tortoise shells.

It was only half past twelve, but already the house was jammed. Everyone in Tangier was there, it seemed, except the hosts of the four earlier parties, brooding alone in their homes now that their guests had fled to better things.

Robin was struck by how easy it was to recognize where everyone had been—they were all distinguishable by their modes of dress: formal evening attire on those who'd been at "Castlemaine," absurd costumes on Françoise's bunch, business suits on the Manchesters' friends, garish resort clothing on the scummy TP crowd.

He plunged in, anxious to accomplish a self-appointed task, to fix up Hervé Beaumont with the hustler Pumpkin Pie. He finally found the "tart of gourds" brooding in a window seat, bare arms poking through the sleeves of his tank top, muscles gleaming in the night.

"Hi, Pie," he said, sitting beside him. "What's the matter? You're looking sad."

"That bitch Françoise," Pie replied. "She didn't invite me to her thing."

Robin saw the boy was hurt and felt sympathy, since he understood the cause. He'd been the Countess's gardener, and her lover after that. She was the person who'd introduced him to society and had given him his extraordinary name.

"It's that fuckin' Inigo. Everyone's against me now."

"Not so," said Robin, patting him on the arm. "Inigo was in love with you, so he can't bear to see you anymore. Françoise is his friend, and doesn't like to see him sad. She didn't invite you tonight, despite the fact that she adores you, so Inigo could have a little fun."

"Hey, man—you really think so? Well, OK. Everything's cool now."

Robin was pleased to have so easily cheered him up. Also he was amazed by Pie's mastery of jive talk. Moroccan boys were like that, he knew, instant mimics of Europeans, but what astounded Robin was how quickly Pie had abandoned the refined Latin American mannerisms he'd acquired from Inigo. It was as if that relationship had never existed. *How little we really leave these boys,* he thought.

"Remember my picnic, Pie?"

"Yeah, man. That was a bitch."

"There was a French boy with me. Hervé Beaumont."

"Yeah. Lives on the Mountain. I know the cat you mean."

"Well, he's with me tonight, Pie, and very interested in meeting you. I think you'd like him. He's quite *rich,* by the way."

Pie, who'd been staring out at the room, on the lookout for some queen he could hustle for the night, suddenly turned his attention back to Robin, who congratulated himself for knowing the secret word that opened all Moroccan hearts.

"Rich, huh?"

Robin nodded.

"Sounds nice, man."

"I'll bring him over."

"He's not cherry, is he?"

"No, but he doesn't know the Moroccan scene. We know how special that is. Yes, we do—don't we, Pie?"

"*Yeah.*" Pie grinned, held his palm out straight, and made little cutting motions at it with the edge of his other hand. It was the first reference he'd ever made to the time he'd held a knife against Robin's balls. Robin raised both his hands in mock submission, backed off a little, smiled, then both of them began to nod their heads. They were acknowledging, Robin supposed, the curious relationship that they had.

How marvelous, he thought, as he hunted Hervé down, *how marvelous these transactions of the flesh.*

After he made the introductions, watched Pie and Hervé share a pipe of hash, he wandered off to explore the party, search out material for his column. People had become wary of him ever since Townes had convinced him to write with a harder edge, but his stock had risen after a biting column on Vicar Wick, and now his sources were speaking to him again.

He circulated for a while, picking up tidbits—nothing of substance, however, nothing to rival the scandal at the church. The big story was the TP party, and Laurence Luscombe's unexpected finesse. Robin finally found Joe Kelly, drinking heavily, holding forth to Madame Fufu and the Drears.

"Know what Aunt Jemima said to Uncle Ben?"

The question was directed at Madame Fufu, who didn't understand it and shook her head.

" 'You're a credit to your *rice,*' " said Kelly. "Ha! Ha! Ha!" He yowled, pounding at the sides of his chair, nearly unloosing the antler arms.

Robin winced. It was such an awful joke. Madame Fufu didn't get it and shook her head.

"That's a Yank joke," said Jessamyn Drear as Madame Fufu excused herself and wandered off.

"Better be careful," whispered Jessica to Kelly. "We might need her husband for *Emperor Jones* in the fall."

"Oh, fuck that burr head," Kelly said, "and fuck O'Neill too." He took a long sip from his drink. Robin sat beside him in Madame Fufu's place.

"So, Joe, I hear Luscombe won the game."

"Yeah," said Kelly, "him and that lousy Derik Law. I had a great plan going till those two screwed it up."

"What happened?"

"I don't know. He gave some sugary speech and turned the thing around. But I'll fix that little proud nose, wait and see.

Makes me sick with all his crap about 'The Theater' and his phony arty airs. I know his type, knew 'em in New York. British character actors, phonies all of 'em, holed up in the Great Northern spewing out their Shakespeare by the hour. Want a quote? Something you can print? Just say Tangier's not big enough for the two of us, and that I'll get that old hack yet."

"Now calm yourself, Joe," said Jessamyn while Robin wrote Kelly's statement down. "You're managing director—that's the *real power*. Larry's just a straw man now."

Robin listened a while, then withdrew, remembering a line of Friedrich Nietzsche that Martin Townes liked to quote. How did it go? He stopped in a doorway, trying to recall the words: "It's a relatively simple matter for a weathered charlatan like myself to keep up interest in so small a carnival as this."

He gazed around. Hervé and Pie were still together, still sharing a pipe. Well, he thought, at least I've done one good deed. Then he noticed Jean Tassigny, sitting by himself. He walked over to him, sat down, and listened to his tale of woe.

"I'm leaving tomorrow," Jean said after telling Robin about the telescope. "There's a ferry for Algeciras in the morning. I'll catch the train for Paris there."

"Don't be ridiculous. Why the hell are you so upset? She was cheating on Joop. How can you be surprised she's cheating on you?"

"Oh, *God!* That's why I have to leave. A perfectly intelligent person like yourself saying a thing like that—that's the whole damn trouble with Tangier!"

"Oh, come, Jean," said Robin, feeling a sudden need to defend the town. "You're not going to give me that old in-Tangier-they-know-everything-about-sex-and-nothing-about-love routine. You're too sophisticated to spout that crap, the swan song of every poor beggar who ever left this city hurt. Really, I'm surprised. You take things much too seriously. Your situation is so *classic,* you ought to be able to see the humor in it instead of feeling sorry for yourself. The handsome boy, lover to the older woman, married in turn to the ugly wealthy man. You mistook her lust for affection, Jean, and your own misguided passion for love. You participated in something that held a certain drama, considering the fact that the three of you were living in the same house, and now that it's over you want to flee the scene, if only to further dramatize your hurt. Stop it, Jean, and don't stare at me with those bedeviled eyes, as if to show me how Tangier has corrupted your otherwise pure and unblemished soul. You've traveled a mere inch down the highway of sin. What you need is a new lover. May I be so bold as to suggest—*a boy?*"

Jean looked up at him with astonishment, then began to laugh. "Really, Robin, you're very funny."

"And you're very handsome—no offense."

They shook hands and Robin wandered off, fairly certain that Jean Tassigny was not going to leave Tangier.

He headed toward the terrace, where Jimmy Sohario had installed a Moroccan band. Passing through the doors, he came upon an amazing sight. It was Foster Knowles dancing crazily while everyone else stood back and watched. The Moroccans were drumming away, clearly entranced with this American who shot out his feet, one after the other, and whipped around his right arm like a cowboy making ready to lasso a calf. "Whoopee," he yelled, "whoopee," as if celebrating the end of a drive down the Chisholm Trail.

Robin had never before seen Knowles behave like that. The Vice-Consul had always seemed to him a terrible stuffed shirt. His wife, Jackie, was standing facing him on the fringes of the crowd, bent over slightly, clapping in tune to the drums, letting out with little squeals from time to time. "Yippee!" and "O-yippee-hi-ho!"

Robin, fascinated, wondered what had brought this behavior on. When Foster grabbed Old Musica Codd out of the crowd and whirled her into a jig, he moved over to Jackie and shouted in her ear.

"Is he stoned?"

"Oh, Mr. Scott," she said, batting her sky-blue eyes. "I'd have thought you'd have heard our news by now, you being a gossip columnist and all."

"What news? Don't hold out on me, Jackie. I've always been sweet to you in my column."

"No, you *haven't*," she said smartly, showing him a petulant smile. "You could have got me into a lot of trouble if Foster wasn't so—"

"Dense?"

"Oh, you *are* nasty, Mr. Robin Gossip Scott."

"Yes, I am," he said. "Now tell me what's going on."

"Well, my 'dense' husband, as you call him, has just been named Acting Consul General of the United States. That makes me equal to Mrs. Whittle, so you can start by showing me some respect."

"Acting Consul? What happened to Lake?"

"Oh—Dan. Well, I think he's on his way out of the country, to Frankfurt or someplace, some hospital, I guess. *Poor Dan.* Anyway, it's really *exciting* for us. Happened just a couple hours ago. We were down at the Manchesters' when suddenly the Ambassador's limousine pulled up. He took us up to this fantastic house where we met Mr. Perry and the Crown Prince!"

"But why? What happened?"

"Gee, I don't know exactly. Seems Dan resigned over some fracas or other, so the Ambassador's put Foster in charge. We're really excited. They're going to change all the locks on the Consulate doors, and as soon as the Lakes' stuff is moved out we get to live in the residence too."

Their conversation was broken off then by a mob of people who'd heard the news and had come around to congratulate the Knowles' on their precipitous rise to power. Rick and Anne Calloway, from Voice of America, were dutifully kissing ass, and Peter Barclay was already busy organizing a congratulatory lunch. *So incredible,* thought Robin, *these rapid changes due to fate.* The last time he'd seen the Knowles', Jackie was Dan Lake's mistress. Now her husband had Lake's job, and she couldn't wait to take possession of his house.

He spent the next hour shuttling back and forth between the rooms, watching the party turn rowdy. He saw Hervé sneak off with Pumpkin Pie and congratulated himself again for that. He had a little conversation with Kranker, then watched Fufu try put the make on Florence Beaumont and Baldeschi work on the hopelessly cool Tessa Hawkins. Heidi Steigmüller was still wearing her De Gaulle mask. It was amusing to watch her talking to General Bresson, no doubt about military "maneuvers and affairs." Percy Bainbridge in his Mary Poppins costume was chatting away with Jack Whyte. Perhaps, Robin speculated, he was retaining Jack to build a prototype of his "three-cornered kiss."

Between the elevation of the Knowles' and the collapse of the Kelly coup, Robin felt he had enough material for a column. What he needed now were some details about the Perry party, things he could use to put it down. He was in the process of extracting information from Vanessa Bolton, who was happily telling him all about the little boats in Perry's tub, when Kranker rushed over out of breath and grasped Robin by the arm.

"Come quick," he said. "It's finally happening. Wax and Barclay are having it out."

Robin grabbed hold of Vanessa, dragged her with him as he followed Kranker to another room. When they arrived they found a quiet little crowd in a circle around Barclay and Wax, who were standing apart facing each other like gunslingers in a Western town.

Wax was still in his costume, holding his "beanstalk" like a staff. Barclay, legs apart, arms folded confidently across his chest, wore a somewhat frayed and dated smoking jacket and clutched a silver-headed cane.

"What's going on?" someone whispered.

"Shush," said Robin, craning forward so as not to miss a precious word.

"Just the sort of comment we'd expect," he heard Barclay say, "from the son of a chimney sweep."

"Ha!" said Wax. "Everyone in Tangier *knows* about you, how you tried to force Camilla Weltonwhist to buy that worthless property below your house so you could plant trees on it and pretty up your view."

"That's a damn lie," said Barclay, beginning, Robin thought, to look unnerved. "But then we all know your history, that you're nothing but a liar and a thief."

"You're right. I've never pretended to be anything else. The trouble with you, Mother Barclay, is that you don't know *what* you are. But I do. I see right through you. For all your fancy lineage you're just like an Arab boy who spreads his ass for half a crown."

It was a terrible insult, terribly unfair, Robin thought, and Barclay didn't take it well. He grew red in the face, and the veins in his forehead began to throb. Suddenly he pursed his lips and let fly with a glob of spit. It landed on the carpet, a little short of Wax.

"Oh, you *are* angry, *dear*," said Wax, regarding Barclay with utter scorn. He raised his "beanstalk" and started toward him, would have bashed him on the head with it, Robin thought, if Barclay hadn't managed to deflect it with his cane.

Immediately their friends dragged them apart, and into separate rooms. There were huddles then, cliques and factions formed, while the whole party turned into a debate about which one had bettered the other and what had started the argument off. Robin, uninterested in either of these things, was busy writing their dialogue down. He'd have to ask his editor for double his usual amount of space. He had enough now for a delicious column.

Hamid was relieved. He'd done his duty well, protected the princes and princesses who were finally all safely bedded down. He was relaxing with his men in the kitchen of "Castlemaine," dining on leftover food which Henderson Perry had graciously offered, when Aziz Jaouhari suddenly burst in.

"Something terrible, Hamid," he said. "There's been a murder at Villa Chapultepec."

Hamid jumped up from the table, and together they ran out to his jeep. As they drove down the Mountain toward the Beaumonts' house, he shot questions at Aziz.

"The victim?"

"All I have is that it's a European. The body's been disfigured. Supposedly it's a mess."

"Who reported it?"

"The resident caretaker down there. He heard some noises, then saw someone running across the grounds. He couldn't make out who it was, but decided to check the villa. He found the body in the salon."

"How could this happen, Aziz? We've had patrols on the Mountain all night."

Aziz shrugged. "There're no lights on the road. If someone knows the estates up here, he can cross the walls at will."

When they arrived at Chapultepec a truckload of police

were already there. Hamid nodded to the cringing caretaker and walked straight through the house. It was a gruesome sight he found, the walls of the salon covered with blood, the nude body of a young European male lying on the marble floor. He'd been castrated, his stomach, chest, and face punctured numerous times. There was a trail of bloody footprints leading out through the glass French doors.

Aziz raised his hand to cover his mouth. "Do you know who he is, Hamid?"

The Last
Column

"Really, you look terrible," said Hamid. "Worse than I've ever seen you."

It was eleven o'clock in the morning, two days after the murder of Hervé Beaumont. They were sitting in the Haffa Cafe, Robin with his back to the Straits of Gibraltar, Hamid facing the coast of Spain, cut off from sight by haze. A pregnant cat under the little iron table licked softly at Hamid's moccasins. Ramadan was due to end in one more day; then the new moon would come, and the feast of Aid es Seghir.

"Actually," said Hamid, still appalled by Robin's bloodshot eyes and the drained pallor of his face, "he was passive when we caught him. He made no attempt to struggle, and within five minutes he confessed. He took us to the place where he'd hidden the knife, under a rock in a cliff on the way to Cap Spartel. He was going to hide out in the mountains and then try to slip over the frontier. Inigo came around last night and asked to visit him in his cell. I refused, with mixed feelings I admit. There's something likable about the boy, though of course he's dangerous and mad."

Robin nodded. "I knew he was both those things. Inigo

called him 'schizophrenic.' Last year he nearly cut off my balls."

"You're still blaming yourself—"

"Of course, Hamid. I introduced them, encouraged Hervé. Told him it would be good for him, would clear up his confusion and straighten out his head."

"Well, Robin, you couldn't have known—"

"I *did* know. If I'd thought about it, just taken a minute and thought, I might have predicted the whole thing. I certainly knew that Hervé was in trouble, and that Pumpkin Pie was violent. I'm responsible, Hamid. I feel that I am. I knew what I was doing. Subconsciously I knew."

Robin thrust his head down on the table and began silently to sob. His body quivered and made the table shake. Hamid watched for a moment, then reached out and placed his hand on Robin's hair.

"Really, Robin, there's no point in assigning blame. I had this boy in my office on a vice charge last month. I could have locked him up. But I didn't. I was tired and let him go. Does that make me an accomplice? I really don't think it does."

Hamid wanted very much to comfort Robin, relieve his terrible distress. He didn't think he was responsible for the Beaumont murder—he put the blame on something else.

"It's not you, Robin," he said. "You're judging yourself too harshly now. This comes from something a lot deeper than your little immoralities, something sick, even evil, that exists in the expatriate milieu. People using people. Europeans and Moroccans competing for advantage. That sort of thing breeds rage, and when unstable personalities are involved we get violence just like this."

Robin calmed down after a while, stopped his weeping and raised his head. "I hate myself, Hamid. I detest what I've become. Ridiculous hustler. Phony poet. Trashy gossip. Despicable queer. The only thing I don't regret is that I've been your snitch all these years."

"Yes, that's something to be proud of—"

"I've been helpful to you, haven't I, Hamid? Devoted? I even helped you crack this case. I fingered Pie the moment that I heard."

"Oh, yes, you've been helpful from time to time. Certainly you're my favorite informer, though perhaps not the most reliable one I've ever had."

"Have you felt grateful toward me at times? Happy you let me stay?"

Hamid laughed. "I'm not sure grateful is the word. But yes—I'm happy I didn't throw you out years ago when I had the chance."

"Good. I'm glad." Robin looked into his eyes. "Will you do me a favor, Hamid? Something for old time's sake?"

"That depends. Tell me what you want."

"I want you to expel me from Tangier."

Hamid smiled. "Don't be ridiculous. You're not a prisoner here. If you really want to go, all you have to do is leave."

"That's the problem, damn it, Hamid. It's not so easy just 'to go.' "

"I don't see any difficulty about it. In fact, I think it's a fine idea."

"You don't understand. I've *tried*. For years I've *tried*. I've wanted to go for a long time. But I can't. My life here is too easy and set. If I go somewhere else I'm sure to have difficulties. The only way I'm ever going to leave is if you kick my ass."

Robin fixed Hamid with his most sincere and anguished gaze. Hamid searched his eyes for irony, and finding none looked closely at him and raised his brows.

"Let's be serious, Robin. I understand you, but you're not saying what you mean. You're perfectly capable of leaving Tangier on your own. What you want from me is something else. Not an order of expulsion. You want punishment. You want me to expel you as a punishment, to help relieve a little of your guilt."

"That's it, of course." Robin smiled. "You're so sensitive, Hamid, such a remarkable cop. I'm your Raskolnikov, and you're my Inspector Porfiry. You've read Dostoevski, of course."

Hamid shook his head. "I can't even get through our local authors. My reading is confined to dossiers."

"This one's worth the trouble. *Crime and Punishment*. It deals with subjects you know so well."

"Thank you. I'll try to find a copy. But getting back to your departure, where do you think you'd like to go?"

"Canada. Montreal. I have some friends there. I could probably find a job."

"Any family?"

Robin laughed. "They all disowned me years ago."

"What sort of job then?"

"Oh—journalism. I'd be a good police reporter, don't you think?"

"If you worked at it—maybe. Have you money for the trip?"

"Not now. No. But it wouldn't cost too much. I could catch a freighter out of Lisbon or Algeciras. One-way passage. I could raise it, I suppose."

"You're serious, aren't you?"

"Yes, I am. I don't know whether it's too late for me, but at least I'd like to try to start again."

"Then do it, Robin."

"Expel me and I will."

Hamid was disgusted. "So, we're back to that—the old Tangier tricks. You'll never have another sort of life, Robin, if you don't start right now and change."

"What?"

"Listen to me! Stop these stupid charades, these little Tangier deals you've been making all these years. 'I'll do this for you, Hamid, if you do this for me.' 'Let me stay and I'll be your snitch.' 'I'll save myself and leave, but you have to expel me first.' Such nonsense! Why don't you just do the thing straight out? I'll help you. I'll drive you to the frontier at Ceuta. I'll even lend you the money for your passage to Montreal. Tell me when and I'll escort you where you like. But I won't issue an order of expulsion or deal with you as a police inspector. Only as Hamid, your friend. How about trying that?"

Robin was startled. "You'd really do that for me, Hamid? I'm grateful. Really I am. That's good. Very very good."

They sat in silence for a while, smiling at each other, pleased.

"Do you want to leave this afternoon?"

"The sooner the better. Why not?"

"What about your stuff? Will you have time to pack it up?"

"I'll leave it. It's worthless anyway. Won't do me any good in Montreal. But there is one chore I have to do. I owe the *Dépêche* a final column."

Hamid nodded. "Three o'clock then? In front of the Poste. But be sure and call me if you change your mind."

Hamid drove to his bank, picked up some money, then went on to his office to complete some work on the Hervé Beaumont case. He signed a document that released the body to the sisters, who wanted to take it up to Paris on the evening plane. Then he phoned the prosecutor about Pumpkin Pie. He suggested the boy be taken to the asylum at Beni Makada so that the psychiatrists there could observe him for a week and report on their observations at his trial.

There were a few other small matters that claimed his attention—a velvet and silver-threaded cape stolen during the costume party at Countess de Lauzon's, and the beating of the estate agent Max Durand by a gang on the Mountain Road. Unruly gangs had been terrorizing foreigners for a month, but until now the Mountain had remained secure. Now, it seemed, even that enclave had become fair ground.

He ate no lunch, since the fast was still in effect. The thought that it was nearly finished made the deprivation less intense. At three o'clock he drove over to the main post office on Boulevard Mohammed V. Robin was waiting there with a small leather suitcase, his typewriter, and a tattered musette bag slung across his back.

"Is that all you're taking?"

Robin nodded. "Everything worthwhile," he said, sliding into the car.

Hamid took the coast road at Robin's request, through orchards of olive trees, then along the cliffs that lined the African side of the Straits.

"Write your column?" he asked as they passed Malabata point.

"Oh, yes, and I turned it in. Be sure to read it Saturday. In some ways it may be my best." Robin turned in his seat for a last look at Tangier. "You know," he said after the city disappeared from sight, "I've been away only a quarter of an hour, but already I want to reminisce."

"Well," said Hamid, "when you're settled in Montreal I hope you'll think kindly of the place."

"I'll try, Hamid. But I don't guarantee I will."

Hamid laughed. "It's funny, isn't it—nearly every foreigner who's ever moved here has become disillusioned in the end. The strong ones find the will to leave. The others stay and rot. I like to think that you'd have left sooner or later on your own—that it wasn't just Hervé's murder that showed you that you must, but a sense of waste and self-disgust."

"You've always been after me to leave, Hamid. I think you used to suggest it because you liked to see me get annoyed. Anyway, you were right. Now tell me—you're an observant man. Have I changed very much these past ten years?"

"Oh, yes. You were a beautiful hippie when you came. Mad, of course, but interesting, and so extreme."

"And now?"

"Now you're a gossip."

"A bitch you mean."

"All right—a bitch. You started out here as a person, but after a while you became a 'Tangier character.' Our stock and trade. We have so many 'characters,' many more than a little town like ours is able to support. Now I wonder about Montreal. Whether you'll fit in there. Whether you'll really change."

"I think so. It's a big, sophisticated city."

"Very expensive, I imagine, too. Actually, I was wondering whether you'll be able to do without some of your exquisite pleasures. You know what I mean—your peculiar tastes."

"My homosexuality? Of course not. I am and always shall be gay. You hate that, don't you?"

Hamid shook his head. "If you think I do, you're wrong. But what I don't like, aside from the issue of children, is the preying stance you people take. Rather than sticking together and sleeping with each other, you insist on taking advantage of Moroccans who are ignorant and poor. It's racism, really—exploitation. Our boys are booty to be plundered, animals to be penetrated and used. Have you any idea what this does to

us? It's far worse than going into a poor country and exploit-
ing cheap labor, resources—phosphates or oil. We're talking
about human beings, after all, people like my own brother,
one of the very few who's had the good fortune to escape the
business more or less intact. Still he's been affected. I see it
in him all the time. By the way, I caught him with Hervé one
night in the rug room of his shop, stumbled in on them by
accident a month or so ago."

Robin, silent, was staring straight ahead. When he finally
spoke he did not use his usual bantering style. "To think that
all these years I thought it was just a matter of your personal
distaste. Well, Hamid, on our last day together I discover a
side to you I didn't know before. Too bad in a way, but I
agree with everything you've said. My escapades here have
been exploitative, and endlessly complicated by sex—
something I've never understood or learned how to control. I
have to ask myself, you see, why I didn't take better care of
Hervé. I was his friend, but I sent him to a hustler, one I
knew was dangerous besides."

"Oh, stop it, Robin."

"No. It's very important, because it ties in with what you
said. Pie was the reluctant chicken, and Hervé the incompetent hawk. I've learned a lesson from this, I think. In Montreal, I assure you, I'm going to become a different man. No
youngsters, first of all, though that much is obvious, I suppose. No—it's really much more important than that. It's a
question of people and who they are. I'll be gay, of course,
but when I look for lovers I'll choose them from among my
equals, my friends."

Hamid drove on, and after an hour the Mediterranean
came into sight. Then they started to descend, by groves of
eucalyptus, toward towns with Spanish façades. Down at sea
level they passed tourist villages built up along the coast.
Hamid finally stopped the car a few feet from the frontier.

"Well," he said, "I'm going to miss you."

Robin nodded. "I shall miss you too. Tell me, Hamid, about
yourself. What will your future be?"

"I'm changing too, Robin—just like you."

"Good. Good. A strange ten years it's been. Thanks again
for the loan. I'll pay you back when I get a job."

"I'm not worried. I wish you luck."

"Thank you, Hamid. Good luck yourself."

They shook hands, then Robin left the car. Hamid watched as he approached the frontier, set down his bags on the customs rack, had them chalked by the inspector, then moved on to passport control. He emerged a few minutes later. A guard raised the jackknife barricade. Robin stepped out of Morocco, turned, and gave a final wave. Hamid waved back, and when Robin's red mop had finally disappeared into Spain, he turned the car around and drove back to Tangier.

A few days later when the *Dépêche* came out, Hamid bought a copy and opened it on the street. He turned to "About Tangier by Robin Scott" and was surprised by what he found. Most of the space was blank where the column normally appeared. There were only a few lines printed near the top: "Robin Scott announces his permanent departure from Tangier and bids farewell to all his friends."

Indeed, Hamid decided, it was the best column Robin ever wrote.

The Fire

On the first of September the weather in Tangier changed. The haze, which had hung above the city for a month, lifted in a single day, and after that the sky was clear and blue. The yachts sailed out of Tangier harbor, and the summer residents dispersed. The hotels emptied, the tourist buses disappeared, and the restaurants along the beach began to close.

Ramadan was finally finished too—a blessing, thought Hamid. No more frantic nights of eating; no more torturous days of thirst. The heat was gone, and so was tension. He smoked cigarettes, sipped mint tea. There were even times when he smiled at Aziz across an empty desk.

Kalinka still glided about in her Vietnamese dresses, slim, enigmatic, sublime, but it seemed to Hamid that her work in Dradeb had brought a new beauty to her eyes. Often in September when the nights were cool they would lie together, wrapped in each other's arms, on the rough Berber rug on the floor of their salon. They'd lie beneath a Riffian wool blanket he'd bought for her in the souk at Sidi Kacem, bound together chest against chest so tight he could feel the beating of her heart. He was moved by her tiny throb, and the pale, tawny quality of her skin. How big he felt then, a large, dark man. When she looked up at him, showed her smile, he was rent by stabs of love.

They were lying like this late one night near the end of the month, holding on to each other, feeling each other's warmth, while the wind blew furiously outside, rattling the windows of their flat.

"I left the laundry out," she said after a while. "I can hear it flapping there, out on the terrace. Poor sheets. Poor towels."

"I'll bring it in," he said, kissing her and standing up. She felt the same sorrow for everything that was damaged or abused, could not bear suffering in anything, whether a lame dog, a broken man, or a petal torn out of a flower.

He hesitated a moment at the glass terrace doors, turned back to look at her, a small figure on the enormous rug. "Back in a minute," he whispered, then unlatched the doors. The wind was blowing so hard he had to push at them with extra force.

Outside the laundry was alive, dancing crazily in the cold night air. He fought with it for a while, tried to undo the clothespins she'd attached, finally managed to gather it into a great bunch in his arms, then stared out at the Mountain, where yellow lamps blinked on and off, covered and uncovered by wind-lashed trees. The sky was clear, black, sparkling with stars. Then he saw the fire.

For a few moments he was fascinated by it—flames leaping in the wind, far across the valley of Dradeb. It made a brilliant spectacle in the night, swirling pillars of sparks shooting toward the sky. He watched, impressed by its fury, wondering where it was. Then he knew, it came to him in an instant, and he felt helpless standing on his terrace a mile away, his arms loaded with sheets and pillowslips and towels, while the wind blew the faint aroma of burning wood across his face.

"Mosad," he whispered to himself. "Mosad."

A second later he was back inside, wrestling with the terrace doors. "Must go, Kalinka," he said, dumping the laundry on the rug. He started toward the closet to find his leather jacket and his gun.

⟨ 332 ⟩

"What is it? What's the matter, Hamid?"

"Call Aziz," he said. "Tell him to meet me on the Mountain. Tell him the man from Israel has come. And don't wait up for me, Kalinka. I won't be home till late."

Then everything was too slow for him—the elevator which took too long to reach his floor, and even longer, with its slowly grinding gears, to take him to the street. Running out of the lobby into Ramon y Cahal, he was met by a blast of wind. The palms were thrashing, and the neighborhood dogs were making a cacophony in the night.

For a moment, when his car refused to start, he pounded at the steering wheel, enraged. How long had it been since the fire had been set? How long, in this wind, before it devoured the Freys' great house?

The engine caught finally and he was on his way, down Avenue Hassan II, looping around the Italian cathedral, then swerving into the road that led to the Mountain through Dradeb. He made good time until he reached the intersection at Rue de Persil, where he found himself trapped behind a long line of honking cars. A bus was stalled ahead. He wished he had a police jeep with a siren.

He pulled onto the sidewalk, left his car, then ran toward the bus through air thick with pungent fumes. He was about to shout at the driver, order him to pull aside or clear the way, when he saw there was a barricade in the street, a huge pile of vegetable carts, benches, tables, and chairs from a neighboring cafe and, beyond that, a mob of youths rushing toward the fire. He heard sirens then, far away—firetrucks, he realized, trapped behind. The bottleneck was impossible, the road was too narrow, and someone had slashed the tires of the bus. He thought about trying to dismantle the barricade, but knew it would take too much time. The firemen would have to deal with that; he would continue to the Freys' on foot.

There seemed to be a lot of people ahead. He could hear laughter and cries, the sounds of a country carnival. He climbed onto the obstruction, picked his way across its top, then jumped down just as a swarm of young people emerged from an alley of the slum. They carried him along with them until he stumbled in front of a miller's shop. They ran on in a surge toward the Jew's River bridge to view the fire on the cliffs.

He picked himself up and ran on, determined to break through the mob, cross the bridge, get onto the Mountain and up to the burning house. But the farther he ran, the thicker he found the crowd, a barrier of humanity with a choking density of its own. It seemed as though everyone in Dradeb had poured into the street. The throng was impenetrable. People's eyes were wild. There was fury in them too, he felt—violent passions about to be released. He yelled that he was a police inspector, but could barely hear his voice. The sound of it died in the yells of the people around, their delighted whoops and cries.

It would be impossible, he realized, to fight his way through. He shouldered his way to the curb, then up some steps against more people surging down. Finally he found an empty alley, darted in, then paused a moment to catch his breath.

He knew Dradeb, had spent his childhood in the slum, had known all its alleys, its intricate passageways, years before. But the place had changed. Its shacks had been rebuilt and repositioned many times. Still, he knew, there had to be a route to the ravine, a path he could follow through the labyrinth of tin and cardboard buildings that would take him to a point above the bridge from which he could descend to the river, then cross to the Mountain through the muck.

He dashed up the passage, moving as quickly as he could, sniffing his way, moving by instinct, prowling the maze like a hungry cat. He rushed down little alleys barely wide enough to accommodate his girth, charged up paths, through archways, reached a tiny square containing a water trough and a public well. Then he ran directly through a house whose walls were made of blankets, across a graveyard long since encroached upon by shanties, through heaps of garbage, across an open sewer behind an outhouse, emerging finally far higher than he'd planned, on an outcropping above the chasm not more than a hundred yards from the sea. Some women were standing there, one with an infant in her arms. They were all gazing across the gorge, mesmerized by the fire.

Spirals of sparks, gushing from the Freys' crenelated roof, swirled until they died against the sky. The walls of the palace were silhouetted by flames. Hamid could see fire through the windows, leaping, flaring, devouring the precious collections inside. The house was finished—in a few minutes it would be completely burned. He stared at it, remembering that a month before, when he was short of summer help, he'd approved Aziz's suggestion that they remove the men they'd posted to watch it from the road.

Impossible now, he knew, to get across. The chasm was too steep, he was too far from the bridge, and in any event there was no way he could cross the river without becoming trapped in a treacherous marsh. Even if his quarry were still there, an unlikely event, he was too late, too far away—the crime had been committed, the arsonist had struck. Somehow, eventually, the firemen and police would get through. Then he could organize a manhunt, pound his desk, order the frontiers sealed. But for all of that, he knew, he would obtain no result. Watching the house burn, he felt sorrowfully that he'd failed.

Suddenly one of the women shrieked. When he turned to her she pointed down to the left, at the little cluster of shops at the base of the Mountain and the mob massed on the bridge. There was pandemonium down there, shouts and cries, people running back and forth, waving torches, crazed. There were other fires too, and he could see figures in the night running up the Mountain, wielding torches and swinging chains. He heard sirens closer than before. Something was happening. He could feel the savage anger of the mob. They'd been galvanized by the spectacle of the fire. It was as if all of Dradeb was tensed, coiled to attack.

He began to rush down toward them, tripping, stumbling, then picking himself up and charging on, over piles of rusty cans and broken glass, through mounds of trash so high he sank into them to his knees. The smell of the fire merged now with the foul aroma of outhouse filth. The clamor grew louder; the sirens wailed as he struggled on, picking his way, oblivious to the possibility that he might fall from the narrow ridge between the back walls of shanties and the deep Jew's River gorge.

The earth here was not firm. The cliffs were eroded. There were always mudslides when it rained. Several times he felt the land give way, but still he stumbled on, grasping the fence along the ridge built to keep rats from entering the slum. As he approached the bottom he was better able to decipher the cries, a chorus of angry male voices yelling "Burn!" and the mob, lashed to fury by this chant, roaring back its approval in savage animal response.

He was blocked forty feet above them by a cement barrier that diverted flash-flood water from the bridge. Below he saw them in extreme disorder, a vicious, thrashing mass. Someone was being trampled. Someone else was being kicked. Then he saw flames leap up from behind La Colombe as young men bailed gasoline against its walls. In seconds the fire grew—they were burning Peter out. The flames leaped, engulfed the shop; then, a moment later, he saw Peter in silhouette, clutching at the security grill, desperately trying to escape.

The mob was mad, deranged. Were they going to stand there while Peter burned alive? Already the young people who'd set the fire were streaming up the Mountain with their cans of gasoline. Hamid drew his gun, raised it, fired it into the air three times. People stopped, gazed up at him, a menacing figure on the ledge, as he motioned frantically and yelled to them to let the Russian out. But the wind and the shouts below drowned his words. In desperation he raised his revolver again, this time to shoot at them. He held the gun straight out, gripped in both his hands, prepared to fire, massacre, do anything he could to bring them to their senses and make them stop. But Peter fell back just then, disappeared into his flame-filled shop. There was silence as the crowd watched him burn, then turned back to Hamid with fearful eyes.

The cry of "Burn" began again. The chant grew thunderous, and the mob began to stir toward the Mountain Road. Hamid's gun was still raised. He hated the rioters, and wanted to kill them, but though his hands were steady his mind was not. He began to tremble, knowing that it was impossible, that he could never fire at unarmed people out of hate. As he lowered his revolver they turned away from him, and a huge pack of them ran up the road. He watched helpless, crying out to them against the wind as they stormed the Mountain, dispersed among the villas. Then he lost his footing, slipped, felt himself falling, tumbling amidst wastes of cans and glass, smelled the stink of sewage as he rolled over and over, felt his head bounce against a rock as he fell into the slime.

He lay there a long while, slipping in and out of consciousness, hearing an occasional shout and cry. Finally awakened by a siren whirring very close, he raised himself and stumbled along to the bridge. He found it occupied by militia and police. The firetrucks had gotten through; men were at work putting out the flames. Soldiers, armed with guns and staves, were restoring order to the Mountain and Dradeb.

There had been a rampage—that much was clear the following day. It had lasted several hours. Great damage had been done. Mobs of Moroccans had attacked the Mountain, then been violently repelled by troops. Now Tangier, filled with soldiers from barracks around the town, was under military command, while the police directed traffic and a team of inspectors from the Ministry of the Interior began an investigation of "the events."

Hamid, a bandage on his head, made an inventory of the damage with Aziz. They visited the smoldering ruins of the Freys', found that the electric driveway gates had been expertly crosswired, and that all the Alsatian dogs had been shot. There was no trace of the inhabitants—Hamid assumed they'd been burned up inside. Out on the lawn he found an empty frame which, according to the servants, had contained the Freys' Renoir. The painting had not been burned but had been cut away. Hamid had no doubt it would reappear, exquisitely reframed, on the wall of some Israeli museum.

La Colombe had burned to the ground, and with it all of Peter's accounts and stock. Peter's body was badly burned. Hamid identified it for the record at the morgue.

Laurence Luscombe had died too, of a heart attack the medical examiner said. The only foreign resident of Dradeb, he'd been awakened by the noise. Emerging from his shanty, he'd been stricken on the street, then lying there, unnoticed, had been trampled by the mob.

Françoise de Lauzon's "Camelot" had been totally destroyed by fire, as had the cottage of Lester Brown. Both had escaped and hidden in shrubbery nearby to watch the violent wind fan the flames and burn down their houses before their eyes.

General Bresson's villa had been ransacked, his collection of Indochinese ceramics dashed to pieces against the floor. Percy Bainbridge had been a guest at Peter Barclay's house during the riot. In his absence the mob had broken into his cottage, looted all the models of his inventions, then moved along to the villa of Joop de Hoag, where they'd pushed Madame de Hoag's car into the sea.

For some reason the pillagers had ignored Inigo's house—the painter, miraculously, had slept through the melee. They'd tried unsuccessfully to penetrate the iron gates that protected the palace of Patrick Wax. The old man had fled in one of his gold-trimmed robes. With the help of his loyal "houseboy," Kalem, he'd scaled down the cliffs to spend a fearful night shivering on the beach.

The people at Barclay's dinner had been badly frightened, though they'd all escaped unharmed. The mob had struck there with their torches and their chains just as Barclay's guests were tasting cheese and port. Barclay, with an instinct for survival, had blown out the candles and turned off all his lights. Then he and his friends had huddled under his table, the big one that seated sixteen, watching the youths outside plunder the garden, their angry faces illuminated every now and then by flames.

"It was like being surrounded by a pack of redskins," Barclay said. "Wild men, all of them, screaming around, slashing at my climbers and shrubs. I suppose we're lucky we're still alive. They would have burned us out if they hadn't been attracted by the fire at Françoise's."

Hamid took note of all this, but still he was perplexed. Had it been the fire at the Freys' that had inspired the attack, or would the mobs have struck in any event, whipped to fury by the agitators on the bridge?

Early the next morning Aziz came by to fetch him at his flat. A boy wandering the marshes of the Jew's River had found two bloated bodies there. Hamid recognized them at once as Kurt and Inge Frey. They'd been strangled with piano wire—the strands were still around their necks.

Evidently, he decided, their bodies had been heaved into the ravine, then carried some distance by the river until they'd become stuck in the swamp. Hamid waited while they were carried out, then told Aziz to return to the Sûreté. There was something important he had to do, someone he had to see.

"Ah, Hamid," said Achar, shaking his hand in the clinic waiting room. "I've been expecting you. I'm really glad you came."

He gave instructions to one of his nurses, something about a prescription for a patient, then led Hamid down the corridor to his cluttered office in the back.

"Your head all right?" he asked. "The wound properly cleaned?"

"Just a bump," said Hamid. "The police doctor fixed me up."

"Good. I'm tired, though I'll look at it if you want."

Hamid shook his head.

"Not much sleep these last forty-eight hours. We've been very busy. Lots of broken bones to set." He paused, lit a cigarette. "The repression was violent, you know. Those wooden staves can cause a lot of damage, especially when swung by pitiless people who don't care whom they hit."

He smiled then, his ironic smile, which annoyed Hamid, though he wasn't sure exactly why.

"Tea!" Achar yelled to an orderly in the hall. He leaned back behind his desk, his face tired, his features set and grim. "I see that you're displeased, Hamid. Perhaps you hold me responsible for what the Rabat papers are calling 'certain bizarre events that have transpired in a residential quarter of Tangier.' Tell me—is this an official visit? Or have you come here as a friend?"

"Why do you use this tone with me, Mohammed? I've come in confidence, of course. I have nothing to do with the investigation. If I wanted to speak to you officially I'd summon you to the Sûreté."

"Yes, yes—forgive me, Hamid. I've had very little sleep."

The orderly brought in a pot of tea and two glasses on a tray.

"Close the door when you leave," said Achar. "Tell the staff I'm not to be disturbed."

He poured out half a glass, looked at it, then returned it to the pot. "About three more minutes, I think," he said. "I crave sugar all the time now, Hamid. Stress, perhaps, or some sort of psychological need." Their eyes met then, and Achar smiled. His steely gaze disappeared. "All right," he said. "Here we are. Ask me anything you want."

"I didn't come here for a political discussion. A number of things have happened that disturb me very much."

"Zvegintzov, for instance?"

"Yes. Zvegintzov first of all."

"That was regrettable, I agree, since he was of trifling consequence in the scheme of things. But these things happen when there's a mob. Of course Kalinka must be upset."

"Actually she's taken it pretty well, but I didn't come here to talk about her. What disturbs me is the vicious way that he was killed. I was there. I saw it. So don't talk to me about pitiless soldiers. I saw Moroccans behave like animals, stand there and watch him burn."

Achar fingered the teapot, then raised his eyes and sighed. "I know you were there, Hamid. Some friends of mine were on the bridge, inciting the people to use the torch. Well, there you are—I admit we're agitators, or perhaps just respected men who use our influence to channel rage."

"Damn it, that's what I don't understand! Why channel it against Zvegintzov and a few pathetic foreigners on the hill? If there're grievances, correct them. Attack your oppressors if you feel oppressed. But you have no right to send up bands against the Mountain, terrorizing people and taking lives."

"So, you're angry, Hamid. Well, well—it's not so simple as you think." He poured another half glass of tea, nodded, then filled the glass. He handed it to Hamid, then filled another for himself.

"Driss Bennani told me something he learned from Fischer, the old architect who was working here last year. When there were riots in the American slums a few years back, the black people there set fire to their homes. Well, I don't believe in that—turning one's rage against oneself. How much more logical and healthy that we should attack the world outside. I'm sorry about Zvegintzov—he meant nothing, was nothing but a stooge. The foreigners mean nothing—most of them are clowns. But they're *symbols*, Hamid, symbols of wealth and power, up there above us, in their big villas looking down, cultivating their gardens, relaxing in their pools, serviced by the Russian, furnishing themselves from his luxurious stock of goods. Should we have burned down this clinic? Ridiculous, of course! Attacked city hall so we could be shot like dogs? Well, that may happen one day too. The point, Hamid, is that the Mountain was not only the closest place at hand, it was the appropriate place. We really had no choice."

He had spoken forcefully, and Hamid knew he believed everything he'd said. But there was something cold about Achar, something ruthless in his reasoning that caused Hamid to look at him with fear.

"Don't be upset, Hamid. There's nothing new in any of this. There've been attacks before, in many parts of the world, enraged third-world hordes rising up against the smug, soft people of the West. It's a cliché by now, and the aftermath too, the repression, with the inevitable result that an even more powerful anger is instilled. Then more attacks, often in different forms. Not just boys with chains, ripping up gardens, putting a few villas to the torch, but armed guerrillas attacking barracks, assassinating officials, making war. It's an old story. Algeria. Cuba. Vietnam. We'll see it again in other places, and, I guarantee you, we'll see it here. Our regime, stupid as it is, will recognize the danger too. Watch out now for a combination of repression and superficial reform—increased food subsidies, phony land reforms, and, too, new detention laws, and American advisors to teach the tactics of counterinsurgency to you in the police. This little business in Dradeb will be forgotten very soon. We can look forward now to more outbreaks, a good deal more effective and severe. The children of the slums have seen and understood the efficacy of violence. But excuse me, Hamid. You didn't come here for a political discussion. Forgive me for rambling on. I get carried away these days."

For a while Hamid stared at him, then finally he spoke. "You think I'm shocked by what you've said? Believe me—I'm not. I'm only amazed by your arrogance. And your righteous certainty, which makes me sick."

Achar laughed. "Well, Hamid—perhaps you're right. I try not to be arrogant, at least not in the Dr. Schweitzer sense. But *yes,* I am certain that I'm right. How else can I sustain myself? However, let's lower the level of abstraction. I know that politics isn't your game. So let's talk about you. Let's see where you fit in."

"I don't fit into any of this."

"Maybe, but don't be too sure. I said you were observed by my friends during the burning of Peter's shop. You're well known in Dradeb. You're from our quarter. Most of the people here know you're an inspector of police. All right, there you were, standing up there on that ledge with a revolver in your hand. You were threatening the people down on the bridge, making it quite clear you didn't like what they were doing and were going to shoot them if they didn't stop. Well, they did stop. There was a little pause, the sort of moment that even a single man can use to turn a mob around. So, there you were, prepared to shoot, but then you lowered your gun, and suddenly they felt released. Yes, Hamid! That's what your action meant to them. It was a signal. It told them you wouldn't shoot. You, a policeman, releasing them to go on, an even more powerful trigger than the one on your gun."

"What are you talking about? They'd burned the shop! Peter was already dead!"

"Yes! And a few of them were already on the Mountain. But not the mob that ran up there later on."

"You're crazy!"

"Why didn't you shoot them, then?"

"I don't know. I couldn't do it. I don't have the heart for things like that."

"Ah! There you are! You didn't have the heart. It was your duty to do what you could to protect the Mountain. When you chose not to do your duty, you showed your heart was with the mob."

"Well, Mohammed, it isn't as clear as that. You're simplifying everything, trying to catch me in a trap."

"It *is* simple, Hamid. The people on that bridge were quite certain what they saw. At that moment *you were the regime.* You held a gun on them, and when you lowered it you announced that you stood with them."

"I don't think so."

"Well, I do. By the way, I hope this doesn't land you in trouble. It shouldn't if you brazen it out when you're called up to explain."

"You're crazy, making me out as a collaborator. Anyone who knows me knows I could never be that."

"All right, Hamid. Have it that way if you like. But think about it just the same. Maybe you'll change your mind."

Hamid glared at him. He was angry now. "What do you want from me?" he asked. "What are you trying to do?"

"There's no trap, Hamid, but I do want something. I want *you.* You could be such a help. Listen—there's a new era ahead, a new Morocco, a new society to be forged. You could have a place in it, play an important role. It isn't enough merely to understand the rage. One must *feel* it, and I know you do. I've seen you change over the last few months. I've seen you grow impatient with your work. Forget the foreigners. The logic is with us. I need you, Hamid. I want you to join me in this thing."

Late that afternoon he and Kalinka stood alone in a corner of the European cemetery at Bourbana watching four Moroccan gravediggers lower the body of Peter Zvegintzov into the ground. Hamid had bought the coffin; Kalinka had commissioned a little granite marker on Hassan II. The text was simple and written in French: "Peter Zvegintzov, entrepreneur," it said, and then the date of his birth in Hanoi, and of his death in Tangier.

"Poor Peter," Kalinka said when the grave was finally covered. "He had no friends here. No one at all."

"Still he'll be missed," said Hamid. "He once told me that the Europeans on the Mountain couldn't survive here without his help. He was a cushion, he said, between us and them. Perhaps now they'll find it a harder town."

"But still," she said, "they never liked him. He was not a sympathetic man."

He glanced at her—they were walking between long narrow rows of graves. Peter had been her last connection with the past, but now to Hamid she seemed strong, perhaps stronger than she'd ever been.

"They had a service for Luscombe at the British church," he said. " 'A good turnout,' as the British say. The new vicar, they tell me, speaks very well. As for the Freys—no one has come to claim them yet. I suppose we'll have to bury them at government expense."

They walked on in silence, down the long rows where Europeans who had lived in Tangier were laid to rest. The cemetery was crowded; there was little room left in it now. Perhaps, he thought, this was a sign that the European presence was nearly at its end.

"I keep asking myself," he said, starting up the car, "why I didn't shoot at those people, the real reason I lowered my gun. Achar says I was with them, but I'm not sure he's correct. It was just impossible for me to do it, even though I was furious. Watching Peter die—it was too terrible. I didn't care then about property or law."

She gazed at him, and he saw admiration in her eyes. "You're gentle, Hamid, just and humane. You did what you did because of who you are."

He drove to Ramon y Cahal, accompanied her to the flat. Then while she prepared their dinner he stared out across his terrace at Dradeb and the Mountain beyond.

Achar was right, he thought. *I've wasted my life on foreigners. It's no longer important that I understand them. Now I must understand myself.*

There came to him then the revelation that what had happened on the Mountain and his own role in it were things that would forever change his life. In that moment when he had stood there, faced with lawlessness and disorder beyond his wildest dreams, he had discovered something important about himself and the sort of man he might become.

He didn't speak much at dinner, instead listened to Kalinka talk of Peter and her memories of him years before.

"Hanoi was beautiful in the spring," she said, "the blossoms on the fruit trees, the laughter on the streets. On Sundays Peter took me for walks around the Petit Lac. Sometimes we'd enter the little Buddhist shrine on the island to take refuge from the rains. We'd stand in there, he'd hold my hand, we'd look at people running from the storm, turn to each other and smile."

She smiled then herself, as Hamid met her eyes—the sad smile that he loved. In that smile was her refusal to ask for pity, her commitment to survive, whatever the shocks that touched her life.

"Oh, Hamid," she said suddenly, "you must go and help Achar. You must keep your job with the police, of course, but you must help him too—*you must*. He needs you, your qualities, your sense of justice. He's too cold, and he knows it. He needs a warm man beside him like yourself."

Yes, she was right, he knew, and her clarity amazed him— that she, once so confused, so befuddled, now saw things more clearly than himself. She'd said his vision of Tangier had been too narrow, and then she had helped him to see the city in a different way. Was it the example of her mother, he wondered, that extraordinary woman who'd fought so hard for what she thought was right, or was it simply an innate sense Kalinka had of the inequities of the world? He wasn't sure, but knew one thing: that it was her intuitive sense of life, and not the logic of Achar, that now made him want to change.

Yes, somehow she had come to understand the city, had grasped its needs and mood, and now she understood him too, he felt, and the role that he should play. That was what was so marvelous about her—her mysterious grasp of things—and why her presence, no matter how quiet, had always been so good.

He looked up, saw that she was watching him.

"Hamid, I need you too." She smiled and very gently nodded her head.

He knew then what she was going to say, and he wanted to say it first. He took her hand. "What do you think, Kalinka—a traditional Moroccan wedding, with lots of dancing and beating drums all night?"

They made love.

Later, falling asleep, wrapped in her arms, he felt serene at last. His tensions unwound, and with them his old conception of Tangier. He began to dream his way through the city's labyrinth, seeking a way out of its trap, its maze. He wanted to soar about the town, look down upon it, understand it as a place where he could act, no longer as a mere observer but as a player in the struggle he knew must come.

Epilogue

Martin Townes
Leaves Tangier

Early one afternoon in late October the American writer Martin Townes arranged his packed suitcases near the entrance to his villa and climbed up to his roof. Here he sat for hours in the glass-walled studio he'd constructed years before, looking down upon the city which he would leave before the sun was due to set. Tangier shimmered as it always had, but there was a different aura about it. Armed men with close-cropped hair, dark desert men with cruel eyes, were patrolling everywhere in pairs.

Townes had sold his villa. Many others had done the same. Rich Moroccans from the south, Casablanca and Rabat, were taking advantage of the Europeans' fear and buying up the Mountain for a song. Townes didn't envy them, these wealthy Arabs, these new lords of the hill. He knew that when the next rampage took place they'd be the object of Dradeb's wrath.

Townes, like most of the European community, had used Tangier as a shelter from the storm. Often, sitting in his tower, looking across the city at the rising sun, he'd felt that he was cheating his way out of a fair share of the world's misery and pain. But now everything was changed. The refuge had collapsed. The city had been revealed, and now he felt shaken out of voyeurism and ennui.

Yet even though he was leaving Tangier, Martin Townes knew he would never escape the city's spell. He'd decided to write a novel about Tangier and some things he'd imagined there, and though he knew there would be those who would say his characters and scenes were based on real people and events, this would not be true. Everything in his novel, he'd decided, would take place only in his mind. He would attempt nothing more than to chronicle the fantasy which he dreamed while staring down upon Tangier that final afternoon.